Emerald Sea

Emerald Sea

John Ringo

EMERALD SEA

This is a work of fiction. All the characters and events portrayed in this book are fictional, and any resemblance to real people or incidents is purely coincidental.

A Baen Books Original

Baen Publishing Enterprises
P.O. Box 1403
Riverdale, NY 10471
www.baen.com

ISBN: 0-7434-8833-4

Cover art by Clyde Caldwell

First printing, July 2004

Library of Congress Cataloging-in-Publication Data

Ringo, John, 1963-
 Emerald sea / John Ringo.
   p. cm.
 ISBN 0-7434-8833-4 (hc.)
 1. Mermen--Fiction. 2. Fascism--Fiction. 3. Despotism--Fiction. I. Title.

PS3568.I577E46 2004
813'.54--dc22

2004005564

Distributed by Simon & Schuster
1230 Avenue of the Americas
New York, NY 10020

Typeset by Bell Road Press, Sherwood, OR
Production by Windhaven Press, Auburn, NH
Printed in the United States of America

10   9   8   7   6   5   4   3   2   1

Dedicated to Mark Turuk,
without whom this book would never have been written.
What doesn't kill us makes us strongerrrr!

Freakin' Canucks . . .

Prologue

The fifteen-thousand-ton asteroid had been named, in the deepness of time when men still did such things, AE-513-49. In the latter twenty-first century, when every chunk of ice and rock that was of any conceivable danger to the earth had been mapped and tracked, it had been concluded that AE-513-49, which looked a bit like an elephant's foot and was composed of nickel-iron, had a probability of impact with the earth low enough that the heat death of the universe was a more likely problem.

AE-513-49 had been considered for mining until it was determined that, as a Helios asteroid, one close in to the sun, bringing out the materials would be more costly than those on the relative "downslope" towards the outer system. Then asteroid mining, after a very brief heyday, went away as the human race started to dwindle and, with it, the need for metals from beyond the atmosphere.

Thus AE-513-49 had been permitted to continue on its lonely orbit, circling the sun like a very small planet, hanging out at the very edge of the "life belt" between the earth and Mercury.

Until a curious thing happened.

A couple of years before, small gravitic nudges were applied to it. They first sent it inward towards the sun where it would, of course, have impacted without any noticeable trace. But then it encountered the gravity well of the small planet Mercury and "slingshotted" around it, headed back "outward" in the system.

More small nudges, some of them infinitesimally faint, adjusted its trajectory until it was precisely aligned with a point in space through which the earth would pass. Then, for almost a year, nothing.

As it approached the earth, however, more nudges were applied. A few adjusted the course so that it would assuredly hit the earth and, what's more, on a particular circular zone of the earth. Other nudges sped it up or slowed it down so that it would hit a particular *point* on that circle. Then, as it approached the atmosphere, the nudges became more distinct. It was now targeted on that one small point.

As it entered the atmosphere, thin and high, it began to fluoresce, coruscating waves of fire leaping off of it as the lighter materials it had picked up on its two-billion-year journey through the solar system burned off leaving the solid nickel-iron core revealed. This, too, began to burn as it hurtled closer and closer to the face of the earth, the metal subliming off in waves of fire.

Thus it was a melted ball of nickel-iron, hurtling downward at far more than orbital velocities, trailing an immense line of fire behind it, that slammed to a stop in midair thirty-five meters from an unassuming home that was sitting, against all reason, in a pool of lava.

In keeping with the laws of physics the nickel-iron, which was half ionized by heat, exploded outward in titanic fury. But this, too, stopped in midair and the enormous detonation, which would have destroyed much of the local area, was captured by some invisible force and quickly dissipated.

The nickel-iron that had once been AE-513-49 spread itself across an invisible hemispherical barrier, practically covering the house and shutting off all light to its interior for a moment, then slid away, bubbling as if from the application of some tremendous energy, to join the rest of the lava.

Inside the hemispherical protection field, the asteroid impact was noted as only a simple thump. At the thump, Sheida Ghorbani opened up a view-screen, as she did at least once a day, and looked at the lake of boiling lava that surrounded her home. The whole valley around her home was a mass of red and black liquid rock, fuming and spitting plumes of yellowish sulfur-laden steam. As always she called to mind the lofty Douglas firs, winding paths and crystalline mountain stream that had once been. Back in the days before the Fall.

The human race had brought itself so far. Rising through

the mists of history. Surviving wars and famines. Until they had finally come to a technological point where so much was available, war, and even government, had been all but forgotten. The AI entity called Mother, which had started as a security protocol for the nearly mythical "internet" had morphed over the years until it was She who was the final arbiter of need. Mother, with her Argus eye and processors ranging from extradimensional quantum field systems to the honeycomb of bees, knew all and could see all. Beyond who was naughty and who was nice, it was She who saw the sparrow fall.

But the dangers of such an entity were known long before it was possible to create one. And Mother's creator, knowing the danger that She represented, She who was the *first* true AI, had established human controls upon her. Thirteen "Keyholders," each with a physical pass item, who could "tweak" Her protocols and, in extreme cases, open up her kernel and reprogram Her. The latter, however, required complete unanimity.

The Keys had first been held by major corporate heads and by governments in the early days of Her youth. But over the years some of them had fallen into a shadowy underworld. As Her power grew, more and more capabilities and decisions were loaded upon Her shoulders until in the last millennia She had become the defacto world government. She was controlled, primarily, by the overt "Council" of thirteen Keyholders. They were the human link in the chain and mostly ensured that Her protocols were tweaked and maintained while She did the grunt work of managing distribution of goods and services. The last human-controlled world government had dissolved nearly two hundred years ago from sheer lack of utility.

The reason for the lack of utility was simple; with no want there was limited conflict and crime. Replication, teleportation, nannites and genetic engineering had created a world where any human could live as they desired. A house on a mountaintop was easily created and the mountaintop could be anywhere in the world, since with teleportation going elsewhere was a matter of wishing. Body modification had taken wide forms, with humans Changing themselves into mer, unicorns, dolphins and a host of other shapes. All conflict, and crime, comes down to a breach of written or unwritten contracts. It was Mother that ensured that contracts, by and large, were not breached. In the rare case in which they were, the individual involved was hunted down by an efficient, if small, police force and "adjusted," in extreme cases by a memory wipe and replacement to create a nice, docile, well-adjusted human.

But there had been problems with unlimited wealth and ease. Over the years both human birthrates and scientific progress had fallen by the wayside. World population had peaked at twelve billion in the latter twenty-first century and then had started a long, slow, decline until the population, pre-Fall, had been a mere billion or so individuals, mostly residing in widely scattered homes and small hamlets. With limitless recreational activities, and birth, thank God, removed from the bodies of women and moved to uterine replicators, raising children was at the very bottom of most people's wish lists. And strong protocols, enforced by Mother and voted upon in earlier times when massive social mistakes had occurred, prevented any group from willy-nilly producing children. Each human being created in a uterine replicator had to be from the base genetics of two humans and one or both had to take responsibility for rearing the child "properly." Failure to do so resulted in the loss of birth privileges to *both* individuals.

In the year before the Fall, less than ten percent of the population had produced children. Using straight-line projections, in an estimated five hundred to a thousand years, the last human would have closed the door on an extinct species.

Scientific progress had gone the same way. While there continued to be individuals who liked to "tinker" with the borders of science, the last major breakthrough, teleportation, had occurred nearly five hundred years ago.

Looking at both of these trends, the most senior council member, Paul Bowman, decided that Something Must Be Done. He had decided that humans needed to learn to work again. That humans needed to learn to be "strong" again. That implementing a work ethic, by limiting power to only those who "produced" for the community, would bring back the science, and art and literature and birthrates, which had languished over the past millennia.

Over the years he had gathered members of the Council who, for their own reasons, looked to him for leadership. And in the end, when the rest of the Council refused his demands, they had struck, attacking the others at a Council meeting with insects that carried a deadly binary neurotoxin.

Sheida was one of the Council who opposed him, arguably the leader of the opposition. And she, a student of history as most of them were not, had feared that his fanaticism would lead to violence. She had consulted with a friend who was even more steeped in the history of violence and had prepared as well as she could. Very little that was dangerous could be brought into the Council chamber. The toxic wasps had only worked because individually they were not poisonous; it was only with the sting from two different types that the neurotoxin activated.

She had been stung, twice, by one type. Others of her faction had died.

But at the same time, they had struck back, killing members of Paul's faction. The late Javlatanugs Cantor, a werebear, had killed one, falling himself in the battle. Ungphakorn, a Changed quetzacoatl, had killed another, and seized that one's key.

However, in the end, Sheida and her surviving cohorts had retreated. And the war had begun. And the Fall started.

The Council now waged war amongst itself with the energy that had once powered the society. The lava outside her home was the side effect of the massive energy beam being directed upon the shields of her fastness by Paul's side, which had taken the name "New Destiny." Just as other energy beams attacked the power stations under the control of her faction, which had taken the name "The Freedom Coalition." The Coalition had attacked in turn and now virtually all of the energy that had supported human society had been used in attacks and defense by the Council.

This had left the rest of the world in a truly apocalyptic state. Food had been teleported or replicated for centuries. Homes were often in places impossible to live without ongoing power. Failure of personal energy shields had doomed humans from the bottom of the ocean to the photosphere of the sun. Failure of food delivery, or being left on a mountaintop, or far out at sea, had doomed others more slowly.

Thus had begun the Fall, and the Dying Time that followed it, when more than ten percent of the population of the world, some one hundred million human beings in their various forms, had died. Some, mercifully, before they knew what was happening. Others to falls or drowning or slow deaths from starvation and exposure.

And the lives of those left after the Dying Time were anything but easy. The world had descended to a preindustrial environment with farmers scratching a toe-hold in the land, and armies fighting a thousand small battles with bandit gangs to hold the line and maintain some semblance of civilization.

The most important single group who saved the remnant population of earth was made up of small groups of "reenactors," people who had wrapped their lives around earlier times. There were small communities where people lived the lives of their forefathers, using hand tools and domestic animals to replicate the lives of the ancients.

Many of these people had been living their hobby for decades, or even centuries, and knew techniques that no single person from any period in history would know. They had used every trick, every technique, to save the lives of the refugees, an old word that had been forgotten prior to the Fall, who arrived at their doorstep.

In the area that had fallen to Sheida's purview, the areas of the former North American Union, the reenactor societies had gathered the refugees, taught them how to survive, and in extraordinary cases even thrive, and slowly rebuilt society and government. Not so slowly, even. In no more than a year there was a core government, a constitution and a burgeoning ground and naval force.

The latter two were vital because in Ropasa Paul had been doing the same thing. But he was taking a different tack, establishing himself as dictator and using the power in the bodies of people to Change them into a form "more suitable for the current conditions." His Changed legions, growing in size every time they took another section of Ropasa, had quickly overrun the entire area and established an iron-fisted rule. And then he had begun his plan to invade the Norau heartland of his enemy.

Sheida often wondered if she had been right to oppose Paul. On the face his plan was not nearly as horrible as what had actually occurred. And he was getting most of what he wanted from the war, anyway. Populations were booming since the release of energy and most protocols had caused women to become fertile again. People were certainly learning how to work.

But all she had to do was look at what had happened in Ropasa. Over the centuries the strictures against using Mother as a universal eye, a universal tool of coercion, had grown strong. Mother knowing your innermost secrets was one thing; a person could handle that if they were sure no human was watching. But everyone had secrets they didn't want the world to know. Everyone had the occasional minor moral slip. Under the protocols pre-Fall, Mother could not be used for criminal surveillance, period. For the small, volunteer and chronically overworked police to track a criminal, to prevent a crime, to read a person's mind, meant using other methods, other systems, rather than the All-Seeing Mother.

If Paul had taken full control of the system, Mother would change from a distant, uncaring, deity to one that was poking into everyone's lives constantly. The way that Paul was going, She would be used for the most extremes of coercion. To Change a person, now, required direct, personal, intervention. If Paul had control of Mother, he could turn the whole human race into a series of separate, specialized, insects.

It was *a just war*, she thought, turning off the view-screen and going back to the myriad duties of the chairwoman for the Freedom Coalition, and the newly crowned "queen" of the United Free States. *It has just cause, it has a chance of winning and the group against which it is fighting is clearly and unmitigatedly evil, for all that the evil, on Paul's part at least, stemmed from "good" intentions.*

Now, if they could only win it.

CHAPTER ONE

The horseman reined in at a side road and looked at the fields stretching to the east.

The rider was massively built, but he sat the war-horse lightly despite his armor. He was wearing a gray cloak fastened with a bronze brooch worked in the figure of an eagle, loricated plate—segmented armor that was overlapped like the plates on a centipede's back—steel greaves and bracers and a kilt made of straps of leather with iron plates riveted on the outside. Tied to the right side of his saddle was a large helmet with a narrow T slit in the front while on the left was a large wooden shield with iron rim and a boss worked in the figure of a stooping eagle. The armor, the bracers, the helmet and the shield were nicked and battered but well polished and maintained.

His right hand rested loosely on his leg while the hook and clamp that substituted for a left hand held his reins. The device was decidedly out of character considering the tech base of the rest of his equipment; it was a complex curved prosthetic clamp with a sharpened inner blade. It looked as if it were made for cutting small limbs and would probably make opening bottles a treat. There was a small scar under his right eye and more scars could be seen scoring the skin of his right arm wherever the bracers didn't cover.

Also tied to the saddle were a short sword in a scabbard and a large bow case. On the rear of the saddle there was a large pack, a blanket roll, a quiver of arrows and a bag of feed for the horse. Despite the size of the rider and the weight of the equipment, the horse bore the load with no sense of worry. It stamped after a moment, but that seemed more impatience than fatigue. The rider shushed at it and the horse settled down without another shiver.

The rider, his panoply and the horse were all covered in a thick layer of dust.

Despite the battered armor and weather-beaten look, the rider was a young man, good looking in a hard-faced way with short black hair and green eyes. It was hard to tell from his expression but he had just passed his nineteenth year. And a good bit of the fields he was looking at were his.

They were being harvested in a late autumn Indian summer with the skies blue and warm above. On the far side of the large field two men were managing the take from a combination harvester. One drove the harvester while the other drove a wagon that was capturing the grain. The grain was short and as the ox-drawn harvester passed it left behind stubble and straw that was laid out in rows for baling.

The rider paused, indecisively, then turned his horse into the field. The near end of the field hadn't been harvested yet and the horse whickered at him until he paused to let it strip a mouthful of the grain.

"Go ahead, Diablo," the young man said, humorously. "Mike shouldn't begrudge it."

The harvester looked up at a shout from the man driving the wagon and pulled the oxen to a stop. They nuzzled at the grain but since their mouths were covered by feed bags they couldn't emulate the horse. He said something to the man on the wagon then climbed down off the harvester and walked across the fields towards the rider. At that the rider pulled the horse's head up with a word and tapped him into an easy trot. When he approached the other man he reined in and smiled.

" 'I will feast my horse on the standing grain,' " he said, then dismounted, hooking his reins onto the saddle to tell the horse to stay.

"Herzer," the harvester said with a smile, holding out his hand. "It's good to see you, man."

"Good to see you, Mike," the young man replied, clasping his friend's forearm and gesturing with his hook at the fields. "Damn, you've been working hard."

"Yeah, but it's paying off," Mike said, looking at his friend and shaking his head. "You look tired."

"I am," Herzer admitted. "And I'm glad to be home. But I'm due for a tour at the Academy, so maybe I can chill there for a while."

"What do *you* have to learn?" Mike asked.

"What do you have to learn about farming?" Herzer replied.

"Lots."

"Yeah, same here. But Edmund's talking about an instructor position. I figure I'll be doing some research at the same time. Time to brush up on my ancient Greek."

"Makes sense," Mike said, wiping at his brow. "What are we doing talking about this out here? Let's go up to the house."

"What about the field?" Herzer asked.

"It'll keep," Mike said. "The rain's supposed to hold off for another couple of days and this is the last one I have to cut. I saved mine for last."

"Yours?" Herzer asked, waving at the horse to follow as they walked back towards the reaper.

"I could scratch up enough capital to float a loan for the reaper," Mike said. "I've been harvesting half the fields in the valley the last month. And, yes, this is actually *your* field."

"That wasn't what I meant and you know it," Herzer said with a grin. "I wouldn't know the first damned thing about farming this place."

"Well, I'm learning," Mike admitted. "I'm learning every day."

The helper had been watering and feeding the oxen during the break and he nodded at Mike and Herzer as they walked up.

"Harry, this is Herzer Herrick," Mike said. "Herzer this is Harry Wilson. He's got a small farm down the river."

"I've heard of you," Harry replied, wiping his hand and shaking Herzer's.

"I'm taking Herzer up to the house. Go ahead and use the basket on the reaper, then cross-fill. I'll be back in a while."

"Okay," Harry said, getting on the reaper and clucking the oxen into motion.

"Slower that way, but it'll get some of the field done," Mike said.

"You want a ride up to the house?" Herzer asked, gesturing at the horse.

"I can walk," Mike replied gruffly.

They strode up the side road towards a distant hill, passing through a screen of trees that was apparently kept as a windbreak. On both sides of the road, before and after the trees, there were fields. Some of them were ready for harvesting, in grain and corn, others had plants that were not quite ready for harvest and a few were apparently fallow. The latter were covered in an odd golden plant that looked like a weed.

"Cover clover," Mike said at a gesture from Herzer. "Very good for fixing nitrogen and it forms a 'standing hay' that horses and cattle can eat in the winter." He gestured to one of the fields where low bushes were covered in purple-green berries. "Olive bushes. I'm hoping to get a good crop of olives off them."

"I thought olives grew on trees," Herzer said, fingering the eagle emblem at his throat. In the left talon it held a bundle of arrows and in the right an olive branch. The eagle's screaming beak was pointed to the left.

"They do. And the trees take decades, centuries really, to grow to maturity," Mike said with a shrug. "These grow in a season and you can get more olives per acre than with trees."

"Seems like cheating," Herzer grumbled. "You know why the olive is the symbol of peace?"

"No."

"Because it takes so long for the trees to grow. If you have olive trees it shows that armies haven't fought over the land in a long time. Take away the long maturity and what does it mean? Nada."

"Great, but I'm getting fifty chits a barrel for mature olives," Mike said, with apparent grumpiness. "And I can get two crops a year off the bushes. Even with the cost of field hands and preparation I'm getting ten- or elevenfold profits per season. So you can take your philosophical objections and stuff them."

Herzer laughed and pointed to a group of trees on the back side of the olive field. They were short and had broad glossy leaves that were a dark, rich green.

"Rubber plants," Mike replied. "I'm trying them out. They're supposed to be freeze resistant and fast growing. They grow fast, that's for sure, but this is the first winter they've been out so we'll see how they do."

There was more. Growing fruit and nut orchards, stands of hay, partially cleared fields with cattle on them. Herzer pointed to the latter in question.

"I got together with some other farmers and we rounded up more ferals last year," Mike said as they passed the last field. "That's where I got the oxen, too. And you've never lived until you've tried to turn a feral bull into a plow-ox."

Herzer laughed again as they came in sight of the house.

It was a low, log structure, rough in appearance but sturdy and well made. The barn to the side of it was much larger and made of a combination of logs and sawn wood. There were two or three other outbuildings as well.

"Leave it to you to have a better barn than you do a house," Herzer chuckled.

"That's what Courtney keeps saying," Mike replied. "But we're not made of money."

The woman in question came out the door as Herzer was loosening Diablo's saddle. She was a short, buxom woman with fiery red hair and an open, smiling face. Having watched her negotiate, Herzer was well aware that that heart-shaped face masked a mind like a razor, but he was fairly sure the smile in this case was genuine.

"Herzer," she yelled, pulling her skirts away from the child at her side and running to the hitching post. "Where did you come from?"

"Harzburg," he said, picking her up and kissing her on the cheek. As he did he noticed a decided roundness to her abdomen. "Got another one in the oven?"

"Yes," she said with a tone of asperity. "This will make three."

"Three?" he asked then nodded. "I hadn't realized I'd been gone that long."

"Little Daneh is in the crib," she said, gesturing at the child that was still hiding by the door. "Mikey, come here. This is our friend Herzer."

The boy shook his head and then, as her face clouded up, darted in through the door.

"I doubt he's used to strangers in armor at his door," Herzer said then frowned. "I hope he doesn't *get* familiar with strangers in armor at his door."

"Trouble?" Mike asked.

"Not down here that I've heard," Herzer said. He finished loosening Diablo's saddle and lifted all the gear off, then led the horse to the trough and tied him off. "That was why I was up in Harzburg. Tarson had been taken over by a band of brigands, for want of a better term. They had been raiding Harzburg and the city fathers requested federal help. They got me."

"That must have been a pleasure for them," Mike said with a chuckle.

"Yeah, they'd requested a century of Blood Lords, as if we *have* a century of trained Blood Lords to send. And they had a militia but they'd never founded a local Blood Lord chapter. Or even sent anyone to the Academy. So I got to go whip them into shape." Herzer laid his saddle, tack and blanket on a railing, then grabbed the rest with his hook and slung it over his shoulder. "Lead on, Macduff!"

"How'd it go?" Courtney asked as they went in the house. She brought over a flagon and set it on the table, then laid out cold pork, cheese and bread.

"Thank you," Herzer said, taking a slice of the cheese. It was sharp and tangy and went well with a slice of the cold pork. "I'd thought about eating on the road but I figured I'd stop by and you might be willing to feed me something other than monkey on a stick."

"Not a problem." She smiled, nibbling at the cheese herself. "And I repeat, how'd it go?"

"Well, it was a little sticky to start," Herzer admitted. "They'd expected someone . . . older."

Mike chuckled and shook his head. "You've got the silver sword and the laurel of valor."

"Which meant just about nothing to most of them," Herzer said around a mouthful of cheese and bread. "So I just worked at it until they realized they could do it my way or die. I made it pretty clear I didn't care which. The Tarsons finally attacked the town, where we wiped out most of their fighters, then more or less walked in and took Tarson over. The leader of them had set up a 'citadel' made of a free-standing stockade and a couple of log blockhouses. They burned quite nicely with the application of a little tallow and brush." He frowned at the memory, then shook his head.

"You make it sound easy," Mike said.

"Easy. Yeah. Only took me a year and a half." Herzer shook his head again and took another bite of the pork. "Nice. So what's been happening around here?"

"It's been quiet, thank God," Courtney replied. "We had a petroleum prospecting party through here."

"I've heard about that," Herzer said. "They sold some processed product to the Academy and we've been experimenting with it."

"Doing what?" Courtney asked.

"Well, it burns a treat," Herzer said, grimly. "Useful if we can figure out a way to get the burning stuff over *there* where the bad guys are," he continued, pointing in a random direction. "There's a device called a flamethrower that we're working on. If we perfect it we're going to have to figure out a new way to fight because it's going to make tight formations suicidal, especially wearing armor."

"Ouch!" Courtney said. She shook her head and changed the subject. "The town's pretty much stopped growing. Hotrum's Ferry has been drawing off a lot of people. We're starting to sell a lot of produce down the river."

"Getting good prices for it, too," Mike said. "They can ship it up river to the dwarf mines from there more easily than we can truck it from Raven's Mill."

"I hope they've got decent defenses," Herzer said. "Paul's going to make a grab for Norau sooner or later."

"Well, that's their beef," Mike replied. "Were the Tarson brigands working for Paul?"

"We never were sure," Herzer replied. "If I had to guess I'd say yes. Paul and Chansa have got their fingers in a lot of the pies that are causing us trouble."

"But it's settled now?" Courtney asked.

"As far as I can tell." Herzer shrugged. "The people of Tarson are certainly on the side of light. Harzburg . . . you can burn the place to the ground for all I give a damn."

"So are you staying the night?" she pressed.

"No, unfortunately," the soldier said with a sigh. "My orders were to report 'without delay.' So I'm going to have to head into town pretty soon. But I figured I could take enough time to stop by and have some real food at least." He grinned and carved off another slice of the pork. "You're both looking good. The farm is looking good. I'm glad." He chewed on the pork with a thoughtful and sad expression for a moment, then smiled again. "Life could be a hell of a lot worse."

"Herzer, tell Duke Edmund that he'd better let you get some rest or he'll be talking to *me*," Courtney said dangerously. "And you had better *take* it, Herzer Herrick."

"I will," Herzer replied, looking around at the low room. It was clean and *homey* in a way that nothing in his life had been in a long time. It was like a slice of some peaceful place that he was afraid he would be shut out of for all eternity.

"I've got to get going," he said after a bit. "Thanks for lunch. Hopefully we'll be able to get together some while I'm around."

"We'll do that," Courtney said with a smile. "We'll make an event of it."

Herzer grabbed his gear and headed back out to the horse. Diablo looked at him balefully when the gear started going on but the horse sat quietly as Herzer saddled up and loaded item after item.

"Is all that necessary?" Courtney asked.

"Not really," Herzer said. "I suppose there are things that I could pick up along the way. But I like the tools that I have."

Finally he was saddled up and gave Courtney a hug and shook Mike's hand.

"See you in town," Herzer said, mounting the horse with a grunt. Diablo sighed and shook himself, not so much telling Herzer to get off as settling his *own* gear to his satisfaction.

"We'll take care of your farm until it's time to come home," Courtney said. "You just come back, okay?"

"Home," Herzer said, shaking his head. "What an interesting abstract notion." He smiled and waved as he trotted back down the road.

CHAPTER TWO

Herzer turned left and headed south when he reached the road, then quickly moved Diablo to the side as a dispatch rider came trotting from the direction of town. The rider, who was a private in the Federal Army by the look of it, gave him a glance then a salute as he passed. Herzer returned the salute abstractedly, concentrating on a problem.

At the time of the Fall, world population had been just about one billion. The aftermath of the Fall had not seen as much die off as anticipated, mostly because of small towns like Raven's Mill. But the effectively total loss of technology had created enormous implications that were just beginning to sink in. The one that was near and dear to his heart was military manpower. The military technology available was pregunpowder because of the explosive prohibitions still slavishly followed by Mother. Historical battles in pregunpowder days meant that each side had a near parity of forces. But raising large armies was practically out; there was too great a labor shortage. Conscripting large groups meant that something vital simply wouldn't occur; farming, manufacturing, something was going to fail.

Thus it was up to relatively small handfuls of soldiers to protect civilization from the barbarians. And to protect the new and faltering United Free States from the various feudal warlords and the technological despotism of New Destiny.

Like a ship captain of old, Herzer lusted for more men, more soldiers. Too many times he had had to fight in battles outnumbered. Mike would make a superlative soldier but he *needed* to be right where he was, farming.

Some of the pressure was relieved by new/old technology. The harvesting that Mike was engaged in would have been done by a team of six, at least, in preindustrial times. Powered looms, Bessemer forges, meant that there were fewer people producing more per person. But even with the productivity increase there weren't enough workers for all the potential positions. Which meant fewer soldiers as well.

It was an insoluble problem, but one that Herzer wrestled with constantly. The dispatch rider, for example, was supported by way stations in the controlled areas of Overjay. Each of the way stations had to be manned, and what's more had to have horses at it. Figuring out a better means of communication would mean freeing up all of those people, and horses, for soldiers. Which might have meant sending more than one barely trained lieutenant to Harzburg and ending the problem in a week instead of a year and a half.

These musings carried him through the fields on the way to town and up to the gates. Most of the fields had been cleared before he left but he saw new orchards on the hillsides as well as new outbuildings. The town, whatever Courtney might think, continued to build.

There was work going on at the top of the hills north of town as well but it was more martial in nature. A wooden gate was under construction and a stockade stretched up the hill to the Academy on the right. On the left the stockade had been torn down and a bed of gravel followed the track of the top of the hill.

"Lieutenant Herrick," the team leader of the gate guards said, nodding his head.

"The duke's pushing ahead on the curtain walls?" Herzer asked, nodding at the gravel that was being dropped by ox carts then leveled out by prisoners. More than a few of the prisoners were Changed, taken in the brief foray by Dionys McCanoc against the town. They were, as far as anyone could tell, normal people who had been caught up by McCanoc and converted, against their wills, into soldiers for him.

The actions of the raiders even before their attack on the town had been such that life sentences had been handed down for all of them. There was, however, a good bit of sentiment suggesting that at some point the "normal" humans might be rehabilitated. The Changed, however, short of being Changed "back," were subject to no such sympathy. Generalized sympathy for what had occurred to them, yes, but not direct sympathy for their plight because they were as vicious as a pack of oversized weasels. They were incredibly strong, short, and brutish in appearance and had the personalities of rabid pit bulls. They had been christened "orcs" on first sight and the name had stuck.

Whenever Herzer, personally, felt sorry for them he just watched a group of them, like this one, working, and got over it. They were unwilling to work except under threat of immediate punishment and even then spent more time fighting among themselves than working. Slowly, over the last couple of years, their numbers had been reduced through one accident or murder or another until it looked like clemency might be unnecessary; in another couple of years they'd have killed each other off.

In a way the use that the prisoners were put to was a shame; they'd make decent sword fodder. For that matter, the Changed were apparently New Destiny's idea of what made good soldiers. Which just showed that New Destiny had its head firmly up its ass. They were tough and aggressive but they also had a strong tendency to break if they took too many casualties and were impossible to discipline. They were just fine with scream and charge but no damned good at holding a shield line.

Using them as garrison in a town that was being particularly resistant to reason had its attractions. Renan came to mind as did Tarson. But Raven's Mill, not to mention the Freedom Coalition, couldn't do something like that; they were the good guys.

Diablo knew the way home and had broken into a trot beyond the construction on the wall so before Herzer knew it he was at the gates of the Academy. He realized it when he heard a familiar voice.

"You appear to be thinking deep thoughts, Lieutenant."

"Just considering the lack of manpower, Gunny," Herzer replied with a grin.

Master Centurion Miles A. "Gunny" Rutherford had been a reenactor prior to the Fall. In his latter career he had specialized as a noncommissioned officer in the Norau Marines, a position called "Gunnery Sergeant," and he had lived his life for years in that role to the point that he lived, ate and breathed the model, in his mind, of such a person.

As it turned out, he had more background for the role than most people had realized. He was born shortly before his parents decided to move to the province of Anarchia, a region that was maintained, prior to the Fall, in a nontechnological environment. Gunny had never been too sure what happened to his folks after they emigrated but it was probably similar to what had happened to Duke Edmund's brother. It was an area used as a "bleed off" for people who didn't want to live in paradise and it was anything but. Anarchia, in those days, had been run by groups of feudal warlords, and newcomers had a tendency to die in distressing numbers. Gunny had grown up in that environment, eventually becoming one of the punk soldiers of the "Baron" of Melbun. It was there that he had first run afoul of Duke Edmund, when the man born by the name of Charles came looking for his missing brother and decided that Anarchia needed a good shaking up. The "Baron" had learned, the hard way, that undisciplined gang members didn't stand a chance against a disciplined army. The survivors of the Baron's men had been inducted in the burgeoning army of Charles the Great.

That had been years ago, centuries before Herzer was born. Afterwards, when Anarchia was pacified and the sad story of his brother pieced together, "Charles" had returned to the world and become "Edmund Talbot," just another reenactor. And with him had come his friend, Arthur Rutherford.

After the Fall, Gunny made his way to Raven's Mill and took up his position again, trainer for the new corps of Blood Lords.

Of which Herzer was, by far and away, the best known member.

"You do what you can with what you've got," the NCO at the gate said with a shrug. "We're doing well enough," he added, gesturing around.

The area at the base of Raven's Hill had been part of the Faire grounds prior to the Fall. As the town began accepting refugees the area had first been used as a processing area, then with the establishment of the Blood Lord Academy the Hill had been turned over to the Academy.

Where a few buildings had once stood there were now headquarters, barracks, stables, and on the top of the hill, one of the highest in the area, was a building fortress.

Herzer considered the answer as he looked around. While it was true, it was also the reason that Gunny was going to always be an NCO. His focus was on the troops, not where they might come from. Training them was his passion, using them in battle was a close second. But Gunny always thought at those, essentially tactical, levels. Herzer was, slowly, learning to think beyond the here and now, a trick he was picking up from Duke Edmund. The New Destiny forces had the same manpower problems as the Freedom Coalition. Their answer had been to support Norau forces that were hampering the Coalition while building, from reports, a large army at home in Ropasa.

Gunny could, and would, focus like a laser on training the raw troops given to him. And the end product was excellent, as Herzer himself had proven. But he distrusted allies and gave most of his thought processes to better use what he was given. It was up to officers to find more bodies and integrate untrained allies.

Because no matter how good the Blood Lords were, and they were *very* good, there was no way the relative handful of fully trained soldiers could stand up to the army that Paul was building.

"Well, we'll be getting some new recruits from Harzburg and some of the surrounding towns, soon," Herzer replied, walking Diablo over to his paddock. "Then we'll have more to do with."

He dismounted and started stripping off Diablo's tack as a pony-sized unicorn, followed by a young colt nearly her own size, came trotting over.

"Hi, Herzer," the unicorn said in a high-pitched voice. "I'm glad you're back."

"Hi, Barb. Admit it, though, you're glad *Diablo's* back." Herzer chuckled, opening up the gate and letting his mount into the paddock.

"H'zer!" the colt shrilled then butted Diablo in the side with his short, stumpy horn. "D'ablo!"

"He doesn't really know who you are," Barb replied, ignoring the jibe. "He does that with everybody."

Prior to the Fall, Barb Branson had been through several Changes and just prior to the Fall she had turned herself into a unicorn. The Fall had caught her in that form and, after several unpleasant experiences in the aftermath, she had been recaptured from Dionys' forces. Despite the fact that she was now in better hands she found herself unable to adapt to "human" society and lived with the horses, and Diablo particularly. The relationship had been the source of some crude jokes initially but now had become so normal the people of the town barely considered it. The colt was the result of mating with Diablo and seemed to be progressing somewhere between a human baby and a horse. He had been able to walk almost immediately but speech was a relatively recent acquisition.

"He's growing fast," Herzer said with a nod. The colt, from reports, had been barely the size of a cat when born and now stood taller than his mother at the withers. He looked as if he was going to try for his sire's size.

"And getting into *everything*." Barb sighed. She went over to the feed supply and slipped her horn into a hole. A lever inside dispensed a measure of grain and she nipped at the colt to keep him away as Diablo walked over to feed. "We had to fix this so his horn wouldn't reach; he figured out how to use it when he was about three months old."

"Well, take good care of Diablo," Herzer said. The horse in question looked up at his name, then took another mouthful of grain and, still chewing, walked to the center of the paddock. When he was in the right spot he lay down and rolled onto his back, writhing from side to side to get the dust good and thick. He rolled until he was well covered in dust, then walked back to the trough to finish his feed. Barb had stood by patiently, keeping the youngster away, until he returned. "Anything you need?"

"Nope, we're fine," Barb said. "Thanks for setting this up."

"Not a problem," Herzer said. He carried the tack into the barn attached to the paddock and put it away, then picked up his baggage and headed to the barracks.

As a Blood Lord officer he had a room of his own but it was Spartan in the extreme. Every time he returned he promised that he'd do something about decorating but he never did. The room had a rough bed, a desk, a footlocker, an armor stand and a wall-locker. He dumped his gear on the floor and then stripped off his armor, working his shoulders around as the weight came off. Then he carefully put away everything that didn't need immediate cleaning. He knew there was an orderly around somewhere and he could leave the cleaning of his clothes and armor to the orderly's attention.

He drew the short sword he'd been carrying and checked its edge but he'd cleaned and honed it since the last time he used it so it didn't need anything. He polished and oiled it out of habit, then considered his next moves.

He was supposed to report to Duke Edmund but he figured he could at least get the road grime off before he did. The question was whether to walk across town and use the baths or just shower at the barracks. Finally he decided on the latter and stripped off his clothes, wrapping a towel around his waist.

The showers had been added to the barracks just before he left. There wasn't much to them, just a series of spigots overhead surrounded by concrete floor and walls. Compared to the bathhouse they were positively primitive, but it beat the heck out of walking all the way across town. For some reason he really didn't want to talk to half the people in town, which was more or less what would happen if he headed to the baths.

The barracks were deserted this time of day—the instructors were out chivvying students or working in their offices, which were across the quad, and the permanent guards were drilling—and he wandered down the corridor alone. The showers were at the center of the wooden building, past officer territory and into the area where the NCOs bunked. He nodded at the charge of quarters as he passed, then turned into the bathroom.

There was an orderly in there cleaning up but, again, he just nodded at him, then walked into the shower room, pulling the towel off and hanging it on a hook before turning on the water.

The water took forever to get hot, but at that it was still better than anything Harzburg had had for a long time. There was a sliver of soap on a ledge and he used it liberally including on his hair. The latter was starting to get long again and it was about time for a cut. But that, at least, would have to wait. By now the duke would have heard he was back. He turned off the shower and grabbed his towel, heading back to his room.

In the main bathroom there was a row of spigots spilling water into a concrete trough with a long metal mirror mounted over it. Herzer paused by it to survey his face. He'd had hairgrowth on his face stopped prior to the Fall so he didn't have to worry about five o'clock shadow. His hair *was* a tad long, starting to touch his ears at least, but it would pass inspection. Only the Blood Lords conformed to Gunny's remarkable standards of personal grooming.

He headed back to his room and began donning a fresh uniform. It was a tad loose—he'd lost weight on the Harzburg mission along with everything else—but it still fit well enough. Cosilk underpants and shirt, gray cosilk trousers and the kimonolike overtunic. The latter's lapel and trim was in light blue, from time immemorial the color of infantry, and there was a blue stripe down the outside of the trousers. Blue for the infantry, yellow for cavalry, green for the archers and red for engineers. He stopped before putting the tunic on and pinned the two pips of a lieutenant to the lapel. He looked at it for a moment, then shrugged.

"Might as well go full blast," he muttered, opening up the footlocker and extracting a small leather box. From it he pulled a device like a shield, which he pinned on the left upper breast of the kimono. Below it he pinned four medals. The one on the uppermost row was a representation of a gold laurel. The three on the row below were a silver eagle, wings outspread, another shield, formed in bronze and pair of crossed swords.

As soon as the medals were arranged to his satisfaction he slipped into the kimono and belted it with his sword-belt. He picked up his sword, gave it an automatic check, and slipped it onto the belt. Normally the weapon sat high on his right side, attached to his armor but he'd spent so much time in both configurations either one was relatively comfortable.

He stepped out of the room and down the corridor to the main entrance.

"If anyone asks for me I've gone to report to Duke Edmund," Herzer said as he headed for the double doors at the front of the building.

"Yes, sir," the charge of quarters replied. He was reading something and didn't look up.

Herzer paused and turned on one heel. "That's the sort of thing you're supposed to write down, Private," he growled.

"Yes, sir," the private replied in a much more focused voice. He opened his ledger and reached for the quill standing in an ink bottle.

Herzer nodded at him, then turned and walked out the door.

"Come," Sheida said at the door chime.

Her aide Harry Chambers came in, followed by a tall, thin, dark-haired man. He could have been anything from thirty to two hundred. He had an expression of slightly distracted amiability on his face as he nodded at the council member.

"Joel Travante," Sheida breathed. "Welcome. Most welcome, sir. Sit, please. Harry, if you don't mind?"

"Not at all," Harry said, stepping out and cycling the door shut.

As the door shut the man in the float chair changed subtly. Whereas he had been smiling, the smile dropped from his face to be replaced by a blank, hard mask, and his languid pose, while not shifting a millimeter, dropped away. He went

from seeming to be a nice, simple, professional to something
that looked more like a drawn sword.

"How are you?" Sheida asked, nodding at him, hard. "Where
have you been?"

"In the Asur Islands, ma'am," the inspector said, sitting
forward and nodding back. He had a deep, baritone voice and
his eyes were blue and cold.

Prior to the Fall, the world had had little crime. With nearly
infinite wealth, personal protection fields and the availability
of semilegal means to fulfill even the darkest fantasies, there
was very little opportunity or need to cause it.

There were, however, individuals who for various reasons
committed offenses of one sort or another.

Given that people could live any sort of life they desired,
it required an odd person to commit crime, especially particularly vicious and predatory crimes. And with a life of luxury,
it required an even odder person to devote their life to finding criminals.

But just as there were persons who could not resist breaking
laws, there were others who had something in them that drove
them to search, find and just as often destroy the worst of
the criminals. These were the Council Inspectors. There were
very few of them, no more than a hundred in the year prior
to the Fall, and most of them worked part-time. But among
them there was an elite, the Special Inspectors, who had powers
nearly equaling those of the Council. And Inspectors only got
to be Special Inspectors by both having a long career of tracking
down the worst of the criminals and by showing exemplary
conduct doing it.

Joel Travante had been a Special Inspector for nearly forty
years prior to the Fall.

Direct access to Mother's DNA database was closely
restricted. To obtain a general DNA search required a plurality of council member approval, and a direct location search
required a super majority. But prior to the Fall the inspectors had enormous resources to find their subjects. The slightest
clue at the site of a crime could be used to track down the
perpetrator. A shred of DNA, a fiber of clothing, any distinctive chemical or biological residue, and the inspectors had a
lead that they would follow until they died or hell froze over.

Or the whole world came apart.

"What were you doing there at the Fall?" Sheida asked.

"There was a person who had committed a string of
offenses," Joel said, one cheek twitching for just a moment.

"Primarily rape and murder, concentrating on very young females. He would . . . seduce them in order to get them to drop their shields and then . . . ensure that they were too overwhelmed to raise them . . . afterward." His jaw worked for just a moment and he shook his head angrily.

"I had a hard gene coding on the person, he'd been going by the name Rob Morescue, mostly, but he had seemingly dropped off the face of the earth. None of the secondary surveillance systems picked him, or his DNA, up, anywhere. I was able to secure the information that the person had turned himself into a kraken. I had reason to suspect that he was residing somewhere in the deep trenches near the Asur Islands. I had been asking around; there was a pretty large delphino population in the area as well as orcas and various fishermen and sailors. At the time of the Fall I had gotten three confirmed sightings of a kraken in the area and was about to perform a search of the depths. Then, with the Fall, I was forced to forego my investigation."

"And since?" Sheida asked.

"I took a job with one of the local sailors who had converted to commercial fishing," Travante replied. "In time I was able to secure my own vessel, a small sailing caique. When New Destiny forces took over the island I maintained my cover as a visiting tourist and post-Fall fisherman. When the time was right and the weather looked good I set sail for the mainland."

"In a fishing caique?" Sheida said, aghast. "How large?"

"Four meters, ma'am," Joel replied. "I had reason to suspect that some of the orcas that had willingly joined the New Destiny forces had suspicions that I was not all that I had said. Some of my questions, pre-Fall, had apparently been insufficiently circumspect. And, frankly, ma'am, I didn't think much of New Destiny's charter or actions. So as soon as I felt it was probable I'd survive, I set sail. It's not that difficult a sail from the Asur Islands to Norau, provided nothing goes wrong."

"Charts?" Sheida asked. "Navigation?"

"I was able by that time to secure a compass and had some training from my previous employer at stellar and oceanic current navigation," Joel said, shrugging as if a three-thousand-kilometer voyage across empty ocean in a small boat was no great feat. "Dorado tended to congregate around the boat so that I had a ready supply of food. I had a large store of water when I left and picked up more from occasional rain showers.

I made landfall on the coast of Flora ninety-three days after setting sail, made my way up the coast to the base at Newfell, contacted a person that I had known prior to the Fall and was put in touch with the Freedom Coalition rump of the Council. Upon being summoned by you I traveled by stage-coach and horse to Chian and was ported here."

"Amazing, Inspector," Sheida said. "Will it bother you if I say 'a bit too amazing'?"

"No, ma'am," the inspector replied. "If you wish to perform truth detection, feel free." Like most intrusive protocols, truth detection required permission of the subject or agreement by a plurality of the Council.

Sheida frowned and then shrugged, drawing a smidgeon of power and running a lie detector test on the surface of the inspector's thoughts. There was no indication that he had any reservations about his story. He had some personal problems that were beating at him, though.

"What's wrong?" Sheida asked. "You're calm on the surface but you're not so calm underneath."

"It is . . . personal, ma'am," the inspector said, then sighed. "My wife and daughter are missing. I'm aware that most families were broken by the Fall, ma'am, but it doesn't make me any happier. Now that I'm back in contact with higher, I am hoping that I can search records to try to find them. The problem is . . . as far as I knew, my wife was in the Briton Isles at the Fall. What is worse, my daughter was in Ropasa visiting friends." He paused and then shrugged again. "Frankly, ma'am, I'm afraid that if New Destiny finds out who they are, and that I'm working for you, they will use it as a hold on me. If they do so . . ." He paused, his face hard. "I will be in a very uncomfortable position."

"An uncomfortable position indeed," Sheida frowned. "For reasons that I'll get into in a moment, don't discuss that with *anyone* except myself. If you encounter anyone who knew you before the Fall, tell them that you have definite proof that both of them died during the Fall."

"Yes, ma'am," Travante said, his face hard. "They might have."

"I hope not," Sheida replied. "We have very few assets in Ropasa or the Briton Isles. I think it unwise, furthermore, to put out any sort of feelers about your wife and daughter. Our intelligence assets have been being . . . 'rolled up' is the term, compromised and just as often interrogated and then Changed, with unfortunate regularity."

"In that case, ma'am," the inspector said, "please do *not* put out any feelers."

"The unfortunate regularity is what I wish to discuss with you," Sheida said. "I'm beginning to suspect that while we have not been able to get much intelligence out of New Destiny's areas, the reverse is not the case." She summoned a holographic representation of Norau and pointed to a series of red dots.

"While we can prevent Paul's associates from teleporting into our territory, we cannot prevent communications or avatars," she said. "But by the same token, since we've locked out virtually all programs under pass codes, we *can* detect when non-Coalition pass codes are being used, and non-Coalition avatars or projections are entering our territory. These are records of all such transmissions over the last six months."

"That's . . . bad," Travante said, looking at the traces. They dotted the map like pustulant sores and were found wherever there were latter day concentrations of survivors. "This is just the last six months?"

"Yes," Sheida frowned. "Some of them might be avatars appearing for a look at some occurrence. Paul still has a slight surplus of energy over ours and he is apparently using it for the development of intelligence."

"Wise of him," Travante said. "Trying to throw it at your shields, unless it's extremely high power, would be a waste of assets."

"But the problem is that we're losing agents," Sheida frowned. "And bleeding information to the enemy. You're not the first inspector to turn up, although you're the first Special. And I've set most of them on this problem. Eventually, I want you to have a close look at . . . possible problems in our higher command."

"You mean in the Council?" Travante frowned.

"No, I'm sure of all of our council members," Sheida replied. "I'd like you to investigate other possibilities. But before you do that . . . are you up for a long ride again?"

"At your command, ma'am," the inspector said.

"I want you to go *back* to Newfell Base," Sheida replied. "There's a mission being prepared there. We're *definitely* losing data from Newfell. There is probably more than one source. But I want you to insinuate yourself into the mission, probably as a sailor on the ship given your recent experience, and try to determine if there is an agent or agents amongst the crew. When you return from that mission, you'll probably stay at Newfell, or in the Fleet, pending the outcome of the investigation."

"Yes, ma'am," the inspector said.

"Just that?" Sheida smiled. "Back on horses and stagecoaches, all the way across the continent?"

"How do I contact you, ma'am?" was all Travante asked.

"Hold out your left wrist, face up," Sheida said. When he did she waved her fingers over his wrist and, for a moment, a picture of an eagle was superimposed on it as if by a tattoo, then faded.

"If you need to contact me, touch the eagle and say or think my name," Sheida replied. "Sheida, Sheida Ghorbani, whatever. Just think of *me*. Edmund Talbot, who is a long-term friend and as trustworthy as they come, is going to be on the mission. If you need assistance, contact him. He will be informed that there is an agent of mine present. Try not to step on each other's toes."

"I won't, ma'am," the agent said, rubbing his wrist. There had been no feeling to the invisible tattoo, but there was a psychosomatic tingle left behind.

"As it turns out, you won't have to take the coaches back," Sheida said with a smile. "Although you might prefer it. There's a dragon, a wyvern rather, that is headed that way. He'll take you to Washan. You'll need to hop once you get there to make it to Fleet headquarters before the mission leaves."

"Yes, ma'am."

"I will keep an inquiry out in my own awareness for your wife and daughter," Sheida said. "If I find any information about either of them, I will contact you."

"Thank you," Travante said.

"Harry will give you your traveling money and brief you on how to get more," Sheida said. "He's not aware of your mission; you're only going to be sent as far as Washan. Make the rest of the journey on your own."

"Yes, ma'am," Travante said, standing up. "By your leave."

"Good luck, Inspector," Sheida replied, standing up and touching his shoulder as she led him to the door. "I will pray for, and search for, your family."

"And I will pray for you and yours," Travante said, his face changing into a mask of amiable competence as the door opened.

CHAPTER THREE

The walk to Duke Edmund's was mercifully uninterrupted. Herzer couldn't figure out, for most of the walk, what was wrong. He knew that he was feeling intensively antisocial but it was more than that. Raven's Mill was the town where, in many ways, he had grown up. Admittedly he spent less than a year in the town after the Fall, but he should have felt at home upon his return. God knew he'd thought longingly of getting back half the damned time he'd been at Harzburg.

But for some reason "good feeling" just wouldn't come. For some reason the town felt like his uniform: Just a little too loose. Little changes, like a new sign over Tarmac's tavern, stood out and left him feeling even more irritable.

Just as he reached the town hall he started to get a handle on the problem. Part of it was uncertainty about his future. The plans that had been sent to him during most of the Harzburg mission had spoken of bringing him back as a trainer. Not one of the sadistic madmen who ran the first phase—Herzer understood the importance of running the trainees into the ground while having no desire to perform the job himself—but as an instructor in the forming Officer Basic course. He was, in his opinion, more suited to *taking* the course, but the pool of trained officers was so small he could understand the need to throw him into the breach.

However, the peremptory "return at earliest possible moment" did not bode well for a routine training assignment. What he particularly did not want was to run into someone who might

ask him why he was back so soon. And be in the position
of being able to satisfy neither their curiosity nor his own.

As he approached the entrance to the town hall the two
guards at the door braced to attention. Gone were the days
of half-awake guardsmen with rusting weapons leaning up
against the wall. The guards were permanent members drawn
from the militia and trained with the Blood Lords. Just enough
to know they didn't want to *be* Blood Lords was the joke.
Blood Lord training and "winnowing" was merciless and even
after a recruit passed the tests to join the fraternity, training
continued unabated. Running up and down Raven Hill in full
rucksacks was just the start of a daily regimen that was brutal
to the point of sadism.

But that, and a belief in teamwork that went all the way
to the bone, meant that Blood Lords could outfight and, often
more important, outmaneuver enemies that were their numerical
superior. "Fight until you die and drop" was just one of their
unofficial mottoes. And nobody fought like Blood Lords.

He walked inside and took the left turn to Edmund's office
but was stopped almost at the door by a secretary. That was
another new iteration.

"Can I help you?" the woman asked. She was faintly familiar
but Herzer couldn't quite place her. Dark hair, just below
median female height . . . nope, wasn't coming.

"Herzer Herrick," Herzer replied. "I'm under orders to see
Duke Edmund 'at the earliest possible moment.' "

"He's very busy," the woman said with a sniff. Whoever
she was, she didn't appear to recognize *him* either. "Why don't
you just take a seat?"

Herzer didn't bother to smile; he just took a parade rest
position, hands behind his back, legs spread shoulder width
apart, and simply *looked* at her.

"Why don't you go tell Duke Edmund that I'm out here," he
said in a totally neutral voice. He let his eyes do the rest. "Now."

It was a technique he'd picked up from Gunny and as usual
it worked. The woman was more than willing to pass the buck
to someone who, she clearly hoped, might put him in his place.
It wasn't the most politic way to deal with a petty-power-
hungry functionary, but it tended to work.

In this case the woman looked at him poisonously for a
moment, then got up and knocked on the door.

"Duke Edmund," she said, opening the door without a word
from the interior, "a Herzer Herrick *insists* on seeing you
immediately."

"That's because I told him to, Crystal," Edmund replied, mildly. "Send him in."

As Herzer walked through the door he remembered where he had met her before.

"Nice to see you again, Crystal," he oozed insincerely as he stepped through the door. "How's Morgen?"

He carefully shut the door behind him and then saluted with right fist to left breast.

"Lieutenant Herrick reporting," he said neatly.

"Can it, Herzer," Edmund growled, standing up and stepping to a cupboard. "Care to cut the trail dust?"

"If you please, sir," Herzer replied. "What's with the Cerberus at the gates?"

"She's anything but a dog," Edmund replied. "But whether she knows it or not, she's temporary. I had a protégée of June's holding down the desk but she's on maternity leave." He handed the lieutenant a glass dark with liquor. "Salut!"

"Blood and steel," Herzer replied, taking a sip. "Very mellow."

"Laid it down nearly thirty years ago," Edmund replied. "It should be."

Herzer observed Sir the Honorable General Edmund Talbot, duke of Overjay, carefully but could see little sign of change in the last year. The duke was heavy-set with a full beard and a shaved head. He was wearing gray linen trousers and a blue tunic of a fine woolen material, the edging of which was embroidered in yellow. The clothing was worn smooth from use but had the look of being comfortable clothing rather than old. He could have been anything from a hundred to two hundred years old, judging by the fine lines on his face and the flaccid skin on his forearms, but Herzer knew he was closer to three hundred. He had a solid, calm look that he somehow projected to those around him. Wherever the duke went, even if it was in the middle of a battle, chaos lessened and order followed. It was another trick, like his ability to pitch his voice to be heard above a battle and the knack of always knowing *where* to be, that Herzer was desperately trying to figure out.

"You're wondering why I called you in so abruptly but we really should wait until . . ." the duke said, then paused as the door opened.

"It's fine, we know him," Daneh Ghorbani said as she stepped through the door. "I sleep with him every night, he won't mind me barging in."

Doctor Ghorbani was middle tall for a female, perhaps a meter and three quarters, with long red hair that was currently braided down her back. She was heavily bosomed and inclining to a plumpness that was decidedly odd in the post-Fall society. Prior to the Fall human genetics had been tinkered with to such an extent that all but minimum fashionable body fat tended not to form. She wasn't fat; the term "padded" came to mind, and on her it looked good. She, like her paramour Edmund, seemed to project a field of calmness around her, even when putting down annoying underlings. And she looked well, which Herzer found, to his surprise, was of sudden immense importance.

She was followed by what could have been her younger sister but was in fact her daughter. Unlike her mother, Rachel Ghorbani was anything but calm.

"Father, you have to get rid of that insufferable woman," she said hotly as soon as the door was closed.

"So I've been told," Edmund replied with a smile. "Daneh? A glass of wine?"

"Isn't it a little early?" Dr. Ghorbani asked, glancing at the drinks in their hands.

"I'm sure the sun is over the yardarm somewhere in the world," Duke Edmund replied, pouring a glass of wine that caught the light through the window like a ruby.

"Yes, thank you, Father, I will have some," Rachel said, acerbically.

"Of course." Edmund chuckled, pouring another glass and handing them to the women. "A toast: to a smooth sea and a fair journey."

"What journey?" Rachel blurted out.

"The one that Herzer and I, at a minimum, are going to be taking."

Chansa snarled and shook his head as the modeling projection completed its run. No matter *how* many times he ran the model, the current projections made invasion of Norau impossible.

The room that he worked in was low and cramped for his huge bulk, a subbasement under the council chambers that had only recently been found and reopened. It wasn't that he'd been relegated to a subbasement, it was simply that lately it fit his mood. Let Celine scamper about her laboratories and Paul create his insane workrooms to "do the work of the people." This tiny room controlled more raw power than any other room on earth. But with all that power, he still couldn't make the impossible possible.

It wasn't a matter of forces. The implementation of the Change program, while hampered by the various program lock-outs that bitch Sheida had started, was continuing apace. And the Changed males made more than adequate soldiers, while their females were sturdy enough to do most of the drudgery of food supplying. And arms were not an issue, either. Not only did Ropasa have supplies of them for historical reasons, inserting the same sort of training as the combat and farming training of the Changed was not difficult. A special class of Changed had been created that made excellent artisans.

No, the problem was logistics.

Lifting his entire force would leave Ropasa stripped of garrisons. Not only did that mean that Coalition forces could make strikes against them, it also meant being unable to prevent internal revolt, which was a very real problem among the Unchanged. Second of all, supplying that entire force over nearly two thousand kilometers of ocean was chancy at best. Impossible if there was any coherent resistance. And the likelihood of such resistance was high.

So any invasion would have to be attempted with less than his full force. Since projections showed that less than the full force would be inadequate to destroy current Norau forces, something had to be done.

Thus far the attempts to weaken the United Free States had been failures. If anything they had left them stronger. First the disaster with Dionys, which still left him cringing, then other attempts to take over territory had been stymied. There were neutrals in Norau, groups resisting integration to the UFS, but by the same token they also resisted aligning themselves with New Destiny. And projections showed that at the current rate of UFS increases in manpower and military buffering there was no point at which an invasion had better than a fifty-fifty chance of succeeding.

It was maddening.

He looked up as an avatar of the Demon appeared, and tried not to grimace. Just what he needed.

"Yes, Lord Demon?" he asked. The Demon was, like his namesake, a fairly chaotic entity. It always paid to stay on his good side, such as there was.

"I understand you suffered another setback in Norau?" the Demon rumbled. It was impossible to tell what the actual person looked like under the black armor, other than being an outsized humanoid. The armor was full articulated plate from the horns on the helmet, through the tusks, down to the talons on the boots. The rumor was that the being underneath was simply a smaller version. "Would you care to detail it?"

"Not particularly," Chansa said bitterly, then shrugged. "Harzburg is a town with some strategic importance to one scenario of an invasion of Norau. I attempted to take over the town using proxies. I supplied them with a small amount of power and some arms as well as guidance. They attempted to take over the town. They failed."

"Edmund Talbot again?" the Demon said, soothingly.

"He sent one, *one* damned Blood Lord, and a year's work went down the drain!"

"The man is incorrigible," the Demon replied. "But he does train good subordinates. I have always found that choice of subordinates is important in any endeavor. The Council, for all its strengths, has been a group that had little in the way, or need, of subordinates, so it is not surprising that you have less . . . experience with the handling of them. In that regard," he continued, gesturing in the air as another avatar appeared, "might I commend the services of my protégé, Brother Conner."

"You do me great honor in the term, lord," the man said. He was tall but apparently entirely unChanged with a lean, ascetic look and less than his first century in age. Dark hair fell to midshoulder length. He was almost normal until you looked at his eyes, the irises of which were almost perfectly white. His pupils were tiny black dots in the middle of them.

"You are too kind, Lord Demon," Chansa said after a moment. "But I'm not sure what to do with him."

"I would *suggest* that you do what you do best, prepare the armies of New Destiny for the invasion," the Demon replied acerbically. "And let Conner handle the destabilization. He has . . . experience in these matters."

"Ah." Chansa paused again, then shrugged. Favors from the Demon generally had a hidden cost, but they also weren't to be turned aside. "Thank you, Lord Demon."

"I'll be leaving you two to your work," the Demon replied, fading out of the air. "Have *fun*."

"Paul is preparing a fleet on the coast of Ropasa," Edmund said, pulling out a map and setting it on his desk. "Here in Brethan and in Neterlan. And he's assembling armies of Changed near both areas."

"Invasion?" Herzer asked.

"That's the apparent intent," the duke replied. "And it's borderline that he could be successful."

"At an invasion?" Daneh said. "How? He's got to cross the

whole Atlantis ocean and then attack a prepared enemy. I'm not much on the military end, but that doesn't sound feasible to me."

"We don't have much in the way of troops, Daneh," Edmund replied with a shrug. "There's unorganized and organized militia, yes, but they're not going to count for much but positional defense. You can't even really use them for sallies. And the 'positions' that most of the towns have aren't much. And you'd be surprised how many over the beach invasions have been successful. If the country was castellated, that is if we had lots and lots of castles as Ropasa does, it would be impossible. As it is, it's just very risky.

"One of the ways to play a war like this is deterrence. That is, make it clearly so impossible for something to happen that nobody in their right minds would try it. And hope that your enemy is in their right mind. In this case, we have to eliminate any chance of such an invasion succeeding. To do that, we have to control the sea-lanes.

"We're working on that on the coast. The Navy has been working on a new class of warship that should make things very unpleasant for anyone attempting to cross. But a few warships, probably in the wrong place, aren't going to deter New Destiny. Nor should they.

"What we need are allies that control the sea-lanes." He looked up significantly at Daneh, who shrugged.

"I think that's supposed to mean something, but I have no idea what."

"The mer," Herzer interjected. "Weren't they reported as concentrating, post-Fall, down in the Southern Isles?"

"Exactly," the Duke said. "If we have the mer on our side, between them and the delphinos, who are going to follow their lead, and the dolphins they have attached to them, at the very least we have total reconnaissance of the potential invasion fleet. Fighting it might be another matter, but I'd be surprised if they couldn't do something along those lines too."

"So it's a diplomatic mission?" Herzer asked. "Why you? Why me for that matter?"

"It's a diplomatic mission with military implications," Edmund said. "I'm the best known, I almost said 'notorious,' person available on the East Coast and I'm probably going to be one of the point generals for any defense."

"You're probably going to *command* the defense," Daneh corrected.

"Probably. And Herzer for some similar reasons."

"So what this means is that while the rest of us suffer through the winter," Rachel said, somewhat bitterly, "you're going to go gallivanting down to the Southern Isles?"

"Sheida wants me to go handle the negotiations. She told me I could take whatever staff I thought was necessary. What I consider *necessary* is Herzer."

"So you *are* leaving us behind and sailing off to the Isles for the winter," Daneh said humorously.

"Well, maybe," Edmund replied, in a much more serious tone. "Herzer is a damn fine junior officer, but there's nothing absolutely vital he has to do here. Between Kane and Gunny the town should be good against anything but a major attack. And I know what's out there well enough to know that isn't going to happen short of invasion. So I can leave the town and be pretty sure it will be here when I get back. The question is, can the town do without both of its doctors?"

"I'm not a doctor," Rachel replied, but she nodded. "But I see what you mean."

"Say that you're the best of the trainees, then," Edmund admitted. "There are reasons that I want to take one or both of you along. Frankly, I'd prefer Daneh. But I don't think it wise to take both unless we can make provisions for adequate medical care here."

"Well, how long is this going to take?" Daneh asked. "I mean the negotiations. Port down, port back and a week or two there."

"One problem," Edmund grimaced. "Sheida says that it's important, but not important enough to port us. She's working on some sort of device that will reduce porting power drain; she has an experimental one up and running so she can get in and out of her house. But even that will be point to point. In the meantime, we're still down to the speed of horse and wind."

"How long?" Daneh repeated.

"A month? Two? Possibly more if the weather turns against us."

"I know my responsibilities," Daneh sighed. "And there's Charles to consider; I'm not sure I want to be away from him for that long. I'll stay." Daneh's son had been born as the result of her rape, shortly after the Fall, by Dionys McCanoc and his men. When the child was born it was clear who had bestowed the male genes. Just as clear as the fact that the father was no longer living. Herzer rather liked the kid who, except for a tendency for mischief, appeared to have gotten nothing but his looks from his father.

"I want you to consider carefully what I said," Edmund replied. "I would prefer *you* to go and Rachel to stay. Including taking you away from Charles."

"Why?" Daneh asked and was rewarded with a blank stare. "Edmund, quit being mysterious."

"I'm not being mysterious. I have my reasons and I have reasons not to *give* them."

"That's just Edmund's way of saying 'I'm being mysterious,'" Daneh said with a chuckle.

"I'll give you one that's up front," Talbot replied after a moment. "We want an alliance with them, a military alliance certainly and a trade agreement by preference. We need to know what they need, that we can supply, for that to happen. I won't say that I want you to go talk with the women while I do the 'men talk' . . ."

"Good!" Daneh said with a smile.

" . . . But I will say that we have different strengths and areas of knowledge. I'd take Myron if I thought agriculture was going to be important, but I think that areas having to do with . . . lifestyle are going to be far more so."

"I'm a doctor, not an anthropologist," Daneh said. "For that matter Rachel has a firmer grasp on preindustrial cultures."

"You have a point. But I trust your judgment more than Rachel's." He turned to his daughter and shrugged. "That wasn't meant to be offensive, it's just Daneh is . . ."

"Older and wiser?" Rachel said, then shook her head. "I'm really not offended, because I understood what you meant."

"I can turn over control of the local power system to Emily," Daneh suggested. "She's up to just about anything that Rachel would be. And I assume that if something major comes up, we can consult. She's certainly up to deliveries and small repairs. Dr. Beauharnois is up in Hotrum's Ferry if something serious occurs."

Talbot thought about it for a moment then shrugged. "I guess you're in, Rachel."

"When do we leave?" Herzer asked.

"Not for at least a week or two," Edmund said. "I didn't think you'd make it back this fast and it's going to take at least that long for the rest of our party to get here."

"And who is that?" Daneh asked.

"You'll see," Edmund replied. "It's a surprise."

CHAPTER FOUR

Joel was surprised to see Harry practically hovering outside Sheida's office.

Sheida used what had once been her mountain home as her central headquarters. Since she often hosted parties and other functions it had been large enough to support the minimal staff that she needed.

But since it was now surrounded by bubbling lava, getting anything in and out required porting, which was extremely high in energy use.

The answer, as he had discovered on his way in, was a permanent portal. Step through the arch and you were suddenly "elsewhere." He wasn't sure what the energy level to the portal was, but it couldn't be high; he had been only one of a dozen or so people who had passed through it while he was there.

Instead of heading for the portal, Harry waved him in another direction. Joel noted that he had a slight limp.

"I've set up your transportation," the aide said, leading him to a small office. It had, apparently, once been a bedroom. There were now three desks in the room, along with boxes of paperwork. There were no external windows so it smelled dank and musty.

Harry pulled out a sheaf of papers and a small bag that clinked when he set it down.

"Gold has, again, become the international currency," Harry said with a sarcastic smile. "Make sure you're not set upon by ruffians."

"I'll try," Joel replied, smiling amiably. He opened up the pouch and dumped it out. "I take it I sign for this?"

"And we'll need expense records," Harry replied. "Did you know Sheida before the Fall?"

"Yes, we were acquaintances," Joel said, piling up the square chunks of gold. "I'd studied the history of management and business before the Fall. She wants me to look at logistics at Washan and other facilities along the East Coast."

"Mind you don't step on Edmund's toes," Harry replied. He slapped his thigh and grimaced. "He gave me this."

"The limp?" Joel asked. He pulled over the receipt and signed it, apparently without reading it. In fact he'd read it upside down while the aide was holding it and while the total was close it wasn't exactly the same. He'd just signed for a chunk of gold, the equivalent of two months wages for a field hand, that wasn't there.

"Happened right after the Fall," Harry said. "Drove a sword through my mail and tore a hole right into my thigh. He always said that the only way to fight was to intend to kill the other person; I never thought he was serious until then."

"Didn't he know what would happen?" Joel asked, widening his eyes in horror. "And haven't you gotten it fixed? I mean, power is short, but . . ."

"Well . . . we didn't know the fields were down," Harry admitted. "And, yes, Sheida fixed it. But it's still not quite right."

Nannites either fixed something or they didn't, at least when it came to gross tissue damage. They didn't just stitch things back together but reformed them to the cellular level. Which meant that any remnant injury was psychosomatic.

"I'll try not to get my legs chopped out from under me," the inspector said. "How am I getting back?"

"Sheida wants you to fly on a wyvern that's headed that way," Harry said, looking at him oddly. "Apparently she's really worried about this logistics problem."

"Just a good use of resources." Joel shrugged. "How do I find this wyvern?"

"Not worried about riding on one?" Harry asked, frowning slightly.

"Looking forward to it, actually," Joel smiled. "Better than the coaches."

"Well . . . take the portal then ask around for Robert Scott, he's the travel coordinator. He'll know where you're supposed to go." Harry stood up and offered his hand. "Good luck."

"Same to you," Joel replied. "I'm sure we'll be meeting again."

"Oh?"

"Sure, the logistical issues around here are just amazing."

"There are several issues that I'd prefer to set aside," Chansa said, looking over at his new assistant. "They're taking up my time and energy; time and energy I need to devote to the invasion plans."

"Understood," Conner said. He had a very old-fashioned writing stylus and pad of paper and nodded as he took notes.

"The two aspects that are taking up most of my time at the moment, though, are trying to establish a political climate for our eventual invasion and a mission by Edmund Talbot to gain an alliance with the mer."

"We have pods of orca that are allied with us," Conner said. "Surely they can deal with the mer."

"The mer and the delphinos have a long-term friendship," Chansa said. "The delphinos, in turn, are well thought of by those few idiots that have turned themselves into true whales. And the latter travel throughout the oceans. Between those groups they will know, to a minute, where our ships are. It's important that they are neutralized. And I mean *totally* neutralized; either on our side or unable to affect us. The invasion fleet is going to be on the ragged edge of possibility as it is. The mer have to be taken out of the equation."

"I see," the agent said, apparently doodling. "Where are the mer at this time and what assets do we have in place? For that matter, I'll need access to power for communications and a budget, not to mention updated intelligence."

"I can give you everything except the power," Chansa said. "Since that idiot McCanoc got himself killed, that's been in short supply; even we council members are limited."

"Well, it will be quite impossible to perform my job without power, my lord," the agent said, closing the pad. "And there are other things. To get to the mer will require ships. I'll need soldiers as well as contacts with the orca. And the way that I work, my lord, is that you tell me what needs to be done and I do it. My own way."

"That's pretty damned impertinent," Chansa said, flexing his jaw.

"I'm sorry if you feel that way, my lord," the agent said. "But that's the way that I work."

"Why don't you get your power from the Demon?" Chansa temporized.

"I don't work for Milord Demon, sir," the agent said with

a sincere smile. "I work for you. Asking *him* for power *would* be impertinence. And he can be so direct about such things."

Chansa chuckled and nodded.

"I'll get you a list of what's available. Find yourself an office; there's all sorts in this warren. Give me a list, a *reasonable* list, from that. And besides the orcas, I've talked to Celine and we have some *special* assistants for you. After that you're on your own. You'd better be worth it."

"I'm sure that I'll be worthy of the trust you place in me, my lord," Conner said.

"I'm not," Chansa replied. "Now get."

The one problem with the portal was that you couldn't see who was on the far side; it was simply a shimmering wall of opalescent light. As Joel approached it he wondered who all the people going in and out of the house were and, for that matter, how they were cleared for entry. As far as he could see, anyone who reached the town could use the portal to penetrate Sheida's innermost sanctum. He was sure there *was* security on the passage, but what and how had not been discussed.

There was a short line waiting to pass through and he joined it, nodding at the woman in front of him.

"You're new," the slightly built woman said. She was barely up to Joel's chest in height.

"Just passing through," Joel replied. "I had a meeting with Harry about improving the logistics."

"Not much to be done with just the one entry," the woman sniffed. "Getting fresh food in and out is real bother."

"You're a cook?" he asked, automatically fishing for information.

"For Herself," the woman replied with a note of pride. "I'm on my way out to have a word with the butcher. The last load of meat was simply dreadful. Not that Herself eats much, she eats like a bird to tell truth, it's really terrible. I try to get her to eat more but even my best pastries she barely nibbles. It's a real shame."

"Do you cook for the rest of the complex?" Joel asked as the line moved forward.

"I'm one of the cooks, but I'm mainly to supply Herself," the woman said. "Sometimes when she has a big meeting I'll take charge of that. There's a head 'chef' but he's such a pain, a real prima donna if you know what I mean."

"Uh-huh."

"But when they do have a big party it's a real pain. First

getting everything through on portal and then getting all the guests in and out. You have no idea how much food it takes for a big party, oh, but I guess you do if you handle logistics?"

"Rather large parties, yes," Joel said with an amiable grin. "But I just do paperwork, you know. I don't have to do the cooking."

"Well, you have no idea. I mean, at least we have a decent kitchen but it's still too small and the stoves could use a good upgrade. Fortunately I'd made a study of *real* cooking before the Fall. None of this three sprigs of over-spiced carrot and a piece of chicken the size of your thumb, no sirree . . ."

After they passed through the portal into the receiving room Joel managed to extract himself from the woman and mentally groaned. He wasn't sure who was in charge of Sheida's counterintelligence but it left a great deal to be desired. These people simply didn't *think* in terms of security. That her senior cook wandered in and out talking to any stranger was bad enough. But if there wasn't a good filter on the portal anyone could go in and out. Or anything. Slipping a toxin into the food would be no problem. A time-release binary would take down everyone in the complex.

He was half tempted to turn around and go see Sheida about it but after a moment's thought he decided to continue the mission. He'd be reporting at some point and he could ask her, or one of her avatars, about it later.

He looked up the "transportation coordinator" and found out that his dragon wouldn't be leaving until late morning the next day. With that information, and where to meet the dragon, he set off into the town.

Like most of the post-Fall towns, new construction was evident. Most of it was packed earth, what was called adobe in other areas. Chian was at the base of the western mountain ranges where they met the plains, drawing from both areas. The town was filled with herdsmen from the plains, most of them wearing rough bison coats against the early fall cold, and people that he designated "townies." After casting around for a bit he found a money changer. The building was one of the few made of stone and obviously old, not only pre-Fall but probably from the semimythical "settlement" period. There were guards armed with short swords and they frowned at him as he stepped through the open door.

The interior was dim, lit only by small windows set high on the walls. He waited for his eyes to adjust, then walked over to the barred counter at the end.

"I'd like to change some gold for credit chits and some chunk silver," he said to the woman behind the counter.

"Let's see it," the woman replied, pulling out a scale and jeweler's loupe.

He slid over one of the chunks of gold, wondering if they'd ID him as from Sheida.

"Federal mint," the woman frowned after a glance at the imprint on the bar. "We haven't seen many of these."

"Neither have I," Joel replied with his patented vapid smile. "I did some contract work for the Federals and that's what they paid me with."

"I still need to assay it." The woman sniffed. She rubbed the metal on an emery block, then dropped a solvent on it. There was a brief hiss and she compared the color to a chart. She gave another sniff and put the gold on a scale, frowning all the while. Finally she looked up with a reduced frown.

"There's a fixed value on these," she said, rummaging in a drawer until she pulled out a sheet of paper. She compared the date, then shrugged. "Four hundred twenty-three credits."

"Close enough for government work," Joel replied. "I need it in as small a package as possible."

The woman opened her cash drawer and extracted a handful of bills, stamped bronze coins and some loose silver in irregular chunks. She put the silver on the scale and added a tad more then slid the whole under the bars.

"Three hundred credits in cash," she said, counting out the bills. "Five twenty-cred pieces and twenty-three in silver."

"I've never seen these," Joel admitted, picking up one of the bills. It was printed on one side with the eagle of the UFS and on the other with an image of some person he didn't recognize. It said "Fifty Credits" on it. He rubbed at the printing and the ink stayed in place.

"It's the new scrip currency they're distributing," the woman explained. "It can be exchanged for fifty chit credits anywhere in the UFS. If you go to one of the unincorporated towns, most of them are willing to accept it, too."

"Seems a bad trade for gold," Joel temporized.

"Well, if you walk back in with that we give you the exact same amount, less a two percent transaction fee," the woman replied, clearly used to explaining the facts of life to utter newbies. "Or, if you have an account with us we waive the transaction fee."

"So you act as a bank as well?"

"Yes, we're Federally licensed and act under charter of Idoma," the woman said. "It's a bit different than before we chartered, but not much. And we're insured against loss, which is a nice feeling. Too many moneylenders and changers have been robbed since the Fall. Now it's a Federal offense and the inspectors will chase anyone who robs a Federal bank to the ends of the earth."

"Or one of Paul's regions," Joel noted. "Okay, I'll take it. Can you direct me to someplace to sleep? I'm leaving tomorrow."

"The Hotel Brixon is nice," the lady said, pointing out and to the left. "And they have a good dining room."

"Thank you for all your help," Joel replied, picking up the cash and slipping it in his pouch. "I'm sorry I can't open an account."

"Well, perhaps if you spend more time here," the woman replied. "Chian is really growing, almost like a second capital city. There's always work to be had."

"I'll consider it," he said. "Have a nice day."

"What is it that you do, again?" the woman asked.

"Contract work," Joel replied, as he turned away. "I like to think of it as . . . salvage."

The man currently using the name Martin St. John sipped at surprisingly good wine and looked around the crowded tavern. He wasn't casing his fellow diners. The Brethon merchant who had had the misfortune to meet the seemingly friendly young man on the road from Setran was returning from a good sales trip. It was the merchant's nuggets of silver, each the size of a knucklebone—the preferred currency in Ropasa over the inflationary paper scrip of New Destiny—that had paid for the bad stew and good wine to follow.

The wine was the reason the inn even existed. The building had been at the crossroads for literally millennia, first as an inn dating back to the time of the Hundred Years' War, then as a private residence that was maintained across the millennia. The last owner had used his wine cellar, and the broadsword that hung over the fireplace, to reestablish it as an inn in the years after the Fall. Until he ran afoul of New Destiny's Changed legions and the ownership had passed to cronies of New Destiny.

The food had been better before the coming of the new owners. But they had held onto the wine cellar. In time, they might even learn how to make a decent stew.

But for now, it was good enough. He was out of the rain that was pissing down outside, he had a full belly, and the mature claret was putting him into a nearly expansive mood.

That was until the door opened and a tall, spare figure walked in out of the rain.

The man took off his broad-brimmed hat and shook it, looking around the room with eyes that were almost entirely white. The denizens of the inn looked at the stance and, most especially the eyes, and turned away, the conversation dying for a moment then picking up to an almost unnatural chatter.

Martin hoped that the man was looking for someone, or something, else. But the newcomer caught his eyes and smiled in an entirely friendly way and then made his way across the crowded room.

"Brother Martin," Conner said. "What a pleasant surprise."

"Surprise, hell," Martin replied, bitterly. "What the hell do you want, Brother Conner?"

The Brotherhood of the Rose had existed before the Fall. In the pre-Fall world, there was very little need, or reason, for criminality. It required both incredible cunning and a deep desire to do harm; when literally anything could be had at a whim, crime took on a truly bizarre form.

For the Brotherhood it was a game, a way to while away the time between birth and death in a world surfeited with luxuries. To steal a woman's virginity and betray her trust, to find the one thing that a person cherished and relieve them of it, to kill, in a world where everyone was protected by energy fields, nannites overcame toxins and healing was virtually instantaneous, took cunning and skill, especially since the few remaining police of the Council had access to investigation technology that was nothing short of magical. And it was a matter of points among the "Brothers" to do such things with style.

In the Brotherhood, Conner had racked up a truly amazing point total.

Since the Fall, the skills that Martin had developed had kept him warm, fed and as comfortable as it was possible to be in the Fallen world. He realized that all of those things might be coming to an end. Or not.

"How have you been?" Conner said, sitting down across from him and crossing his legs at the ankles. He waved to the server, a young man who looked harried by all the customers, and looked back at Martin. "How's tricks?"

"Oh, you know," Martin said, leaning back also. "I get along. This and that."

"Yes," Conner said, smiling. "I'm sure. I passed a bit of a gaggle on the road. It seemed that some local merchant had been set upon by vagabonds. Such a terrible thing. Paul's doing all that he can to reduce crime in the areas under his control. I'm sure that the ne'er-do-well will be caught in time."

Martin tried not to gulp as he took a sip of wine that suddenly tasted of vinegar. Before the Fall, getting caught generally led to close supervision. In extreme cases, and he knew he fell into the latter category, a brain-wipe might have been ordered, with a nice, docile personality imposed upon the criminal.

Since the Fall, crime was generally a local thing. If a thief was caught, the locals tended to be direct and final. Rope was cheap and, after all, could be reused.

With the coming of Paul's legions, though, things had changed. Paul had much better uses for criminals than making corpses. His legions were always looking for new bodies, bodies that gave up their own energy to be Changed into the brutal, bestial beings that served as the bulk of his army.

It included a brain-wipe, of course, but instead of a nice docile personality and a life of ease, if not interest, the former thief became just one more orc to be sent into the camps.

"I'm sure," he said. "How are you?"

"Well, I have to admit that I've found an employer," Conner said, taking the cup of wine that the harried serving boy had fetched for him ahead of a dozen other customers. "I hate to think that I'm going legit."

"Legit, yeah," Martin snorted. "I can just see you pulling down a pay-chit."

"Well, I have to admit that regular food, the money to buy clothes . . ." he said, eyeing Martin's weather-beaten ensemble, "has a certain pleasure to it. Especially since the jobs so far have been . . . right up my alley."

"I hate to think of the body count," Martin said.

"Well, as it happens, I've currently got too many projects to handle on my own. So I've convinced my employer that I could find suitable . . . subordinates. Such as yourself."

Martin eyed him for a moment, then shook his head.

"No. I don't know what racket you've gotten yourself into, but I know I can't trust you as far as I can throw this inn. I think I'll just keep going my own way, thanks."

"I'll add," Conner said, more or less ignoring him, "that the offer would include a pardon for any little offenses that you might have, accidentally I'm sure, committed against the caring government of New Destiny." Conner smiled in an open and friendly manner. "Such as a certain merchant on the Setran road."

"Who in the hell are you working for?" Martin asked, his eyes narrowing.

"Why, New Destiny of course," Conner smiled. "Such a fresh and forward looking name, don't you think. Do say yes, Martin, it would mean the world to you."

Martin flexed his jaw and took another sip of wine, then nodded.

"Okay, what's the job?"

"It seems that those *rascals* from the United Free States are getting concerned about a certain fleet that is building on the coast," Conner said.

Martin just nodded; the movement of the Changed legions, and all the provisions to support them as well as the building of a fleet of ships, was impossible to miss anywhere within a hundred klicks of the ocean.

"They seem to think that the mer will do them some good," Conner continued. "I've been tasked, among other things, with ensuring that the mer, one particular group of mer to be clear, don't ally with the UFS. One way or another."

"Where are they?"

"Well, that's the nice part," Brother Conner said. "It seems they're located in the Isles off Flora. So you can look forward to a relaxing sea voyage and then a pleasant tropical vacation."

"I'm not going to be able to do much about this by myself." Martin frowned, but given the cold autumn rains outside, a tropical vacation sounded just about right.

"Of course not," Conner snapped. "You'll be . . . managing a group of orcas and a new breed of Change called ixchitl. You'll be the control. I've a fleet of six ships that will take you to meet them and then carry you to the Isles. They're some of the first completed and you'll have Changed marines as well as their leaders under your command. Stop the alliance with the mer, wipe them out if you have to, and destroy the UFS group, and their ships, at the same time. Our information is that they're sending a new type of ship, a 'dragon-carrier.' The dragons, wyverns actually, aren't going to be a problem; they don't have a way to attack the ships. Is all of this clear enough for you or do I have to write it down in words of one syllable?"

"No, that's clear enough," Martin said, looking at the shutter-covered windows beaten by rain. "When do I leave?"

CHAPTER FIVE

Jason coasted to a stop parallel and slightly above Bruce the Black who was observing a group of mer, men and women, repairing one of the fishing nets. The material available for the nets was horrible, a type of long seaweed, a green algae in reality, whose "stems" were soft and pliable. Braided it was marginally effective as a net unless someone tried to capture, as in this example, a school of dorado, which were some of the fastest fish in the sea.

But between the nets, and scavenging for crayfish and the sea plums, and the occasional large fish that hunters like Jason speared with bone-tipped harpoons, hunger was kept at bay. That was about all that could be said about the happy life of the mer-folk. Oh, and the Work went on.

"Representatives Freedom come," Jason pulsed. The mer, unlike dolphins or other marine mammals, used gills and had no air available to create sonar. Instead they had a small bone, equivalent in basic design to those of the inner ear, located in the nasal passages in their forehead. They could send commands to the bone that pulsed their words and turned them into high frequency sonar. It was also adequate, barely, to maneuvering in zero visibility, be that in the dark or in a cave or even in light silt. And they could receive and process, to an extent, the sonar images created by the delphinoids, who had a much more advanced system. But for conversation, the mer relied on verbal shorthand.

"Destiny, too," Bruce answered. The name "the Black"

51

referred to a joke that had circulated early in his years as a mer. He had said that his real purpose was to find the treasure of an ancient pirate named Blackbeard and spent a fair amount of time in the search. He was anything but black. His skin was a nearly perfect white, his hair was blond and his tail-section was covered in golden scales. But someone had called him "Blackbeard" and it had stuck, even after he became one of the leaders of the Work, the apparently eternal project of putting the coral reefs back into a "prehuman" condition.

The Fall had set back the Work, beyond question. Even Bruce the Black had been forced to recognize that hunting and gathering on the reefs was a necessity, not a barbarous hobby. And sea plum, a human-generated weed for all intents and purposes, which had been ruthlessly pruned, was now tended with nearly the same care as mer-children. But the Work went on.

Bruce the Black had been one of the most notable members of the mer community and he had been an outspoken proponent of continuing the Work to the best of their ability. It had been taken up as an article of faith among the mer, that the Work was more important than any temporary squabble among the Powers-That-Be.

Sometimes Jason wondered if there might not be more to life than the Work. Such as, for example, trying not to get trampled by the oncoming war.

"Fight will," Jason said.

"Fight/lose," Bruce replied. "Always fight/lose. Neutral are. Neutral stay."

"Freedom . . ." Jason replied.

"Destiny! Freedom! Fight/lose! Neutral stay!" The last was said with a blat of sound borrowed from the dolphins. In tonal shorthand it said "I'm the leader and you're not and you *will* obey!"

Jason, however, recognized the undertone, that of a porpoise mother chastising her infant, and was less than happy about it. There was, however, not much that he could say in return.

"Freedom representative Talbot. Going am."

"Where?" Bruce asked, finally turning to look at the younger mer.

"Hunt will," he said with a contemptuous gesture at the nets. "Food need. Neutral stay." With that he turned and gave a powerful flick of his tail, enough motion that the water assuredly washed over the older mer.

If Bruce took it as an insult, that wouldn't bother Jason one bit. He was half tempted to pee in his wake.

Herzer turned down an offer to have dinner with Edmund and gravitated to the officers' mess instead. For one credit chit he was served overcooked and oversalted roast beef, lumpy mashed potatoes with slightly burned gravy and greens cooked to mush. However, he consoled himself that it was better than monkey on a stick. He didn't recognize any of the people in the mess, except occasionally by sight. He'd checked around and there were none of his class currently present, not that there had been many survivors. After dinner he drifted back to his room, uncertain about where to go or what to do. He could get all spiffied up and go to the O-club bar and get shit-faced, but that had little appeal. There were always some women hanging around and if he flashed his medals he'd probably get laid. But he liked to think that he was beyond that. He lay down on his bed and tucked his hand behind his head, and tapped his prosthetic in thought. He should have gone to dinner at Edmund's. He'd barely said hello to Rachel and Daneh, who were two of his favorite people on earth. He should go to the bar; at least with a few belts in him he could probably sleep. The bottom line was that he had gotten so used to having something to do, constantly, that he didn't know how to relax anymore.

Finally he stripped off his tunic and opened up his wall locker. It took him two checks to determine that he had, precisely, zero civilian clothes.

"Herzer, you're getting way too into this shit," he muttered. Finally he pulled out an undress tunic and a field cloak and stomped out of the quarters.

He headed downtown in the general direction of Tarmac's tavern, then took a left and, on an impulse, headed for the public baths. When he got near them he stopped and whistled. What had once been a rather small set of three wooden buildings was now a complex of at least half a dozen. And from the traffic going in and out half the town was there.

He headed up the front entrance and passed through one of several doors. There was a small antechamber, heated against the growing cold of fall, and he stripped off his cloak before passing through the second set.

The far room, which smelled of chlorine and was, frankly, overheated, had tables down either side with at least six people at each of them. He didn't recognize any of them and he hoped

that it was mutual. He stepped to the right where a teenage
girl wearing a bathing suit nodded at him.

"Lord, you're a big one," she said with a smile. "I haven't
seen you before."

"I haven't been here in . . ." He had to stop and think for
a moment. "Oh, at least two years. So I think you'll have to
walk me through the procedures."

"Well, I have to stay here or I'd be happy to." She grinned.
"But it hasn't changed much." She dipped under the desk and
came up with a bag marked with a complicated symbol and
a wooden marker. "Take the bag, go through the doors. There
are disrobing rooms in there and towels. Grab a towel, put
all your stuff in the bag and give it to an attendant. They'll
seal it and you keep the marker."

"What are all the buildings?"

"Well, there's a shower room, please pee and take a shower
before you climb in the baths," she said with her first frown.
"There's one building for women-only baths, another for men;
they're marked. Then there's the pool room, which is unisex.
You can eat in there as well. And the fitness center."

"Fitness center?" Herzer asked. "I'm getting a sinking feeling.
Do people wear bathing suits in here?"

"Some do, some don't," the girl smiled. "And there are some
for sale in the gift shop, which is right around the corner,"
she added, pointing.

"I think I'll stop there, first," Herzer said.

He followed her directions and found a fully appointed gift
shop. Not only were there bathing suits, there was a complete line of toiletries, soaps, shampoos, towels with the Raven's
Mill logo and even shirts and coffee mugs. He picked one of
the latter up and grimaced. "Raven's Mill, Home of the Blood
Lords" was baked into the ceramic.

"Can I help you?" a cold female voice asked from behind
him.

"Morgen!" he said, when he turned around. "I thought you'd
run off to another town!"

Morgen Kirby was about a hundred and seventy centimeters of slim redhead. They had had a very brief relationship
just after the Fall, before he had joined the Blood Lords. Very
brief. Basically a half a day at the end of which they had a
flaming argument. He couldn't, off-hand, recall about what.

"I did," she said, sighing. "I went to Resan."

"Oh, shit," was all Herzer could say. The town of Resan
had been one of the first that Dionys McCanoc's forces had

hit and because the town elders had a policy of "strict non-violence" his forces had gone through it like a hot knife through butter. And that reminded him what the argument had been about. "I'm sorry. I didn't know. How . . ." He paused, unsure how to go on.

"McCanoc attacked just before dawn. I was working for one of the established people in the town and had gone out to one of the farms for milk; Mistress Tabitha had to have *fresh* milk for breakfast every morning."

"So you got out," Herzer sighed.

"Not . . . entirely unscathed." She frowned. "After that I went to Washan but after you and Edmund stopped McCanoc I decided the one place I wanted to be was back in Raven's Mill. Even if *I* didn't have my head screwed on straight, I could at least be somewhere where others did." She paused and shrugged. "You were right. Shilan and Cruz and all the rest were right; this world can't afford peaceful innocence. There are too many bad people in it. I always sort of expected you to turn up and gloat. But after a while I figured out you weren't the gloating type."

"No, I'm not," Herzer said. "I'm the worrying type. I actually thought of you earlier today; I saw Crystal. She's Edmund's secretary."

"You were right about that, too," she snorted. "She *was* being snippy because I was with you. When I got back here I was a bit loopy and she tried to 'comfort' me. Big mistake. She found out *how* over 'nonviolence' I am."

"Um . . ." Herzer scratched his chin and frowned. "I . . . well we get briefings about combat aftermath. You know, you really need to talk to a counselor . . ."

"I have been," she smiled. "For damned near a year I've been going to the post-rape trauma groups. I'm actually bucking for a junior counseling spot and Mistress Daneh thinks I can make it." She suddenly frowned again and looked at his prosthetic. "What the hell happened to you? Where's your *hand*?"

"McCanoc," Herzer said with a shrug, raising the prosthetic. "It's okay, it's got a little latch for holding my shield, takes all the trouble out of it. Better than a hand in some ways."

"I didn't know." She frowned again, looking at the clamp and hook of glittering metal.

"And you work here?" Herzer said, changing the subject.

"And I work here." She shrugged, still looking at the prosthetic with a troubled expression. "Three nights a week. And the sawmill during the day. So, were you looking for me, or . . . ?"

"Actually, I was looking for a suit," he admitted. "I haven't been to the bathhouse in a year or two and it's really changed."

"Not as much as you might think." She smiled. "Some people use them by the pools, but most don't. And, frankly, I don't think we have anything that will fit you."

"Story of my life," he grumbled.

"Well, you never were an off-the-rack kind of guy," she said with a grin.

"I guess I'll go brave the baths then," he said. "I've been in Harzburg for a year and they're . . . pretty uptight about body modesty. I guess some of it rubbed off."

"Oh, I'm sure you'll get back into the evil ways of Raven's Mill." She grinned again.

"Well . . . see you later?"

"Maybe," she said with a shrug. "I'm . . . not sure it would be a good thing to just pick up where we left off. I'm . . . over it but not that far."

"Believe me, I understand," Herzer said, frowning. "I've never had that particular experience, but I've seen the aftermath enough times. Take care of yourself, and . . . I'm here. Shoulder, bed, sword, okay?"

"Okay," she said, dimples appearing on her cheeks. "Go have fun."

"Fun, right," he said, throwing the bag over his shoulder.

The changing room had altered as well. There were closed stalls for changing; before it had been totally open. And there were two attendants waiting for his clothes and gear. From prior experience he knew he could trust them to not pilfer anything out of the bags so he added his money pouch after a moment's thought. That done, he tucked a towel around his waist firmly and headed through the door marked "Showers."

More changes. The showers were individual stalls; before they had simply lined one side of the room. There were males and females in the room and when one of the latter, a tall, lithe blonde, came out of a shower stall stark naked he actually started to feel more at home. He still put the towel back on before leaving his own stall.

Beyond the room was cross corridor with several doors. One was marked "Baths, Male" another "Baths, Female" and a third "Pools." He pushed open the male bathing room and saw a line of large wooden tubs, much like he remembered. There were a few guys in the far tub but the room was otherwise empty. He didn't recognize any of them so he headed for the room marked "Pools."

He wasn't sure what to expect but it wasn't what he got. The room was long, apparently one large building, the walls made of paneled wood and lined with oil lamps. More oil lamps were hung throughout the room and in several spots there were round fireplaces with metal covers and chimneys to let the smoke out through the roof. The floor was tiled and the "pools" were just that, nine pools of varying sizes scattered around the room. There were benches and low tables as well and most of the people who had been coming in and out apparently gravitated here. The conversation was loud and echoed across the room.

He stepped through the door and looked around trying to decide what the standard mode of dress was but there didn't seem to be any. Some of the people had on light bathing suits but the majority were naked and there didn't seem to be any discrimination. A blonde in a suit so sheer she might as well have been naked was talking to a male who was. Two guys in bikini bathing suits were talking to the woman who had walked out of the shower starkers. He finally recognized one of the instructors at the Academy and had started across the room when he heard his name screamed and the next moment found his arms filled with naked female.

He was having such a hard time trying to figure out where to put his hand, and hook, that it took him a moment to recognize her.

"Shilan!" he yelled. "Damn, it's good to see a familiar face." Hsu Shilan had been part of his apprenticeship class, a lovely trim brunette with whom he'd had an "off-again" relationship until he joined the Blood Lords and basically lost track. Last he'd heard she was a textile designer at one of the mills. She'd put on a bit of weight since then, but since she had been skinny to the point of anorexia it looked good on her. Too good. Herzer found himself stroking her back and wished he had more clothes on.

"Well, if you'd stay in *town* for a while," she said, sternly. If she noticed the stroking it was only to lean into it a bit.

"My master's voice," he replied, carefully removing his hands lest he get a little too enthusiastic. "I go where they tell me. This time it was Harzburg for a year and a half."

"You haven't met my husband, David," she said, dragging him to one of the pools.

"Husband?" he squeaked.

One of the bathers had risen out of a nearby pool and held out his hand.

"So you're Herzer Herrick," the man said. Herzer noted as he took the hand that it was soft and that he out-massed Shilan's husband by at least twice. So if it came to cases, he could probably punch David through the nearest wall. He still intended to be extremely correct and punctilious. Damnit. The mission in Harzburg meant that he was trying to uphold the reputation of the Federal forces. And although an ancient general had said "A soldier who won't fisk, won't fight," the Harzians were such stuck-up pricks that he'd had to play saintly soldier boy the entire year. It had been a *looong* year.

"Shilan has told me an awful lot about you," David continued.

"It's all lies and damned lies," Herzer said, squatting down as modestly as he could with a towel on. Shilan had slid back into the pool but her breasts, which were noticeably rounder and fuller than the last time Herzer met her, were fully exposed.

"Come on," Shilan said, waving at the pool. "Jump in. The water's fine."

"Um . . ." *One hundred twenty-eight times three is . . . three times eight, carry the two . . .* By the time he was barely a quarter of the way into the equation he'd gotten to the point he wouldn't embarrass himself and he pulled off the towel.

"See, told you he was hung like an ox," Shilan said with a chuckle.

So much for not being embarrassed.

"Yep, the reason we never had a relationship was she saw me in the showers and fainted," Herzer replied with a growl.

"With excitement, maybe," David laughed. "I see some of us got 'enhanced' before the Fall."

"Natural genetics," Herzer replied, tightly. "I had the muscles built on, but that was because I had a degenerative condition. I'd worked for them, they just wouldn't stay. When I got cured, I had a bod-mod, but it was only for the muscles. Then I *maintained* them. The rest is genetics. The size overall and . . . in places."

"Big hands," Shilan chuckled. "That's what you meant."

"Hand," Herzer noted, holding up his prosthetic.

"Sorry," Shilan said, suddenly contrite.

"Not a problem, it's great for opening beers," Herzer replied with a shrug.

"You're Herzer Herrick?" The woman from the showers slid

into the pool, looking at him with a quizzical frown. She looked to be in her twenties but her movements were so smooth and precise she had to be nearing her first century. "I was expecting someone . . . older."

"At your service, Mistress . . . ?"

"Miss," the woman said with a smile. "Stephanie Vega." She held out her hand, reaching across the pool to do so.

She was blond, a natural apparently or at least with either transformed genetics or very ready in her use of dye, long and slender in the hipless, bustless look that was fashionable pre-Fall. A face that was a little too perfect to be natural. Herzer wouldn't kick her out of bed for eating crackers. Well, maybe if she was really messy about it.

"And, yes, I'm Herzer Herrick," Herzer said, giving her his patented big-dumb-goofy grin. To most women big seemed to equal dumb and if dumb was what they wanted, he was their man.

"The Blood Lord?" she continued, her eyes widening, as if she still didn't quite believe it. Her pupils were dilated so far it was hard to tell she had green eyes.

"You might say the Blood Lord's Blood Lord," Shilan said somewhat cattily. "When they recruit they ask 'Do you think you can be as good as this?' "

"I wasn't disbelieving you," Stephanie said, smiling disarmingly as she leaned back against the wall of the pool. "But the stories that you hear . . ."

"We only eat babies if they're particularly tender," Herzer said. The woman was oozing charm, which suddenly set off alarm bells.

"Fight until you die and drop and all that," Stephanie said. "You've been out of town?"

"Harzburg," Herzer said. "Great place to visit, wouldn't want to live there."

"What were you doing?" Shilan asked.

"Tarson had declared for New Destiny," Herzer shrugged. "They were raiding Harzburg. Harzburg screamed for help. They got me."

"One war, one Blood Lord?" Stephanie asked.

"One minor little campaign," Herzer said with a frown. "They had some issues with their 'support.' They got over it in time."

"How?" Stephanie asked, leaning forward again and putting her hand on his knee, under the water.

It had been a long year so he recited some more multiplication tables.

"Tarson had been sending parties to raid the outlying farms," Herzer said. "Look, do you really want to hear this?"

"I want all of it," Stephanie said, throatily.

"I want to hear it, too," David replied when Herzer just looked at her, his face blank and hard.

He looked up at the ceiling when he realized other people, including the Blood Lord instructor he had seen across the room, had gathered around. He thought about the blood, the hacked remnants of what had been human beings scattered across a farmer's field. He realized what his face must look like so he, with difficulty, slid a friendlier mask onto his face.

"Tarson had been sending raiding parties out," he repeated, turning to look at Shilan. "They'd burned a couple of the farms in the area that wouldn't, or couldn't, pay their 'taxes.' I took to riding around . . ." He paused and shrugged.

"Blood Lord training is designed for formation; fighting as an individual is entirely different. But we cross-train." He looked over at the instructor from the Academy who nodded at him. "I'd . . . done more cross training than normal, for that matter. Anyway, I was out at one of the farms, just visiting. I'd been riding around to them, helping out sometimes, meeting people. And there was a scream from outside and Diablo was whinnying." He closed his eyes and tried to smile but it just wouldn't come.

"The farmers had a daughter, just about eleven. When I got outside some of the Tarson had her on the ground. Others were headed for the house, torches in their hands. I . . . well, it gets pretty blank in that kind of combat. My shield was on Diablo but I was in armor. They weren't." He stopped talking.

"That's it?" Stephanie said after a long pause. "What's the rest of the story?"

"The rest of the story is in the after-action report," the instructor said. "Fifteen raiders, motley weapons. Axes, swords, spears. One Blood Lord. You did us proud that day, Lieutenant."

"Thank you, sir," Herzer said, modestly, trying very hard not to remember. "I don't really remember most of it," he lied.

"What happened to the girl?" Shilan asked.

"She's never going to look at slaughtering the same for the rest of her life," the instructor said, grimly.

"She was fine," Herzer said. "Shaken up, but fine. They hadn't had time to get their pants down much less get stuck in. I talked to her a few times afterwards; she needed to talk it out and she didn't feel like she could with anybody else. She's fine."

"You're not much of a storyteller are you?" Stephanie asked.

"It's hard to talk about some things with people who haven't been there," Herzer admitted with a shrug. "The . . . feel of your sword crunching through a rib cage is difficult to describe. What it feels like to have your sword stuck in a corpse's spine while someone is hammering on you with an axe. What a field looks like after you've chopped a dozen human beings into their constituent parts. Having to decide whether to try to save someone's life or just give them mercy."

"I take it back," Stephanie said, leaning back. "You can feel free to leave out the little details."

"I didn't care about the ones headed for the house," Herzer said, suddenly loquacious. "If I raised enough of a ruckus they would either run to help or run off. I do remember bowling a couple of them over as I went through, and . . ." He looked up and his right hand made a motion like a butterfly drawn in air. "And a bit more to a couple of others. I made a mistake with the girl, though. I was so *angry*. The guy who was trying to rape her . . . his teeth chattered on my sword blade like a toy. Chit-chit-chit-chit-chit. That was when it got stuck, in the back of his brain really." There were grimaces in the audience but he didn't notice, being somewhere else.

"I'd kicked one of the guys holding her down on his face but another one was hitting me on the back with an axe. It was just bouncing off my armor so I turned around and punched him and took his axe away. I chopped a space around me and got my sword freed up." He shook his head and shuddered.

"What?" Shilan asked.

He shrugged and made a stomping motion as his gripped hands moved back and forth as if he was trying to free something. More grimaces, including from Shilan who clearly wished she hadn't asked the question, and a few of the audience wandered off, hurriedly.

"Diablo had turned up by that time and I made sure he didn't step on the girl. The ones who had been planning on burning the house were headed back by then and some of them threw spears. I remember one of them bouncing off the armor and another stuck. That just gave me another weapon. I hit them with that for a while, until it broke, then went back to the sword. When there weren't any more people bothering me, or the girl, or my horse, I went over to the spring and cleaned up."

"Tired?" the instructor asked, professionally.

"Not really," Herzer said. "A bit of a case of the shakes, but it hadn't taken five minutes, all total." He stopped and shrugged. "It was more like a not particularly intense drill. They weren't very good."

" 'Nah, fifteen of 'em,' " Stephanie mimicked. " 'Wasn't really what you'd call a fight.' Lord! Brag for God's sake!"

"Why?" the instructor said, lightly. "I'll admit that it was a tough fight. There are few among the Blood Lords who would have done as well. I doubt that I would have. But for Herzer, yes, it was child's play. He *is* the Blood Lord's Blood Lord, the icon that we hold up to the students, just as this young lady said. I'm sorry, I didn't catch your name," he added.

"Shilan," Shilan said. "I hadn't realized that you heard."

"I'd moved over. The point is that the Blood Lords train to do one of three, or all of three, things to their opponents. Outmaneuver them, chop them to ribbons and if all else fails *outlast* them. We do that partially by being able to rotate units, but the individual Blood Lord is trained to fight, literally, for at least an hour without being significantly fatigued. A five-minute fight—he shouldn't have broken a sweat."

Stephanie leaned sideways in the pool and supported herself on one elbow, arching her back slightly towards the instructor.

"In pretty good . . . shape then, eh?" she asked, tossing her head so her hair swung back and forth.

The instructor just looked at her for a moment, then nodded sharply.

"Pretty good, yeah."

Stephanie languorously slid back to her place and took a deep breath as she smiled up at him.

"I'm so *glad* to have such big strong *men* guarding us!"

Herzer gripped the bridge of his nose to keep from laughing, hiding his face behind his hand. He looked sideways and saw that Shilan was just staring at the woman, her mouth open. She closed it after a moment with a clop.

"Whatever were we talking about?" Stephanie asked.

"I dunno," Herzer said with a laugh. "Economics comes to mind for some reason."

"Why economics?" Stephanie asked, clearly puzzled.

"Because it's the most boring subject I can imagine," Herzer answered, laughing.

"Oh, I dunno," Stephanie replied, pushing her hair back with both hands behind her ears and then posing with them out to the side as she thrust her chest forward. "*Derivatives* can be fascinating."

Herzer laughed again and shook his head at her incredible forwardness.

"So, I kill people and break things," he said, looking for any subject that *wouldn't* get another rise out of her. "What do you do?"

"I work at the bank," she said, flatly, frowning. "Let's not talk about work."

"Bank?" Herzer said. "What bank?"

"Raven Federal," Stephanie replied.

"Used to be Tom Sloan's Loan Shark and Credit Destroyer," Shilan said with a grin. "They've come up in the world."

"Huh," Herzer said. "Tom handles all my accounts. I've got to see him tomorrow."

"Accounts?" Stephanie said, raising an eyebrow. "Plural."

"Plural," Herzer said flatly. "What are you doing Shilan?"

"I'm still a textile designer," Shilan said. "That's where I met David. He's in sales at the plant."

"Which is a losing cause," David said unhappily. "We used to be the only mill in the area. But these days Hotrum's Ferry has three, and transportation costs are making us unprofitable out of the immediate region."

"Well, this is just fascinating but I've got a date with a bottle of wine," Stephanie said, standing up. "Herzer, pleasure to meet you," she added, holding out her hand.

"Same here," he replied, shaking it. She turned immediately and climbed out of the pool.

"Okay, what just happened?" he asked.

"Social butterfly," the instructor said, sliding into the pool. "She got exactly what she wanted out of the conversation, then went off to find one where she could get more."

"Whatever," Herzer replied. "I'm sorry, I cannot for the life of me recall your name."

"Mike Fraser," the instructor replied, holding out his hand. "I'm in second phase at the Academy."

"I was *supposed* to be coming back for an instructor's gig at the O course," Herzer said, shrugging.

"What are you doing instead?" Shilan asked.

"I just got told," Herzer admitted. "But I'm not sure I should talk about it."

"Open secret," Fraser said. "You're going to the Southern Isles with Duke Edmund."

"So much for military security," Herzer grumbled.

"Like I said, open secret," Fraser shrugged. "You can't organize something like that without it getting out. And there are no secrets in the baths."

"None at all," Shilan said. "Worst gossip spot in the town. Even including the 'ladies get-togethers' that resulted from counseling classes. Although those are more catty. I knew that Edmund was going to the Isles, but not that you were going."

"Daneh and Rachel took it as a surprise," Herzer said.

"They don't come in here much," Shilan shrugged. "Rachel rarely and I've never seen Daneh in here."

"I can imagine why," Herzer said.

"It's not that," Shilan replied. "I think she's about as over her rape as it's possible to be. If not she certainly controls it well. I think she's just very body-modest. Rachel, too, to a lesser extent. And, of course, they have their own baths at the house. Daneh probably would have picked it up at one of the meetings but she's been missing those the last couple of weeks. I only heard about it . . . two nights ago."

"I don't care how hard it is to keep a secret in the baths," Herzer said. "This is still a problem."

"Yup, sure is," Fraser nodded. "I'm not sure what can be done about it, though."

"Education comes to mind," Herzer replied. "I don't know what the security classification is on this mission, but I don't really care. It shouldn't be talked about in public, period. That's basic OPSEC, sir."

"No rank in the baths, either," Fraser noted. "But I get your meaning. You're probably right about the education aspect, but we're all still feeling our way. A couple of years ago, none of us were soldiers."

"Not my problem," Herzer shrugged. "It just bugs me."

"Speaking of feeling our way . . " Shilan said, then blushed. "That didn't come out right."

"It's okay," Herzer chuckled. "It would take a very dirty mind to find anything wrong with that comment. Admittedly, I have a dirty mind . . ."

"Speaking of trying to figure out stuff about this life," Shilan said, clearing her throat. "Why is he a captain and you're a lieutenant?"

"A very good question." Fraser nodded. "The answer is that I came to the Academy as a lieutenant and have gotten promoted since. I think you were enlisted, Herzer?"

"Yeah," Herzer said. "I just got my commission before going

to Harzburg. That was another one of their gripes. I basically got the commission *for* the mission and that was pretty obvious."

"But you got them to see the error of their ways?" Fraser asked.

"It took a while," Herzer admitted. "The town is run by guilds and they took to their prerogatives, post-Fall, really damned quick. It was more feudal than it sounds. They didn't want some no-class low-life newly promoted lieutenant telling them how *they* were supposed to run their militia. For one thing, the militia was only open to those they thought 'acceptable.' Which meant those they could trust with a weapon at their back."

"Under the constitution *all* voters are supposed to be armed," David interjected. "I mean *required*."

"Yeah, and that has holes you can run an elephant through," Herzer said. "They were using the 'bondage labor' provisions to exclude most of the people in the town, not just the refugees but others they didn't like and had squeezed out of power. You had to be a full guild member to be a member of the militia."

"About a fifth their available bodies at a guess," Fraser mused.

"About that," Herzer said. "And all too busy to bother actually training. I mean, most of them were *honestly* busy, you know how it is. They had real jobs, hard ones. And the labor pool guys, who were mostly sitting around hoping for work, were restricted from training. I'd been railing about it, quietly, for quite a while. There was also a real split between the farms, who were the ones getting hit, and the town, where they thought nobody would attack. Well, shortly after my little encounter at the farm Tarson *did* hit the town. Things were pretty screwed up but we managed to stop them after they'd burned the tanneries."

"We?" Fraser interjected.

"I'd . . . been training some of the bond labor on the side," Herzer admitted. "And that was item one in the meeting after the attack. But it was me and a few of them that drove the attackers off."

"Blood Lord tactics?" Fraser asked.

"Modified," Herzer admitted. "More of a phalanx approach. Really, I just had them make long spears and learn to march in formation with them. And, yeah, that was tough to arrange. But we got our tools together and drove the Tarsons off. Then the shit hit the fan. There was a pretty . . . intense meeting. But they had a few unpalatable choices. They could throw me out and try to get something else from the Federals. Pretty damned unlikely. Or they could actually train their 'organized' militia. Equally unlikely. Or they could trust the scum with weapons."

"The scum?" Shilan said, angrily.

"That's how they felt about the labor pool guys," Herzer said. "And some of them *were* scum; Harzburg had a hell of a crime problem for that matter. They started off the meeting wanting to kill me. 'Violation of local ordinances' was the crime I was accused of. I more or less told them 'You and what army?' By the end of the meeting they'd given me approval to recruit among the laborers. And I made a tiddly little company out of them if I do say so myself." He looked up at the rafters again and shrugged. "Maybe I'll have a command again, someday."

"Count on it," Fraser sighed.

"So when the Tarsons attacked again we routed them and drove them back to their town. Took the town, burned the ringleaders in their 'stronghold' and I put a few of the better of the laborers in charge in Tarson. The people of the town were mostly glad as hell to be liberated. The guild guys tried to make like it was their town but we told them where to stuff it. I worked out a charter for Tarson, got their application in to the UFS, waited until the election—which was as cold and stacked as I could make it—was over and just afterwards got the word to head home. Mission accomplished."

"In spades," Fraser said. "What are you getting for this one?"

"Another mission," Herzer laughed.

"Excuse me, Mr. Herrick," a soft voice said from over his shoulder.

He looked around and was faced by a tiny tuft of pubic hair. Looking farther up he was stunned by the vision. If the girl standing over him wasn't absolutely perfect in every way she could see it on a clear day. Brunette, about a meter and a half, perfectly rounded breasts, high and incredibly firm, flat belly, rounded mons. He realized he was staring.

"Yes?" he asked, his voice ending in a squeak.

The girl slid into the water to his left and smiled at him.

"My name's Sheena. I don't think you know me."

"I don't think so either," Herzer replied, all charm out the window. *Three hundred fifty-seven times four . . . down boy!*

"Back before the attack on the town, you went out with

a cavalry patrol," she said in a soft little-girl voice that practically drove arithmetic out of his brain.

"Yes?" *Carry the two . . .*

"My brother was one of the guys on the patrol," she said, leaning forward and kissing him on the cheek. "I want to talk to you, but I'll be right back."

"Okay," he croaked, then turned back to the group in the bath, all of whom were smiling and trying not to laugh.

"How old do you think she is?" Fraser asked, trying not to be smug.

"Seventeen?" Herzer said.

"Try twelve," David replied.

"No fisking way!"

"Way," Shilan replied. "Way, way, way."

"What the hell is she doing naked in the public baths!" *Accosting perfect strangers and ruining their whole day.*

"They're public baths," Shilan replied with a shrug. "I guess her parents decided she was old enough."

"They need to have their *heads* examined!"

Sheena suddenly slid back into the water next to him and laid her hand on his arm.

"I'm really glad to finally meet you," she said, huskily.

Down, down, down, down, DOWN! Twelve! TWELVE!

"Me, too," Herzer replied. "So are you going to school now?"

"Oh, yeah." Sheena frowned. "I didn't have much before the Fall, you know? So I'm in the little kid classes . . ."

Okay, I'm clearly not going to get laid tonight, thank God . . .

CHAPTER SIX

Herzer fell out the next morning at first call in PT gear. It felt good to have nothing in front of him but some simple physical training. He ran the Hill once, then picked up a pack and rucked it four more times, each at increasing speed. He was out of shape and knew it, but he did a credible imitation of Blood Lord speeds on the Hill. After that he moved over to the salle area for the permanent party. None of his class was present but he found someone who was a close match and got in a solid two hours of sword and shield work. He might be light on wind but he hadn't lost his touch with sword and shield and his opponent damned well knew he had been kissed, even through the padded armor.

"Very nice, Herzer. I never figured you for beating up on the babies."

He turned around and slapped Bue Pedersen on the arm.

"Bue! Damn, where the hell have you been?"

"We're forming a legion in Washan," Bue said. "I've been 'assisting' in that endeavor."

"Wish I had been," Herzer said. "Spar?"

"If you think you're up to it." Bue grinned. They had both been in the first Blood Lord class, and at the defense of Raven's Mill. But their careers had seldom crossed paths since. Bue was a triari sergeant while Herzer had been "promoted" to lieutenant. The Blood Lord had few formed units; they tended to be the cadre for other forces and the first class had found itself scattered up and down the eastern seaboard. Herzer had picked up that some were even as far away as the central plains.

Bue donned padded armor and found a practice sword to his liking. The Blood Lord technique was not precisely suited to one-on-one dueling, but both of them were trained in individual fighting as well.

The rules of the game were that they could not move to either side, but had to act as if they were in a unit, moving forward or backwards only slightly. Herzer centered himself and started the battle with an attempted shield bash which Bue turned to the side deftly and then they began hammering.

With no ability to move around it was just that, the swords licking out to jab and chop relentlessly. The shields stayed in front of the body and could be moved up and down, or, slightly, to either side. And they did move, fast, the two fighters wielding the heavy shields as if they were made of balsa wood instead of oak and iron. Blows slipped past repeatedly, though, slamming into shoulders and arms, but none of them would have been disabling so the fighters drove on, each attempting to either get in a crippling blow or force the other to give up from sheer fatigue.

Herzer noticed that most of the other fighting had died down as the two continued to hammer at each other. He had already had a good solid two hours of mock combat and his wind was not what it had been before the Harzburg mission. Bue, on the other hand, seemed to be made of iron. No matter what he tried he couldn't get in a crippling blow nor did the NCO seem to be tiring.

"You're getting soft, Herzer." Bue grinned.

"All that easy living up in Harzburg," Herzer admitted, gritting his teeth. He knew one blow that might work, but it was chancy and right on the edge of illegal in competition. When he realized he was about to die or drop he hooked Bue's shield with his and lifted both of them, an almost impossible maneuver. Then he dropped to one knee and drove his practice sword upward into the NCO's unprotected stomach, doubling him over retching.

"I'm still . . . better than . . . you . . ." Herzer gasped, bending over and panting.

"Cristo, I'm unmanned," Bue said, clutching at his stomach.

"And now you see why we keep Class One as far apart as possible," Gunny said to a background of applause.

Herzer didn't know how long the NCO had been watching but he managed to struggle to his feet.

"And I thought it was because we were the best of the best," Herzer said, grinning despite his fatigue.

"You're pretty good," Gunny admitted grudgingly. "But you want to try that maneuver on me?"

"Not in a long lifetime," Herzer admitted. He walked over to the armor rack and hung up his shield, helmet and sword, then stripped out of the sweat-soaked armor. "You okay, Bue?"

"I'll be okay," the NCO admitted, walking over to rack his own gear. "Where in hell did you learn that little trick?"

"Tarson," Herzer said. "Desperation is the best teacher."

After showering off, he had breakfast with Bue and Gunny. The mess hall was neutral ground and Blood Lords did not maintain strict separation between enlisted and officers so several other officers were having breakfast with the "troops." They caught up on what had been happening and talked about the "old times," just a couple of years before, when the Blood Lords were being formed.

After breakfast Gunny and Bue went off to their duties and Herzer headed downtown. He thought, again, that while Gunny was still sharp as a tack, he seemed to be losing the edge just a hair. He'd picked up that Gunny no longer ran the basic entry test for the Blood Lord trainees; the first ruck run up the Hill. He just couldn't make the time anymore. It had only been two years, but two years of running class after class had clearly taken it out of the old NCO.

Retiring him was out; he'd either be one of those guys who just hung around all the time or he'd die or commit suicide. All he had known before Fall was living what he had researched as the life of a senior noncommissioned officer. Something was going to have to be done, but offhand Herzer couldn't think what.

Herzer wondered, not for the first time but the first time clearly, what Gunny had been like when he was a youngster. Or Duke Edmund, for that matter. He had looked at both of them, when he first started out, as the near order of gods. And now there were people who looked at him the same way. Had they been screw-ups? What was the force that drove them to be who they were? You had to have something seriously odd in your background to live the lives that they had lived before the Fall, not to mention what they had done after it.

Who were they *really*? People looked at him as if he was

something special. Even as he walked downtown, people would come up to him and nod and whisper as he passed. Herzer, the victor of the Line. Herzer the Undefeatable. He knew he wasn't any of those things. But he wore the mask, wore it so well sometimes it felt as if he was becoming their belief. But he knew, inside, that he was the same screwed-up kid who had run away from Daneh's rape. Who had needed to be hammered on the anvil of the Blood Lords, and of life, to attain any sort of competence. Who still screwed up from time to time.

Who were they, really?

Those thoughts carried him as far as the bank and he wandered in abstractedly, scarcely noticing when he reached the newly installed desks.

"Can I help you?" the woman at the desk asked.

"Stephanie?"

Gone was the flippant social butterfly. The woman had her hair up in a bun and a severe expression of less than friendly competence on her face.

"Lieutenant Herrick, I believe?" Stephanie replied.

"I'm looking for Tom," Herzer said.

"Do you have an appointment?"

"Nooo," Herzer replied with a slight grin. "But I thought I'd drop by for old time's sake."

"Mr. Sloan is quite busy, but I'll see if he has a moment." She got up and went through a side door as Herzer took his first real look around.

Tom Sloan had started small. Prior to the Fall there was no such thing as "currency." There were energy credits but they were traded, to the extent that any trading occurred, through the Net. Everyone had a relative sufficiency. Even Herzer, who as a young man had been "released" by his parents, had enough to not only pay for advanced medical treatment but also to maintain elaborate "enhanced reality" simulations. It took real energy to use up all your energy credits.

After the Fall, currency had at first been based on food. Food was distributed based on "credit chits." One chit, one meal. Or rough food, slightly more than one meal, if you knew how to cook it. Over time the chits had transformed into the standard currency and as the society got more complex they had become the standard monetary form. You still could buy a meal or food from the government with chit in hand. But most of them were traded through what was becoming more and more of an economy. And even the term "chit" was falling out of the lexicon, replaced by "credit."

Tom had gotten into the trading of chits early. He had accumulated stores of them, based on loans from the government and deposits by people who had a surplus. And he'd put the money to use, loaning it out in turn at often usurious rates. But he was scrupulously fair and honest, which went a long way to people letting his interest rates slide; too many of his early competitors had played fast and loose with people's money. He had also handled investments and contracts for people like Herzer, people who had a small surplus and wanted to put it to work.

He'd clearly come up in the world. The small office he used to have had been expanded into a large building. There was a counter with some women behind it and a few offices off of the main lobby which apparently had Stephanie to guard it. There were also two inconspicuous *real* guards, hulking men nearly Herzer's size. One of them he recognized from the town militia. He'd tried out for the Blood Lords but hadn't been able to make the full training. He still looked more than capable of ripping any troublemaker in the bank limb from limb. Herzer nodded at him and the guard nodded back, not warily but fully aware that the Blood Lord would be difficult to rip if push came to shove.

"Herzer!"

Tom Sloan was a tall, good-looking guy anywhere between thirty and a hundred and fifty years in age, wearing a fine linen tunic and a pair of light-blue cosilk pants that just matched his eyes. He had sandy hair, a ready smile and a firm grip. Herzer was sure that he practiced the smile and handshake in the mirror every morning.

"Hey, Tom, got a minute?" Herzer asked.

"Always," Sloan replied with a toothy smile. "Miss Vega, could you pull the lieutenant's files and bring them to my office?"

"Certainly, sir," Stephanie simpered, then scurried away. Herzer had been sure that the woman could never scurry, but she did it well.

"Come on," Tom said, laying his hand on Herzer's arm and leading him through the door. There was a corridor with more offices to either side. Most of them had their doors open and in each there were people, mostly women, poring over piles of paper.

"If one more thing changes in this town I'll scream," Herzer said.

"You've got no idea." Tom sighed. He opened a door with "Sloan, President" on a brass plaque and led Herzer inside.

The room was comfortably but not flashily appointed. There were a couch and table, a couple of chairs and a medium sized desk. An étagère behind the desk had a few personal effects in it, including a small oil painting of Tom and a woman. Herzer vaguely recognized her but couldn't place the face.

"You're married?" he asked, taking one of the chairs. He fit in it poorly, which was normal, but he realized his legs were shoved up higher than usual. Then he realized that if he was "normal" sized he would have been looking up at the bank president.

"Last year," Tom said. "I had an invitation for you . . ."

"But I was out of town?" Herzer grinned.

"Somewhat."

"So what's with the banker look?" Herzer asked.

"Changes." Sloan grimaced. "Practically the first thing the new Congress did was pass banking laws and set up an independent federal bank board. I had to get investors, set up a charter, and do all the paperwork. Stuff that I could keep up myself blossomed into a full-time job to manage the reports that the feds require. I had to shift most of the investments that I was managing to another firm. I sent you a letter about that."

"Got it," Herzer admitted. "But they're still filtering the returns through you?"

"Yes, but I can't advise on any of it or manage it," Sloan admitted. "But I can bring you up to date on what we're keeping in-house. Your deposits, fixed securities, things like that."

"Okay, what is a fixed security?" Herzer said.

"Well," Tom grinned. "You remember when I used to say: 'Look, Herzer, leave it with me and I'll give you five percent a year, guaranteed'?"

"Yeah."

"Fixed security," Tom said as the door opened up. "Ah, thank you, Miss Vega."

"You're welcome, sir," Stephanie replied, laying a thick file on his desk and walking out without a backwards glance.

"Put your eyes back in your head, Herzer," Tom chuckled.

"Actually, I got a pretty good look last night in the baths," Herzer admitted.

"I've been keeping up with your accounts," Tom said, ignoring the comment. "But they're managed by Posteal, Ohashi and Deshort . . ."

"Deshort?" Herzer asked. "Isn't he the economy guy that Edmund was, is for that matter, always muttering about?"

"I don't know," Tom said, frowning. "His background is in preindustrial economic modeling. He's on the board. But I didn't know that he and the duke had problems."

"Not problems, really," Herzer said with a grin. "More like a mutual disadmiration society."

"He's on the board of the bank, as well . . ."

"In that case, I think I need another bank." Herzer chuckled. "If Brad Deshort is involved in managing my money, I'd rather play the ponies."

"Are you seriously disturbed about this?" Tom asked.

"I don't know; how much have I lost?" Herzer said, still chuckling.

"You haven't lost anything, Herzer," Tom replied, seriously. "I've been very careful about your investments and so has PO and D."

"I'm joking, Tom," the lieutenant said, shaking his head. "Never joke with a banker about money."

"If it really bothers you . . ."

"It doesn't," Herzer said, definitely. "Let's look at the books, okay?"

It took nearly an hour to go over all the investments that Herzer had accumulated. He was surprised at that; he had no idea he'd gotten his finger in so many pies. But the eventual total was pleasant.

"Anyway, it's a well distributed portfolio," Tom finished. "There *have* been some losses; the sand-gravel business folded completely in fact. You came out of that with only a few pence on the credit, but everything else is going well. Fortunately most of your investments still fall into tax credited areas. We'll see what the idiots in the legislature come up with next year."

"And then there's Mike Boehlke's farm," Herzer added.

"Yes, we don't manage that, but Mr. Boehlke has made it into quite a business. A solid, if long-term, investment."

"And another subtle joke," Herzer pointed out.

"Excuse me?"

"One of the expressions we use in the military for getting killed is 'buying the farm,' " Herzer said, his face distant. "Soldiers talk about finally getting out and buying a farm to settle down on. So when one gets killed, we say he 'bought the farm.' " His face suddenly cleared and he grinned. "Either I'm already dead or I'm never going to get kilt."

"I see," Tom said, shaking his head. "So are you ever going to settle down on the farm you already have 'bought'?"

"I dunno, Tom," Herzer replied with a shrug. "I guess we'll both have to live long enough to see."

The worst problem for Joel about the dragon ride had been landing at the base at Washan. It was one of the growing army bases along the coast, though, and he quickly faded into the background. He'd ridden wyvern a few times before the Fall and the only new iteration was the length of the trip. Since wyvern could only make a couple of hundred klicks per day it had been a multiday trip across the country. But wyverns were still faster, and marginally more comfortable, than coaches.

When he landed at the base he made himself scarce, then started looking for transportation. The base was not actually at Washan but across the Poma River and there was a small town that had grown up outside the base, mostly to support the needs of the sailors and soldiers that roamed the area.

He walked down a street lined with pawnshops, bars and barbershops, watching the small groups that moved on it. There were a remarkable number of barbershops and they seemed to do a brisk business. As he passed one he noticed that the "barber" was a scantily clad young woman and had to make a rapid reassessment of the situation.

It was the middle of the day, though, and there weren't many crowds. He considered stopping in one of the bars, or one of the barbershops for that matter, and seeing what he could pick up. But that wasn't part of his mission so he continued down the road to where a small complex of buildings was set off to the side of the town. There was a corral with about a dozen horses, most of them in decent condition, a small barn and an even smaller building with a porch out front. He walked to the latter and slipped inside.

The interior was dim; there were only two unglazed windows in the front area and the afternoon was overcast. So he was startled to hear a female voice from the rear of the room.

"Help you?" she said.

The woman wasn't young, wasn't old, probably somewhere in her first century. She was seated behind a counter looking at him over the top of a piece of paper.

"I need to catch the stage down towards Newfell," he said, stepping up to the counter.

"Next stage isn't for three hours," the woman replied, setting down the paper. "Stage goes all the way to Newfell Base."

Reaching the base on the stagecoach was not part of his plans. He glanced at the wall, where a map was mounted, and then down. "Well, I'm only going to Tenerie, not Newfell. I'm actually headed for the coast; I just found out I've got friends over there who made it through the Fall."

"Tenerie's thirty credits," the woman said, pulling out a ledger book. "Can you afford it?"

"I think so," Joel said, pulling out the silver he had gotten in Chian and one of the bronze coins. "I've got a twenty piece and some silver."

The woman sighed at the latter but pulled out a scale and measured out the silver to make thirty credits. "You need to get this changed, you know. Hardly anybody out here uses chunk metal anymore and I can't give you what you'd get at an assayer's office for it."

"Okay," Joel said. "I'm from up the road towards Raven's Mill. Plenty of people still use it up there."

"Yeah, well, welcome to the big city," the woman grinned. "Nobody around Washan, or Newfell for that matter, uses that stuff anymore. You might over on the coast, I don't know about those hicks."

She wrote him out a chit for the stage and picked up the paper in apparent dismissal.

"Thanks so much for your help," Joel said, turning and going back out into the street.

Three hours. Assuming it was on time. That might mean two hours. Or four. Or nine for that matter.

Beyond the corral was an inn, clearly for the use of overnight customers from the stage. Across the street from it was a bar with two barbershops closely adjacent. But on the other side of the barbershops was a building with a large, freshly painted, sign that said "Sundries."

Joel wasn't sure what "Sundries" meant in this case; it might be a larger and more complicated version of one of the "barbershops." But he suspected it might mean such lost luxuries as, oh, a razor, soap, maybe even new clothes.

He walked over to the shop and was pleasantly surprised. It was well stocked with shelves of clothing, toiletry items and even premade shoes.

"Can I help you?" the clerk said, coming from around the counter at the rear.

"I need a new set of clothes," Joel said, fingering a folded pair of pants made of some heavy material. "And some toiletry items. And a bag to carry it in."

"Of course," the clerk replied. "We sell a lot of such things to soldiers and sailors who are being moved other places. That's a material called 'denim.' It's just starting to come off the lines, quite the new fad. Heavy, double-woven cosilk with double stitching. A pair of those will last you for years and years, just getting more comfortable with each wearing."

"I need a pair of those, a shirt, some underthings, *not* made out of that . . ."

"Of course, sir," the clerk smiled. "Might as well be leather, like the dwarves."

"Or hair shirts like the Blood Lords," Joel said.

They found clothes in his size and Joel picked up a selection of toiletries. He had never had his beard growth permanently stopped before the Fall. It made more sense to intermittently stop it; growing a beard always looked more natural than even the best implant. But that meant he had to either grow one permanently or shave, and of the two he preferred a clean chin.

He bought everything that he needed, including some travel food and a water bottle for the trip, and still had plenty of time before the coach was *supposed* to arrive. On his trip across the country he had discovered the unreliability of the service. Some people had discussed building railroads. But the explosive protocols prohibited all but low-power steam. And a low-power steam engine could only pull a couple of loaded cars, making the plan economically unviable. Canals were being built but they could only reach certain areas.

He had a plate of not particularly good food and a cup of worse ale and sincerely considered visiting one of the "barbershops." He had not been celibate since the Fall. Before the Fall he and Dedra had maintained an open relationship and he was sure she would not begrudge him the release under the conditions. But for some reason, despite the fact that most of his relationships post-Fall had been . . . economic, he chose against it. Finally, he walked back to the stage office and took a seat on the porch, closing his eyes and thinking.

Sheida had as much as said that she suspected a high leak in the Council. His immediate suspicion was her aide, Harry. But just because he was peculating, that didn't make him a traitor. Still worth checking out. Frankly, if he ever was put in a position where he could effect a change, counterintelligence would be a very high priority. That led him to wonder why so many of the agents in Ropasa had been rolled up. Some of that might have been from leaks, but he suspected that if the counterintelligence people on Sheida's side were as oblivious to trade-craft as they seemed, the *intel* people were probably as bad.

Face it, he did not like this minor mission that he had been assigned. If he had his way, just about every ship and unit would have at least one covert agent in it. But that would mean a host of agents. Which meant a training program. Well, you'd need one of those for actual intel gathering, might as well combine the two to an extent.

Working out the details of the proposed plan carried the sun down and it was just before sunset when the stage pulled to a stop. There were only two passengers, both of whom got out to stretch their legs as the horses were changed.

He gave the driver his receipt and put his new bag on the back of the coach, climbing in and settling himself while the other passengers were still outside. He'd taken the front, less comfortable, seat in deference to the two people who had preceded him on the trip. When they got in he nodded his head. One was a young man in a Navy officer's uniform and the other was older dressed in nondescript civilian clothing.

"Ensign Jonah Weilis," the officer said, offering his hand.

"Joel Annibale," Joel said, shaking the officer's hand. He hoped like hell the ensign wasn't assigned to Newfell Base and that, if he was, they wouldn't run into each other.

"Rupert Popadiuk," the other man said, nodding his head.

"Going to Newfell?" Jonah asked. It was clear that the two continuing passengers had used up any small talk they might have had. "I'm being assigned to headquarters there. I was at the base in Balmoran."

"I'm on my way to live with some friends on the coast," Joel shrugged. "Getting off at Tenerie and hiking overland. They've got a fishing boat over there; I've got some experience at fishing boats."

"You ought to join the Navy, then," the officer said, smiling. "It's a hard life but a good one and very important. If you're really experienced with small boats, you could probably buck for almost instant petty officer rank. Where were you before?"

"Flora last," Joel said, lying glibly. "I sailed with a packet up to Washan. I looked at the base here, but . . . Anyway, I've got these friends. It's not much of a life, but I get by. What do you do in the Navy, Ensign?"

"I'm in counterintelligence," Jonah said as the coach started into motion.

"That's interesting," Joel said. "But what's it mean?"

CHAPTER SEVEN

"Celine," Chansa's avatar said with a nod.

Most of the business of the council members was managed through avatars. The fully sentient projections had been prohibited pre-Fall, since they tended to have some bad side effects. But the council members, with myriad duties and no experience of delegation, used them to keep an eye on the various activities of their regions.

Chansa had gotten a request from Celine to attend a "demonstration" and, with reluctance, he had agreed. He admitted that the New Destiny faction had benefited by her "creations" but he often found them personally uncomfortable. The basic Changed that made up the bulk of his legions were bad enough. He had given what he thought were understandable modifications, but in Celine's hands what had been delivered were monsters. He had considered simply overriding her; the Changed of the legions were his responsibility after all. But Celine could be particularly nasty when balked. So he tolerated hordes of half-wild beasts. He had to admit that very few groups had been able to stand up to them and, in general, simply the threat of having the hordes sent against them tended to make most resistance falter.

But some of her "specials" were simply ungodly. Abominations that turned his stomach. And while most of them required too much power, or time, to have truly become common, she had been promising a "new breakthrough" soon.

He had therefore met one of her avatars at a refugee camp

81

in the southern Briton isles. The south had been relatively easy to overrun, but the north still held out stubbornly, holding onto small glens and highlands that were monstrously difficult to maneuver in. The ancient fortresses that dotted the landscape, many of which had been rebuilt by reenactors prior to the Fall, were an additional challenge. Then there was the stubborn nature of the defenders. They seemed to positively relish fighting all the forces he had sent against them. If he was to use Celine's "specials" anywhere, it was to be against the damnable Gael.

The refugee camp was standard, a long curtain palisade with a collection of wooden huts. The refugees were fed and sorted out, most of the men and some of the women ending up going through the Change process. The basic process was designed to produce beings that were more suited to the post-Fall world. They were sturdier and stronger than standard humans with some innate skills. That, at least, had been the basic specifications. He had added, to his continued dismay, a suggestion for "aggression" so they would make better soldiers.

The humans in the line to be Changed had to be bound and guarded by soldiers. As he watched, a woman darted forward and tried to drag a man out of the line, only to be clubbed to the ground by the guards. One of them picked her up by her hair and dragged her down the line to a farther hut, part of the barracks complex for the guards. The man she had tried to grab slumped to his knees but was clubbed and then dragged forward by more guards.

"Chansa," Celine answered, also watching the byplay. She turned to him, her black eyes bright and smiled. "You look so glum, Chansa. It's not as if they're being eaten or something."

"Where did they take the girl?" Chansa asked, knowing in his heart the answer.

"How should I know?" Celine smiled. "I don't keep up with every little operational detail."

"You had something to show me?" Chansa ground out.

"Over this way," the avatar waved, leading him back behind the Change rooms from which roars of pain could be heard. In most of the huts the humans were being Changed into the forms that were the basic sword-fodder of the legions. But Celine had thoroughly let herself go and there were other huts for "specialties." Armies needed soldiers. But they also needed construction workers, servants, medical personnel and other specialties. In the secondary huts each of the base humans was transformed to a more "suitable" shape. At the same time their original memories were removed, so that they wouldn't be depressed by the conditions of this Fallen time, and replaced with simple operational instructions, training on how to live in this new world.

There were paddocks behind the huts where the newly made Changed stumbled into the world. They were thin and scrawny and often had to be kept from killing each other, but he knew that with a diet heavy in protein—and he often wondered where some of that protein came from—they would flesh out into tough, if undisciplined, fighters. Two of the new Changed charged each other as he watched and more mature ones that had been posted as guards closed on them, clubbing them with fists and tearing at them with their talons until the two half-dead fighters were separated.

Back behind the area was a section designated for women and children who had not been subject to the Change. Children were simply too fragile, with insufficient internal reserve of energy, to be Changed and at least some women had to be left to manage them.

He saw more guards wandering in the area, some of them going in and out of the huts and as he passed behind one he heard a whimpering shriek from the interior. The "refugee" camps were managed by Celine and if he had his way he'd change that. But since it was beyond his power to correct, he tried not to think about it. This extended walk was making that hard. He closed his ears to the sound of cries, some of them from children, as Celine led him to a much larger hut.

"As you know, we've been unable to find a home for most of the female refugees," Celine said. "They are of limited utility in this world. And the children are nothing but a resource drain. But I think I've finally found a solution."

Inside the hut there was a ring of guards around a small group of people. One male, a female who might or might not have been his wife, and three children ranging in age from a skinny, feverish-looking toddler to a girl just under puberty. One of Celine's acolytes was in the room as well and as soon as the two avatars appeared he began to mouth nonsense syllables.

A globe formed around the group and the air around them filled with light, presumably from nannite interaction. Suddenly the air was split by screams of pain which dwindled and changed into pure rage. When the globe cleared, standing in the center was a thing. As large as Chansa and if anything broader. The beast was heavy bellied with a piglike face and long, curved tusks. His arms dangled nearly to its bowed knees and his fingers and toes were tipped by razor sharp talons. He was definitely, even disgustingly, male, with an enormous penis and a large scrotal sack. He looked around the room and lunged at the doorway but was stopped by an energy field. The beast struck at the invisible shield repeatedly with fist and shoulder, bellowing in fury, until the acolyte spoke again and the monster settled into a quiescent state that, nonetheless, radiated rage.

"Where . . ." Chansa said and then cleared his throat. He didn't want to ask the question, knowing in his heart the answer, but he found himself unable to stop. "What happened to the people?"

"The male was used as the nucleus for my newest creation," Celine said with a beatific smile, stepping forward to stroke her hands over the monster; her avatar passed through the field since it had been keyed for flesh and blood alone. "His internal energy was also used. As was that of the other resources. And their material was added to his. Perfect. Flawless," she said, stroking the creature on its arm. "The penis is fully functional, and he can reproduce with human females, assuming they survive the experience. The offspring . . . well, my models have several potential outcomes. I'm looking forward to empirical data."

"Celine, even for you . . ." Chansa said, then pulled himself up. "This is *madness.*"

"Paul said that he wanted horror," Celine replied, turning to look at him as she stroked the creature's arm. Her eyes were bright and mad. "I can do horror."

"Yes," Chansa replied. "That you can." He tried to consider the situation objectively but could not. And, strangely enough, it was not the image of the family disappearing that kept coming back to him, but the woman being dragged away by her hair.

He wished that he could delude himself, as Paul did, that what they were doing was good, was just, was right. But he could not. He had long ago concluded that it was an evil beyond redemption, a force of ill more powerful than the world had ever known. He knew that he had dug himself into a hellish pit that it might never be possible to dig out of. And he knew what had brought him here: delight in power.

Each taste of it had been like a drug to him so he had

clawed his way up until, with Paul's help, he was a council member. But with each step on the ladder, as an inspector, as a special inspector, as an associate council member, a web of responsibility, checking that power, had woven around him, taking some of the heady drug away. When Paul presented him with the ability to throw off those webs, as if they were truly gossamer, he had taken it, knowing full well with whom he had allied.

And it had led to this.

If they won the war, if Paul managed to survive, if they could . . . weed certain members of the Council, Celine with her monsters, Reyes with his girls and his whips and his knives and, most especially, the Demon, if they could choose the *right* people to take the Keys of the Freedom Coalition, *maybe* they could dig out.

Which meant winning. And that meant using, yes, every weapon at their disposal. Even Celine. Even this . . . monstrosity.

"It's magnificent."

"They're magnificent," Rachel sighed.

Herzer shook his head as the dragons winged in to a landing on Raven's Hill.

"You're joking, right?" he asked. "I see what you meant about the surprise."

There were six of them, four with riders and two riderless. Five of them were wyverns, which, unlike the classic "dragon," had two powerful hind legs and a vast span of wings to support their flight. Wyverns were nonsentient and trainable, barely. They had something of the intelligence, and personality, of horses. If, of course, horses ate flesh instead of grass and needed to consume close to their own body weight in food every day. Their bodies were also the size of a large horse but their wings, even folded, took up more cubic meters than their bodies. When opened, the batlike wings spread some thirty meters to either side.

The one on the end, though, was a true dragon. Four legs, long neck, massive wings, large enough to overshadow the five wyverns. Dragons had been developed slightly before the elves and were sentient beings, with all the rights, and responsibilities, of humans. But further creation was halted shortly after the AI wars in reaction to the various horrors of that war. Afterwards there had been a brief population increase but over the succeeding two thousand years the race had dwindled away to almost nothing.

And here was one landing in Raven's Mill. Apparently with the purpose of flying them down to the sea. And then accompanying the expedition to the Isles.

"You have got to be joking," Daneh repeated for him. She was still puffing from the trip up the hill and now looked at their "rides" with total befuddlement. "Tell me we're not riding those down to Newfell."

"Okay, I won't," Edmund said, chuckling. "But you might want to start climbing on."

"Cool," Rachel said, then looked more closely at the True dragon. "Excuse me, Miss Dragon?"

"The name is Joanna," the dragon said, lowering her head down to Rachel's level. Despite a mouth full of very long teeth she had flexible lips and a mobile tongue that permitted quite clear speech. "Joanna Gramlich. Most humans have a hard time telling dragon sexes. How did you know?"

"We saw you at Marguerite's birthday party," Herzer interjected. "So you're now part of the Freedom Coalition? That is wonderful to hear."

"That is a long story," the dragon replied acerbically. She had a fairly high-pitched voice that still rumbled. It was a tough trick. "I prefer to use the term 'independent contractor.' Duke Edmund prefers the term 'mercenary.' "

"A mercenary *dragon*?" Rachel gasped. "Why?"

"Do you know how much food it takes to run this damned form?" the dragon said. "I was caught like this by the Fall. I got really tired of trying to catch my own food."

"Joanna works for room and board and a fairly high salary, which she takes in gold and gems," Edmund noted dryly.

"And don't forget combat bonuses," Joanna said.

"I won't. But this is a diplomatic mission."

"Sure. Like it's going to stay that way with you around. Are we going to sit here jawing all day or are you ready to go? I can take two. I'd prefer the females; they look lighter. One of the wyvern riders can double up with the duke. I hope the big boy can stay on wyvern-back."

"I don't know," Herzer temporized. "How do you control it?"

"Don't try," Joanna snapped. "It will follow me; it knows who the pack-momma is. Just strap in and hang on."

Herzer hefted his bag and walked over to the wyvern, looking up at it askance. The body wasn't much longer than a horse, but the giant legs bulked it to nearly twice the weight and three times the height. The "saddle" was a pad on the back, held in place by double straps running from the neck back to the legs; the wings attached all the way down the rest of the body. There were four reins that ran up to the beast's head but Herzer knew darn well that he had no idea what they were for.

The skin of the body was smooth with small, pebbly scales like a lizard, and it was clear that the wyverns derived most of their genes from lizards. The wing skin, on the other hand, was almost scaleless and what could be seen seemed more like a bat's. There wasn't much to be seen of it because the way the wings folded and refolded, most of the open skin was folded under the flight bones.

The wyvern turned its short neck to the side and glared at him out of one baleful, and very human-looking, eye. After a moment it made a sound, something like a *very* large dove, which sounded either questioning or querulous. Or, probably, both. Or so it seemed to Herzer.

"Hi," someone said, walking up behind him. It was one of the wyvern-riders, and Herzer started when he realized that it was a she. In their leather uniforms and helmet it was hard to distinguish sex at any sort of distance. "I'm Vickie. Let's get you strapped up."

"O-kay," Herzer said. "Where do I put this?" he asked, holding up his bag. He'd packed one spare uniform and some light clothes including a bathing suit someone had dredged up in his size.

"Don't ask Joanna, or you might not like the answer," Vickie said with a smile. She took the bag and stepped nimbly up the wyvern's legs to the top where she attached the bag just behind the saddle. The dragon made another questioning sound and shifted the leg she was standing on at which she slapped it on the side. "Shut up, Chance."

"The way this works is you *lie down* on his back. *Don't* try to sit up. It looks great in pictures and it works like shit in reality. See the slots on the side?"

"Yup," Herzer replied. He'd been giving the harness a good look. "How do I handle the reins?"

"Like Joanna said, don't," Vickie replied. "I'll hook them up, though. The top reins are for up, the bottom reins, which hook to your feet, are for down. Pull right with the top reins to go right, left reins to go left. Don't try to do a stoop, you won't like it."

"What's a stoop?"

"If you don't know what it is, you don't want to try it.

Just hang on and don't mess with the reins. Chauncey will follow us just fine as long as you don't mess with anything."

She waited as he climbed up the wyvern, then attached straps across his thighs. There were clear grab straps on the front but the only thing actually holding him on were the thigh straps. She finished by hooking the bottom reins onto his boots and pushing the top reins, which were one continuous circuit of leather, under his body.

"The worst part about riding dragon-back is learning to keep your legs *still*. You go and stretch and this bad boy is going to head for the ground like a falcon. Got it?"

"Got it," Herzer said settling his body in the seat. He was glad he hadn't brought his armor; it would have been very uncomfortable. "Is it *Chance* or *Chauncey*?" he asked.

"It's Chauncey," Vickie admitted. "I call him Chance for short."

"What's taking so long, Vickie?" Joanna bellowed and Herzer realized everyone else was already mounted. "You're supposed to be mounting him up, not arranging a mounting!"

Vickie looked at him with a dyspeptic expression. "Gotta go."

"See ya." Herzer grinned, wriggling closer into the seat. "We'll arrange the other some other time."

Vickie chuckled and patted him on the butt as she climbed down.

"Thanks, but I don't go both ways," she said as she jumped nimbly to the ground.

"Pity," Herzer muttered as he watched her mount her wyvern. As soon as she was on, Joanna spread her wings and with a massive blast of wind, lifted off the hill and swept down over the river.

Chauncey was apparently well trained because with a bound that caused Herzer's neck to snap back he leapt forward and upward into the air, following the larger dragon. Immediately the air was filled with wings as the formation of dragons reached for the sky.

For a moment it was all that Herzer could do to control his vomit reaction. The combination of the height and the up and down motion of the wyvern as it got up air speed was sickening. But after that brief spasm he found himself caught up in the spectacular view. The dragons were making a curving climb to the right that carried them first out over the Shenan River, which glittered in the early morning light, then over the town of Raven's Mill itself. Looking around he realized that they were already higher than Massan Mountain. As he thought that he grabbed the straps because the wyvern suddenly stopped flapping. For a moment he thought something had gone wrong but it was just a glide period as the formation turned towards the mountain across the river.

As they passed back over Raven's Hill Herzer felt an upward motion that wasn't from the dragon and realized that they had passed over a thermal. Apparently to take advantage of it the dragons began their slow wing-beats again and they rapidly gained height until they lost the thermal and ceased flapping. They crossed the river at a gentle glide and Herzer had to wonder where they were going. The ocean was to the east but they were going west.

Just as he really started to get worried, it wasn't impossible that New Destiny might have co-opted this "mercenary" dragon to kidnap Duke Edmund and his family, they passed over Massan Mountain and hit another, much stronger thermal.

This was, apparently, what Joanna had been looking for because she began a climb at the end of the mountain, in the midst of the thermal, and the dragons seemed to rocket into the air under the power of their wings and the much greater energy of the rising air.

CHAPTER EIGHT

Daneh had ceded Rachel the front seat on Joanna's back and Rachel had initially been quite happy with that. She was looking forward to flying dragon-back. However, shortly after climbing on, as the dragon muttered various imprecations about sharp shoes, she rethought her position. For one thing, while she wouldn't have preferred to have the view to the front blocked by her mother's buttocks, it was now hers that were directly in view. What was worse, she badly needed to pass wind. The change in altitude, the frisson of fear on the lift-off, the whole experience was causing her internals to rear-range quite disastrously. And while she and her mother had had some tough times, gassing in her face was not going to be anything but killer embarrassing.

To take her mind off of it, she decided to brave the dragon's wrath.

"Joanna!" she yelled. "Can you hear me?"

"Yes," the dragon rumbled in reply, without turning her head. "But if you think I'm going to look you in the eye you need to stop reading fantasies. Flying is hard enough without having to look backwards!"

"That's fine," Rachel shouted back. "Can I ask you a personal question?"

"You can ask," the dragon said.

"Are you always this touchy or is there something in particular that has you pissed off?"

Rachel felt the seat under her shaking and clutched at the

grab-straps, but after a moment she realized that it was just the dragon laughing.

"A little of both," Joanna admitted. "I've been called a bitch before, plenty of times. But this mission has me ticked in a major way."

"Why?" Rachel yelled. "Southern skies, warm seas, tropical sun . . ."

"Long damned flight," Joanna admitted. "We don't get to go on a pleasure cruise. The ship's supposedly set up to let us land from, but my guess is we're going to have to fly most of the way. That's like doing a five, six, ten day *marathon*. We can *do* it, but it's still a pain in the ass."

"Oh."

"And that's not all," Joanna said, warming to the subject. "What the hell are we going to eat? The ship we're meeting can't possibly carry enough fresh meat for us for the whole trip. So that means, what? Salt beef? *Fish? Raw fish?* I hate sushi!"

"Sorry!"

"Not your fault," Joanna said. "I hate this Fallen world. I want to be able to *Change*. Any time I want. I want to eat *chocolate*."

Rachel just nodded at that; she felt the same way.

For that matter, if she was in the pre-Fall days, even riding like this, she could have her gas bypassed rather than be impolite. Oh, well, at least geneticists had long ago fixed the smell problem.

"Damn thing," Joanna muttered.

"What?" Rachel shouted back. Due to the rush of the wind, Rachel had to shout but any statement from the dragon was fairly clear.

"Oh, nothing," the dragon replied. "Your boyfriend's mount is riding my slipstream. It's just an extra weight to pull."

Rachel looked from side to side and noticed that the other dragons had spread out in a v, with the exception of Herzer.

"He's not controlling his mount!" she pointed out.

"I know, it's just Chauncey being lazy. Doesn't mean I have to like it."

"Why are the other ones in a v?" Rachel yelled. "They look like they're going to run into each other."

"Slipstream again," Joanna answered. "There's a low-pressure area that passes out to either side. Ever see geese fly over?"

"Plenty of times."

"Same thing. That doesn't drag directly on me, though, like Chauncey is. Damn idiot wyvern."

They continued in a slow spiral upward, riding the thermal and the power of the slowly flapping wings for what seemed half the morning. But by the rise of the sun it couldn't have been more than a half an hour. Finally, Rachel felt a drop, more a feeling of lightness.

"Top of the thermal," Joanna said, banking to the east. "I got at least three thousand meters out of it, which is pretty good for a morning in October."

Rachel had been avidly looking at the view in the distance but at those words she looked down. And then screwed her eyes tight shut and grabbed at the straps.

"Don't look down," Joanna chuckled.

"Too late," Rachel replied.

"Oh, what the hell is that idiot doing?" Joanna growled.

Herzer had realized during the climb-out that Chauncey was riding the bigger dragon's slipstream. But he for sure wasn't going to try to mess with a spiraling climb. However, when the dragons lined out and glided into the sun, he decided that it was worth seeing if he could shift down the line. The worst that was going to happen was that he would release Chauncey and the wyvern would go back to his accustomed place.

There remained one problem. He was directly behind Joanna, no more than twenty meters. Her tail actually whipped back and forth past Chauncey's nose, close enough to nearly hit it. The tail end of the extended V formation of the wyverns was actually *behind* his present position. Which meant that he would have to slow down, then catch back up. He knew neither command.

Going on a hunch, he slowly pulled back on the climbing reins until the slack was out, then pulled back on those *and* the diving reins, very slightly. His clamp held the reins snugly but he was always careful not to flex *too* hard lest he cut the reins like snapping a twig.

Herzer wasn't even sure what Chauncey did, but they began to drift backwards from the larger dragon, while staying more or less at the same height. He was actually dropping slightly below her, but staying on an even keel, not in a "dive" or whatever.

Herzer let back out on the reins and then pulled, ever so slightly, on the left rein. Obediently, Chauncey entered a slight bank to the left, but they also began to lose height.

Herzer loosened up on the rein, pulled a bit to the right, and shortly found himself just outside the left-most of the riders on more or less the same heading. Unfortunately, he was about sixty meters below the wyvern and nearly a hundred behind.

Oh, well.

The rider just happened to be Vickie and he could hear her shouting at him, but he wasn't sure what she could do about his experimentation.

The problem was simple. He had to get up to their level and get Chauncey to speed up so that he could enter the proper formation. They were now, steadily, pulling ahead of him and either gaining altitude or he was losing it in comparison. But Chauncey seemed content to obey orders and follow the present course. Despite the fact that it was the wrong one.

He pulled, gently, on both up reins. All that did was cause him to lose more ground, but they did gain some height, briefly. Then Chauncey pulled against the reins and reentered the glide. Herzer suddenly remembered a term "stall speed" and wondered, briefly, just how close he had come to making the dragon "crash." If such a thing was possible.

He suddenly had a very clear vision of a tree limb in his face. Shortly after the Fall he had been one of the people chosen, because he had some limited riding experience, to "help out" with a round-up of feral animals. While he had been trying to keep a boar from killing a female friend, Diablo had jumped over the spitted boar and Herzer's forehead had impacted a tree limb at nearly a full gallop.

The recovery had been slow and painful. But if he screwed up *this* ride, he was looking at a several-thousand-meter fall. That was not even *vaguely* survivable.

But he *really* needed to catch up to the formation.

"Up, Chauncey," he yelled. "Go! Forward! Hut! Hut!" There didn't seem to be any way to beat at him. He'd never really seen the riders make *any* motions except small rein movements.

But. His boot was actually over skin, not on the saddle. He doubted that was unintentional.

"Hi, Chauncey," he yelled, digging his boot into the side of the dragon as hard as he could.

The startled wyvern began flapping its wings, rapidly gaining speed. So rapidly that the formation was coming up much too quickly. And he was still slightly below it.

"Up!" he called, pulling back on the reins. At the last

moment he checked his instinctive reaction to yank back and instead applied a gentle pressure, as if he was trying to get Diablo to go to a moderately slower gallop.

The control worked, Chauncey adjusted his angle of flight and went upward, losing some forward speed at the same time, but when they returned to level flight, by simply letting out on the reins, they were above and past the formation. Also slightly farther out to the left and he had no idea how that had happened.

"What the hell are you doing?" Joanna bellowed. "I told you to just go along for the ride!"

"He was in your slipstream!" Herzer yelled back. "I didn't think you should have to tow him!"

"If it had been a problem I would have *told* you!" Joanna raged back. "Now what are you going to do, hotshot?"

He had to go backwards, down and to the right. The "slot" he was trying to get to was about ten or twenty meters to his right and about the same back. About sixty meters down. He seemed to be in a slightly less efficient glide than the other dragons, probably because he wasn't coasting in the same vortexes.

Well, he'd tried the up reins, and the up and down. And turned left and right.

"I guess I'll try the down reins," he muttered and pushed back, lightly, on the right down rein.

Rachel had been watching Herzer's fumbling entry into flight with some amusement but she gasped in horror as the dragon turned over on its right wing and plummeted towards the ground.

"Oh, my God!" she shouted.

Joanna turned her head slightly to the side and tisked. "That's what we call a stoop."

"Is he going to be okay?"

"Well, the reason we call it a stoop is that it's fisking stoopid."

Herzer grabbed at the straps as the dragon seemed to turn, briefly, upside down. He had a very clear view of the underside of Vickie's dragon as he passed and he realized he was screaming, but there didn't seem to be anything else to do at the moment.

However, he was only briefly inverted, if he ever actually had been, and he quickly gained control of the beast, taking the climb straps and pulling back on them slightly less gently than he had been.

The dragon pulled out of its dive in a strong swoop upward and to the left, pushing upward with strong strokes of its wings and Herzer let out a bellow of joy at the incredible feeling of having that power at his control.

"Yes!" he shouted, as the dragon pulled up to the level of the formation. More confident now he let it rise to slightly above the formation then angled it into the slot at a downward glide. At the last Chauncey seemed to sense the vortex and entered the slot of his own accord.

"Oh, my God!" Herzer shouted over to Vickie, a smile plastered on his face.

"You're fisking crazy!" Vickie shouted back. "You could have killed yourself."

"That's what's so great!" Herzer yelled back, still grinning. "Normally it's human beings trying to kill me. This time it was just physics!"

"Give him a break, Vickie," the next rider over shouted. "The first time she stooped she pissed herself."

"Thank you so very much, Jerry!" Vickie shouted back. "You'd better check your straps well for that!"

"It was great!" Herzer yelled. "Let's do it again!"

"Not a chance," Jerry yelled. "The reason we're flying like this is it's a long flight today. You've already pushed him harder than was a good idea. Just let it be. Time for aerobatics on the trip."

"He's not a dragon-rider!" Vickie yelled back.

"Dragon. Rider. Dragon-rider!" Jerry pointed then laughed.

"How long are we flying today?" Herzer yelled.

"Long time, four or five hours," Vickie replied. "That's pretty close to the limit of a dragon's endurance."

"Oh," Herzer muttered. "I didn't know," he added in a yell.

"It should be fine," Vickie yelled. "It's not that they wear out, they just need to feed by then. And full dragons don't fly very well. We usually fly a couple of hours, then feed them, then fly again. This way we'll fly four or five hours, then they'll have to gorge. And once they gorge they won't be any good for hours."

"What if they don't get fed?" Herzer yelled.

"You don't want to be around a hungry dragon," Jerry replied. "You really don't."

The dragons hissed like giant tea kettles, swinging their heads angrily from side to side. But the chains they were attached to kept them far enough apart that even their tails couldn't strike at the ones to either side.

On the other hand, to get the large platters to them would require getting close enough to get bitten.

The destination of the group had been Newfell Naval Base, a growing facility near the mouth of the Gem River. It was at the very tip of a massive bay that marked the joining of the Gem and Poma rivers, the latter of which was fed by, among others, the Shenan that ran by Raven's Mill.

The base had been formed in response to the apparent intended invasion from Ropasa and it was a scene of remarkable industry.

There were twelve large piers, each of which was in use by a veritable fleet of small vessels. Most of the vessels seemed to be barges and lighters that were carrying material from the interior, but a few were larger sailing vessels that had probably reached the base by sailing up or down the coast. Herzer recalled that to the north were the growing cities of Balmoran and Manan, either of which might have sent the ships.

The material being unloaded from the ships made its way to a set of warehouses lining the waterways. From the warehouses some of it spread to support the rest of the base. There were foundries that provided the iron-work for the ships, saw mills that roughed the trees that were rapidly being turned into hulls and masts, rope manufactories that took the rough hemp from the interior and made it into strong manila lines, and sail-factories where heavy cosilk bolts were sewn into the vast sails needed for the growing ships.

But all of it paled to the efforts of the shipyards themselves.

The wyverns had been parked at the edge of the shipyards along the Gem River. On every side ship hulls lying on ways were in the process of being built, surrounded by scaffolding. From every direction came the sound of sawing and hammering, and besides the smell of tidal marshes there was an overpowering smell of curing wood and sawdust.

And all of it was contributing to the unease of the wyverns.

The platters were large, over a meter in diameter, with raised edges and metal handles. The smell from the steaming mess they contained mixed with the stench of the tidal marshes to create an aroma that Herzer found truly nauseating.

But what he really wanted at this moment, rather than a mask to cut the stench, was his armor. Those wyverns had *big* teeth.

"What's in this?" he asked, lifting one side of the platter

as Jerry took the other. Herzer probably could have lifted one himself but it for most riders it was a two-person job.

"Offal, soybeans, vegetable oil and ketchup," Jerry said. "Now they know the smell of this stuff and they don't like it. So they're going to be inclined to get a bite of fresh meat. We stop just outside of lunge range and slide it to them. On three."

"Ketchup?" Herzer asked.

"They like ketchup. One, two . . ."

From behind them there was a roar and Joanna landed to the side in a blast of wind.

"Cut it out!" she bellowed, leaning over to peck the nearest wyvern on the back. The wyvern ducked its head to the ground and got as close as it could to scraping its belly, letting out a faint mewing sound.

"*Now* feed 'em," Joanna bellowed, pecking at another of the wyverns that had leaned towards the platters. "I need you guys alive."

Jerry and Herzer crabbed forward and dropped the platter under the wyvern's nose and then picked up another and dropped it in front of Chauncey. By that time the other three had been fed as well.

Like it or not the wyverns immediately buried their nose in the mess, sucking at it since it had little in the way of texture.

"Well, that's done," Jerry sighed. "Now we check them over."

The dragon's pebbly skin was fairly strong but it could be badly gouged by a misplaced strap. Jerry, with Vickie occasionally giving acerbic advice, showed Herzer how to check for gouges or scrapes. They then spent some time working on Chauncey, trimming his toenails. Jerry had a large set of bolt cutters for the job but Herzer gently lifted one of the talons and inserted the tip into his clamp.

"They're strong," Jerry said.

"Not a problem," Herzer said. "Probably." Herzer flexed his forearm and the tip of the nail flew off with a "snick" sound.

"Cool," Jerry said. "Very useful."

"Also opens bottles and makes julienne fries," Herzer said with a grimace. "I'd rather have a hand."

"How's it work?"

"If I grasp like I'm grabbing with forefinger and thumb it clamps," Herzer said. "If I grasp with middle and ring finger it engages the cutters. If I pull with the pinkie it engages a *gear* on the cutters and the clamps. Gives me about six times the grip or cutting strength."

"Did you use the clamp?"

"Nope, didn't need it," Herzer said, running his hand up Chauncey's leg as he cut the other nails. "That's done this one."

"Chauncey's one of our newer wyverns," Jerry explained as Herzer worked on the other talons. "He's just out of the rookery but since he's biddable and didn't have a designated rider and we were told we needed one spare we brought him along despite the fact that he's not full grown."

"Big enough," Herzer said. "How fast do they grow?"

"Ten years to get this big," Jerry said. "He'll add another sixty, maybe eighty kilos before he stops in another ten."

"Ten years?" Herzer said. "Then . . . he was born before the Fall?"

"Yeah," Jerry said with a smile. "Nobody's been able to do time travel yet. There was a wyvern racing league; we came from that."

"I'd thought that Sheida had had them bred," Herzer said then paused. "Why did you join up?"

"Well, we had to keep them fed somehow," Jerry replied with a shrug, giving Chauncey a last wipe with a rag. "And between Sheida and New Destiny there wasn't much choice, was there?"

"No, I don't think so," Herzer answered honestly. "I . . . I was involved with some folks that were allied with New Destiny at first. I didn't know they were until after I'd left. They weren't very good people even before that, though."

"Well, I joined up with Sheida almost immediately," Jerry said. "I had a rookery near her home in the Teron mountains. After the Fall I flew over and she saw the benefit immediately. So I and a couple of others flew around to the rookeries and recruited."

"Where did Joanna come from?" Herzer asked.

"I don't know. Sheida found her someplace."

"Do you mind her . . . sort of being in charge?"

"Not at all," Jerry replied with a shrug. "She's like a god to the wyverns, which helps as you might have noticed. And when she gets into a battle the other side doesn't have much of a chance. The wyverns really aren't very good at fighting; all they can do is bite or claw down, and when they do they lose airspeed. Joanna goes through the enemy like a mechanical reaper. She can really use that tail for some serious damage. I'm glad she's on our side."

Herzer and Jerry were gathering up the rags and cutters

when Herzer spotted Rachel picking her way through the wyverns. The dragons had settled down after their feed but a few of them hissed at her as she passed.

Rachel ignored them, making a beeline for Herzer. When she got close she stood with her hands on her hips and shook her head.

"So this is where you've been hiding?" she asked. "I thought you were happy in the infantry?"

"I am," Herzer admitted. "But we're going to be working with the dragons a lot. I figured it was a good idea to get to know them as well as possible."

"Well, Father thinks it's a good idea if you two attend the mission briefing, whatever that means," Rachel said. "Which is why I'm here."

"Are we done?" Herzer asked.

"Done enough," Jerry answered. "Let's go."

CHAPTER NINE

Joel had permitted the enthusiastic ensign to recruit him; it seemed like the simplest way to manage the insertion given the complications. Ensign Weilis had even picked up the ticket from Tenerie to Newfell. So after arriving at Newfell Base, the ensign led him to the recruiting station and then took off to report for duty.

Joel shook his head at that, wondering at many levels about the ensign's naiveté. They had stopped overnight south of Washan, staying at one of the coaching inns; the price of the cramped room was included in the fare. So it had been midmorning by the time they arrived. Technically, the ensign did not have to report until just before midnight the day of his arrival. If he reported now, he'd either sit around in an office all day or be assigned busywork until somebody figured out what to do with him tomorrow.

The other level of concern about Weilis' naiveté was Joel's conviction that whoever was running counterintel couldn't find their ass with both hands. The ensign had gladly told him all of his duties in Balmoran and some of what he thought he would be doing in Newfell. In fact, the kid was such a chatterbox, Joel now knew half the story of his life. He either had his cover down pat, or he was an idiot. No, the kid wasn't an idiot, he'd been *trained* by idiots. And that was worse.

Joel shook his head again and opened up the door to the recruiting office. There was a desk in the room with two comfortable chairs placed in front of it. Behind the desk was a stern-faced older guy in a uniform just about covered in medals. His face broke into a friendly grin when Joel came through the door.

"Hello there, son," the NCO boomed, coming to his feet and walking around the desk. "Glad to see you, I'm Chief Rishell, but you can call me Chief."

"Hi, Chief," Joel said. When the chief limpingly cleared the desk it became apparent why he was behind it; his right leg was gone from the knee down. "Got bad news for you, I think this must be the recruiting office, right?"

"That's right, son," the chief said, pumping his hand. "It's a man's life in the Navy, but we only take the best. Good strong hands there—you working as a plow-hand before?"

"No, Chief," Joel said. "The point is, that nice young lieutenant directed me here. I'm looking for receiving."

"You already got recruited?" the chief replied, dropping Joel's hand.

"Yeah, I used to work fishing boats, before and after the Fall," Joel replied with a grin. "They said something about making me a petty officer."

The chief looked at him with a blank expression for a moment, then pointed to his left.

"Receiving's three buildings down."

"Gotcha, Chief," Joel said, trying not to grin.

"You on orders?" the chief asked, looking at his shabby traveling clothes.

"Verbal is what they told me," Joel replied with a shrug. "Basically they swore me in and put me on a stage coach for Newfell."

"Hmmm . . ." The chief peered at him for a second and then went back behind his desk. "Siddown, son."

Joel did so, cocking his head to the side.

"The thing is, you're not required to report until just before midnight," the chief said with a slight frown. "If you go over there this time of day, they won't have any way to use you. They might tell you to take off and take care of personal business. But they'll probably put you on some temporary detail nobody wants to do, like raking grass or shoveling shit. Now, everybody has to do those sometimes, anyway. But there's no damned reason to put yourself in the way of them, if you know what I mean."

"I appreciate that," Joel said. "But I don't know what there is to do."

"If you've got any cash, I'd suggest going over to the Post

Exchange. They've got a snack bar and there's even books you can buy now in the PX. Maybe take a walk around the base, but if you're out of uniform people are going to ask you questions and if you run into some officious young prick he's gonna tell you to report in right away. Go get a book and some lunch and find an out-of-the way spot to hide. I'm only letting you in on this, you realize, 'cause you're a fellow sailor."

"Thanks, Chief," Joel said, rising. "Can I ask you what happened to the leg?"

The chief looked at him intensely for a moment, then shrugged.

"Got a line caught around it in a gale off Cape Far," the chief said. "Just remember, the sea, she's a mother."

"Been there, done that, Chief," the spy replied. "Take care."

"Sure," the chief replied as he walked out the door. "You too."

Joel found the PX and, sure enough, there were some books. He had no idea of authors or titles so he simply picked the one with the most lurid cover. It was as bad as he'd expected. It was the "true" story of Raven's Mill's defense against one of New Destiny's proxies in the first year after the Fall. It centered, to an almost mind-numbing degree, on the training of the Blood Lords. On the other hand, if there was any accuracy, he needed to talk to their trainers. They already had a functional nucleus of professional training going and if the spy school he had in mind ever got off the ground, some training along the same lines would be useful.

The book, however, was another story. No way was he letting the writer anywhere near anything that *he* did. The guy introduced characters for no particular reason and then killed them off, just when he was getting to like them. Sure, it was a real story and the people really died, but give it a rest. He also had clunky prose and a really strange sense of humor. This guy was never going to win any awards.

On the other hand, it *was* a page turner and the snack bar guy had to throw him out when they closed. He tucked the book away, unsure whether to burn it or finish it later, and headed over to receiving, still chuckling. He hoped that this idiot never got ahold of *his* life story. He'd probably kill him off, just when everybody was getting to like him.

Herzer and Jerry followed Rachel back towards the headquarters and Herzer took the opportunity to have a closer look at the shipbuilding. There were more than a dozen ships under construction, ranging from a small boat that probably was meant to be used in the bay all the way up to a massive vessel, fully sixty meters long. The latter only had its frames up, but it was clearly designed to be fast and powerful. He had no clue what it was going to look like when completed but it had the look of a warship.

Behind the warehouses there was another row of buildings on slightly higher ground. Most of the structures were extremely rough, obviously made in the first rush of building after the Fall. Some of them were already being torn down for materials; the large tree sections that had been used to construct the early cabins could be sawn into wood to make three buildings out of one. One of them, however, was having additional construction added on and it was to that one that Rachel led them.

"This is the base headquarters," Rachel told them as they approached through streams of workmen and sailors in blue trousers and off-white shirts. "It's also Fleet headquarters for the time being. They're a bit bunched up."

"I can imagine," Herzer said, chuckling. They were having much the same problem in Raven's Mill with the Academy and the Overjay local defense headquarters occupying the same suite of buildings. "What gets me is how many people there are here; it must be two or three times the number in Raven's Mill. And that's more than there were in Harzburg. Most of them are prime soldier material and we're *dying* for soldiers!"

"From what I picked up in the headquarters they've been filtering in from the north and south ever since the Fall," Rachel said as they approached the entrance. The two guards in blue uniforms saluted Herzer as they passed and he gave them a wave in return. "There's a lot of emphasis being put on getting a fleet built."

"Well, I'd rather fight Paul's forces at sea than on land," Herzer admitted. "So I won't begrudge it."

She led them through the building to an office in the rear that was part of a recent addition; the air was still thick with the smell of sawdust and the stud-covered walls were weeping sap.

The party from Raven's Mill was grouped around a desk, behind which sat a short-coupled man with a heavy tan and a shock of iron gray hair that had been cut short on top and to stubble on the sides. He had cold blue eyes that searched the newcomers unhappily.

"Lieutenant Herzer Herrick, Jerry Riadou, this is Skipper Shar

Chang. His rank is colonel in the Free States forces. He's the skipper of the *Bonhomme Richard*, which is going to be conveying us to the islands. Skipper, Jerry is the senior dragonrider and Herzer is one of my officers who is acting as my aide in this mission."

"Sir," Herzer said, snapping to attention and rendering a salute.

"General Talbot outranks me, Lieutenant," the colonel said, dryly. "One of the many wonderful aspects of this mission."

"You're in charge of the ship, Skipper," Talbot said, calmly. "We're just along for the ride."

"The dragons aren't," Chang replied. "Let me explain to you all the problems we've got to deal with. The *Richard* is a brand-new ship, a dragon-carrier and the first one to be launched. It's specifically designed to support dragons. The first problem is that we've had to design it in theory, since these are the first wyvern we've had on the base. She's designed to carry thirty-six wyvern and their riders or four great dragons and a support team at sea for one hundred days. The five wyverns and one great dragon are going to rattle around in her like peas in a pod but that's the good news. We've just completed builder's trials. There are problems left to fix. She hasn't had a shakedown cruise. Her rigging needs adjustment. Dragon support is *going* to need adjustment. And in the midst of all of this we're tasked with this high-priority mission. You begin to see why I'm so enthusiastic."

"I can understand that, sir," Jerry interjected. "We were informed that the mission had both aspects in mind, working out doctrine and supporting the diplomatic mission. We'll do it, sir. We have to."

"Agreed. What's your rank, son?" the skipper asked.

"Well . . ." Jerry temporized. "We don't actually have ranks as such. I'm just the most senior guy. In most cases, I defer to Joanna when she's around."

"Grand," Chang sighed. "So you're not officially members of the UFS forces?"

"We are, sir," Jerry replied, cautiously. "At least, that's how we get paid. But the subject of ranks has never been raised. We just go where Sheida tells us and do what we can. We've *done* combat missions, sir. It's not been a problem."

"And what happens if one of your riders decides they don't like the mission?" Chang asked.

"It's . . . never come up, sir," Jerry admitted.

"I'm going to send a long memo to Atlantis Command,"

Chang said. "That's for sure. Until further notice, Mr. Riadou, your new rank is warrant officer first class. I don't know what you've been being paid but that's also your pay-grade, starting now. If it's more than you've been being paid, you just got a raise. If it's less, we'll figure something out. Flight pay, maybe. Choose one of your riders as your senior noncommissioned officer. The rest will be given the rank of sergeant. Do you have any questions?"

"No, sir," Jerry replied.

"You should. You're now under military law and discipline. That's a far cry from being a civilian. I can have your riders flogged or hanged for failure to obey an order. So can General Talbot. For that matter, you'll have to obey orders from Lieutenant Herrick, here, since he's a commissioned officer and outranks you. I'll have a copy of the regulations sent to your barracks."

"What about Joanna?" Talbot asked.

"She'll get a rank of commander," Chang said after a moment. "She'll be equal in rank to my XO but outrank everyone else on the ship except you or me. In general, she'll have full control of the dragons and their riders. She'll also be responsible for their actions. Will that be a problem?"

"Unlikely," Edmund replied. "But she's got a very specific pay structure. It's in my orders."

"Understood," Chang said. "Now, to the mission. As Mr. Riadou noted, we've got a dual priority, getting the dragons trained in and handling the diplomatic mission. Comments?"

"Getting to the islands is the highest priority," Edmund replied. "Dragon training cannot interfere with that to any great extent."

Chang sighed and shook his head. "More or less the point that I'd come to. Well, we'll just have to handle it." There was a knock at the door and it opened almost immediately to reveal a brown-haired young man with a distant expression. He stopped, startled, at the group in the crowded room and looked at the commander behind the desk.

"Sorry, I'll come back," he muttered, starting to leave the room.

"You were supposed to be here fifteen minutes ago," Chang sighed. "Come in, Evan. Evan is . . ." He paused and looked Duke Talbot with a puzzled expression. "We're not sure exactly what to call Evan. Generally we just refer to him as a ship's designer, but he's more like an efficiency expert."

"I like to think of myself as a systems designer," Evan said with a smile that relieved his puzzled countenance. "About that, there's a change I want to make to the feeding system on the *Richard* . . ."

"Evan, we have to have the things in place long enough to write doctrine, you know," Chang replied. He had an amused expression on his face as if this were a long-running complaint.

"I know, Shar, but I think I can cut one crewmember . . ."

"Tell it to me later, Evan, there's something more important at the moment." Chang turned to Jerry with a gesture. "This is Warrant Officer Riadou. He's the senior dragon-rider of the first dragon-flight we've received. You should get him dialed in on the facilities on the *Richard* as soon as possible. Jerry Riadou, Evan Mayerle."

"Okay," Evan said, holding out his hand. "Does that mean we actually have *wyverns* to work with?"

"And a greater dragon," Chang said with a nod. "You hadn't heard?"

"Uh, no," Evan replied. "We'll have to break down the stalls on the hangar deck and—"

"Take it up with the XO," Chang said, cutting him off. "We're sailing on the morning tide. I'll be out in no more than an hour. Pass that on to the XO, will you Mr. Riadou?"

"Will do, sir," Jerry said. "Should I move my people out to the ship?"

"There's no way I can think of to get the dragons to the ship without them flying out, so the first thing we're going to have to do in the morning is fly them on. What do you think?"

"I'll go out to the ship, make sure that everything is arranged and that I'm familiar with the system and then come back on shore?"

"That's right," the skipper replied with a chuckle. "I want to see you this evening so stay on the ship until I arrive."

"Yes, sir," Jerry said.

"This is the Navy, Warrant Officer," the skipper replied with a smile. "When you get an order you say 'aye, aye, sir.' "

"Aye, aye, sir," Jerry replied. "Should I go now?"

"And the term is 'by your leave' or 'by your permission.' " Chang sighed. "Yes, go. You too, Evan. I'll see you both on board."

When the two had left Chang shook his head and looked at Duke Talbot.

"Is it just me, or is everyone having to make this up as they go along?"

"Everyone is." Talbot chuckled with the rest. "Daneh is

having to half-train doctors, Herzer constantly has to make soldiers out of straw and mud. Everyone is."

"Do you have any idea how complex a large ship is?" Chang asked. "Just gathering the necessary materials for it to go to sea is mind-boggling. Enough food and water for a hundred days, for *thirty-six* dragons? Not to mention the two hundred and twenty-five crew members, twenty officers and warrant officers, dragon-riders, *passengers*. On that subject, water is at a premium on-board. There is a ration of one gallon a day per person and it is not adjustable. There are saltwater showers and you can have thirty seconds of secondary water for washing the salt off. Don't drink it; it's not potable. We have a low-power steam engine for powered support and it produces the shower water, but there's only so much. The cabins are small and tight; there's no room for much gear. And the food ranges in quality from poor to very bad."

"So much for a pleasure cruise to the islands," Rachel said with a laugh. "It's better than things were right after the Fall, Skipper."

"That it is," Chang said with a nod. "Speaking of gear, this was *ported* over. Or formed here, I'm not sure which."

He reached behind his desk and pulled out a gray plastic box, setting it on his desk. It was apparently seamless.

"I can't open it," he added in a less than amused tone. "I have no idea what it contains."

Talbot placed his hand on the top of the box and it opened down an invisible seam on the top. Inside were four transparent bags, some mixed items on the bottom and a sealed envelope. Talbot pulled out the envelope and broke the seal, then shrugged at the contents.

"More instructions from Sheida," he said, folding it and putting it back in the envelope. Chang was visibly annoyed that he was not made privy to the communication but Talbot ignored him. "Breath-masks for working underwater and suggested trade materials," he added, closing the box. "Could you have this sent out to the ship, Skipper?"

"Of course, General," the officer replied. "Will there be anything else?"

"No, I don't think so," Talbot said. "It would probably make sense for us to go out to the ship as soon as possible."

"I'll make arrangements," Chang replied, gesturing at the box. "That way your luggage can come with you."

"Thank you," Edmund said with a broad grin. "Now?"

"Horace!"

CHAPTER TEN

Herzer shook his head at the sight of the massive ship.

"They've only got a couple of hundred people to man it?" he asked.

The ship was nearly eighty meters long with three masts, the rearmost and highest of which stretched forty meters in the air. Sails were furled in every direction and Herzer had a hard time sorting them out. There were some that looked like they dropped down from crosspieces on the masts, but others were twisted around sloping ropes or something on the front.

The ship also looked awfully odd because where more masts should have been at the rear, there was a large platform. In fact, the wheel and deck that he'd expect to be at the rear was entirely missing. It might be under the platform, but if so it was well hidden. And a large, cantilevered platform angled out forward on the near side of the ship. And the whole ship was painted a dull gray, which Herzer found strange.

The group was being rowed out to the ship in one of the many small boats in the harbor. This one was rowed by two people, a man and a brawny female who seemed to be in charge. The boat was one of many headed to or from the ship and as they approached they could see a group of seamen lifting pallets onto the ship from one of the lighters along-side. Next to it was another lighter that had snaked four hoses over the side. It had a small steam engine going and was apparently pumping something aboard ship.

As they approached the ship a set of stairs with a floating platform was lowered over the side and the two oarsmen pulled the boat up to it.

Herzer had been surprised when Duke Edmund had had them board in reverse order of seniority but he understood now as the duke was the first to hop from the craft onto the platform and rapidly ascend the stairs. Herzer followed Daneh out of the boat and up the stairs. He was trailed, in order, by Vickie, Rachel and one of the other dragon-riders, the latter of which was carrying the featureless gray box. From the top of the stairs came an odd sound, like very high-pitched whistling. He got to the top of the stairs just in time to see the duke drop his salute and hear a leather-lunged petty officer bellow: "Overjay Command, Arriving!"

At the top of the stairs there was a double line of sailors and the blue-uniformed soldiers that he had seen at the Navy base. The sailors were in their day uniforms but the soldiers were turned out in armor, which was well polished, and boarding pikes, which were held vertically at attention.

Edmund had briefed them on the way out so Herzer first saluted the rear of the ship, where the UFS Navy flag, a diamondback rattler on an orange field, was flying, then the officer greeting them.

"Permission to come aboard, sir?"

"Permission granted," the Navy commander replied, returning the salute. He was wearing the same undress uniform as the sailors, blue trousers and off-white shirt, but wore a broad brimmed hat, turned up at one side, on which were fixed the two vertical silver bars of a commander. He was nearly as tall as Herzer but much thinner and he held out his hand with a friendly grin. "You're going to have as much trouble moving around this ship as I do."

He turned to the duke and waved towards the rear of the ship as the petty officer in charge of the greeting party ordered it to stand down and fall out.

"I'm Commander Owen Mbeki, executive officer," the commander said.

"I'm Edmund Talbot, obviously," the duke said with a smile. "My wife Doctor Daneh Ghorbani who is acting as my cultural attaché, Lieutenant Herzer Herrick my military attaché and aide, my daughter Rachel Ghorbani, Daneh's aide, Staff Sergeant Vickie Toweeoo, senior NCO of the dragon contingent."

"Charmed, I'm sure," the commander replied, shaking their

hands. "I'll show you to your staterooms, General. Sergeant Toweeoo and the other dragon-riders are quartered by their beasts." He waved to the leather-lunged petty officer and gestured at the two riders. "Have someone relieve this poor man of the baggage, Chief Brooks, and show them the dragon facilities. Then round up Evan and that dragon warrant."

"Aye, aye, sir," the CPO said.

Once on the deck it was clear that the overhang, what was apparently a dragon landing platform, covered a good third of the ship. The commander led them towards a gangway that was actually under the shade of the platform and gestured above.

"That thing's going to be a bloody nuisance, General," the commander noted. "Not only does it mean losing a mast, perhaps two, with the concomitant loss of speed, but it's got a huge sail area. Maneuvering this tub is a stone bitch."

"What do you think about it?" Talbot asked. "Are the dragons worth it?"

"We'll have to see, won't we, sir?" the commander said with a tone of amusement. "From what I understand they don't have much of a means of attacking anything below them. At the moment I'd have to say no. On the other hand, preparing for them has given us this lovely huge ship to play with and if they don't work out we can simply add a couple of masts and have a real fighting ship at our fingers."

He led them down the short flight of stairs to the next deck. The top of the opening to the passageway was covered in padding and painted bright yellow and black.

"Watch your head," he said, ducking in example. "Especially you, Lieutenant. Turn to face the ladder, please; it's safer that way."

The corridor beyond was low and narrow. There were two crewmen, a male and a female, coming from the opposite direction and both of them flattened themselves against the wall as the party passed.

"Sorry about this," Daneh muttered.

"Not a problem, ma'am," the female crewman murmured while the male gave Rachel a raised eyebrow.

"Moving protocols," the commander said as he pushed aside a curtain and entered a room to the right of the corridor. "When you're moving in a corridor, the junior gives way to the senior. Since that means I only have to stand aside for the captain I think it's a lovely deal." He pointed to two bunks along the side of the tiny cabin. "I'm not sure about arrangements. We're a mixed crew but we have separate bunking for males and females. There's this cabin and the master cabin, which is designated for the use of Duke Talbot since it's large enough for meetings. Either the two ladies can bunk in here, or the lieutenant and Mistress Daneh's aide share, or, I suppose, the duke could give up his cabin to the ladies and bunk in here. There's also a large cabin in the dragon-rider's area but I'd prefer to set that aside for the riders if you don't mind. Or one of them could bunk with the riders."

Edmund looked at Rachel and raised an eyebrow to which the girl shrugged.

"I've been living, one way or another, with Herzer most of my life; I don't have an issue with rooming with him."

"I could bunk with the riders," Herzer said at almost the same time.

"No, I want you to work with them but I'll want you handy as well," Edmund said, rubbing his beard. "Bunk here. If there *are* issues, deal with them."

Herzer shrugged and went into the room, tossing his gear on the top bunk. It had a low wooden railing on the outside and the cushion was made of some relatively soft padding; he wasn't sure what. It wasn't straw or feathers, of that he was sure. There was just enough room for him to turn around, with his head bent, in the small cabin. Climbing into the bunk was going to be an interesting operation. His gear, not much of it, just one bag, went at the foot of the bunk, which gave him about a hundred ninety centimeters to work with. Given that he was two hundred ten centimeters in height, it was going to be cramped. He'd just have to prop his feet on the bag.

"And just down the corridor," Mbeki said, this time opening a door into a room, "we have Duke Edmund's cabin."

The room, while low, was relatively spacious. Besides a large bed it had a table large enough to handle six people, eight if they crowded. There was also a fairly large window made of thick glass, and a few meters of open floor space.

"You're on the port side of the ship here, just forward of the captain's cabin," the commander said. "My cabin is right across the corridor. Wardroom is just down from the aide's cabin on the port side. The rest of the officers' quarters are forward of the companionway."

"This will do well," Duke Edmund said. "Put that over there," he continued, gesturing to the seaman who had been following them.

"Duke Edmund," Herzer said. "I'd like to look up Jerry and get a look at the dragon quarters."

"Warrant Officer Riadou is supposed to be meeting with the captain soon . . ." Mbeki said.

"I'd like Herzer to attend that," Talbot interrupted. "Herzer's going to be my liaison with the dragon-riders. I'd like him in on discussions of their use."

"Very well," the commander said, nonplussed. "Seaman, show Lieutenant Herzer to the captain's dayroom."

Herzer followed the seaman though a bewildering series of corridors to a door guarded by a sentry.

"Lieutenant Herzer to see the captain, orders of the duke," the seaman said, stepping aside.

The guard looked the lieutenant over and raised an eyebrow. "Blood Lord?"

Herzer leaned forward until his nose was an inch from the sentry and nodded.

"Blood Lord. There is one captain. There are two lieutenants. I'm the other one. And if you give me a look like that again I'll wipe the floor with you. I don't take lip from privates. Especially ones with newly issued armor and who haven't seen shit to make them salty. Do I make my point?"

The sentry flexed a jaw muscle and nodded. "Yes, sir," he said, then knocked on the door.

"What?" Chang called from the interior.

"A Blood Lord lieutenant to see you, sir," the guard said.

"Let him in."

Herzer marched in and saluted the captain, who was bent over a table, head nearly touching Evan's, both of them poring over a schematic, presumably of the ship.

"Message from Duke Edmund?" the skipper asked.

"Actually, sir, he sent me to . . . look in on the meeting, sir. I'll just stay out of the way."

The skipper stared at him flatly for a moment, then shrugged. "No, if you have anything to contribute, feel free. We've only been working on this project for a year. I'm sure you have all sorts of useful suggestions."

"I'm much more likely to ask questions, sir," the lieutenant said. "But I intend to avoid even that."

"Questions are good," Evan said. "Doing something like this is all about questions. Like, what's going to happen to the handling of the ship when thirty-six wyverns are coming and going all the time?"

"Something we'll have to find out," the skipper said. "Right now, I'm wondering if we can even get them on and off."

"We can do the landing, sir," Jerry said doggedly. "The wyverns can land on a dime."

"This will be a *moving* dime, Warrant," the skipper growled. "Up and down, side to side, forward and back. I'll limit the movement to the extent that I can, but I can't *stop* it."

"We'll figure it out, sir," Jerry replied.

"Know anything about logistics, Lieutenant?" the skipper asked. "You've fed those wyverns. How much feed per day?"

"Depends upon the type, sir," Herzer answered. "From what I was told, two hundred kilos per day of the mess, less if it's good quality protein and fats."

"Access to the latter will be restricted at sea," the captain said. "You've helped feed them?"

"Sir," Herzer said, nodding his head.

"Think about doing that on a rolling ship in the middle of a gale," the captain said with a smile.

"Sir, have food bowls set into the stalls, sir," Herzer replied. "Have slots to feed the mess through the slots. Better yet, have some sort of a moving trolley that automatically feeds them; that prevents humans accidentally sliding into the stalls. Have the edge of the food bowls sufficiently high that the mess is unlikely to slop over. Feed in increments rather than lots at one time. More time intensive but if there's an automated feeder that's not a problem. Sir."

The captain raised one eyebrow. "Is that an official recommendation, Lieutenant?"

"But . . ." Evan said then shut up as the captain raised a hand.

"Sir, no, sir, it's just an idea," Herzer barked, standing at the position of parade rest. "I was specifically asked, sir."

The skipper leaned back in a chair and actually appeared to look at Herzer for the first time.

"Who *trained* you, Lieutenant Herrick?" the captain asked.

"Gunnery Sergeant Miles A. Rutherford was my advanced combat trainer, sir," Herzer replied. "He developed the Blood Lord training system. Along with Duke Edmund."

"*Gunnery* sergeant?" the skipper asked. "That's a *Marine* rank."

"If you have an issue with the use of that rank, sir, I respectfully suggest that you take it up with the Gunny, sir," Herzer said sardonically.

"Think you're salty, Lieutenant?" the skipper asked, tilting his head to the side.

"No, sir, never been to sea, sir," Herzer replied. "But . . ."

"Yes?" Chang said, with a raised eyebrow.

"I've been wounded with arrows, axe, spear and sword, had my hand cut off by a powered blade, fought my way through a cloud of nannites to try to dig my dagger into a man protected by a force field. I've been smashed off my horse, trampled and seen my best friends die on every side of me. I've flown dragons, fought cavalry battles and clashed shield to shield with ten times my number of Changed, all slavering for my blood. For two *damned* years I've been fighting this war on the front lines, *sir*. If you're trying to intimidate me, Colonel, you're going to find it a hard row to hoe."

The skipper stared at him for just a moment, then nodded his head.

"We're trying to figure out how to land and recover drag-ons on this ship and how to keep them alive, *healthy* in extreme conditions. We're also trying to figure out how to make them more of an offensive weapon. Warrant Officer Riadou has apparently fought with them before, but if the enemy isn't disheartened by their appearance there's not much that they can do except flap their wings and hiss. They're not even very good at using those impressive talons of theirs. Air to air, dragon y dragon, they might just be formidable. But we need to figure out how to make them a formidable force against *ground* and *sea* enemies. Now, they make decent scouts but I don't want a ship that's relegated to a scouting mission. I want an *offensive* weapon. Understand?"

"Sir," Herzer said with a nod of his head.

"Is there some way that you can help with that?"

"Not at this time, sir," Herzer admitted. "I wasn't planning on contributing, as noted. I'm here to be Duke Edmund's eyes and ears. But . . . sir?"

"Yes?"

"There's nobody that I know of who is better at wringing an offensive edge from a weapon than Duke Edmund."

"Perhaps he'll have some ideas, then." The skipper shrugged. "By the way, you came up with the same plan that Evan has for feeding the wyverns. Mr. Riadou has some issues with it."

"Wyverns are pack animals, sir," the rider said. "I'm afraid that if they spend much time battened down and completely separated they're going to be pretty unhappy. Depressed. A depressed dragon is a noneating dragon."

"We'll cross that problem when we come to it," Chang said. "And that's your problem unless there's something specific that I have to approve."

"Yes, sir," the rider said.

"I want you to be thinking along offensive lines," the skipper continued. "I want you to figure out ways that your dragons can sink *ships*. Capture them for that matter."

"Well, we can drop rocks," Jerry said. "But we have to toss them over the side and hope we both miss the wyvern's wing and hit the enemy. It's not very efficient."

"You and Evan talk it over," the skipper said. "I've spent enough time on this problem. Take Herzer with you. Figure something out."

"Will do, sir," the warrant officer replied. He straightened up and saluted, fist to chest. "By your leave, sir."

"In the Navy we salute to the brim of the cap," Chang said, tossing him a salute in return. "And not indoors. Gads, classes on basic military courtesy for riders. Add that to the list."

"Is he in the Army or the Navy?" Herzer asked. "Sir."

"He's damned well under my command on this ship, Lieutenant," the skipper replied tightly. "He can damned well follow Navy protocols."

Herzer nodded in reply and pushed open the door.

Joel had been assigned a bunk in the transient quarters and the next day hurriedly assigned uniforms and filled out a myriad of forms. The only one that gave him any trouble was the last will and testament. He had no one, at least no one he was in contact with, to leave his belongings to. On the other hand, "Joel Annibale" didn't exist, anyway. Finally, he left the form blank and when he turned it in the clerk in charge pointed to the empty line.

"You gotta leave it to someone or something," the clerk said.

"I don't have anyone," Joel said, his face hard.

"Most of us don't," the clerk replied. She was a young woman and she shook her head, sighing. "You can leave it to the Navy fund. This is my family, now. I guess it's yours, too."

Joel filled in the line and signed the form with a strange feeling. He knew he probably wasn't going to be with the Navy long, but for the time he had a home.

He was sent down to the docks with his ill-fitting uniforms, bulging seabag and new boots that slipped on his feet. He was assigned to a boat and got the first look at his new ship.

The damned thing was huge, a clipper ship if he recalled the design right. But the masts were all screwed up because of the big platform on the back.

There was a working party loading on the starboard side and before the new hands were even assigned quarters they were put to work hauling up the supplies. There were hogsheads of salt beef and pork, steel barrels of ration biscuit, bag after bag marked "Soya" and innumerable other items. Winches had been secured to the crosstrees and the material came over in large cargo nets. Then it had to be hand carried below and stuffed away in the holds. On his first trip down he was surprised to see that the material was only supplementary to what was already on-board; the ship was stuffed tighter than a tick.

As soon as the lighters had pulled away from the ship he was accosted by a female petty officer.

"I'm PO Su Singhisen," the petty officer said. "You're Seaman Annibale, right?"

"Right," Joel said. "Joel Annibale." The PO was a medium-height blonde with her hair pulled back in a tight bun.

"You looked like you knew what you were doing, there," she said, waving at him to follow her below.

"I've worked ships before," Joel said. "None this big, but it's pretty much the same."

"And they made you a steward?" Singhisen laughed.

"They did?" Joel replied. "Nobody told me what my duty station was going to be."

"Grand," the PO chuckled. "The navy finally finds somebody with *experience* on ships and they make them an officers' steward."

"Sounds like any bureaucracy to me," Joel chuckled.

"What did you do before the Fall?" Singhisen asked as she led him below. The companionway was short and while the PO didn't have to stoop, Joel did.

"I mostly sailed in the Asur Islands," Joel replied. "After the Fall I took up fishing for a living."

"How'd you get here?" she asked. She opened a door on an incredibly cramped room with four tiers of bunks spread across it in six rows. "Home sweet home."

"Grand," Joel replied as she led him down the narrow aisle between the bunks.

"You're the newbie," she said, pointing to the top bunk. "So you get the worst spot."

Joel had already seen that the seabags were set at the base of the bunks. He climbed up and lashed his in place.

"What next?"

"Galley and then I get somebody to show you the route to officers' country. Then we put you to work."

CHAPTER ELEVEN

Herzer followed the two far back into the bowels of the ship. The corridors were impossible to figure out, or so it seemed; most of the time he didn't know if he was facing the rear of the ship or the front. But finally they entered a high, wide corridor that was unmistakable.

"This is where the dragons walk?" he asked.

"We call it Broadway," Evan replied with a nod. "There's a ramp for them to walk down. The hatch is a major structural weakness, but we think we've shored around it sufficiently."

"Jerry, how much weight can one of the wyverns carry, over the weight of the rider?" Herzer asked.

"About two hundred kilos *depending* on the weight of the rider," Jerry replied.

"So why was I told to fly one alone?" Herzer mused. "I could have doubled up with, oh, Vickie. Or you, for that matter."

"We'd brought a spare," Jerry replied with a shrug. "Why overload them?"

"Hmmm . . ." Herzer followed them down to the stalls and checked out the arrangements. Sure enough, there was a method to slip food through to the permanently installed food troughs as well as spigots for water at each of the pens, feeding into a separate watering trough. The stalls had points to hook up chains in case the wyverns got out of hand as well as ways to close the stall down and press the wyvern up against the back if one got completely out of control.

"I think this will work," Jerry said, reluctantly. "Actually, it's better set up than our rookeries. I'll take some of these ideas back. Where's the mixing area for the mess?"

"Down the corridor," Evan said. "You'll love it. The material is brought up on lifts in premeasured quantities and then you just pour it in the mixer. That's powered as well, if we have take-off time. If not there's a four-man capstan for mixing and running the feeding chutes."

"I hope you remembered the ketchup," Herzer said jokingly. The mechanical feeding contrivance looked like a recipe for feeding body parts to the wyvern to him, but as an officer he hoped he'd be spared the job of using it.

"We've got two tons of ketchup powder," Evan said earnestly. "That should cover a hundred days even at the standard use of one kilo of ketchup per day per wyvern, which was what we were given as the measure. How do they like fish?" he asked.

"I have no idea," Jerry said. "We're from inland. Why?"

"I was wondering if it becomes necessary if they would be willing to substitute dried fish or fish sauce for meat or ketchup?"

"We'll find out," Jerry said with a laugh. "I'm sure we will find out."

"Evan, we met a 'Chief Brooks' earlier," Herzer said, rubbing his chin. "Who is he?"

"Brooks is the command master chief, the senior chief on board," Evan said. "Why?"

"Know where I'd find him?" Herzer asked.

"Just go up on deck and ask, somebody will know where he is."

"Jerry, I've got the funny feeling that I'm going to be ordered to get a, pardon the pun, crash course in dragon flying," Herzer said. "But I assume one of you will be bringing in Chauncey?"

"Absolutely," Jerry said with a frown. "I'm not even sure about . . ."

"Trust me on this," Herzer said. "I've learned to read part of the way into that opaque mind of my boss. We'll have to figure out how to get me trained on a ship."

"We'll try," Jerry sighed.

"Okay, I'm going to go find Chief Brooks," Herzer said. "Later."

"Later," Jerry replied as he walked away.

"I wouldn't want to be in his shoes," Evan said. "Chief Brooks doesn't like his time wasted. If he's not happy with a lieutenant it doesn't keep him from, with great respect, of course, eating the lieutenant a new asshole."

"I'm not sure I'd want to be the chief that tried to eat Herzer a new asshole," Jerry said musingly. "Now, human being quarters?"

"I think I can live here for a while," Daneh said, looking around the cabin after the others had left.

"It's more comfortable than I expected," Edmund admitted. "I was figuring we'd be in bunks."

"You're a duke now." Daneh smiled. "*And* a general. People want to pamper you."

"Like I need pampering," Talbot said. He reached down and opened up the box again, then dug into the bottom, pulling out a small gemlike device.

"A datacube?" Daneh said. "I can't believe she's expending so much power on this! I've had people die because I didn't have power."

"Daneh, if we get this wrong far more people are going to die than will ever go under your knife in a very bad lifetime," Edmund said. "And it's not *just* a datacube."

"What's it for, then?" she asked.

"Communications among other things," Edmund temporized. "And . . . in the event of a direct energy strike by Paul or any of his faction, they'll draw power from Sheida's protections. *That's* how important this is to her. But we're not to use it unless we *really* have to."

"This is more than just an invasion," Daneh said. "I mean, about more."

"There are so many balls being juggled I'm not even sure which are in the air," Edmund admitted. "But just concentrate on your mission and we'll be fine."

"I hate it when you get all inscrutable," Daneh said, sighing. "Speaking of which, I have an interest in Herzer's well-being. Why did you *really* bring him along?"

"When Jerry and his friends were racing wyvern, Herzer was fighting orcs in enhanced reality," Edmund said, frowning. "With the pain protocols turned up. He's a hard, cold, thinking bastard of a fighter. Harry tried to get those flyboys to pay attention to the mission, which is to force the enemy to admit defeat. He didn't manage it. I'm hoping that Herzer has better luck."

"And?"

"And . . ." Edmund smiled. "After the job he did in

Harzburg he needed a nice vacation to the Southern Isles. A pleasant cruise, a beautiful roommate, who knows what might happen?"

"Edmund, are you matchmaking?" Daneh said, aghast.

"For Herzer? Always."

"Your own daughter?!"

"Why not? They're young, they're compatible . . ."

"And Rachel treats him like a brother," Daneh said, throwing up her hands. "Herzer is a stallion stud, Rachel, as far as I know, is still a virgin. And apparently uninterested in changing that fact. It's not going to work."

"It's worth a shot." Talbot shrugged. "Frankly, Rachel needs him more than vice versa. She just doesn't realize it."

"She's making a fine life for herself," Daneh answered. But even she knew it sounded defensive.

"Certainly," Edmund replied with a nod. "If she wants to live it alone."

"That's up to her," Daneh said. "I tried it."

"How was it?" Edmund asked. "It was hell from my end."

"Not that good," she admitted with a smile. "Speaking of which, how long until we need to make an appearance?"

"Long enough."

Joel's duties were simple enough, if rather time consuming. He had the middle watch, from midnight until eight in the morning. He was to support the cooks that fed the watch and run coffee to the deck officers or any officers who were in the wardroom. He was only the steward for the XO on down; the captain had a separate steward who stayed on his schedule. It meant though, in effect, that he had the run of the officers' quarters and wardroom and if there was a leak among the officers, he had a good chance of picking it up. In addition he had battle stations with the sickbay as a stretcher-bearer, was part of the capstan crew for raising anchor and had a position lowering the whaleboats in air-operations. He was pretty sure he wasn't going to be getting much rest.

After getting him familiarized in his duties PO Singhisen released him to go try to get some sleep; he had to be back on duty at midnight.

In the cramped quarters he tried to drown out the noise of a card game at the end of the compartment, not to mention the quiet conversations of other off-duty seamen around him. Finally, he rummaged in his seabag and pulled out the penny dreadful he'd picked up, opening it to the dog-eared page and finding a grammatical error in the first sentence. Jeeze, this guy was bad. But at least it passed the time.

"I think we've waited long enough," Shedol said.

"No, we haven't," Shanol answered, flicking him with his tail.

Shanol Etool had spent plenty of time wondering if he'd made a huge mistake taking a Change to orca form. Admittedly, after the Fall it was easier to survive as a Changed orca; knowing how to climb out of the water carefully and get back in just as carefully had yielded more than he could eat of seals.

On the other hand, an almost continuous diet of raw fish and marine mammals palled *quickly*. He might have starved in the Dying Time if he hadn't changed, but while hunting dolphins for sport was one thing, eating them raw was another. And they could be *brutal* if you got separated from the pod.

The alliance with New Destiny had meant no more hunting, having servants on land to prepare food and take care of the occasional parasite, a comfortable and guarded harbor to rest in. But he knew, even at the time, that the markers were going to be called in eventually.

The pod of Changed orcas were tired and hungry. They had gotten a bluntly worded order to move from their usual grounds near the Asur Islands and make their way to the deep water near Bamude. The problem was that the open ocean between the two areas was nearly devoid of life. They had happened upon one pod of natural dolphins but the damned beasts were hard to catch. Other than that they hadn't eaten since leaving their home waters. And the swim had been brutal.

But the ships they were meeting were supposed to be bringing supplies, as well as orders. Not to mention the fact that the tersely worded orders had still contained enough to make clear they were not a request. So they would wait.

"Do you hear that?" Sikursuit pulsed. "Sounds like a boat."

"Yeah," Shedol said. The second in command was nearly as large as Shanol, and both were outsized for normal orcas. They had both Changed at the same time as various forms of underwater hunting had gotten boring and they decided to try it "au naturale." It had been their combined energies that had gathered the pod together. They had separated out the female orcas and the females now languished in pens in the harbor, reserved for mating to Shedol or Shanol unless one of the other males in the pod was especially graced. "Waves slapping on the hull."

Sikursuit lifted himself up to the surface and looked in the direction of the sound but when he came down he shook his head from side to side.

"Still below the horizon," he said with raised pectoral fins. Like all the Changed he had stubby fingers on the end that were barely capable of holding implements.

"I'm tired of waiting," Shanol announced. "We'll go to them."

"You're late," Shanol squealed from his blowhole, rolling an eye up at the figure leaning over the side of the ship.

"The winds were terrible and this tub isn't exactly graceful," Martin replied. He slipped a membrane over his head and dove in the water.

"There, that's better," Martin replied. The membrane separated out oxygen from the water column around his head and transferred it as he breathed in a manner that made it seem like breathing air. And as he spoke the membranes converted his words into sonar pulses that were comprehensible to the orcas. "Unless I'm much mistaken, you're away from the rendezvous."

"We heard you coming and we were hungry," Shanol replied as the pod circled the unChanged human.

If Martin noticed the emphasis on "hungry" or the circling orcas he gave no sign.

"The point is that it was a *general* rendezvous," Martin pointed out. "Old friends and new as they say. I'm Martin St. John. You're Shanol Etool."

"I know who I am," Shanol pulsed, tightly. "Where's the food?"

"In time, in time," Martin replied. "Let's get things straight, I'm your control from here on out. We've got a complicated little problem to work out and you're going to do it my way."

"Or?" Shedol asked, clashing his teeth. "You're in the water with *us* little landsman; as far as we're concerned, you're just slower lunch."

"I understand your position," Martin said. "There are many in the sea that take it." He waved his arms, and up out of the depths rose a kraken, a human who had taken the extreme change into a giant squidlike creature. The kraken whipped out one thirty-meter tentacle and wrapped it around Sikursuit drawing him down into the depths as he squealed in pain and fear.

"I think we should be clear," Martin continued as the shrieks from the orca rose to a crescendo. "I'm in charge. Now, there are all sorts of theories about leadership and management. But, really, they all boil down to 'I tell you what to do and you do it.' You're not honorable, so I can't appeal to your honor. You're not patriotic, so I can't appeal to your patriotism. You're not moral, so I can't appeal to your morality. But fear and intimidation are universally acceptable methods of leadership. As you, Shanol, and you, Shedol, have proven," he added as the shrieks were cut off in abrupt finality.

He looked around at the orcas who were pulsing into the deeps. The kraken had faded from eyesight but it was apparently still in range of sonar.

"Oh, that's just Brother Rob," Martin said. "He was . . . a compatriot in some . . . businesses with me before the Fall. He made a couple of minor little errors in, shall we say 'sexual gamesmanship,' and decided that taking a very long vacation somewhere extremely unlikely was called for. And while Mother could find him in a deep-sea trench, the busybodies from the Council weren't able to. But he, too, has decided to aid us in our endeavors. Of his own free will, of course."

"Of course," Shanol pulsed. "But I'm now short an orca."

"Well, we can't have you short on personnel," Martin said, waving his hand again. From out of the gloom of the depths rose a school of what appeared at first to be manta rays. But as they approached, the vertically slit teeth made it clear what they were.

"What hell *are* those things?" Shedol said. "Jesus."

"No, far from it," Martin chuckled. "They are ixchitl, a recent little development of the Lady Celine. They will be supporting your endeavors. They, of course, don't have sonar or vocal apparatuses. But they do hear you quite clearly. You might not want to say anything that would get them angry."

"Not me," Shedol replied.

"What's the job?" Shanol ground out.

"The mer and the UFS are meeting. The UFS wants an alliance. The main group of mer is located in the Isles. We're going to make sure that the alliance doesn't come about. You're going to be our . . . ambassadors in this endeavor."

"And the ixchitl?" Shanol asked.

"They're for if diplomacy doesn't work."

"Chief," Herzer said.

After getting lost twice he had found the chief supervising

some sailors working with a huge mound of rope in a forward compartment. They were coiling it, carefully, and Herzer could appreciate why. The rope was at least two decimeters in diameter and the Bull God only knew how long; it was taking ten of them just to move it and another five to get it coiled properly.

"Lieutenant Herrick," Chief Brooks replied. He was medium in every way. Medium height, brown hair, brown eyes and the medium-brown skin that was normal after millennia of genetic crossing. If he'd ever had a body mod of any form it was to make him more medium. But he still had a commanding presence that was unmistakable.

"Was wondering if you had a minute?" Herzer asked.

"Sure, Lieutenant, this is under control," the chief answered, walking away from the working party. "What's up?"

"Well, when I was but a young lad, my Gunny told me that if I had something I couldn't handle I should talk to the Gunny," Herzer said with a grin.

"There's not a gunny on board," Brooks replied.

"Yep, but you're the equivalent. I need some materials and some of them are going to be rare and some of them are going to be hazardous. And I'd bet you'd know where and how to get them before we weigh anchor."

"And they're not coming on this ship without the CO's permission," the chief answered. "Not if they're hazardous."

"I'll get the permission, if you can get the materials," Herzer said, handing the chief a list.

The chief glanced at it and swore. "What the hell do you need this for, sir?"

"A little experiment," Herzer answered. "But if you can get your hands on a lot, it might be a good idea. If the experiment works out, we're going to need it in quantity."

"I'll see what I can do, sir," the chief said. "But it's got to be cleared."

"Will do, Chief."

A sentry had been posted on the duke's door when Herzer got back but he ignored him as he started to knock on the door.

"Sir," the sentry said. "You might want to rethink that."

"Why?" Herzer asked, then he heard what could only be termed a moan through the thick oak doorway. "Oh." He paused for a moment, then shook his head. "Unfortunately, we don't have time." He knocked and waited.

There was muffled swearing from inside the cabin and then Duke Edmund said: "What?"

"Herzer, sir. Just say 'approved.' " There was what might have been a stifled giggle.

"What am I approving, Herzer?"

"Do you want the long version or do you just want to say 'approved' and have me go away?"

"Approved, Herzer."

"Thank you, sir."

"I'll see you at dinner. *Not* before."

"Yes, sir," Herzer said and nodded at the sentry. "Now, how do I find the skipper again?"

"Generally, he'll be in his day cabin, sir," the sentry said, nodding back up the companionway.

This time Herzer only got turned around once. He knocked on the door and entered at the command: "Come!"

"Sir, with the approval of Duke Edmund I'm planning on conducting some experiments," Herzer said without preamble. "I need your approval to bring onboard some hazardous materials. Chief Brooks will be seeing to their stowage."

"What materials?" the skipper asked.

Herzer told him.

"What in hell do you want those for, son?" Chang asked.

"You did say you wanted this ship to be an offensive weapon, sir."

The skipper regarded him for a long moment, then nodded. "Approved."

CHAPTER TWELVE

"Martin."

Martin had been taking a nap in his cabin when Conner's projection appeared. He had suffered from seasickness at the beginning of the voyage, not to mention getting bounced around in the unhandy vessel. But in time he'd gotten his sea legs and now was enjoying the rocking of the waves, wishing that he'd had the sense to bring a woman along to pass the time.

He opened his eyes and rolled up to sit on the edge of the cot, but didn't get up since he had an unfortunate tendency, still, to hit his head on the rafters of the low room.

Conner's projection, normal sized, was "standing" with his head just under the rafters and his feet stuck through the floor up to his thighs.

"I made contact with the orcas and ixchitl," Martin said. "Thanks for rounding up Rob. He was useful in establishing my credentials."

"So I heard," Conner said with a dry smile. "Shanol is not going to be happy."

"Shanol thinks he's the biggest fish in the sea," Martin replied with a shrug. "Disabusing him of that notion was useful. What's up?"

"We have a new source in the UFS ship," Conner said. "Obviously I won't say who; need-to-know and all that. But I can now tell you of their position and plans in something like real-time."

"Very useful."

"Indeed. They still don't have anything like offensive capability; they're not sure the dragons can get on and off the ship for that matter. There are only a couple of dozen marines on the ship and the crew is hardly trained in combat. You should be able to take the ship, or at least sink it, with only one of your own vessels, much less all six."

"Good to know," Martin mused. "That way I can spread them around. I've been talking to the captain and even with their position and plans known, finding one ship at sea is, apparently, not an easy task."

"I'm sure you'll be up to the task," Conner replied. "This is using energy I sorely need for the other tasks I've been set. If you need me, use the data crystal to contact me. Keep it with you, that way I'll know where to find you."

Herzer was up before dawn to the twitter of bosun pipes and the cry of "All hands weigh anchor."

He picked an out-of-the-way position, he thought, to watch the crew set sail. Most of it was a mystery, but he was fascinated by the way that the sails were raised.

Much of the crew was up in the rigging letting the sails out, which looked like lunacy from the deck, and another group was engaged in raising the anchor. Since the sails had to be tightened up, this left a relatively small group to do that. And he could tell that the sails were going to be pulling hard, really hard. No matter how many blocks and tackles were involved, and he quit counting at fifty, there was no way that the ten or so men could pull the sails tight.

But most of the ropes attached to the sails ran back to a position by the last mast. And there was the answer; a small, low-power steam engine. At the end of the engine was a metal pulley that was creating a constant turn. Each of the lines was taken, in turn, around the pulley and used for tensioning, sometimes two at once. In a relatively short time, and with very few hands, the sails were set, the anchor was up and the *Bonhomme Richard* was sailing out of the harbor. As the ship got under way he could see the first of the wyverns lifting off from the beach, accompanied by Joanna.

He walked back to the stern of the ship and climbed a ladder to a position at the rear. The skipper was up there bellowing orders at the crew to get the ship "into the wind" whatever that meant, and Herzer gave him, and the ship's wheel, a wide berth. But at the very rear of the deck there was another position with a pintle-mounted chair and board table. The XO, Commander

Mbeki, was there, occupying the chair and sipping on a cup of sassafras tea, along with Duke Edmund and Evan Mayerle, all of them watching the approaching dragon.

"Welcome to primary flight operations, Lieutenant," the XO said as he walked up. "We're going to try to recover them in the bay; if they can't get onboard in this mill-pond there's no way they can land at sea."

Joanna had lined up to try first and the line of dragons half-hovering in the light wind was a sight to behold; he could only imagine what it would be like when the ship got a full wing. Herzer watched her come gliding in but he knew, instinctively, that she was too fast and too low. As she got to within a hundred meters of the craft she realized it as well and tried to correct but she was still too low and almost crashed into the water before flapping upward and spiraling off to their right.

Jerry tried it next and he was too high. He tried to correct at the last minute as well but fell out of the proper glide path and *also* nearly landed in the drink. Herzer thought he might be riding Chauncey, but the wyverns still looked the same to him.

"This isn't working," Mbeki growled.

"I don't think they can figure out what's right from where they are," Edmund muttered.

"No, sir," Herzer said. "Sir, it occurs to me that it's got to be something like catching a running prey and I don't think wyverns do that. We might be going too fast for the first time. If we could slow the ship down, maybe turn it towards the wind . . ."

"Skipper," the commander called. "Request you come into the wind, make minimum sail for steerage only."

"All hands! All hands!"

The sailors, once again, climbed the rope ladders and this time pulled in all the sails but one of the triangular ones on the front. The boat slowed noticeably and the wind now seemed to be coming from directly in front of the ship.

"We can't point directly to the wind, can we?" Edmund asked.

"No, but we're still making about four klicks," the commander noted. "There's not much wind today so it *feels* like it's from right in front of us. But the wyverns will be pushed to one side as they come in."

Herzer watched Jerry start to line up again and quietly backed away from the group. There was a ladder up to the platform at the rear of the deck and he rapidly ascended it. The ladder was on the outside of the platform and the deck so he found himself precariously dangling over the water three stories below.

When he reached the top of the platform he found it open with no recesses or obstructions of any sort. He moved to the rear of the platform and waved his hands over his head, looking up at the approaching wyvern. After a moment he saw Jerry's head come up and was sure that he was looking at him. When he was he lowered his arms until they were outstretched and then waved them upward; the wyvern was well below the "right" glide angle to make a landing. There was a moment's pause then Jerry coaxed the beast upward. The movement got him out of line and Herzer directed him left, then held his arms out straight. As the wyvern neared he, again, dropped low so Herzer ordered him upward. Jerry followed the command and as he swept in in a flurry of wings Herzer dropped to the platform and shielded his head. He was rewarded with a massive "thump" and the platform shook under his body.

Herzer rolled over and looked up at the wyvern, which was eyeing him like dinner.

"There is *no* way to tell the right way to land from up there," Jerry yelled. "None!"

"We figured that out," Herzer replied as the rest of the party from below made their way up the ladder.

"Great landing, Mr. Riadou," the commander said, smiling. "I thought we weren't going to be able to get you in."

"I wouldn't have made it if it weren't for Herzer," Jerry said. Handlers had come forward and were attaching traces to the wyvern. The center-rear of the platform suddenly slanted downward and the handlers walked the wyvern down the slope and into the broad hatch to take it below.

"What did Herzer do?" the commander asked, looking at the lieutenant.

"He waved me down," Jerry replied, artlessly then looked at the group who were all eyeing Herzer. "It *worked*, sir."

"Yes it did," the commander admitted. "Do you think you can do it again?"

"If the riders follow the commands, sir," Herzer temporized. "It might be better if Mr. Riadou did the ordering; they're more likely to follow him."

"But he hasn't seen it from the ship side," Commander Chang said. "Has he?"

"The next one up is Vickie," Jerry said. "Sergeant Toweeoo that is. I think that she'll follow Herzer's directions and I can follow through. One thing, though."

"Yes?"

"It was hard to see his arms; I was catching more glints from his hook than seeing his hands. Could we get some hand flags or something?"

"I'll have them brought up," the XO said after a moment's thought. He looked up at the circling wyverns and shook his head. "We need to set up a signaling system. Why didn't we think of any of this in advance?"

"We thought it would be easy," Evan said, his eyes glazing as he got caught in thought. "We're working on a flag signaling system for the fleet; the dragon signals can be worked into that."

"Work on that later," Chang said. "I'll get some hand flags up here and then you get those other dragons down."

The others descended while Herzer and Jerry waited on the top-deck. Herzer noticed that despite the fact that it was October and there was a faint breeze it was damned warm up here; controlling the landings in the summer would be unpleasant.

Finally they heard the ladder squeaking and Chief Brooks' head appeared at deck level; he had two flags grasped in his right hand.

"Here you go, sirs," the chief said, holding the flags out. "Have fun."

"Will do, Chief," Herzer said with a chuckle, taking the flags from the chief who, clearly, wasn't coming any closer to the landing deck than that. He took one flag in his right hand easily enough but found that the rounded handle of the flag was one of those surfaces his clamp had trouble with. Finally he slid it into the interior of the clamp and applied slight pressure of the cutting surfaces against it. It was awkward but it would work.

Finally he had it juggled in place and looked up at the group of circling dragons until he spotted the one that he thought was Vickie.

"Is that Vickie just turning out?" he asked Jerry.

"Yeah, I think so," the rider muttered. "Another thing to add to the list: binoculars."

Herzer took the flags and pointed them outward at Vickie, tracking her around the sky until he saw her wave, then pointed them down at the deck and spread them outward.

He saw immediately that she was lined up badly so he waved her off to the right. Then she was too far over that way so he waved her back to the left.

He continued to coax her down but she was all over the sky. Too low, too high. As she came in on final it was clear that she was far too low and he waved her off wildly but she still

came in until the wyvern with a gobbled cry backwinged right
at the stern of the ship, nearly hitting the pri-fly deck. It
backwinged hard but didn't have enough airspeed to recover
so, with a tremendous splash, it landed in the bay.

Jerry and Herzer ran to the rear, fearing the worst, but from
the curses emanating from below Vickie was fine. The wyvern,
when they got there to look down, actually seemed to be
having a good time paddling around in the water.

"What do I do now?" Vickie yelled. "This water is bloody
cold! By the way, thanks for the steer, Herzer!"

"His steers were fine," Jerry replied, angrily. "You were all
over the sky!"

"Whatever!" Vickie snarled back. "What *now*?"

"Away the longboat!" Colonel Chang yelled, then leaned over
the transom to look at the rapidly receding dragon. "I was
informed those beasts could swim!"

"They can," Jerry said. "Vickie, swim Yazov back to the
ship!"

The ship was turned even closer to the wind so that it was
practically standing still, but Herzer noticed that it was drifting
off to one side. The wyvern was swimming powerfully, though,
occasionally ducking completely under water and swimming
that way so his wings could give him a fair semblance of flying.
He made such good time underwater that the last burst was
entirely submerged and when the dragon finally emerged next
to the ship it gave a pleased burble as if it was having fun.

"Oh, yeah, sez you," Vickie choked; she had had to hold
her breath for the entire swim. "Get me out of here! This water
is freezing!"

Sculling his wings on the surface the dragon could easily
keep up with the slowly drifting ship, and the longboat, which
had launched immediately on the crash, was able to recover
the rider easily. The dragon was another matter.

"Recovery team, over the side!"

With the longboat standing by, four seamen, three males
and a female, wearing close-fitting full-coverage clothing, went
over the side. They were followed by a large cargo net which,
with difficulty, was slipped under the wyvern. Through it all
Yazov was fairly placid, poking at the divers as if they were
some sort of interesting sea life provided for his amusement.
But when the sling pulled up on him he was anything but
amused. The net, though, closed his wings into his body so
all he could do was protest as he was raised up via a der-
rick and swung across and then down into the hold. Only

an idiot would allow an angry wyvern loose on the surface of the ship.

"We definitely need to work on this plan," Jerry mused.

"Do you want to call the next one down?" Herzer asked, aghast at the effort necessary to recover a downed dragon.

"Nope, you're doing fine," Jerry said. "That was entirely on Vickie's hook."

"Says you," Vickie snarled as she reached the landing platform. "You were pointing me all over the sky!"

"That's because you were overcorrecting," Jerry snapped. "And when he waved you off you tried to land anyway. I was there, Vickie, don't try to snow me."

"Just because you got put in charge it's going to your head!" the female rider snarled. "I don't have to put up with this shit!"

"You can leave if you want," Jerry said, coldly. "I'll get you a boat back to shore. But *Yazov* stays and you're not going to be flying a wyvern ever again in your life."

"You can't do that," Vickie said, softly. "You *know* what that means to us!"

"And that, Vickie, is the point," Jerry replied, much more calmly. "We need you. I don't want you grounded. But you have to learn that there are things that you're going to have to do to retain what is now a *privilege*, namely dragon riding. And if you're going to be flying off of carriers, you're going to have to learn to take steers. Or I'll have you trucked back to Dragon Home and you can fly off of nice steady aeries that don't move around."

"Are we done?" Herzer asked. "Because we've only got so many hours of daylight left and I really don't want to be waving torches around."

"We're done," Jerry said. "Vickie stay up here and watch."

"Which one do you want?" Herzer asked.

"Take Koo, the one just turning this way," Jerry answered.

Herzer again pointed at the appropriate rider until he waved back then motioned him down. This rider, though, took the steers well. The ship had barely gotten back underway so the slower speed might have helped but the most important thing seemed to be that he reacted immediately to each of Herzer's waved commands. He came in on final and Herzer waved him down, then the three of them hit the deck.

"That was a blast!" Koo yelled happily.

"I see what you mean," Vickie said unhappily. "You can't trust your instincts, or your beast's, up there."

"No, you can't," Jerry said. "And that means you have to turn over control to the guy with the flags."

"That sucks," Vickie said. "I don't trust anybody that much."

"You'll have to," Herzer said.

"And I bet there's one that has even more trouble," Vickie suddenly said with a malicious note.

"I think we'll land Joanna last," Jerry said, dryly.

The last wyvern, Donal, ridden by Vida Treviano, had pretty much the same problems as Vickie but Vida took the wave-off better, probably because he'd seen what would happen if he didn't. He tried twice more but each time came in off-path and had to be waved off.

"Donal's getting tired," Vickie said. "I don't think they can do it. I don't know if *I* can do it."

"Herzer, try to tell him to head for the beach," Jerry said. "I have to get back there somehow and pick up Shep. I don't know if Donal will be up for another try at landing by then or not. Hell, we're going to have to ferry in and out, those of us that can manage landings, bringing out the verns."

Herzer pointed his flags at Donal and then waved in the direction of land. He had to do it twice before Treviano either understood or was willing to agree. Finally, Donal turned to the south and headed for the beach.

"What happens if we're out of sight of land?" Vickie mused.

"Water landing," Jerry said. "And, yeah, if the water had been colder that would have been a problem. We need a better method of recovery for the dragons. Herzer, time for Joanna."

"Okay," Herzer said, "but the two of you get below. If she actually manages to hit this thing I'm not sure there's going to be room for *me* much less you two."

Herzer pointed the flags at Joanna until she waved a talon at him and lined up for a landing. She had good correction for the drift of the ship but she had a hard time maintaining height; she kept sliding under the glide path. Herzer realized when she was halfway down that the ship was just going too *slow* for her to easily land. She either had to start by pointing forward of the ship and hit the landing point as it passed through her glide or the ship had to be going faster so she could increase the glide angle without going into a stall. There wasn't anything to do about it, now, but it bugged him that she had to keep flapping her wings to stay on the landing slope.

She had a good angle, though, on the final run. Herzer, looking up at the immense, and rapidly approaching, dragon realized that there was a very good chance that he was going to get squished like a bug. The platform wasn't much larger than the body of the dragon and if she deviated in the slightest at the last she would land right on him. He put the thought out of his mind, though, and gave her final corrections. As she started to flare out on final he waved her down and dove to the ground.

The air was filled with blasts of wind but they went on far longer than they should. He jumped to his feet just in time to see Joanna, flailing wildly off to the left, dip her wingtip into the water and pinwheel into the bay.

"Joanna!"

Herzer wasn't the only one bellowing but the dragon's head quickly popped up above the light chop and shook from side to side.

"Sorry about that, Herzer!" the dragon bellowed. "Frankly, I lost my nerve at the last second. I was going faster than the ship and I didn't think I'd be able to stop on that little platform. Oooh, this water's cold."

The dragon's body submerged but her head stayed above the surface as she swam to the boat. Instead of using her wings, as the wyverns had done, she sculled her body back and forth like a snake. When she reached the side of the boat she disdained the recovery team, instead extending one claw-tipped wing and grasping the side of the ship. Using this leverage she got her forward talons dug into the wood of the bulwark and hoisted herself upwards.

Herzer was nearly pitched off the landing deck as the ship heeled hard over to one side. The dragon quickly writhed over the side, leaving a trail of splintered wood behind her.

"Sorry about that, Skipper," Joanna said, sticking her head into the quarterdeck. "I think we need to work on the design of that area if we're going to be recovering me very often."

"I hope we won't have to, Commander," the skipper said, furiously. "That's several thousand credits of damage!"

"Make the rail removable," Joanna said, reasonably. "Reinforce the wood. Maybe give me some handholds. For that matter, maybe a lowerable ramp. If it's good enough we might be able to use it for crashed wyverns."

"We'll see," the skipper said.

"It's not my fault if your ship's a little fragile," the dragon said, then shook herself hugely, spreading out her wings so that a fine mist settled over half the ship. "Ah, that's better."

Herzer had climbed down from the landing deck and looked around at the group at pri-fly and on the quarterdeck.

"What now, sirs?" Herzer asked.

"I have to get back to the shore," Jerry said. "I need to see if Vida can land Donal. If not, we either go for a water landing or I'll leave him on the beach and bring Donal out myself. If I bring Donal out someone else will need to bring out Shep."

"I'll go in with you," Vickie said. "I need to figure out how to do this right."

"No," Jerry said after a moment. "You're more familiar with Yazov and you're not comfortable with landing yet. I'll take Koo. His landing was better than mine."

"But . . ." Vickie said, coloring up.

"Sergeant Toweeoo?" Edmund said.

"Yes, Duke Edmund?" Vickie replied, icily.

"You're beginning to grasp what it means to be under military discipline, and why it's sometimes necessary. We do not have all day to discuss this. Warrant Officer Riadou, accompanied by Sergeant Franken will go to the shore and fly out the two wyverns. You, in the meantime, will observe their landings and try to ascertain how to improve your performance. Is that clear?"

"Yes, sir," Vickie said.

"Koo, you can fly Shep," Jerry continued. "I'll bring out Donal. If I have to I'll put him in the drink. They don't seem to suffer for it, except the lifting out part."

"How are you getting back?" Edmund asked. "We need to get moving."

"They can take the longboat," the skipper said. "Or the cat. Both have sails. If we don't make full sail they can catch up. But it will be late today."

"No, I'll take them," Joanna said. "I want to find out if I can take off from that ramp you have set up. They don't add much weight."

That stopped everyone as the image of the dragon running out the lever stuck on the side of the ship struck them. Herzer dredged up the term "turning turtle" to what it might do to the ship.

"I'm . . . not sure that's a good idea," Commander Mbeki said.

"It . . . will be," the skipper said. "We'll turn so the wind is from the port quarter. That will give her more wind to work with and it will heel the ship to starboard. It'll be interesting, but we'll survive it."

"And then there's the catapult," Evan said happily.

"What catapult?" Joanna growled.

CHAPTER THIRTEEN

There was a wooden block on the top of the landing platform and a slot running down the middle.

"The steam generator can be used to pressurize air," Evan said. "There's a piston underneath. We'll rig a sliding platform, since you're so large. It will accelerate you off the platform and give you immediate airspeed."

"I can run off the platform and get that," Joanna temporized. "How much airspeed?"

"An estimated forty klicks," Evan burbled. "More than enough for you to start flying immediately. No need for a run-up or dropping off a cliff!"

"Accelerate to forty clicks in, what? Twenty meters?" Joanna snarled. "Blow that!"

"Really, you just hold on, lean forward and spring up about halfway through."

"Easy enough for you to say," Jerry interjected. "I'm not sure how to explain it to the wyverns."

"We were thinking maybe an automatic release harness or something," Evan replied. "But the wyverns should be able to take off, with one rider, without it. Greater dragons will have problems."

"Bloody right," Joanna said. "One of them being to get them to use this thing."

"I think it looks like fun," Herzer said. "But I'm not the one using it."

"Fun? I just crashed in the drink once, Herzer!"

"Think about it," Herzer said. "You lean forward and spring off almost immediately. And you're already going thirty, forty klicks. Sounds like fun to me. I'll be surprised if people don't start using it for kicks by the time the voyage is done."

"I suppose you want me to go 'yee-haw' or something," Joanna grumped.

"Well, only if you want to," Herzer replied. "Daylight is wasting."

"I need something to eat before I try this," Joanna said. "I can tell most of my grumpiness is low blood sugar."

"It's time for lunch anyway," Jerry replied.

Herzer was surprised to find that he was right; it was past noon. The day had passed in a blur since dawn.

Lunch was . . . interesting. So that Joanna wouldn't feel left out, the skipper had a table set up on the flight deck and Edmund's party joined her for lunch. There was still fresh meat and vegetables available but to give them an inkling of what the voyage would be like the skipper ordered "ship's food" to be served alongside.

The ship food wasn't nearly as bad as Herzer had expected. He'd read about early sailing vessels and the poor quality of the food, but the "ship biscuit" that were served, for example, were rather light and slightly sweet.

"This isn't hardtack," Herzer commented, nibbling one of the biscuits. "I've had hardtack."

"No," Skipper Chang said. "We know a bit more about food storage than the early ships. Those are what used to be called 'captain's biscuits.' They'd go bad in a month or so if you stored them in bags, but they're stored in vacuum-packed steel barrels. The dwarves are able to make them in quantity."

"We need access to some of this tech," Edmund said. "For field rations. Current field rations aren't very good."

"We're working up some food service regulations," Mbeki commented. "I'll make sure you get copies."

"Ships used to be hard pressed for water," Herzer commented.

"Again, the dwarves came through for us," the skipper replied with a smile. "The ship is supplied with two rather large water tanks, located in the bilges. Potable water is pumped in and out. They have to be cleaned from time to time, which is a chore and a half, but they carry more than enough water for the voyage and are easily refilled. We also chlorinate the water so that it doesn't go bad. We pack dried corn, beans, wheat and rice in steel barrels as well, all of them vacuum packed. Then there's canned beets, turnip greens, tomatoes, what have you.

Dried fruit, also vacuum packed. Storing it all is, of course, difficult. But the worst part is meats. We're working on oversized canning processes for those, but for the time being we're stuck with salting."

Herzer had tried the salt beef and wasn't impressed.

"Better than monkey on a stick," he said.

"And that is?" Commander Mbeki inquired.

"Field rations," Edmund interjected. "A form of jerked and dried meat mixed with fruit. Together with parched corn it's the standard field rations on the march."

"You haven't lived, Colonel, until you've lived for a month on fried monkey on a stick." Herzer grinned.

"I'll take your word for it," the skipper replied. "Well, this has been a pleasant interlude, but I think we should get back to work. Commander Gramlich, have you concluded whether you're willing to risk the catapult? This is not something where I'm prepared to give you an order."

"I'll do it," Joanna said. She'd finished off half a cow's carcass while the others had been having their more limited meal and now looked in a far better mood. "Like Herzer said, it might be a blast."

"Very well," the skipper said. "Chief Brooks!"

"Sir," the NCO said, climbing up onto the landing platform.

"Have this knocked down and prepare the launching and recovery teams. Commander Gramlich is going to be giving the first demonstration of the launching catapult."

The table was knocked down, the riding harnesses were attached to the dragon, the longboat with the recovery team onboard was launched and the catapult was prepared. This mostly consisted of ensuring there was pressure, drawing back the launching platform and cocking it.

"All hands, make sail," Chang ordered, to be repeated by bellows all down the ship. "Helm, come to heading zero-one-three."

"Zero-one-three, aye."

"Prepare for launching."

The ship came around until the wind was blowing directly onto the launching platform with the ship sailing towards it to maximize the effect. As the sails were unfurled and tightened the lively ship picked up speed until she seemed to be flying over the light waves, even given the gentleness of the breeze.

"She's a tidy ship," Chang said, smiling for the first time in a long time. "Commander Mbeki, launch when ready!"

✧   ✧   ✧

The catapult had been modified for the dragon. Now there were two separated perches for her feet. She gingerly got on them and gripped tightly.

"Commander," Chief Brooks said. "When the lead perch reaches the edge it's going to detach and fly away. We'd like you to have let go before then, but if you haven't, let go of both of them right after or you're going to be trying to lift them as well as the riders."

"Got it, Chief," the dragon replied. "Let's get this show on the road."

"Lieutenant Herrick?" the chief said, pointing to a large lever to one side of the platform. "If you'll do the honors."

"Everyone ready?" Herzer asked, putting his hand on the lever.

Jerry and Koo gave him a thumbs up and Joanna just growled.

"Okay, on three . . ."

"Wait!" Jerry said. "Does that mean . . . ?"

"That means when I say three I'm going to fire you," Herzer replied. "Now get ready. One, two, THREE."

Herzer pushed forward, hard, on the lever and was rewarded by a high-pitched whistling noise. Then the catapult engaged and the dragon flew forward with a bellowed "Oh, shiiit!"

The catapult accelerated fast, but not excessively so, and Herzer could clearly see that Joanna had let go before the end of the launch. She pushed forward with her own strength as her wings flipped open and she soared upward, instantly in full flight.

"That was COOL!" she bellowed. "Let's do that AGAIN!"

"First get the men on shore," Mbeki yelled. "Then you have to *land*. *Then* you get to try out the catapult again."

Joanna waved an assent, then headed for the rapidly receding shore.

"Prepare to come about," the skipper said. "Might as well be in closer when we try to recover them."

In no more than thirty minutes, two wyverns and a dragon could be seen approaching. As they got closer it was clear that there were only two riders.

"Lieutenant Herzer," Commander Mbeki said. "Get aloft and prepare to land the dragons. Skipper, recommend we come into the wind and reduce speed."

"Sir," Herzer interjected. "The last time Joanna seemed to have more problems with us being really slow than not.

Recommend . . . well I'm not sure what I recommend, but Joanna needed a higher speed."

"What about the wyverns?" the skipper asked, testily.

"Either we increase speed for Joanna, sir, or we see if they can land at a higher speed."

"Prepare to come about!"

The ship tacked back into the wind and left all its jib sails flying.

"Speed twelve klicks, sir," the officer of the deck said. The speed of the ship was measured by a small propeller at the rear that carried the information to a readout via a complicated set of cables and gears.

"We'll see how they do at this clip," Mbeki said. "We were barely doing six before. Up you go, Herzer."

Herzer climbed up on the landing platform, picked up his flags and pointed at Jerry. This time he maintained a good entry and there was barely a thump when the wyvern landed.

He climbed down and walked over to Herzer, shaking his head.

"When I saw how fast it was going I thought you were nuts," Riadou said. "But I think it's easier. More speed means we have more control on the way in."

"Makes sense," Herzer said, pointing at Koo. Koo's landing, too, was much easier. Finally there was only Joanna to land.

Joanna also had an easier time on the glide path but she had more of a tendency to drift to the side. The ship could not point *directly* into the wind and the wind across her was pushing the larger dragon sideways. As she got on final approach the disturbance in the air from the ship's sails threw her off path and it was clear she wasn't going to hit the platform so Herzer waved her off. She had enough airspeed to recover and flapped back up to altitude. On the second try she figured out how to correct for drift and came in straight as an arrow. At the last moment she backwinged and then dropped, heavily, onto the platform as the two humans hit the deck. The entire ship shuddered at the impact of the multiton dragon but the platform held.

"That was . . . interesting," Joanna said. "But I *did* it!" she added with a grin.

"Meeting in the wardroom," Duke Edmund said, from the stairs. "There's a skylight so Joanna can stick her nose into things."

Everyone had some point that they felt could be improved on the dragon landing and launching system. And they hadn't even tested the launching on the wyverns or seen if they were willing to land a second time.

"Tomorrow for that," Skipper Chang said. "General Talbot, with your permission I'd like to spend one more day in the bay doing work-ups. I know that puts you behind schedule but . . ."

"Better a functioning dragon-carrier when we get to the Isles." Edmund sighed. "Agreed. But just one more day."

"Most of the changes aren't crucial," Evan said, looking up from his notes. "The biggest one is some place for the flag guy to hide."

"We're going to need a better term than 'flag guy' as well," Commander Mbeki said.

"How about landing orders officer?" Jerry said.

" 'Keep your eye on the loo!' " Joanna chuckled. " 'Follow the loo!' No, just doesn't have that ring to it."

"Okay, landing signal officer then," Jerry said. "We've also got the problem of five dragons and three riders."

"Do you think you can work Herzer up on-board?" the duke asked.

"I don't know, sir," the warrant officer replied, seriously. "Training usually takes several hundred hours, not just a few hours in the air. And then there's landing. I'd rather he learned that on land, if possible."

"And keep in mind that once we get to sea it just gets harder," the XO pointed out. "This is a mill-pond. Out in the Atlantis it's solid rollers, even if we're not having a storm."

"We won't launch in foul weather," the skipper said. "But storms do come up suddenly. It's something to keep in mind. Think about a good foul weather recovery system."

"Other than going for a swim?" Herzer asked.

"In the North Atlantis, which is where we'll be engaging the invasion fleet, that's not going to be possible," the XO pointed out. "The water will kill a person before we can get them out. It will be on the deck or nothing."

"I think that's about it," the skipper said, rapping his knuckles on the table. "Unless you have something to add, General?"

"No, nothing," Edmund replied. "I think today went quite well."

"Better than I anticipated, frankly," Chang replied. "General, I'll see your party at dinner?"

"Of course, Skipper."

"Very well, people, good work today. Flight operations commence at dawn tomorrow."

CHAPTER FOURTEEN

"And what were you two doing today?" Edmund asked when he entered his cabin, Herzer trailing behind. Rachel and Daneh were sitting at the table, looking at papers spread over the surface.

"Mostly checking out the ship's medical facilities and general health issues," Daneh answered. "They've got an excellent infirmary and the two medics were smart but they're not very well trained. We also checked out the meal preparation area. The cooks are well versed in sanitation, which I was delighted to discover. All in all it's a well-designed ship and a well-trained crew."

"That's good to know," Edmund replied, tiredly. "Frankly, it's more important to the mission than that the dragons work. They might be helpful in the Isles. Then again, they might not be. I still don't see where they're an offensive weapon."

"I've got some ideas in that area, sir," Herzer said, diffidently. "But I want them to get more comfortable in carrier operations before I bring anything else up. It's going to mean the wyverns carrying a fair amount of weight if it works, which means they'll have to use the catapult."

"We watched one of the landings," Rachel said. "It was very cool."

"It was very hairy from where I was standing," Herzer said. He felt as drained as if he'd run the Hill a dozen times. "I think there's going to be a fair number of the riders that won't hack it. You have to be very confident in your flying and confident that the LSO is giving you good steers. When you land normally, the wyvern does most of the work. You just point in a general area and they land. This way . . . the rider has to really steer the beast to a landing. It's not easy."

"None of it's easy," Edmund replied. "The system that's been set up for moving them around, feeding them, launching them. The system that Evan has for moving them in and out of the weyr bays, all of it is even more complicated than I think you realize. Which is good."

"Good?" Daneh said. "Why?"

"So far, New Destiny has been very good at collecting, and even feeding, large masses of troops," Edmund said. "I'm surprised that they are, because they're not very good at using them. Paul's group tends to be very controlling; they don't think an idea is a good one unless one of them has it. They wouldn't have let someone like Evan have his head and just figure things out. They would have stopped Herzer when he went up and tried to control the wyverns on the way in. I think they would have even stopped him after it was clear it worked. Again, if they don't have the idea it is, by definition, bad."

"Your point?" Daneh asked.

"It's pretty clear; I don't think they are ever going to be able to match this sort of ability. They may have, probably do have, wyverns and even dragons. But I don't think they'll be able to come up with all the things necessary to use dragon-carriers. And even after we use them against them, if we do, they won't be able to match our quality. It's like the Blood Lords in a way. Having a capability that your enemy cannot match in war is a wonderful asset."

"*If* they can't match it, sir," Herzer said. "I don't really see that they won't be able to."

"Oh, they may figure out how to land them and take off," Edmund admitted. "But I don't think they'll be as good at it as we'll be. And we'll keep improving. Because we let people like you, and Jerry and Evan and even Commander Mbeki just figure out what to do. Rather than telling them what to do."

"You're talking about initiative," Rachel interjected.

"Absolutely. It's something that we support, stress even. It's something that New Destiny suppresses. In time, I hope to prove to them how wrong they are."

Herzer waved Koo down and ducked into his station as Nebka's wings brushed just past his head.

"That's a center shot for Koo," he called down to pri-fly from his station at the front of the platform. The cuplike station had been hung off the end of the landing platform by a team under Chief Brooks and it lifted his head and shoulders just over the platform itself.

"General," the skipper said. "I think these flyers have got the technique down. We've launched wyverns, landed wyverns and launched and landed Commander Gramlich. I say we head to sea."

"Concur," Duke Edmund said.

"Commander Mbeki, cease flight operations. Helm, come to heading zero-seven-five. Set full sail."

"Zero-seven-five, aye."

"Now you'll see what sailing is all about, General."

"Looking forward to it, Colonel."

Herzer was at pri-fly when the ship passed out of the bay and into the open ocean. As soon as it was beyond the protecting arms of the bay, they hit the full swells of the Atlantis and the ship, under full sail, started to corkscrew through the waves.

"Oh, my God," Jerry gasped, grabbing the handrail at the rear of pri-fly. "We're supposed to *land* in this?" From below the squawks and bellows of the wyverns filled the air.

"This isn't bad," Commander Mbeki protested. "The seas are only two and a half, maybe three meters."

As he said that one of the seas first lifted then dropped the stern of the ship and Herzer staggered across and slammed into Duke Edmund.

"Steady, Herzer," the duke said in a strange voice. Herzer glanced at him and for the first time in his memory saw Edmund Talbot looking strained.

"I'm going to head below," Talbot said. "I'll just . . . I'm going to head below."

"Very well, General," the commander replied. "Take care."

With a nod Edmund headed for the companionway.

"I'm going to check on the wyverns," Jerry said, staggering across the deck. He slid sideways as a rogue wave pitched the ship to the side and was caught by one of the relief quartermasters who was standing by to take over the wheel. He shook his head and plotted a course for the companionway and after a few false starts made it and started to head below.

By this time, Herzer was feeling the first hint of queasiness and looked appealingly at the commander.

"Gets everyone at first," Commander Mbeki said, in a kindly voice. "The center of the ship's where the motion's the least. And if you have to go, try to do it over the lee side. That's the side the wind's *not* blowing from. And keep it off the decks."

What had been a light breeze felt like a gale as Herzer staggered across the deck and headed down to the maindeck. He managed to make it halfway up the ship by holding onto the railing on what he'd come to learn was the "starboard" side—in landsmen's terms the right if you were looking forward in the ship. The wind that had been pleasantly warm seemed to have dropped twenty degrees and he was feeling decidedly chilly. But the motion was less here. His stomach was feeling better. On the other hand, he was starting to shiver and the wind seemed to be cutting to the bone. There was only one choice. He'd run below, get his coat, and head back up here. Maybe he'd just sleep here; he didn't seem to be in anyone's way.

Decision made, he crab-walked across the deck, occasionally scuttling from side to side, and made it to the stairs down. He'd taken to going forwards down the stairs but this time he carefully turned around and lowered himself with hands on both railings. Despite that, he slammed into the wall as the ship hit a rogue wave. He staggered down the corridor to his room, grabbed his jacket—noticing in passing that Rachel was in the bottom bunk moaning, with a bucket by the side of the bunk—and was just opposite the officer's head when he realized he had no more than three seconds before he was going to throw up.

He made it into the head, hung his head over the toilet and began to spew.

It was one of the most miserable times of his life. He seemed to be throwing up far more than he'd eaten. The captain's chef had cooked a very nice chicken, heavily spiced with thyme, for lunch and he'd eaten more than his share. And it was all coming back to him.

The toilet was operated by pressing down on a foot pedal and then pumping a lever. The lever opened a seal at the bottom of the bowl and the pedal let it pump up salt water to wash the bowl clean. As Herzer slumped down to his knees he made the remarkable discovery that the foot pedal could, in these circumstances, become a knee pedal and the lever was operable from that position.

Over the next few hours he made several other discoveries.

The door of the head was difficult to operate while slithering around on the floor.

The foot/knee pedal could also be operated by hand if you couldn't even get up the energy to get to your knees.

The underside of the sink was remarkably free of graffiti. He felt he ought to add a manual for future adventurers. Little truisms to hold dear in those special and private moments when you're looking at the underside of a sink.

Seasickness was one of the most unpleasant experiences in the world.

The man who invented the flush toilet was one of the most important persons ever to live on the face of the earth.

Knee and elbow pads: They're not just for sword work outs anymore.

No matter how many times you pull the lever, sevens are *not* going to come up.

After a while, it all tastes like fish anyway.

When all the food was gone, the thyme just kept coming and coming and coming.

It started with what he came to call "the three-second rule." You had the sudden, intense, knowledge that in three seconds you were going to be seeing the contents of your stomach. You had those three seconds to make a will, pray to the gods that if they got you out of this you were going to lead a straight life from now on, swim for shore or make it to the toilet.

When the three seconds were up the vomiting started. That would go on for what seemed like an eternity, whether you had anything in your stomach to vomit up or not.

When the vomiting was done there was a moment of blessed euphoria. You weren't vomiting anymore. In fact, you felt almost human. You could wipe your face, wipe up any spills, try to get the door open, and do all the usual things that humans do, like think about whether you were going to die or the ship was going to sink.

Then came the lethargy. Suddenly, it was as if none of your muscles would function. All that you could do was sit on the floor and wait for it to pass. It would, in time; sometimes it seemed like days, but it passed. A few times it was so strong he felt himself stop breathing and had to will each breath with all his remaining might. Then, there was a brief moment when you thought it might be over, a few seconds perhaps ten when you felt really human. And then . . . the three-second rule came into play.

Herzer wasn't sure how long this went on but it was hours at least. Finally, as he passed out of a lethargic stage, his stomach, while protesting, seemed to be under control and the "good" period extended beyond all normal ken. He dragged himself to his feet, using the basin and his good friend the toilet, figured out how to operate the insanely complex lock on the door and staggered down the corridor to his room.

The bucket had spilled at some point but Rachel had cleaned up most of the detritus. The room still smelled foul. After careful consideration he grabbed the coat the kindly Navy had issued him, which was made of heavy wool, and staggered back down the corridor, out onto the deck and down to the mainmast. When he got there he wrapped himself around it and fell dead asleep.

Joel had never been so glad to go on duty in his life. It was apparent that most of the crew was relatively inexperienced with life at sea and a good many of them had succumbed to seasickness as soon as the ship exited the bay. He'd been sleeping and hadn't really paid much attention to the change in motion until someone slammed into his tier of bunks. His eyes flew open and he started to roll off the bunk, expecting an attack, when he heard the retching.

"Get it out of the compartment for God's sake," he muttered, lying back down. But the smell was intense in the crowded compartment and others had begun to react from a combination of seasickness and sympathetic nausea. He could even feel himself starting to get queasy. Finally he rolled out of the bunk, grabbed his peacoat and headed up on deck.

The wind was fresh and clean, which was a pleasant change from below, but there were plenty of puking sailors up on the maindeck as well. He headed forward to the bowsprit and stood looking down at the ship's "foot," the wave that the ship pushed up in front of it. Sometimes dolphins would come up and ride in the foot but at the moment all there was was foamy white water, just visible in the gathering darkness. He had another few hours before he had to go on duty and what he'd like to be doing was sleeping. But given the conditions in the compartment, he'd have a better chance up here. So he curled up against the lines at the base of the bowsprit, pulled up the collar of his coat and nodded into a restless sleep.

The dinging of eight bells and the movement of the watch woke him up and he hurried to the small galley at the rear of the ship. It was mainly to keep hot cider going for the crew and officers on the quarterdeck. As he moved across the maindeck towards his duty station the companionway from the officer's quarters opened up and a large figure stumbled onto the deck. He was one of General Edmund's party, an aide or something, and obviously not enjoying the voyage.

Come to think of it, Edmund figured largely in that horrible "true-life tale" he'd been reading. If there was any truth to the book at all, this guy probably knew some of the people involved, maybe even the lousy writer. He'd have to pump him for information sometime. But not when he was so seasick he didn't even notice the steward in the darkness. The guy stumbled across the deck and more or less collapsed at the base of the mainmast. If that was a Blood Lord, the book had to be pure fiction.

Sometime during the night Herzer had made his way back to his cabin and when he awoke Rachel was already gone. She had cleaned up from the night before and the air held only a hint of foulness. He rolled out of the bunk, put on his last clean uniform and staggered down the corridor to the wardroom.

Besides Rachel, Duke Edmund and Commander Mbeki were seated at the table looking at cups of tea. Just . . . looking.

"Morning," Herzer muttered, slamming into the hard seat as a wave caught him.

"Morning, Lieutenant," the commander said. "Enjoying yourself?"

"It was great right up until we cleared the bay," Herzer said. "After that a combination of that bastard Newton and some stomach bug has made it less pleasant."

A steward stuck his head in the room and looked around. "Food?" he asked.

"I'll take a rasher of bacon," the commander said. "And three eggs. Up. More tea and some for Herzer."

"I think I could handle a bowl of mush," Herzer muttered. "If you've got it."

"Coming right up. Duke? Miss?"

"Nothing for me," Rachel said.

"I'll take some mush, too," the duke replied. "I think I can keep it down. And if I can't it's at least soft coming up."

"Is your throat as sore as mine, sir?" Herzer asked, his voice hoarse.

"I suspect so," Edmund said. "I just realized that in my

long and varied career, I had spent it all on land. I had no idea I was susceptible to seasickness."

"Just about everyone is," the commander interjected. "Most get over it after a couple of days at most. There are some, however, who never do. There are also those who say that keeping your stomach full helps. I think they're cracked, frankly. Oh, and if you *had* shipped out before the Fall, you'd never have known; your nannites would have easily corrected it before the first symptoms."

"I wish they would now," Rachel moaned. "I don't think I want to even be in the same *room* with food."

"Head to the center of the boat," Herzer said.

"Ship, Lieutenant," the commander corrected. "The *Richard* is a *ship*, not a *boat*."

"Sorry, head to the center of the *ship*," Herzer said. "The ride's smoother there."

"For now," Mbeki said. "And it will still be smoother than your cabin. But . . . have you looked outside?"

"No," Herzer said. "Why?"

"Bit of a blow coming I think. There's a hoary old adage that an Indian summer will be followed by the worst blow of the season. Didn't really hold true with Mother controlling the weather, but I think the conditions might have reestablished themselves. The sky is quite black to the west."

"Oh," Edmund said. "Great."

"Actually, it might be," the commander said. "We won't be working the wyverns, not that they're up to it from what I've been told. But it will give us a fair turn of speed south. Assuming we can keep this tub upright; the way the sails are rigged will make fighting our way through a storm . . . interesting."

"Is there any *good* news?" Herzer asked.

"Well, I hear that the ship's betting pool has it three to one that you *won't* dump your dragon the first time you try to land," the commander said with a grin.

"Joy."

The storm hit just after noon.

CHAPTER FIFTEEN

Herzer had heard the call of "All Hands! Shorten sail" and had made his way up to the deck to observe. The sailors were already aloft doing their high-wire act by the time he got on deck and he watched it again, in awe. To work with the sails required them to first climb to nearly the top of the mast and then work their way out on thin foot-ropes. All of this while he was having a hard time standing upright. He did notice, this time, that they were all wearing some sort of harness attached to a safety rope. If one of them slipped the harness would, presumably, keep them from falling to their deaths.

He'd noticed a lot of little touches like that on the ship. Danger areas marked off with yellow and black paint. Notices pasted up where hazardous materials were stored. Warnings about lifting heavy weights. The ship matched some of his expectations and violated others. He had read stories from the old sailing days and back then injuries and death were considered just the common lot of the sailor, like bad food, hammocks and no decent bathroom.

This ship had showers, even for the crew, functional toilets and sinks. The crew berthed in cots, albeit ones that were stacked four high. The food was well prepared and as varied as any that he had seen in the post-Fall period. They lived, come to think of it, better than Courtney and Mike. Better than Blood Lords on campaign.

But when he watched them shimmying on those ropes he had to admit that they deserved their improved conditions.

The first real blast of wind hit as the last of the crew were descending from the rigging, and despite the fact that most of the sails were "furled" the wind pushed the ship over on its side to the point that a wave washed up onto the deck. The ship, though, responded to it sluggishly. The wind was howling in the rigging but the ship was digging into the swells rather than running over them, water creaming over the bow on a regular basis. She was riding them out, but it didn't look good to Herzer.

When the rain hit he decided that he'd like a bit more cover and headed up to the quarterdeck. There were now two men on the wheel and it was clear that they were needed; it seemed to be kicking like a live thing in their hands.

"Following sea," the skipper yelled to him when he noticed the look. "The waves push into the rudder and try to push it aside."

"Won't happen with my hands on the wheel, sir," one of the sailors called. "She gripes, though, she surely does."

"The pressure of the wind is pushing her nose down," the skipper translated. "We'll have to move some stores aft to give her more weight back there." He turned and called below for a party and gave some rapid instructions including calling for Mbeki.

"It'll take a while, though," he added. "I'd appreciate it if you moved below, Lieutenant. This may look easy, but it's not."

"Yes, sir," Herzer said, heading for the companionway. It didn't *look* easy for that matter.

Instead of heading for his cabin, though, Herzer headed for the hatch to the wyvern area. The main hatch had been closed and "dogged down," meaning that catches had been firmly sealed from the inside. There was a personnel hatch, though, and he opened that and went below, carefully setting the dual-side catches in place before he climbed down the ladder.

The scene below was a veritable Inferno. The wyverns were not happy at the change of motion in the ship and they were making their disquiet abundantly clear. They also had decided that since they weren't going to be let out to go potty, it was time to do it indoors. Between the screeches and the smell he nearly climbed back out, but he stuck with what he considered his duty.

He saw Jerry slithering across the slimy floor and, grabbing a convenient rail, headed in his direction.

"Anything I can do?" he yelled over the squalling dragons.

"I dunno," Jerry yelled back. "Can you either get the ship to quit pitching or find me a wyvern sedative?"

"No," Herzer answered with a laugh. "Have they been fed?"

"Of course they've been fed," Jerry answered. "Then they puked it back up. And I couldn't believe it but it really *did* look worse coming back up. I'm starting to worry, they're not getting enough water."

"This gale isn't going to quit any time soon," Herzer said. He'd gotten close enough that they could carry on a conversation at normal tones. "What are we going to do?"

"Not sure," Jerry admitted. "Whatever we can. Hopefully they'll get their sea legs after a couple of days. I'm getting better; how 'bout you?"

"Yeah," Herzer admitted. "At least before I came down here. Is there some way to clean this out?"

"I haven't had time to find out," Jerry admitted.

"I will."

Herzer made his way back up the ladder and then paused when he reached the deck. The ship was still pitching and tossing and the wind was shrieking around him like a banshee. But from his experience of storms on land, the first part was usually worst. Once it passed over, if it passed over he temporized, it should get better.

He grabbed a passing seaman and was directed forward to where Chief Brooks was directing a party that was attending to the lashings on the longboat.

"Chief, you need to tell me who to bother when you don't want to be," Herzer yelled over the storm. The ship chose that moment to bury her nose in a wave and a flood of green poured over the side. Herzer instinctively shot a hand out and grabbed a rope, holding onto a young sailor that was passing by with his clamp. As soon as the flood had passed he pulled the sailor upright, noticing in passing that "it" was female, and tossed her back towards the longboat. "Back to work, seaman."

"Well, you're here," the chief yelled back, grinning at the interplay. "Not bad for a bloody landlubber. What'cha need, Lieutenant?"

"The wyvern area is fisking horrible."

"So I heard. But I don't have a party to help you."

"That's not the problem. We just need some idea what to do with all the . . . stuff."

"There's a washing system down there. Didn't anyone show the riders?"

"Apparently not."

"Fisk!" the chief snarled. "Bosun! You're in charge."

"Got it, Chief," a muscular woman yelled to him over the wind and rain.

"Let's go, sir," the chief said, working his way aft.

When they got through the hatch the chief said "Faugh" at the smell, then looked around for the riders.

"Warrant, weren't you briefed on the cleaning apparatus?" he yelled over the screeching wyverns.

"No, Chief, we weren't," Jerry called back. "What cleaning apparatus?"

As it turned out there was a saltwater pump and a draining system that the chief identified. Then he gave a short class on its use. The pump could be operated by two people, but four was better. The water drained to one of four points in the compartment where it was collected in a pipe that led to the exterior of the ship.

"There's a one-way valve at the end," the chief explained. "But in this sea you're going to have to pump it *out* as well." He showed them that pump. "With only the two enlisted riders there's no way you can clean all this up," he finally admitted.

"I can help," Herzer interjected.

"No, I'll get a working party," the chief said. "Could I speak to you two young gentlemen?"

He led them over to a corner of the compartment and put his hands on his hips.

"I appreciate as much as anyone when officers are willing to get their hands dirty," he said, looking them both in the eye. "We've had some young gentlemen come on this ship and think they're too good to do anything but walk around with their noses in the air. But you're officers, sirs, and your job really *is* to supervise. That's not another word for sitting on your ass, sirs; it means just what it means. And, frankly, this isn't even a job for officers to supervise, it's for a petty, one of your sergeants, to handle. Your job's to figure out what's going to happen *next*, sirs, while my job, your sergeant's job, is to handle what's happening *now*."

"Understood, Chief," Herzer said, grinning to finally feel back in the military. "Thanks for the kick in the ass."

"I understand too, Chief," Jerry said with a sigh. "I'm too used to being the doer."

"Well, you're a warrant, sir," the chief said with a frown. "Warrants, really, are doers, too. But not cleaning up shit and piss and puke. That's what enlisted men are for," he added with a chuckle. "Have these boys been fed?"

"They puked it all up," Jerry said. "And, yeah, that's got me worried."

"And they get angry when they're hungry," the chief said.

"They're too sick and nervous to be angry now," Jerry said.

"But when they're over being sick and nervous?" the chief prompted.

"I wouldn't put an arm though the bars," Jerry admitted.

"With all due respect, sir, I'd suggest feeding them. Even though they puke it up. As you can see, now, we can clean that up easy enough."

"Agreed, Chief," the warrant said, then grinned. "Ever thought of being a rider, Chief?"

"Not on your life, sir," the NCO replied. "I'll tell you the truth, I don't even like climbing the rat-lines. I'm so afraid of heights it's not funny. I'd rather eat dirt for the rest of my life. How's the commander?"

"You mean Joanna?" Jerry asked. "She's not sick, except at the smell. She'll be glad to get the area cleaned out."

The chief looked at the deck overhead for a moment then smiled.

"I wonder if she minds rain?"

They moved forward to where the dragon was curled up, looking at the bedlam with a beady eye.

"Commander Gramlich, we're going to get this area cleaned out," the chief said. "But it will be a bit and it will get messy. I was wondering if you might be okay with moving to the landing platform."

Joanna looked at him for a moment then rustled her wings.

"I weigh nearly two tons, Chief," she answered after a moment's thought. "I notice that the ship tends to . . . move when I do. That's why I'm placed damned near the center of the ship. Won't the skipper have something to say about that?"

"Well, ma'am, as it happens, we're in the process of moving some weight aft . . ."

"And I'm a nice mobile weight?" she asked with a chuckling hiss.

"I'd not put it like that, ma'am," the chief said with a smile. "But we can lower the ramp easy enough, even in this sea. The toughest part will be opening and closing the hatch. But if you were to nip through quick-like . . ."

"Be sure to tell the skipper and then, yes, I'm game," Joanna said. "Anything to get out of this damned hold."

"Annibale, Bodman," PO Singhisen said. "Fall out for a working party."

It felt like Joel had just gotten his eyes closed. With the storm he'd been in the galley getting the fires put out and making sure everything was lashed down. So had Bodman, for that matter, who was one of the mid-watch cooks.

"I just put my head down, PO!" Bodman protested, trying to roll over and go back to sleep.

"Fall out," the PO said, sharply. "Now."

Joel rolled off his bunk and pulled on his clothes. The wind was still strong but the ship seemed to be riding better.

"What are we doing?" he asked.

"The damned dragons had as much trouble last night as the rest of the crew," Singhisen said, shaking her head. "We're going to go get their compartment cleaned out."

"Oh, fisking joy," Bodman whined. "Why can't the riders do it?"

"Because there's only two that ain't officers," the petty officer explained as if talking to a small child. "And officers don't clean up shit and piss. It ain't their job."

"Join the Navy," Bodman complained as they made their way forward. "Join the adventure."

Fortunately they didn't have to make their way on deck and the dragon deck was almost uncomfortably warm.

Singhisen had gotten more than just the two of them and there was a group of deck-apes waiting in the wyvern deck when they arrived.

"Okay, McKerlie. Take your team and man the hose pumps. Mbonu, your people are on the outfall pump; you know how to operate it?"

"Yes, PO," the lead seaman said, waving her group over to the pump that was at the forward end of the compartment.

"Annibale, Bodman, you handle the hoses," she continued, waving around the room. "We need to get these decks rinsed down. Then we'll swab everywhere but in the occupied cages. Then we rinse 'em down again."

"Thanks PO," one of the riders said, coming to the aft of the compartment. "I'm getting my riders up here; we'll try to keep the wyverns from taking anybody's arm off."

"Is that a real problem?" Singhisen asked.

"I dunno," the rider said, shaking his head. "They're not in the best of moods."

Joel unreeled the hose and set to work as the deck-apes pumped. The . . . material on the floor was unpleasantly solid and splashed when the salt water hit it, throwing chunks of material around the compartment. He had to get down to a low angle to get it moved and that tended to splash more onto him. He'd wondered why the two stewards were doing the, relatively, lighter job of using the hose but he decided quickly that it was the worse of the two evils. Score one for the deck-apes.

The material did move, though, sloshing back and forth and forming an ugly puddle at the forward end of the compartment as the team there pumped it out. The riders were sliding around in it, moving from cage to cage and trying to calm the hissing wyverns. One of the latter got a muzzle through and took a swipe at him as he was spraying under the edge of the cage, trying to get a lodged chunk of . . . something sort of greenish yellow, worked free. The female rider, who had sergeant stripes instead of a PO's chevrons, whapped it on the nose and it pulled back into its cage. He gave the sergeant a nod, washed the chunk of . . . whatever loose and kept spraying.

Finally, when he and Bodman had the compartment more or less clear the PO got the deck apes on the outflow pump working with mops. It didn't get long to get everything but the cages clean and by spraying under them they even got most of the crap out of those.

It was a nasty, disgusting, job and not one he wanted to repeat any time soon. In his professional opinion, dragons belonged on the land and not in a damned ship.

He was really gonna have to have a long talk with Sheida when this mission was over.

In no more than twenty minutes Joanna was ensconced on the landing platform. The chief had even rigged heavy ropes so that she could hold on; since the rear of the ship was still bucking up and down it was necessary. After a bit she thrust a couple of talons under the ropes, curled in a ball, closed her eyes and appeared to go to sleep.

"Dragons, wyverns for that matter, tend to sleep a lot," Jerry yelled as they headed back down to the quarterdeck. "They use high energy when they have to and try to sleep most of the rest of the time."

True to Herzer's mental prediction the wind seemed to be moderating and with it the seas. And with Joanna's weight to the rear of the ship, along with whatever stores had been moved, the bows were now sweeping over the waves instead of digging into them.

They headed down into the hold again where a team of sailors, with Vickie and a female PO directing, were cleaning out the wyvern stalls. With the materials available the sketchy cleaning didn't take long and Jerry directed the feeding afterwards as the hands, most of whom were probably from an off-duty watch, walked out of the compartment grumbling. Some of the wyverns barely poked at their food but most of them ate as if they were starving. Some of their distress must have been hunger because by the time they were done most of them had settled down. And, just as Jerry predicted, those that had fed almost immediately tucked their heads under their wings and, swaying with the ship, went to sleep.

"Good," Jerry said. "That's the first decent rest they've gotten in two days." He frowned at Chauncey and Yazov, both of whom had ignored their food. They were still mewling piteously although they'd quit the metal-bending shrieks.

"If we found something tastier for them they might eat," Herzer suggested.

"Yeah, and then the next time they didn't like their food they'd wait until we gave them something better," Jerry said. "No, they're just going to have to eat it or not."

Chauncey looked through the bars of his stall and mewed piteously at Herzer.

"I'm sure the cook has some scraps left over," Herzer said. "What if we just gave them a few? That might make them hungry enough they'd eat their slop."

"I dunno," Jerry said. "It goes against the grain."

"If *I'd* been puking," Herzer said, mentally adding *which I have*, his throat was still raw with it, "I wouldn't want something that looked like puke."

"You have a point."

Herzer, getting lost only one time, made his way to the main kitchen, which the sailors insisted be called a "galley," of the ship and caught the eye of one of the NCOs.

"A couple of the dragons are badly off their feed," he said. "We're hoping some scraps will get them eating again."

"All the edible garbage goes in those pails," the petty officer said, pointing to a line of buckets lashed to the wall. "Take whatever you want; we just pitch it over the side."

Herzer went over and checked them over. Most of the garbage consisted of ship's bread and vegetables, but one bucket had a fair amount of stew from the evening meal in it. He untied that one and started to carry it back to the dragons.

"Hang on, sir," the petty officer said. "Johnson, carry that for the lieutenant, then head back here when you're done. Bring the bucket."

Herzer wasn't sure if the petty officer just wanted his bucket back or if he was getting another class in "enlisted men do, officers supervise" but he followed the sailor, who didn't get lost, back to the dragon deck.

The scraps, when added to their slop, were a big hit with the two dragons. They got enough meat that they started sucking on their slop right afterwards.

"Sir, if you don't mind," Johnson said. "We can try to segregate the meat that gets thrown away. And there's bones and things that don't get used, too."

"As long as the PO says it's okay, that would be great," Herzer said. "Johnson, wasn't it?"

"Yes, sir."

"Thanks for your help," Jerry said. "If you ever want a ride, assuming we can get them back in the air . . ."

"That would be great, sir." The sailor grinned. "I'd better get back."

"Thanks again," Herzer said. When the sailor had left, Herzer grinned at the rider. "I think you've got a convert."

"Oh, we've had plenty of people ask us about rides," Jerry said. "Or even becoming riders. Especially since we're down two."

"One of them being me," Herzer said. "Sorry."

"Not a problem," Jerry replied. "Duke Edmund has been fairly clear on that. As soon as the weather calms down, and assuming as I said that we can take off and land in this mess, we'll see about getting you trained. But I warn you, landing on this thing is *not* easy."

"You need at least one more rider than you have dragons," Herzer said. "Or, at least, dragons in the air."

"Why?"

"For the LSO. I don't know that I'd have been able to do it if I hadn't had that one experience with riding. It gave me a grasp of what I was doing."

"Point," Jerry said. "Well, since we've got the wyverns settled and there's not much going on, I might as well start with giving you the ground school portion."

"Ground school?" Herzer said.

"You have no idea."

CHAPTER SIXTEEN

For the next two days, as the weather continued foul, Jerry and Vickie between them tried to cram all the theoretical aspects of dragon riding into Herzer's aching head. At night he went to bed with terms like "yaw" running through his head and every morning it started all over again.

He discovered what had been happening in his brief flight when he'd been trying to move the dragon around in the air. He learned about optimum glide paths, methods of spotting thermals, and the anatomy of the wyverns. The wings were not, as he'd thought, just flesh, blood, skin and bone, but were a complex web of far more advanced materials including biologically excreted carbon nanotubes.

"It's the only way the wing bones could support their weight and powered flight," Vickie explained. "There's no way that bone and skin alone could do it. The largest previous flyer was a fraction of their size. And there's some indication that overall air pressure was higher in the Jurassic."

"So Joanna's got this in her, too?" Herzer asked, looking at the sketch. "They've got to be some of the strongest 'natural' material on earth."

"They are," Vickie said, frowning. "We try not to make too much of a point of it."

"I can imagine why," Herzer said, frowning in his own turn. "There's a lot I can imagine to do with wyvern wings." The bones would make excellent weapons and the primary skins would make tremendous armor. Assuming you could figure out a way to cut it."

"As to Joanna, yes," Vickie said. "But more so. How do you think she keeps her head up in flight?"

"Bloody hell," Herzer said. "That's . . . a lot of nanotubes."

"It's one of the reasons they grow so slowly," Vickie said. "And they're continuous filament monomolecules. One of the strongest substances ever made."

"Cutting them would be a stone bitch," Herzer said. "Which means their wings aren't going to be subject to puncture in combat."

"Trust you to think of that." Vickie chuckled. "But they can be dislocated. It's one of their big weaknesses. But, no, they don't break wing bones or tear wings."

"If they were fighting on the ground the thing to do would be to wrap their wings around them," Herzer thought. "Nothing would get through it."

"They can be superficially scratched," Vickie said. "And that takes a long time to heal. But their wings are, for all practical purposes, invulnerable. On the other hand, they take a lot of care and feeding."

Which they did. On active days they required several feedings per day, totally nearly their own body weight. On inactive days they required far less, but every day it was excreted.

"Fortunately, they tend to let go in air," Jerry said, as he was covering that aspect. "But with them cooped up as they are . . ."

"It gets messy." Herzer grinned.

"That apparently was passed on, and Evan the Ever Efficient planned for it," Jerry said. "The ship really does have enough stores to support them for a hundred days, but that's at the cost of crew. This is a really skeleton crew for a ship this size."

"I'd noticed," Herzer said.

And the skeleton crew was kept busy. While Herzer was cramming his head with information about dragons the crew was busy fighting the storm. Again and again the sails had to be trimmed as the wind backed around, died down and then blew back up.

It was rough and nasty and apparently the life of the Navy. Herzer decided that they could keep it.

Working the night shift was not helping with Joel's mission. He'd picked up a rumor that the head cook was peculating, probably with the help of some of the victuallers that supplied the ship. But that didn't make him a spy, although Joel would include it in his report.

The problem with working the mid-watch was that he had minimal interaction with the officers. If there was a New Destiny agent on-board, the most damaging position would be among the officers. And although they rotated shifts so he'd been around each of them, if any of them were communicating with New Destiny, it wasn't clear.

As he came on watch he picked up another jug of herbal tea and some mugs and stuck his head in the wardroom on his way to the quarterdeck. Commander Mbeki was standing at the rear of the wardroom table, just turning away from, apparently, contemplating the forward bulkhead.

"Get you anything, sir?" Joel asked, holding up the jug and mugs. "Nice shot of herbal tea for a cold night?"

"Thank you, Joel, I'd like that," Mbeki said, his face wooden.

"You okay, sir?" the steward replied, frowning. "You look pretty down."

"I'm fine, seaman," the commander replied, taking the mug that was poured for him. "Just wish this storm would abate."

"Well, if wishes were fishes, sir," Joel replied with a patented young and stupid grin. "Storms don't listen to wishes is my experience. You just ride with 'em or turn into 'em and ride 'em out."

"You've sailed before?" the commander asked, surprised.

"Sailed small fishing boats in Flora, sir," Joel said, taking a mug of tea for himself. "Then took a packet up the coast and joined the Navy. Seemed like the right thing to do."

"What did you do before?" the commander asked. He didn't have to say "before the Fall." "Before" was always the same, before the world came apart.

"Mostly sailed," Joel said, shrugging his shoulders.

"Family?" the commander asked, sitting down.

Joel paused and then nodded. "Wife and daughter, sir. Miriam, I'd guess she was home in Briton. We had a place on the coast. My daughter . . . she was visiting friends in Ropasa. Near the Lore." He shrugged. "I try not to think about it. No more than, oh, a hundred times a day."

Mbeki nodded sadly. "Don't tell anyone that, if you take my advice."

"That I think about it?" Joel asked.

"Where they were," Mbeki said, his face hard. "You really don't want New Destiny finding out. Trust me on that."

"I will, sir," the steward said, mentally filing the datum.

And the face. And the body posture. And the radiating anger. "I surely will."

Finally, on the fourth day after they had left the bay, Herzer emerged in the morning to a strong, cold north wind and beautiful clear skies. The seas were rough but he'd acquired some of the knack for moving on the pitching deck and he made his way down to the dragon deck gathering no more than two new bruises on the way.

"It's a good day to fly," Vickie said as he came down the ladder. She and Koo were engaged in feeding the wyverns and they, too, seemed to think it was a good day to fly since they kept looking up from their feed and cawing at the overhead.

"If you can get off the ship," Herzer said. "And back on. If you thought the water was cold before . . ."

"What's it like?" Jerry asked. "I still haven't been topside."

"Cold," Herzer said, opening his coat in the warmth of the stables. "Windy. Really windy."

"I'm willing to give it a try," Joanna rumbled, from forward. She had moved down after the first night when all the stores possible had been moved aft and the dragon deck cleaned up. Now she stretched to the limit possible and rustled her wings irritably. "And if I've got to hit the water, I can handle the cold."

"I'll go see Commander Mbeki," Jerry said, shrugging into a fur-lined jacket.

"See if you can at least get the hatch open," Joanna said. "I'm tired of being cooped up down here."

Herzer and Jerry made their way aft to the quarterdeck where Commander Mbeki was striding up and down, reveling in the breeze.

"Good morning, sir," Jerry said.

"Morning, Mr. Riadou," the commander replied. "I suppose you want to see about getting off the ship?"

"Commander Gramlich does, sir," the warrant officer replied. "She feels that even if she can't land, she can make a water landing and hoist herself aboard."

"And a joyful moment that will be," the XO said with a grin. "The skipper is taking a much needed nap; he was up through most of the storm. I have the con, but generally evolutions like air operations would mean his presence."

"I understand, sir," Jerry replied. "The commander requested that at least the main hatch be opened so she can get on deck and stretch her wings."

"That I can comply with," the commander said after a moment. "And I would suspect that by this afternoon the wind will have moderated somewhat and the skipper will be awake. We might be able to commence air operations then."

"Thank you, sir," the warrant officer replied. "I'll go see about getting the hatch removed."

The commander was as good as his word. By the time Herzer was finishing his lunch he heard the command "All hands, prepare to come about!" followed shortly by "Prepare for air operations!"

By the time he got on deck, Joanna was on the catapult. The ship had been turned with the wind off what he now knew to be her port bow. Jerry was on the launch lever and Evan was fussing with the new launching mechanism. The detachable balk of timber had been removed and a fixed device had replaced it. Joanna had shown that she could release in time and they were trying the less wasteful system for the first time.

"Are you ready, yet, Mr. Mayerle?" Commander Mbeki called impatiently. The primary flight operations had been moved to a new station on the rear-mast, high enough that it could see to the rear of the ship but low enough that it wasn't in the way of the sails. From that perch the commander could see both incoming dragons and the launching catapult.

"Ready, sir," Evan replied with a wave.

"Commence launching operation," the commander called.

Jerry looked at Joanna, then leaned into the lever. The combination of the cold air, which Herzer had learned was also denser, the strong wind and the rapid rate of movement of the ship caused the dragon to practically leap into the air.

Joanna ascended rapidly and Herzer hurried to his landing station. But when he got there, Vickie was already in the station.

"You're late," she said with a grin. She held up the flags and pointed them at the dragon as Joanna came around into the landing pattern.

It was clear that Joanna was having a hard time with the crosswind. She nearly made it on the first try but was blown off course by the effect of the sails at the last moment and banked off as Vickie gave her a wave off. Herzer could tell that it troubled the rider as well and he patted Vickie on the shoulder.

"You're doing fine," he said, realizing with a start that he had far more experience at this than she.

"Do you want to take over?" she asked, uncertainly. "This is pretty rough conditions." That landing the greater dragon was far harder than the wyverns she didn't have to add.

"No, you're doing fine," Herzer said. "She can either land or she can't. If she can't, she goes for a swim."

The second time the dragon almost made it but was too low on her approach. The wave off was late and frantic and the dragon almost caught a wingtip again but managed to recover and stagger into the sky.

"That time you *were* late," Herzer said, neutrally. "And it was clear that she wasn't going to be regaining the altitude she needed. Don't be afraid to wave off, even Joanna. Better a wave off than a crash into the ship. Remember, you're her eyes in this."

"I'll remember," Vickie said miserably and pointed at the dragon again.

The third time the dragon was high, but Vickie got her on glide path at the end. However, on final a wave lifted the rear of the ship and Joanna had to beat her wings frantically to clear the rear of the ship. She did, however, make it onto the platform, well forward, nearly pitching off the end.

"Well, that was pretty awful," she growled.

Jerry had reached the station by then and touched Vickie on the arm.

"Vick, let Herzer do landing control," Jerry said. "We all need to learn, but I don't think right now is the best time."

"Agreed," Vickie replied, massaging her shoulder. "Those flags really get to you after a while. How do you do it, Herzer?"

Herzer frowned at her, puzzled for a moment, then laughed.

"Vickie, once you've trained to hold a shield and sword up for four hours, straight, this is nothing," he said, flexing his shoulders slightly. It was apparent that they were corded with muscle.

"Time to start working out." Jerry chuckled. "Okay, I'm going to take Shep up. You stay here and watch the landing. When Koo takes off, go get Yazov and you follow Koo. As each of us lands we watch the next person's landing."

By evening the riders were covered in sweat and the dragons had started to lose their interest in the game. When Koo had to be waved off twice and Nebka nearly dumped on the second wave off Jerry called the training.

"Skipper," Jerry said climbing the ladder down to the quarterdeck, "we're going to pack it in for the day. I think we've gotten all the training the dragons are up for today."

"Agreed Warrant," Colonel Chang said. "Good job."

"Thank you, sir," Jerry replied with a tired grin. He had stripped off his helmet and his hair was dripping with sweat despite the cool wind from the north. "With your permission we'll launch a dragon for top cover tomorrow around dawn and start working out scouting mission methods. We also need to start working out a signaling system."

"There are various things to figure out," the skipper replied with a thoughtful frown. "I'd like to come up with a way to recover them at night, and we still need to work out a way for them to effectively attack ships, that sort of thing. I think we'll have a dinner meeting this evening. Before then, get yourself cleaned up and get some rest."

"Yes, sir," the warrant officer said, saluting. "Permission to leave the bridge?"

"Granted," the skipper replied.

"Dragon returning off the port beam," the lookout called.

"He's signaling," the communications midshipman added, looking through his binoculars. "Two figure eights on the dip." He consulted a table and nodded to himself. "That's 'group of delphinos.' "

"Bearing looks to be about one-seven-zero," Commander Mbeki amplified as the dragon flapped nearer. "Eight of them."

"Probably just dolphins," the skipper said. "But at least the signaling system works."

"Herzer's preparing to launch with Warrant Officer Riadou," Mbeki said. "I'm heading up to pri-fly."

"This should be interesting," the skipper said and smiled at the chuckles it elicited.

Herzer hadn't been on a dragon since the first flight but he found his position on Shep easily enough. The extended rein system was confusing at first but he soon found his holds. The reins had been extended so that Jerry had his own set behind Herzer and could take over if needed.

"Just let me handle the takeoff," Riadou said. "I tested this out with Vickie and we shouldn't have trouble. But stay away from motions until we're airborne and I tell you you can take over."

"Okay," Herzer said.

The wyvern hopped to the launch platform and grabbed the launching baulk automatically. The wyverns had come to enjoy the takeoffs, at least the first few of the day. It was a good game until it became tiring.

Herzer gripped the straps and looked at the launching officer. The position had been taken over by one of the ship's petty officers since there were insufficient riders to man it. The PO caught both their eyes and their thumbs up, then hit the release.

Herzer had pointed his face forward and gasped as the wyvern was hurtled forward and suddenly they were in the air.

"What a rush!" he yelled with a laugh.

"That it is," Jerry said. "Almost makes up for the landings."

Jerry got the wyvern up to about seven hundred meters and then turned the controls over to Herzer.

"Now just follow my commands," Jerry said. "I know you can sort of control the dragon, but the next time you're up by yourself you've got to get it back on the ship. And that takes a bit more control than your first time."

"Will do."

They worked through various flight contours. Level flight, slow spirals up, slow spirals down. Finally Jerry signaled for landing and waited until the ship turned into the wind.

"Try to line it up on the ship," Jerry said, signaling to the LSO and getting a wave in return.

"Got it," Herzer said, signaling in turn. He watched the motions of the LSO and grimaced. "I feel like I'm going to overshoot."

"Watch the LSO," Jerry said. "Don't think. Let the LSO do the thinking for you."

Herzer tried to control the dragon but he realized he was all over the sky. "I'm not up to this. Yet."

"True," Jerry replied. "My dragon."

Herzer let go of the reins and watched the landing. Jerry's handling of Shep was much smoother and in no time they thumped to the deck.

"I'm going to need a lot more time in the air," Herzer said as they dismounted and the grooms took Shep below. He realized he was sweating even though he had done practically nothing. The landing had been physically debilitating.

"Yep, you are," Jerry said. "And that's going to be hard

to arrange what with everything going on. I hope by the time we get to the Isles you'll be qualified."

As they sailed south it had become warmer and today it was, arguably, hot. Herzer thought about that as he mounted Chauncey and looked over the side. The water was a deep, cerulean blue, like liquid oxygen. The good news was that if he had to dump, the water was at least going to be warm.

But he put that out of his mind as he gave a thumbs up to the launching officer and looked forward.

He had gotten used to launchings at this point and paid much more attention to the dragon than the launching. Chauncey took the air easily, though, and he directed him into a spiral up and to the right.

"Just get up and into landing position," Jerry had told him, so he spiraled the dragon upward until he had good altitude and directed it to the pattern.

Vickie was being recovered from a recon mission so he waited for her to land, Chauncey gliding at near stall speed on the light winds. He realized that the dragons were becoming more trained to the landings and was considering that aspect when he realized it was his turn to land. He turned on final and waved to the LSO, getting a wave in return. He checked the telltale on the masthead and prepared to correct for the wind being slightly off the starboard side. Joanna had gone for a swim and she was sculling along on her back, watching his approach. On the other hand, it looked like everyone in the ship had fallen out to watch the landing. The crew had gotten used to dragon-flights, but Herzer figured that the first time for a newbie was an event.

He put that out of his mind, too, and watched the directions from the LSO. Again, Chauncey seemed to anticipate some of his commands, as if he had gotten used to the orders as well. But, while this helped, it was still a bastard to make the landing.

He saw that cargo nets had been rigged to the rear and sides of the platform and that the recovery team was standing by. Although that was standard procedure as well, it made him chuckle faintly. If he overshot or dumped it, it was going to be heartily embarrassing.

He automatically corrected as he entered the dead air behind the sails and then he was on final. At what seemed well past the last moment, the LSO waved at the deck and Herzer pulled back simultaneously on all four reins, dropping Chauncey onto the deck like a rock.

He sat there, panting, and ignored the cheers, just quivering in reaction.

"Four line," Jerry said, patting him on the leg. "But not bad. Hop her over to the catapult."

"You mean I have to do that *again*?" Herzer gasped as the cargo nets were lifted up and out of the way.

"Welcome to maritime aviation," Jerry replied with a chuckle.

CHAPTER SEVENTEEN

Herzer did three more landings then switched from Chauncey to Donal. He stripped off the leather helmet the sailmaker had constructed as the wyvern was brought up from below and watched Koo coming in for a landing.

"Herzer," Jerry called as the wyvern was hopping down the ramp. "Vickie's on sweep. I want you to go up with her. You need to get some experience with unpowered flight."

Herzer forbore to mention that he'd already had some on the way because he knew what the warrant was talking about. Figuring out how to stress the dragons as little as possible was as important in its own way as learning to land on the ship.

Herzer approached his new mount cautiously and let it get to know him. Like horses the dragons tended to get used to one rider, but since Treviano had decided he wasn't up to landing on the carrier, Donal had been switched around extensively and it took the new rider phlegmatically.

Herzer mounted, hopped the wyvern onto the launch platform and again had the tremendous rush of the launching. He then pointed the dragon into a slow, upward spiral towards the distant dot of Yazov high above and forward.

It took nearly thirty minutes for him to reach her altitude and when he got there he discovered that Vickie had found a thermal and was coasting in a circle. Donal managed to insert himself into her vortex and followed the pattern of the other wyvern more or less automatically.

173

The dragon-riders had a complex set of hand signals that amounted to one-handed sign language and, rather than shout across the distance, Vickie made a querying sign.

Herzer thought long and hard and managed to dredge up the sign for "training" to which Vickie motioned an assent. She pointed down and to the east of the ship and off in the distance he could see a group of whales moving southward. Looking around he saw that the sea was patched with life. There was a large school of baitfish to the southwest that was being harried by birds and what looked to be much larger fish. He pointed to that and motioned at the wyvern with the sign for food but Vickie just shrugged. The ship had onboard facilities for catching fish, a large seine net that could be laid out by the ship's boats as well as harpoons for larger game, but she clearly thought it a waste of time.

Very far off to the left there was a smudge of land that was probably the coast. It occurred to Herzer, for the first time, that despite the fact that they were paralleling the coast, they weren't staying close in-shore and he didn't know why. He was sure Commander Mbeki could tell him when he landed, assuming he remembered to ask. In the same direction there was a band of water that was a subtly different color than that which the ship was in.

Finally he just paid attention to the flying. Donal was gliding well, maintaining altitude with only occasional flaps of his wings and breathing easily. Herzer had already noticed that when the dragons tired they tended to heat up and breathe much more heavily. Donal was still cool to the touch and exhibiting no signs of trouble.

The ship had passed under their constant circle and Vickie made a gesture to the south so they dropped out of the thermal and glided in the wake of the ship. She was looking from side to side and finally found what she was looking for in a group of vultures that were coasting upward. The thermal was off the path of the ship, southeast of its present position, but not far from where it would pass. They banked gently in the direction of the vultures and before they had lost more than five hundred meters they entered the new thermal and spiraled upward on easy flaps of the dragon's wings.

This pattern continued for, by Herzer's estimate, another three hours until a flag at the mainmast of the ship commanded both of them to return. The ship turned towards the wind, which was from the northwest, and they made an easy landing, Herzer going first.

"Well, that was interesting," Herzer said as he climbed off Donal and let him be led below. The sun was starting to set in the west and the deck of the ship was already shadowed, which was why they had called in the sweep riders.

"Anything to see?" Commander Mbeki asked.

"Not unless you count fish and whales," Vickie answered.

"Big school of fish in towards land," Herzer amplified. "Can I ask a question?"

"Go ahead," the commander replied.

"Why are we so far out?"

"There's a big current, called the Stream, that hooks around Flora and heads up the coast. It's like a river in the ocean. If we stayed in it, we'd take twice as long to go south; it was worth sailing out to the east to avoid it. When we reach the Isles we'll have to sail back into it since the mer's last reported position was on the western edge of the Isles where the Stream passes between Flora and the Isles."

"I think I saw it," Herzer said. "The water was different looking."

"Probably where the school was," the commander offered. "The migrating fish on the coast tend to follow the edge of the Stream. Plankton get caught in the eddies, there's more growth potential in the interface of different temperature waters, and lines of seaweed build up there and provide shelter."

"How much longer to get to the Isles, sir?" Jerry asked.

"Well, if we *don't* have to get off course to launch dragons all the time, about another two days," the commander said with a grin. He looked up at the sky where high clouds had started to cross the sun and frowned. "That's assuming the weather holds and we don't have to heave to."

Herzer slumped into the chair in the wardroom and dragged his helmet off, rubbing at his sweaty head. He'd thought about getting a shower but he was just too bone weary at the moment.

The door opened up and a steward stuck his head through. It was a new one, a tall, lanky fellow who looked both young and old. Herzer was sure he wouldn't be able to place his age in the right century.

"Get you anything, sir?" the steward asked.

"God, would you?" Herzer grinned. "I thought sword work was hard but riding those damned things is harder than it looks. Water? Maybe some tea?"

"Coming right up," the steward said. "Maybe a bite to eat?

There's some cold pork and some ship's crackers I can get my hands on."

"That'd be great," Herzer said, leaning back as the steward left.

The man was back in no time and true to his word he brought both water and herbal tea as well as a platter with meat and crackers.

"Thanks," Herzer said, taking a long pull of the slightly metallic-tasting water and then a bite of cracker. "Join me?"

"Not done, sir," the steward said, but then picked up one of the crackers and took a bite. "Mostly."

Herzer chuckled and took another swig of water.

"You're new."

"The other guy busted his ankle on a ladder, sir." The steward frowned. "I'm Seaman Annibale."

"Got a first name, Seaman Annibale?" Herzer asked.

"Joel, sir."

"Ever flown on a dragon?"

"No, sir," Joel answered. "I used to be a sailor before the Fall. And after, but as a fisherman then."

"So what the hell are you doing as a steward?" Herzer frowned.

"You know, sir, everyone asks me that," Joel grinned. "I suppose I ought to go find the idiot that did it and thank him one dark night." He paused for a moment and then shrugged. "You're with the general's party, right, sir?"

"Yeah," Herzer replied and then stuck out his hand. "Herzer Herrick."

"Really?" Joel said, smiling. "*The* Herzer Herrick?"

"Oh, gods," Herzer groaned.

"I mean, I've been reading this book . . ."

"Oh, gods . . ." Herzer groaned again. "Not you, too?"

"I mean, the guy's not a particularly good writer . . ."

"So I've heard," Herzer replied. "And if I ever track him down . . ."

"Did you really kill fifteen guys?" Joel asked, sitting down.

"Not there," Herzer said then grimaced. "Look, the book was way overblown, okay? I just did my job."

"But that's where you got the hook, right?" Joel asked.

"Yes, that's where I got the hook. But it was *six* riders, okay? Not fifteen. And Bast got most of them. And, yeah, we were outnumbered, but the Changed didn't cover the valley 'like a rippling wave.' There were . . . a few hundred. Look, you ever been in a fight, I mean, where people are trying to kill you?"

"Yeah," Joel answered, soberly. "And I've seen a few dead bodies in my time."

"Ever had a friend killed before your eyes?" Herzer asked, not waiting for a reply. "Look, it's just butchery, okay? It happens to be butchery I'm good at. I don't know what that says about me except . . . I'm good at staying alive. A lot of people that day, and other days, that were just as good as me bought the farm. Sometimes it just seems like luck. But if you've been there, you know that."

"Yeah, I guess I do," Joel said, picking up the mug. "I've got to circulate, sir. But thanks for talking to me. You cleared up a lot."

"You're welcome," Herzer said, then grinned. "And if you ever find the bastard that wrote that book . . ."

"I'll be sure to send you his address." Joel grinned.

There was no chance of dragons launching the next day, as the ship was tossed by the winds in the morning. A bank of clouds was to the north and the crew scrambled aloft to reef the sails. For the next two days the ship was tossed by howling winds and blinding rain as the second front in as many weeks hammered them unmercifully. This one was, if anything, colder and stronger. And while the winds were fair to send them to their destination, on the second day the captain had the ship heave to, sailing into the teeth of the gale. Their destination had been the death of countless mariners over the ages and he was not about to go sailing down on it, unable to get a fix on their position and at the front of a gale.

By the third day the winds had started to abate and the rain had stopped. The captain had the ship put on the starboard tack and sailed to the west, groping forward for a glimpse of Flora or anything else to get a fix on their position. Joanna volunteered to go aloft and try to spot land. She wasn't able to land in the tossing waves but the recovery area had been reinforced and redesigned so that she was able to pull herself out with minimal effort.

"Flora's over to the west," she said, after she had shaken off. "There's an inlet, but there's inlets all up and down the coast. That doesn't tell us anything. There *are* some islands to the southeast; we're about sixty klicks from them. Nothing due east at all as far as I can see. Oh, and there's clear sky well down below the horizon northwest. I think we'll be clear of the clouds, or at least the cover will be broken, by evening."

The skipper and Commander Mbeki consulted their charts and came to the conclusion that they were too close to the Isles for comfort without better conditions or a clear sky to get a navigation fix. They altered course towards Flora, which of the two was the lesser danger, and headed into the Stream.

By evening, as Joanna had predicted, the skies were clearing and the wind and waves had abated. The latter were choppier, but far smaller and the ship rode over them with a graceful dip and yaw that was easy enough to compensate for.

The next morning dawned clear but the winds were increasing and the area around the ship was dotted with whitecaps. The skipper had managed to get a star reading the night before so the ship was now under reefed sails, scudding southward over the tossing sea. When Herzer came on deck after breakfast he groaned, sure that the skipper would want dragons up in this mess.

"We can launch, sir," Jerry was saying as Herzer reached the quarterdeck. The wind, hard and cold from the north, blew his words away so that he practically had to shout. "But I'm not sure about recovery. And I'm not sure we can read the water the way you would like. We can see shoals, and we can signal them, but we can't really gauge the depth."

"Just steer us clear of them," the skipper said. "As for recovery . . . the water's warm," he added with a grin.

"The air sure isn't," Jerry growled, but he was smiling. "We'll do it, sir. But we will probably have to do water landings; I'm not comfortable with the way the ship is moving."

"Do what you can, Jerry," the skipper said, not unkindly. "I know you're worried about the dragons, and their riders, but if we run up on an uncharted coral head, they're all going to drown."

"Gotcha, sir," the warrant replied. "Well, I'll take the first flight.

He was quickly in the air and before he had even reached cruising altitude the dragon was making the dips and swirls indicating shallow water. He angled to the east until he reached a point that looked to be about fifteen klicks off the port bow, circled, then headed south.

"We're well out in the Stream, then," Commander Mbeki said. "This is solid deep water on both sides and ahead of us for klicks, sir. If we had sonar we'd be looking at two hundred, maybe five hundred, meters of depth."

"Yes," the skipper said, "and it shoals out *fast*. Signal him to stay ahead of us looking for shoal water until he's relieved. Signal him to look for mer, as well and to signal if he sees any sign of intelligent life."

"Will do, sir."

"Put a wyvern on standby for launch. If he sees anything I want to recover him as soon as he's had a good look."

It was no more than an hour later when Jerry went into a hover against the north wind. At an acknowledgement from the ship he signaled that there was a settlement below him. Then he signaled that there were several small boats.

"Recall him and launch the standby wyvern," the skipper said. "Tell the rider to ignore the settlement and head southward. The mer are supposed to be somewhere around here. Oh, and send a messenger to General Talbot and tell him that we're approaching the last reported position of the mer."

The man who scrambled up the side of the ship was burned black by the sun with hands callused and gnarled from fishing nets. But he looked around him with lively interest as a midshipman led him to the quarterdeck.

"Colonel Shar Chang," the skipper said, sticking out his hand. "United Free States Navy."

"Bill Mapel," the fisherman said. "This is one hell of a ship you've got here, Skipper."

"Yes, it is," the skipper replied with a grin. "We don't have much information from down here. How is it?"

"Well, it's not as good as it used to be." The fisherman frowned. "I used to run a fishing charter on Bimi island before the Fall and it caught me here. We haven't been starving, but the weather's been a nightmare and finding your way around without autodirectors isn't the easiest thing in the world. I'd never learned star navigation, none of us had, so if we lose sight of shore it's a matter of making our way in and finding a spot we recognize. Storms, reefs, a torn sail, things we never even thought of before the Fall are all disasters. And they're all taking their toll. We've had some problems with vitamin deficiencies, too, but since we started getting some fruit from Flora that's less of a problem."

"What are you trading?" Talbot interjected. "Sorry, I'm General Talbot, UFS ground force."

"The general is also the duke of Overjay," the skipper interjected.

"Duke?" the islander said with a grimace.

"Over my bitter objections," Talbot said, "they've reinstituted a hereditary aristocracy. I at least got them to include methods of turnover."

"How's the war going?" Mapel asked. "There's not much news."

"It's bad in Ropasa," Commander Mbeki said. "New Destiny is Changing many of the people there against their will. But . . . it does give them some advantages."

"In the short term," Talbot snarled. "We've had to fight them and even captured some. They're brutal, aggressive, strong and dumb. Personally, I'll pass, thank you."

"But surely they can be Changed back," Mapel protested. "I mean, I wouldn't want to Change but here we didn't really need to. I can imagine in Ropasa that having enough farmers . . ."

"Their Change is under the seal of a council member," Talbot said. "It will take her, or a quorum of Key-holders, to release the Change. Even *they* cannot release it."

"Now *that's* evil," the islander snapped. "You're sure of that?"

"My wife is a doctor, a fully trained one," Talbot replied. "She was given enough power to investigate the Change. Most of them are bound to Celine's security protocols. Bound by her name in a very old way of putting it. There is no way to release them, short of winning this war. So, since many of them are people who resisted them in the fight in Ropasa, if you fall into the hands of New Destiny . . . well, you know your 'new destiny.' "

"Shit."

"But on the subject of why we're actually *here*," Talbot continued. "Have you seen sign of the mer?"

"They're not here, now," Mapel replied after a moment's thought. "They've moved to the Ber Islands because of the weather; they're seminomadic. They told us they were leaving and we were sorry to see them go; they and the delphinos that cluster with them were helpful in finding fish."

"How are you fixed for nets?" Commander Mbeki interjected.

"Not well," the islander admitted. "Most of the ones that we have are cast-nets from pre-Fall. We don't have good materials for making our own."

"General?" the skipper asked.

Talbot grimaced but then shrugged. "We have some we brought with us, but they're for trading with the mer. I can release a couple of the gill-nets to you. That should help. But I'd appreciate it if you could show the skipper the location that you think the mer have traveled to."

"Easily," Mapel replied. "And I really appreciate it."

"I think that you'll see some traders coming this way soon," Commander Mbeki said. "You might want to think about what you can come up with in the way of trade goods. We'll tell them that you need nets and suchlike."

"Thank you, again," Mapel said. "Now, if you've got a chart of the area I'll point out where the mer went."

After the islander had left they looked at the maps and the skipper snarled, angrily.

"That's the other side of the Banks," he said, pointing to the soundings marked on the chart. "There's shoal water everywhere unless we go all the way around the Isles. The area they are in is on the edge of a deep, but everything to the north, west and south of them is shallow. They're in a sort of crescent. It will take two or three more days, if we have fair weather, for us to beat around to where they are. There's a passage *through* the shoals, but it's just too damned shallow, and narrow, to dare trying it in the ship."

"I'd suppose that makes sense if they're trying to get out of the weather," Talbot said with another grimace. "Jerry, do you think the wyverns can forage off of fish?"

"What are you thinking?"

"It's silly for me to be impatient after this long," Talbot admitted. "But I don't want to spend another two or three days, if the wind holds, beating around the islands. On the dragons we can make it there in an afternoon."

"We can," Jerry admitted. "But they'll be ravenous by the time we get there."

"Can we carry weight over and above us?" Herzer interjected. "We can have some of the salt beef and pork cooked before we leave. Load it in bags and we can carry our own food. It won't be enough for more than getting there, but it will tide them over. Surely we can find something when we get there."

"What about water?" Jerry temporized.

"There's a spring marked on the main island that's by where we're going," Edmund replied.

"These islands are nearly deserted," Jerry said. "When it comes to wyverns getting fed, you don't want to go with *if*."

"Get Joanna up here," Talbot said. "I want her input."

The dragon, when the problem was presented to her, was unsure and unhappy.

"I'm not sure we can catch enough fish to matter," she

admitted. "You're talking about a lot of fish." She looked over the side and then turned to the rail. Tapping it open she slid over into the water.

"All sails aback," the skipper yelled. "Bring her into the wind."

Herzer ran to the ladder to pri-fly and when that wasn't high enough scrambled up the shrouds to the crow's nest on the mainmast. He could see the dragon's form in the clear water. She had submerged and was coursing along the reefs that were visible deep below the ship. Suddenly she lunged to the side and snapped at something, swimming rapidly with her sinuous, snakelike sculling. She appeared to catch whatever she was hunting and moved on. He realized that she was holding her breath for a long time and wondered if that was a normal function of dragons. Finally, she surfaced and sculled over to the side of the ship.

"If these Ber Islands are anything like here, no *problem*," she said happily, working her tongue at a morsel stuck in her teeth. "With your permission, Skipper, I'm going to do a bit more foraging. Sushi's not so bad with enough salt water and salt beef as an alternative."

Talbot looked at the sky and nodded. "Jerry, get the wyverns up. See if they can do the same. If they can find enough food here for their midmorning snack, we'll load as heavily as we can with rations, a few of the nets and other things we brought and then head over to the Ber Islands."

"Will do, sir," the warrant said. "I'm not sure about getting them in the water, though."

In the event it turned out to be not too hard. Once the riders dove over the side, fighting the strong current, the dragons followed. They also quickly learned the technique of fishing from watching Joanna and before long they were darting throughout the reefs, picking off the large fish that dotted it.

"We're in the islanders' fishing area," Herzer pointed out, looking over the side longingly at the water. "I'm not sure they'll appreciate us eating out all the big fish."

"They'll eat better with the nets," Talbot said with a shrug. "I'm sure they won't begrudge us a few grouper."

"Is that what they are?"

"Probably, from what I can see. Grouper and big hogfish. Hogfish is good eating; I wish we could get them to bring a few back alive."

"Permission to go over the side, sir?" Herzer asked. "I'm sorry, but the water looks awfully inviting."

CHAPTER EIGHTEEN

After jockeying his ship back and forth the skipper had dropped the anchor and the *Richard* now floated in the current. Most of the riders were back on board. The few who were not were holding onto a rope let out over the stern.

"Come below," Talbot said after a moment's thought. "Do you think you can hold onto one of the dragons in the water?"

"I'm not sure," Herzer admitted. "And I know I can't hold my breath for as long as they do."

"Well, I'll show you something for that."

Talbot led him to his cabin and opened the box from Sheida. He took from it a rolled up plastic bag and shook it out.

"This is a swimming mask," he said, putting it over his face. The plastic immediately shrunk so that he should have been strangling, but he continued to talk and breathe, albeit with a muffled tone. "It brings oxygen from the water to you, filters out carbon dioxide and exits it when you breathe. When you're underwater it converts your words to mer code speech and will translate it for you as well as the delphino language. The important thing to know is *don't* hold your breath," he continued, stripping the bag off.

"When you're coming up your lungs will expand from the pressure drop and if you hold your breath you'll blow out your lungs. Just breathe naturally."

Herzer took the bag somewhat reluctantly and slipped it over his head. It was an unnatural feeling as it smoothed down but he noticed right away that he could breathe normally.

"How long will it last?" he asked, pulling it back off.

"It's charged for sixteen hours," Edmund replied, pointing at an almost unnoticeable dot of dark plastic on the edge. "But it can recharge from the Net, slowly. And if you're underwater when it runs out of charge it has a high priority for power. You won't run out. And if you do, you just swim up to the surface and head for land; the mer tend to spend their time near the shore. The other reason that's important is that what you're breathing is nearly pure oxygen. If you go too deep, oxygen becomes toxic. Don't go extremely deep."

"Okay," Herzer said. "Let's try it."

"One last thing," Edmund added, pulling a small block of plastic from the bottom of the box. He thumbed it and it sprang into the shape of a pair of fins. "Some purists still used these before the Fall; they're swimming fins. Kick your legs in a scissor motion. They'll help with the current."

Herzer went to his cabin and changed, aware that he'd hardly seen Rachel over the last few days, then headed up to the deck, holding the mask and fins. He put both on and dove over the side.

As advertised he had no more trouble breathing in the surprisingly warm water than in the air. He took some rapid breaths and found that the mask hardly interfered at all. Given that oxygen in the water was far too disperse for him simply to be sucking it in, he wasn't sure what the mask was doing, but it worked. He had drifted backwards in the current and he quickly kicked his way over to the rope. He could see the dragons hunting below him quite clearly and picked out the shape of Chauncey.

He surfaced and grinned at Vickie who was eyeing him askance.

"Blood Lords are always prepared," he said.

"Yeah, I can see that," she grumbled.

"I'm going to down and try to catch Chauncey, any suggestions?"

"Yeah, don't try to ride a dragon bareback," Koo replied. "But if you do, you can probably hang on to his neck. It's the best bet."

Herzer looked down again and watched the dragons for a moment before heading out. The wyverns had their wings half folded into a v and they were moving quite fast through the water with short, powerful strokes. They were fast enough that it was clear the reef fish stood little chance unless they made it into shelter. The dragons would hunt for a couple of minutes then ascend to the surface, blowing hard.

He waited until Chauncey surfaced to the rear of the ship and kicked towards him rapidly.

"Ho, Chaunce," he said as he approached the floating dragon. He wanted the wyvern well aware that it was a rider approaching and not lunch. They both were being carried in the current and it was relatively easy to approach from the front. He grabbed at the wing-root so he wouldn't be carried past, then slithered onto the back of the beast.

Chauncey didn't seem to mind but Herzer quickly found that dragon skin was slippery when wet. He had just managed to get his arms around the wyvern's massive neck when it submerged.

The dragon went almost straight down through the pellucid water, headed for a shadow that was lounging under a ledge.

Herzer suddenly felt a sharp pain in his ears and shook his head, yawning, as they "popped" painfully. He grabbed his nose, half instinctively, and blew against the obstruction, relieving the pressure and popping them again. He blew one more time to be sure, then looked around at the sea-bottom, which was coming up fast.

The bottom was sand with broken coral heads, and the big fish, maybe one of those grouper that Duke Edmund had mentioned, was using the coral for cover. As the shadow of the wyvern swept over it, however, it took off, a brown and gray streak, headed across the sand for another ledge.

Chauncey turned to follow and Herzer was nearly ripped from his perch as the dragon pumped its wings through the dense water. Clearly the reef fish was the faster but Donal suddenly stooped down upon it and it turned desperately to the side. Chauncey made another radical turn to the right and the fish reversed again, but not in time as the wyvern's head darted down and snapped onto the body of the man-sized fish.

The water was clear and the sun high above was shining down so that the sand positively glittered, but Herzer was amazed to see that the blood that flowed from the fish, was bright, emerald green, like new leaves or growing grass after a spring rain. There was a lot of it, as well. It always amazed him the quantity of blood that a being could hold.

The fish had been swimming into the Stream and for just a moment the sea around him turned to the same bright, emerald hue. He was so surprised that he nearly lost his grip again. But the wyvern hungrily finished off the fish, brilliantly colored scavenger fish darting out from the reef to get the dropped morsels, and headed off on another hunt.

Herzer had never been into underwater sports so he was amazed by the sights around him. The shadow of the ship overhead was blue as was the deeper water to the west. The dragons passing in every direction were unreal and amazing, their wings tucked in and "flying" against the current as they hunted over the reef. The water was so clear it seemed that he could see for miles but he realized that the visibility was no more than seventy meters or so, as Shep kept drifting in and out of sight in the distance.

Sharks had started to gather to the feeding frenzy of the dragons and he was a bit worried by that. The wyverns might be able to survive an attack by the much smaller sharks, but if they thought they were prey it would be an ugly encounter. The sharks avoided the dragons, though, perhaps recognizing through some instinct or survival coding ancient beyond belief that the dinosaurlike flying creatures were deadly fellow predators. And the dragons ignored the sharks, in turn.

The exception was Joanna. Chauncey was beating madly after one of the reef fish again, this one no larger than Herzer's thigh, when he saw the great dragon emerge from the gloom to the east and close on one of the medium-sized sharks. A dart of her head on its long neck and the shark was neatly bitten in two, the tail and head continuing to quiver as they drifted for the bottom. Other sharks closed around the remnants and her head darted in again to take one of the smaller ones whole. One of the sharks turned to bite at her but its teeth bounced off her folded wings as her neck turned all the way around and did to the shark what it had been unable to do to her. Apparently satisfied, she sculled back towards the ship, giving a special flip of her tail in the direction of what had once been the most dangerous predator in the sea.

Herzer had released Chauncey to watch the by-play and he suddenly realized that *he* was not one of the most dangerous predators in the sea as a group of sharks moved towards him. He wasn't sure what kind they were, except that they were big and brown and the most "traditional" sharp shape he had ever seen. And they apparently considered him a potential meal. With the exception of his belt-knife, he was entirely unarmed and not sure whether to head for the surface

or the bottom. The sharks were between him and the ship,
so heading for that was out.

He turned to the side and dove for the bottom just as one
of the bigger sharks darted forward. He managed to deflect
it with a well timed blow on its snout, to which the shark
reacted by turning and swimming rapidly away, then to the
side to circle. The punch had not been without damage to
Herzer, however, as the skin on his knuckles had all been
ripped off by the sandpapery skin. He kicked towards another,
which took that as an opportunity to grab his fin.

The fin was of almost indestructible plastic but the same
could not be said of Herzer. The shark reacted to the bite
by trying to rip off a bit of flesh, shaking its head rapidly
and powerfully back and forth. Herzer found himself being
tossed like a rat held by a terrier and distinctly felt something in his ankle pop. After it was clear that nothing was
going to come off the shark released him but by this time
the first one had circled around and was coming in for another
run at more vulnerable parts.

Just as it was about to reach him there was a blue shadow
over it and Chauncey bit it just behind the head. She wasn't
as large as Joanna but her jaws could spread almost like a
snake's and the powerful jaw muscles cut through tough skin,
bony cartilage and flesh, leaving the head attached to the tail
only by a narrow strip of skin.

The water around Herzer was suddenly filled with wings
and green blood as the wyverns reacted to the threat, and
meal, of the gathered shark frenzy, snapping in every direction. The sharks tended to head for extremities, biting at the
wyvern's wings. But, to their dismay, they were just as
impossible to pierce as Joanna's and the wyverns reacted by
dragging the wings over to their mouths and having little clingy
shark snacks.

Herzer decided that the best thing to do was head for the
bottom, like any good reef fish, and watch the battle royale
from the safety of a ledge. There were seven sharks that
considered the dragons fair game, but the five wyverns had
killed four of them before Joanna made her reappearance. She,
in turn, killed two more and the last was finished off by Donal,
who nearly swallowed the relatively small shark whole.

As soon as the last of the sharks were nothing but bits
drifting to the floor, Herzer pushed off from his ledge and
headed up to the group, favoring his leg and doing most of
the work with his right hand. The dragons, however, headed

for the surface even faster and there was no way to keep up
with them. As he was ascending he considered what Edmund
had said and breathed normally. He did notice that he tended
to seem to breathe out more air than he took in on the way
up and wondered what he should do about it. He also noticed
that there weren't even bubbles, which surprised him, but he
guessed that the exhaled gasses were distributed by whatever
mechanism gathered them in for breathing.

His ears started hurting again when he was close to the
surface and he paused to let them clear, working his jaw back
and forth. As he headed up he noticed that he always seemed
to be *at* the surface, but it was always farther away than he
anticipated. It was something of a surprise when first his
outstretched left arm and then his head breasted the surface.

He surfaced downstream from the dragons, well away from
the ship, but Joanna was already serpentining towards him.

"You were almost part of the food-chain there, Lieutenant,"
the dragon said, grinning with her mobile lips. There was a
bit of white flesh stuck in her teeth with a piece of shark
skin still attached.

"Just think of me as bait," Herzer replied with a smile.

"You're taking it pretty well," Joanna said, coasting up beside
him. "Climb on."

"I'm used to people, and things, trying to kill me," Herzer
admitted. "It's a hell of a thing to say, but getting attacked
by sharks is the first normal thing that's happened to me on
this trip."

"You must lead a hell of a life."

"You have no idea."

"You've got a sprained ankle," Daneh said, as she finished
her wrappings. "Not bad, but you're going to need to stay
off of it as much as possible for the next day or so."

The dragons had been recovered, as well as the riders, and
they were preparing to take off to go try to find the mer. As
soon as Herzer's ankle got taped up.

"Not much chance of that," Edmund said, coming up
behind her and holding out something to Herzer. "Souvenir."

Herzer turned the shark tooth over and over in his hand
and shook his head.

"Where'd you get this?" he asked.

"Off the bottom of your fin," the duke said. "It was jammed
in a crevice. There were score marks on the fins, though. Pretty
good considering that it was memory graphite."

"You were nearly killed, you know," Daneh said.

"I know, ma'am," Herzer said with a faint smile. "I was there."

"Are you capable of flying?" Edmund asked.

"If I can get a boot over this," Herzer replied, gesturing at his foot.

"We'll figure something out," Talbot replied, nodding. "I want to get going as soon as—"

"Boat broad on the starboard bow!" the mast-head lookout called.

"Boat?" Edmund said quizzically, looking off to the west. Somewhere over there was distant Flora but it was on the other side of the Stream. And the lookout had distinctly said "boat" not "ship" which they had all learned, quite pointedly, meant a little boat. Nobody in their right minds crossed the Stream in a small boat.

"What do you make of it?" the skipper called up. He had binoculars to his eyes but for the time being the boat was below the horizon.

"Looks like a small canoe of some sort, sir, maybe a kayak," the lookout called down. "One person in it. Coming up from the southwest."

Half the crew crowded the side of the ship, trying to get a look at the suicidal person who appeared to have crossed the Stream in what the lookout noted was, indeed, a canoe, *not* a sea-kayak. As it approached his descriptions got clearer.

"The crew's a female," he called down. "Dark hair . . . wearing . . . a *bathing suit?*"

Herzer suddenly groaned and sat down on a coiled pile of rope, holding his head.

"That's no bathing suit," he muttered. "Five gets you ten it's a leather bikini. Which means it's no human."

"No." Edmund sighed, turning away from the rail. "It's an elf."

"*Bast?*" Daneh gasped. "How did she? I mean . . ."

"Bast?" Rachel asked, having just appeared from below. She shaded her eyes and looked to port where the canoe was now faintly visible. "Are you sure?"

"Who else would cross the Stream in a dugout canoe?" Herzer asked.

"And there's a rabbit in the bow!" the lookout yelled down.

"Well, that's one of life's little rhetorical questions answered," Duke Edmund said with a chuckle. "The answer being 'that damned bunny.' "

✧   ✧   ✧

"Bast," Herzer said, giving her a hug as she swarmed up the side. She kept right on swarming until she had her legs wrapped around his waist and her lips planted on his.

The female he was referring to was no more than a meter and a quarter tall; she barely came to his waist. Her eyes were green with vertically split pupils and her ears were delicately pointed. She had high, small breasts and was wearing a green bikini of soft, washed leather. She carried a bow and quiver over her back and a light saber with a jewel-encrusted hilt belted to her side by a jeweled and tooled leather belt. On her left shoulder was a pauldron, a curved piece of armor to protect the shoulder, on her right shin was a greave, another piece of armor, on her *left* leg was a fur leg warmer and on both arms she wore leather bracers. Other than that she was naked. It was the most impractical getup imaginable, but that was pure Bast.

"Hiya, lover," she said when she'd finally drawn back. She leaned over and winked at Rachel. "I'm not stealing him, yet, am I?"

"No," Rachel replied with a grin. "As a matter of fact, you can feel free to use my bunk. He snores."

"Especially when he's all worn out," Bast admitted, dropping to the deck as the rabbit scrabbled up the side. It shouldn't have been able to but its claws bit the wood like talons.

"Bast . . ." Edmund said, pausing. "Not that I'm not glad to see you, but . . ."

"But you're on this important secret diplomatic mission," Bast said, as Herzer delicately prized her off and set her on the deck, "and you don't want two spirits of chaos ruining it."

"That's probably how I'd put it," Edmund admitted with a chuckle. "At least mentally. Why are you here?"

"Well, you took lover-boy with you," she said, grabbing Herzer's arm and wrapping herself around it. This apparently was too unfamiliar so she swarmed back up him, this time on his left side, and wrapped her legs around his waist, leaning out for all the world like a koala on her favorite tree. "I couldn't leave him to be all alone in the dangerous Southern Isles!"

"Okay, so what's with the bunny?" Edmund said, sighing.

The rabbit in question was a brown-and-white, flop-eared mini-lop who looked for all the world like the world's cutest, albeit dumbest, pet. That is if you ignored the black leather harness loaded with knives and a pistol crossbow. And the mad, red eyes.

"Hey! Island vacation!" the rabbit snapped. "Big-titted blondes, warm beaches, sun, surf, sand and, most importantly, *alfalfa margaritas*!"

"There's no tequila on board," Edmund sighed. "And certainly no alfalfa."

"What?!" the rabbit gasped in a high, tenor voice. "No tequila? In the islands?"

"Tequila comes from Chiara," Edmund explained. "The guava plant grows there. *Rum* comes from the islands."

"Well, that's a point. Navy ships always have a tot of rum once a day. I'll take rum. Rum is good."

"Unfortunately, UFS ships are dry," Daneh said, dryly. "As in, not wet. As in, no alcohol."

"DRY?!" the rabbit shrieked. He whipped out a switchblade and hopped up on Herzer's shoulder, waving the knife at Bast. "You said there'd be *booze*! A pleasure cruise to the islands you said! All the booze I could drink! Maybe even telemarketers! I'm going to turn you into elf cutlets!"

"You can try, black-heart," Bast snapped, launching off of Herzer in what was a quite improbable back flip and landing on the deck with her saber drawn. "Any *time*, you flop-eared monstrosity!"

"Bast, why did you inveigle this . . . this . . ." Edmund waved his hand at the rabbit. "This insanely programmed AI onto this ship?"

"Well, I couldn't leave him in Raven's Mill with both of us gone, could I?" Bast shrugged, putting away her saber. "And I'm sure we can find enough rum *somewhere* in these islands to keep him happy."

"Bast . . ." Edmund said, then paused as she raised a finger at him.

"Ah, ah," she said, cocking her head to the side.

"Bast . . ." he said, a wheedling note in his voice this time.

"Ah!"

"Oh, damn," Edmund sighed. "We're just getting ready to leave and we need all the weight we can spare for the dragons, spare food for them and our gear."

"I'm light," Bast said. "I'll ride Joanna."

"I give up," Edmund said. "What about the bunny?"

"You're going to visit the mer, right?" the rabbit asked. "That means swimming, right? I don't swim."

"Rabbit, you make problems on this ship and they'll make you walk the plank," Edmund growled. "In concrete shoes."

"Them and what army?" the rabbit challenged, hopping off of Herzer's shoulder and landing on the deck with a solid thump. The switchblade waved back and forth menacingly.

"There's a hundred and twenty-five crew and a dozen marines," Edmund said. "If worse comes to worst, they'll roll you up in a spare sail and toss you over the side weighted with ballast. How long can you hold your breath?"

"A long time," the rabbit said, staring him in the eye. After a moment he quit to nibble at his shoulder as if he could care less for the threats. "I'll behave. But you'd better find me some booze. I get all ticky when I don't have booze."

"There're settlements around," Edmund said. "We'll see what we can do."

"General," Commander Mbeki said. "I hate to break up this spectacle but the wyverns are saddled and ready to go. We've got the spare stores and between the wind and the current we should be able to loft all of it, if you leave soon."

"We're ready," Edmund replied. "Someone had better tell Joanna that she has a spare passenger and while you're loading I need to go talk to the skipper."

CHAPTER NINETEEN

"What . . . is that thing?" Chang asked.

"I'd say a spirit of elemental chaos," Edmund replied with a frown. "But that would be superstitious. It, *he*, is an AI cyborg, not any sort of real rabbit at all. He was created a *long* time ago. And I'm being forced to leave him on your ship."

"Thank you so very much, General," the skipper said with a bemused expression. "What happens if he goes berserk?"

"Well . . ." Edmund said with a frown. "His programming is almost unbelievably chaotic. But one tendency is to never harm his own side in a *truly* irrevocable way. He plays tricks, sometimes quite painful ones. And generally is a bully until he gets his way. He'll also betray you, for cash, goods or services, on half a chance. But never in a way that will cause true, irrevocable, harm."

"That's . . ."

"Weird," Edmund sighed. "I do believe that the twenty-second century was the most . . . complex and baroque century in human history. That's one of the results."

"Why would anyone create something like *that*?" the captain said. "It would almost immediately betray its creators, wouldn't it?"

"Oh, yes," Edmund said. "And he was reported to have done so. Something about a large bomb. He was apparently based upon a comic from the twenty-first century."

"A *comic*?"

"You'll see. He's pretty funny if you're into black comedy. Anyway, he had three or four primary programming requirements. In sort of reverse order they're: Have a fun and comfortable life, beat up a designated 'nerd-boy,' track down the cast of a show called *Baywatch* and be affectionate with the women . . ."

"Affectionate?"

"His term," Edmund grinned. "Spend lots of time around large-breasted blondes and kill telemarketers. The last one is his primary programming."

"What's a telemarketer?" the captain asked.

"A form of human gadfly." Edmund sighed, thinking how much of human history had been lost to disinterest. "Like a spammer but they used telephones which were..."

"Oh, I've heard of them," Shar said, suddenly. "Weren't they all wiped out in the . . . oh."

"Right," Edmund replied. "And you're looking at their doom."

"And you're leaving him on my *ship*?"

"Have fun. Keeping him drunk sometimes works."

The dragons were heavily laden but between the wind and the catapult they were able to get into the air and the party started out to the east, following the course that Edmund and Joanna between them set.

The seascape that they flew over was a patchwork of reefs, wide, white flats and small uninhabited islands. There were occasional patches of green in the water, which Herzer was informed were patches of sea grass. From time to time they saw a fishing boat but that was the only sign of humanity. There were fish aplenty in the waters, small schools turning in the sun and flashing up at them. When they had started off it had been nearly high tide and as they flew more and more of the flats became exposed.

The sunlight on the white flats was nearly blinding and after a while Herzer quit trying to look at them, looking out in the distance instead. Within an hour or so he could see the waters ahead were turning the green of the shallows with blue beyond and he knew they were passing over the flats and approaching the deeps beyond.

When they reached the edge of the flats, Joanna turned north tracing the edge of the land that was one small island after another. More flats were to their north, beyond the thin necklace of islands, but to the south the water quickly shaded from green to the dark blue of pelagic seas. Herzer had looked at the charts and the water over there was over a thousand feet deep. Admittedly, it was as easy to drown in five meters of water as a thousand, but there was a special feeling to seeing that immense body of horrendously deep water.

Finally they saw, at the tip of one of the islands, a two story concrete building that was their landmark. It appeared to be an ancient, but until the Fall well maintained, lighthouse. There were no signs of current habitation around it; the bushes were well grown up and the walkways near it were covered in weeds.

"Mer!" Koo called, pointing down and to the right. Sure enough, in the midst of a pod of dolphins the distinct silhouettes of mer-folk were visible. As the shadows of the dragons passed over the pod the mer came to the surface for a look, then dove into the water headed southeast.

"Do we land and swim out?" Joanna yelled.

"Land," Edmund replied. "Then we'll see about getting the dragons fed."

They swept in for a landing by the old lighthouse and as they dismounted saw a line of heads popping up out of the water.

"Herzer," was all Edmund said, starting to strip off his riding gear.

The wind was still from the north, blowing up a fine grit of sand and quite cold. Herzer was shivering by the time he'd stripped down himself and he pulled the mask on, looking forward to what he assumed would be warm water.

It wasn't. The water was bitterly cold when he entered it, striding up to his waist, then putting on his fins. Edmund was already in, heading out to the mer-folk, flapping and splashing like a walrus.

Herzer quickly ducked under and started out himself, staying below the light chop. The bottom was mostly sand at the shore but bits of broken reef started to appear by the time they were halfway to the line of mer.

The mer-men started towards them as they swam, hesitantly at first and then more quickly, a line armed with bone-tipped spears at the front while the rest, who were burdened with mostly empty mesh bags, followed behind. When they got to within a dozen yards or so, Edmund stopped and hung in the water, feet down, and raised a hand.

"We're here from the United Free States; we're looking for Bruce Blackbeard."

Herzer stared at the line of mer that approached. He had

seen them before the Fall but never in a group and never in their natural environment. They were, he decided, no less graceful than dolphins, darting in patterns around each other. But they were far more colorful, their tail ends flashing blue, green, red and every other color of the rainbow. Their hair was all the colors of the rainbow as well and each of them had hair that more or less matched their tails. Besides all the other differences from humans, they had huge ribcages which, as he watched, opened and closed. Clearly they were gills. Their bodies were also far bulkier than those of most humans, but very smooth-skinned and not rippled with muscle. They appeared, as much as anything, fat.

The line of spear bearers had stopped as well and now looked at them in surprise.

"Bruce is at the town," one of them said. "I think he's expecting you."

"I'm Edmund Talbot," Edmund said. "How far is it?"

"Not far, just out on the edge of the deep," the mer replied. "I'm Jason Ranger."

Herzer wondered what it was about his voice that was strange and then realized that it wasn't a voice at all, but the computer in the mask converting it. It had no particular timbre. The mouth of the mer-man didn't move, except for slight changes that might have been subvocalizations.

"This is Lieutenant Herrick, my aide," Edmund replied. "We'd like to visit your town. My wife and daughter are with us as well."

"And wyverns," Jason said.

"Yes, there's a ship beating around to here. We expected to find you over by Bimi island. The wyverns are going to need to fish for food. Is there somewhere they can do that?"

The mer paused at that and shook his head.

"Wyverns fish?"

"They're learning," Herzer replied. "They catch reef fish well enough. And sharks," he added.

"These fishing grounds around here are ours," Jason said. "I'd prefer they not get fished out. And don't let Bruce find them hitting the reefs or you'll lose any goodwill you might have. But if they want to move up or down the coast a few klicks, that should be fine."

"I can show them," one of the spear-bearing mer-men interjected. He had blond, nearly white, hair and a light tan tail.

"This is Pete. When he's not out hunting, he's one of the best chefs in the mer-folk."

"When I've got spices, I'm the *best* chef in the mer-folk," the cook said. "But if we can get me up on one of those wyvern, I can show you where they can fish. There's a drop-off to the east. Lots of grouper and big hogs, but too far to make it worth our while to fish there."

"Herzer?" Edmund asked.

"We'll have to more or less strap you on," Herzer pointed out. "You don't have legs to go in the mount."

"Understood," Pete replied.

"Will you need me in the town?" Herzer asked.

"No, but go get Daneh and Rachel. Tell Warrant Officer Riadou that I'd like him back here no later than sundown and that if he can get the wyverns to *catch* some fish, and not just eat them, that would be an interesting, and useful, experiment."

"Will do, sir. One question, what about Bast?"

"What about her?" Edmund replied after a brief pause. "I don't have a mask for her, or a set of fins. Have Rachel bring out the net," Edmund added as Herzer, following Pete, started to swim back in.

"You have nets?" Jason asked.

"We just have one with us," Edmund replied. "All the room we had. But there's more on the ship."

Evan looked up as a rabbit landed on his workbench with a thump.

"What'cha doin'?" the rabbit asked, raising one paw to vigorously scratch at his ear.

Evan looked at the apparition blankly for a moment, then said, distinctly: "Working on a device."

The rabbit hopped over and looked at the device, then shrugged.

"So you're making a flamethrower. Big deal."

"You know what it is?" Evan said, surprised.

"Of course I know what it is," the rabbit snapped. "I've had them turned at me enough times. Used them a time or two for that matter."

Evan noted at that moment that instead of normal rabbit feet, the rabbit had handlike forepaws with opposable thumbs.

"Well, maybe you can tell me what's wrong," Evan said. "I can't get it to maintain a stream, no matter what I do. I've been working with water, obviously, but it sprays outward when I fire it. I don't want a wall of flame."

The rabbit hopped from one end of the scattered parts to another, then shook his head.

"You do good work."

"Thank you."

"And I know what your problem is," the rabbit added. "But to tell you, I have to extract a price."

"Why?" the engineer said with a puzzled expression.

"Bloody programming, that's why," the rabbit sighed. "I can't just tell people things that they need to know, even when I want to. And I'd *like* to have you make a flamethrower. I *like* flamethrowers."

"Okay, as long as it's not going to get the ship in trouble," Evan replied.

"Actually, I want two things, come to think of it," the rabbit said, scratching at his ear again.

"Well, you're only telling me one," Evan pointed out.

"Okay, you've got a point," the rabbit admitted. "What do you want for the two things?"

"Well, what do you want for the information on how to build a flamethrower?"

"A smaller one," the rabbit replied. "Small enough for me to use. And you'll be surprised how much weight I can carry."

Evan thought about that for a moment, then frowned. "It's not to be used against this ship, or any other ship of the free states. Nor any member of the free states. Nor any ally."

"Jeeze, you drive a hard bargain," the bunny said with a sigh. "I guess that means I can't use it on that damned elf."

"Correct."

"Okay, you'll make it, though?"

"Yes."

"In that case," the rabbit said, holding up a length of pipe. "You need three venturi holes, here, here and here," he said, pointing. "About two millimeters across."

"That's it?"

"That's it. But you still owe me the downsized flamethrower."

"Not a problem."

"What about the other thing I want?"

Evan contemplated him for a moment then shrugged. "What is it?"

"A still."

"A *still?*"

"Do you know that I have not been able to find one *drop* of booze on this tub," the rabbit said, angrily, his beady red eyes positively glowing. "I get all ticky when I don't have booze."

"Stills give off a quite distinctive smell," Evan said. "But it's possible. For *your* use, not to sell to the crew, right?"

"Man, you are forever putting conditions on things," the rabbit snarled. "Okay!"

"What do I get?" Evan asked.

"What? I let you live while giving me conditions, didn't I?" the rabbit asked. "I could just beat you up a little. That's one of my programs; beating up nerd-boys!"

"In which case you wouldn't get your still," Evan said. "And I'm not a nerd-boy, I'm an engineer."

"There's a difference?" the rabbit asked. "Okay, okay, I'll give you one favor, to be called in. If it's completely out of line, I can tell you to jump in the ocean. But I'm not allowed to go back on favors unless it's out of line."

"Okay," Evan replied after thinking about it for a moment.

"And no 'I wish for three wishes' or asking for my pass codes or anything like that. Tit for tat."

"Fine," Evan replied. "I'll make the still. I know just where to put it."

"Okay, I'm gonna blow this joint," the rabbit said, bitterly. "Some island cruise."

The wyverns had been upset about taking off again without being fed—they could smell the salt beef in the bags—and even more upset about backtracking. But after a while they settled down to a steady cooing and twittering which Herzer knew was their form of muttering.

Pete was riding with him on Chauncey. On reaching land the mer-man had given what looked like a closed-mouth cough and water had poured through the slits in his ribs. After that he was an air breather just like the unChanged humans. As they flew Herzer pointed out the view from aloft including one of the vast schools of baitfish.

"Bait ball," Pete replied, shielding his eyes against the westering sun. "Can we fly over it?"

Herzer banked towards the ball and got a bellowed comment from Joanna which he ignored. The school of fish was about fifty meters on a side, a silver ripple at the surface with the water churned to white around it from attacking fish.

"That's menhaden I think," Pete yelled. "But look at those damned *tuna*! That's damned good eating there, especially with a little wasabi."

Herzer could see the larger fish smashing into the bait fish like cannonballs. As he watched one of the larger predators came clear out of the water in its pursuit. It was hard to judge size without a reference, but the fish had to be close to two meters in length.

"We can't really track the pelagics like that," Pete said with annoyance in his voice. "They just move too fast. The delphinos can keep up, but whenever we try to get to them they've moved before we get there and chasing them's a losing proposition."

"Herzer!" Joanna bellowed, sweeping down on him. "We need to get these dragons fed, *soon*."

"Coming, Commander," the lieutenant replied, banking his dragon back towards the coast. But his mind kept moving on the problem. There had been enough food for a hundred dragons in that school of tuna alone. The reef-fish were all well and good, but getting into one of those big schools was going to be the way to *keep* them fed.

In deference to the mer-man, he made a water landing when they reached the fishing spot. It would mean loose straps on the ride back and much oiling to get them back in condition, but it had been undignified enough carrying Pete to the dragon; the least he could do was let him get off in relative comfort.

He loosed the straps holding the mer-man on and then donned his own gear and dove under the water. It had been a cold ride in nothing but his bathing suit and the water was not much better. He got the straps loose with one hand that was fumbling with cold and a hook, grabbed them and headed for shore, dragging the leather along with Pete's help.

Once on shore he laid the straps out on the plentiful rocks and looked at the dragons disporting in the waves.

"They look like they're having fun," Pete said. He had dragged himself up partially on the shore and now leaned on one arm, looking out to sea and flapping his tail idly in the waves, like a person tapping their toes.

"They are," Herzer said. "If I wasn't so damned cold I'd be in there with them. I don't know which is worse, the water or this damned cold wind."

"We're getting a fire started," Jerry said, opening up the closures on his jacket. "You should have worn your gear."

"I was planning on a water landing," Herzer replied, wiping water out of his hair with his hands. "Better to be cold than wet gear. I could do with a hot bath, though."

"No help there," Pete said. "All these islands are limestone built up from coral; the nearest volcanic activity is nearly a thousand klicks from here."

"Just as well," Herzer said. "I'd rather be cold than have a tsunami."

"I can think of a way to warm you up," Bast said.

"I'm sure you can," Herzer replied with a grin.

"But I'm going to go play with the dragons," Bast said, reaching into the pouch at her hip and pulling out a breath mask and a set of fins.

"Where did those come from?" Herzer asked. He knew that Edmund only had four sets and they were all being used; he had his set rolled up and tucked into a pocket of his bathing shorts.

"My pouch?" Bast replied. "I was coming to the islands. I can't breathe water. Of course I brought gear." With that she dropped her gear, took her clothes off, put the mask on, picked up the fins and waded into the water.

"Can someone please explain who she is to *me*?" Jerry asked.

"She's . . . Bast," Herzer replied.

"That's not much of an answer," Vickie said acerbically. "She's an elf? I thought they were, you know, tall and lean and handsome. Not small and pretty and dressed like a character in an anime cartoon."

"She's a *wood* elf," Herzer replied. "They were created around the time of the AI wars. *She* was created around the time of the AI wars."

"Crap," Jerry said. "How old is she?"

"Physically? About two thousand years old," Herzer replied. "Mentally? Somewhere between twelve and two thousand. She told me one time that elves are too happy to spend much time grieving. Given that she's seen thousands of human friends die over the years, I guess that's not a bad way to handle it. As to caring about societal conventions, like not stripping in front of a bunch of people, she's going to outlive them all *and* their conventions. She just . . . well, you've seen. Hell, just wait; that's nothing."

"I can't wait until she meets Bruce," Pete chuckled.

"Why?"

"Bruce is . . . not a bad guy," Pete said. "He's held us together and nobody's starved; not even the young and the old. Really, he's done pretty well, given everything that's going on. But . . . he can be a little . . . stuffy."

CHAPTER TWENTY

Edmund, trailed by Daneh and Rachel, followed the merfolk deeper into the ocean and to the east. They stayed about seven meters below the surface while the bottom sloped steeply downward.

Half way to the "village" Jason let out a grunt and headed downward. He poked in a crevice with his spear, then twisted it and pulled out a lobster nearly the size of his thigh. He wrung the head off and dropped it to the bottom, swimming back up to the group and turning his catch over to one of the bearers.

"It's been a bad day of fishing," he lamented. "We'd been in this area not long ago and most of the easy fish are already hunted out. We're having to go further and further afield to find anything edible."

"Why don't you just move someplace else?" Edmund asked.

"We're not entirely without possessions," Jason said. "So just picking up and moving is not an easy proposition; we only do it if it's necessary. And this area has some features that we find necessary for our survival these days."

"What?" Talbot asked. But he received no reply.

"I've got a net with me," Edmund pointed out after he was sure the mer wasn't going to answer.

"Wait to show it to Bruce," Jason said. He turned to the landsman and pitched his voice lower. "You're liable to find a cold reception; Bruce doesn't care about anything but the Work." The capital was clear.

"Repairing the reefs?" Edmund asked, looking around. They looked in fine shape to him. Billions of fish were swimming across them and sea-fans waved in every direction. "I'd think keeping his people fed would be his first job."

"Mostly he agrees," Jason admitted. "But he doesn't want to have outsiders involved with us. He thinks that if we just lay low, the war will pass over us and we can just continue with the Work."

"And what do you think?" Edmund asked.

There was a long pause before Jason shrugged.

"He's the chosen leader of our people and it's not my job to speak against him, certainly not to outsiders."

"What about to New Destiny?" Edmund asked.

"New Destiny considers the mer to be abominations," Jason said, bitterly. "Let's just say that I disagree."

"So do I," Talbot said with a nod. "And, speaking from past experience, New Destiny tends to spread its feelings far and wide."

"Well, from all reports New Destiny is winning," Jason said.

"Reports are often wrong," the duke replied. "They've never won anywhere that I've had a hand."

"You're only one man."

"True, but I said 'had a hand.' Herzer is, often, my hand."

Jason bleated something that the computer changed to a tuneless chuckle.

"I suspect that being your hand is probably where he lost his. Well, Edmund Talbot, who never fails, welcome to Whale Point Drop mer-town."

The town spread out before them was larger than Edmund had expected. The area of reef had deep crevices gouged through it, generally trending from the shore to the deeps. In the center the crevices came together into an open sandy area with a prominent coral head in the middle. And the area swarmed with mer.

There were mer-men and mer-maids as well as children, although none of the latter were less than a year or two old. Edmund noticed that the mer-maids were just as naked in the upper regions as the mer-men and tried to keep his eyes away from the display of, in the main, perfect breasts.

In the open area, he could only think of it as the village square, the mer were especially thick. Some of them had food for trade, others had handmade goods. But the pickings were slim; there was far more communicating going on than trad-ing. At the sight of the hunting party, many of the people swarmed upwards, but there was obvious distress at the shortage of food they were bringing back. There was also a great deal of surprise at the visitors. The computer picked out the words "Freedom Coalition" but the rest was apparently a jumble.

Jason tugged Edmund through the crowd and down to near the bottom where a group was floating, arguing about something. The argument stopped as they neared and the group saw that Jason had a visitor.

"General Edmund Talbot," Jason said, gesturing at one of the mer, "Bruce the Black."

Edmund nodded at the mer and smiled.

"I've come a long way to see you," Edmund said.

"And for no good reason," Bruce returned, brusquely. "We're entering no agreements with anyone; we've enough troubles of our own without bringing others down on us."

"Well, there are some troubles we can help with," Edmund said, opening up the heavy package and letting fall the edge of the net. "This is a woven monomolecular net. There's nothing on earth that can break it and it will last far longer than you'll live. I've others coming on a ship, not woven mono, but made of good, sturdy cosilk. Those will last for nearly a generation and are, admittedly, easier to fix."

"Gill net," Bruce said. The AI gave it as toneless but it was clearly a spit of sound. "Great for randomly picking up innocent, and many of them inedible, fish. Very much what we need."

"Bruce," Jason interjected. "We weren't able to get more than a couple of hogs and a few damned crayfish. We're *starving*. A gill net is what we *need*!"

"Why? To strip the damned reefs again?" the leader replied hotly. "Woven monomolecule! What happens when it gets caught? You won't be able to cut it, you'll have to tear the reef itself! And what happens when a dolphin gets caught in it? It'll drown while you're off gallivanting!"

"Gallivanting is it?" Jason replied. "I don't see you bringing in any fish!"

"There's sea plum," the mer-leader replied.

"There's always bloody sea plum," one of the group behind him said.

"You've come on a fool's errand," the leader repeated. "You might as well go back. We've nothing for you, and you've got nothing for us."

"Well, I'll leave you the net," Edmund said. "And we have

to stay in the area for a few days; our transportation is having to sail around the banks."

"How did you get here, then?" one of the group asked.

"On dragon-back," Jason replied to a series of clicks. "Pete went with them down the coast to fish."

"The dragons were fishing?" Bruce asked.

"They can swim," Edmund said.

"Mister Black," Daneh interjected. "I'm Daneh Ghorbani and this is my daughter Rachel. I'd like to at least see how you are surviving and how you are doing it. We've had hard times as well and I'd like to see if you have anything that you're doing that we can pick up. We might have a few new ideas to share as well."

Bruce considered that for a moment, then shrugged.

"I can't exactly kick you out," he said, finally. "But I'm not going to join any alliances. Not with you, not with New Destiny."

"Especially with New Destiny," someone behind Edmund said.

"New Destiny isn't so bad," a black-haired mer-man said, pushing to the front of the crowd. He was one of the largest of the mer and even compared to the crowd around him heavy-set.

"New Destiny considers all Changed to be abominations," Edmund replied. "How can they *not* be bad for the mer?"

"If they consider all Change to be abominations," the mer-man asked, "how come they're Changing their own people?"

"Edmund Talbot," Bruce said with a sigh. "This is Mosur."

"Well, Mosur," Edmund replied, just as reasonably. "There's a broad difference, that most people grasp, between being voluntarily Changed into whatever you choose, versus being turned, against your will, into an orc. They've Changed most of the population of Ropasa against their will. I've seen the results and, trust me, you don't want that happening to you."

"How do you know it's against their will?" the mer replied, angrily. "Have you known someone who was Changed the way that you describe? And let me give a more accurate description, one less filled with malice. They are Changed so that they are tougher and more able to withstand the strain of the post-Fall world. Stronger, tougher and knowing how to *survive*. I think that counts for something. Most of the population of Ropasa has *survived*. *They're* not living on the ragged edge of starvation."

"You don't look starving to *me*," Edmund said to a general laugh.

"One's the same as the other," Bruce said, loudly. "They'll fight each other and they'll both lose."

"You'd best hope so," Edmund replied, sadly. "That we both lose. Because while we won't have any issue with you sitting things out, New Destiny will. And if we lose they'll come looking for you."

There was a mutter of agreement and Edmund noticed for the first time that there were delphinos at the edge of the crowd. They weren't entering the discussion, just observing and trading apparently carefully aimed sonar bursts with each other.

"So we have your permission to look around?" Edmund asked.

"It's a free ocean," Bruce said. "It's a free town. That's the point. Look around all you want. But you won't find me changing my mind."

"I understand," Edmund said, sadly.

"Where are you staying?" Bruce asked, suddenly. "Not down here, it's too cold for you."

"You'd be surprised what I can do," Edmund replied. "But we'll be staying up on the land. We landed near the lighthouse; the others will be meeting us there."

"The lighthouse?" Bruce challenged. "Why by the lighthouse?"

"Because it's a *landmark*," Edmund said, shaking his head. "Look, can I talk to you a moment?" He looked around. "Alone?"

Bruce nodded his assent and they swam across the square to an out-of-the-way alcove while the rest of the mer swarmed around Daneh and Rachel, and Jason spread out the net on the bottom.

"What is up by the lighthouse?" Edmund asked.

"Nothing," Bruce answered hotly. "Why are you asking?"

"Because while you've been sweetness and light about everything else, that really cut to the bone and I'm wondering why." He held up his hand to forestall a reply and shook his head. "Look, you probably are the kind of person who hates diplomats and diplomacy. If you even remember what they are . . ."

"I do," Bruce said, tightly. "I've studied history. That's *why* I'm trying to keep us out of this war."

"Fine," Edmund replied. "But the point is, the reason that they wore poker faces all the time was that they had things they didn't want to give away. Now, you've got something,

something important, up near the lighthouse. I'm not going
to investigate what that is. I'm hoping I don't even stumble
across it. But the New Destiny folks, if they find out, will
pry until they know what it is. And if they can, they'll use
it against you."

"But you wouldn't?" Bruce asked. "The Freedom Coalition
hasn't done anything to be ashamed of in this war?"

"No, we probably have," Edmund admitted. "But there's a
world of difference between what we're doing and what New
Destiny is doing. There's a huge difference between acciden-
tal deaths in combat, or a few soldiers out of hand and dealt
with swiftly and surely, versus intentional atrocities and
Changed orcs that are nothing *but* 'out of hand.' There's a
difference between accident and intent. And the point I'm trying
to make is *don't* make the same mistake you just made with
me around them. Or whatever it is you're trying to hide, they'll
hang around your neck like a dead albatross."

"I'll keep that in mind," Bruce said. "But you keep this in
mind. We're not taking the mer off to war. We have important work to do *here*. And we're going to continue it."

"Oh, don't worry," Edmund said. "I have that. Chapter and
verse."

Edmund had gotten into a discussion with one of the tool
makers while Daneh had been dragged off to see one of the
mer's casualties. This left Rachel to be dragged off by Jason.

They went down one of the narrow crevices to where it
turned into a tunnel. About a dozen feet in there was a brief
break in the overhead and in the sunlight was a young mer-
maid plaiting a twisted cord.

"Antja, this is Rachel Ghorbani," Jason said.

The mer-maid dropped the material and drifted towards the
entrance, smiling.

"Welcome," she said. "There's not much to offer, but if you'd
care for some sea plum?"

"I don't know," Rachel said. "I've never had sea plum
before." Her stomach rumbled and she realized that it had
been quite a few hours since she had eaten.

Antja went to one of the crevices along the wall and pulled
down some plum-sized fruits with a suspiciously familiar
appearance. Rachel took one and then paused as she realized
she was wearing a full-head covering. She frowned, then pulled
the mask out allowing the water to strike her face for the
first time. She took a bite of the fruit and recognized the taste.

She carefully put the mask back on, sealing it down, and took a breath, relieved that it hadn't taken any hurt from its submersion.

"I'd never heard it called sea plum," Rachel said. "But I recognize it; it's kudzi."

"What's kudzi?" Antja asked.

"There was once a noxious vine called kudzu that covered all sorts of areas in Norau," Rachel said. "A long, *long* time ago, someone released a retrovirus on it and forced it to produce fruits. The fruit is a cross between kiwi fruit and strawberry with a plum skin. Tasty, but it gets tiring. Where do *you* find it?"

"Anywhere that there's a fresh-water outlet," Jason answered. "Like the spring on the island. In the brackish area around it, there's lots of sea plum. It's got some good points, fish like to nest in it and it doesn't really push anything out of the niche. And it produces sea plum. But, yes, it does get tiresome."

"Unfortunately that's about all that we have right now," Antja said. "Unless . . . ?"

"We didn't get much," Jason admitted, sadly.

"Well, maybe Herzer and his group will bring something back?" Rachel asked.

"Who's Herzer?" Antja said.

After about an hour of fishing the dragons came up out of the water, the wyverns shivering with cold but burbling happily to each other. Two of them were carrying large fish in their mouths and they carried them to shore and dropped them, still flopping, at the feet of the riders. After that they all gathered around the fire, their wings spread, and soaked up the heat happily as their riders dabbed at under-spots.

Pete, once given a decent knife to work with, turned out to be one damned fine filleter and in minutes the fish were trussed up and sizzling over the fire.

"What I couldn't do with a little orange sauce," Pete complained as the fish were served on broad leaves. He had dragged himself up on the shore to direct the cooking and shook his head at the fumble-fingered grilling of the riders. When the fish was done he took a bite of one and then shrugged. "I guess it's better than what we've *been* eating; sea plum and sushi without wasabi."

"What's sea plum?" Herzer asked around a mouthful of steaming hogfish.

"You'll find out," Pete said darkly. "It's fine at first, but after a while it really starts to pall."

The grilled fish, two grouper and a hogfish, were excellent, despite the chef's complaints. The smoky fire added just a hint of seasoning to succulent flesh that was perfectly formed and solid, so solid that it had held up to being grilled with nothing but some sticks shoved through it.

"This is good," Joanna said. "I mean, it's sort of a snack to me, but it's a hell of a lot better than raw, let me tell you. And nice to not be crunching bones."

"I see you decided to start without me," Bast called from the darkness. She strode into the firelight, still stark naked, bearing two huge tuna and with a string of at least two dozen lobster tails around her neck.

"How in the hell . . . ?" Pete asked.

"I heard something about the town not having enough to eat," Bast said simply. "We can carry these back."

"Not *why*," Pete said. "How?"

"Oh, that," Bast said with a shrug. In the firelight, with her hair flat against her head and none of her panoply she looked like nothing so much as a young, *very* young, teenage girl. The tuna that she held, effortlessly, must have weighed nearly as much as she did. "Do you know how to catch a unique rabbit?"

"No?" Pete said.

"You nique up on him," Bast said. "That fish smells good," she added, dropping the tuna and lobster to the ground.

CHAPTER TWENTY-ONE

By the time they were done, with the last scraps given to the wyverns, the sun was just about down and Herzer was not looking forward to the ride back.

"I thought a Blood Lord was always prepared," Vickie said, maliciously.

"Pain is weakness leaving the body," Herzer said. "I can take a little cold."

"You'd damned well better not get hypothermic," Pete said. "There's a reason that we stay down where the water is relatively warm. And we *still* need a lot of fats." He frowned at that and shrugged. "Those tuna would have been good." The now gutted fish, and the lobster, had been loaded on Joanna for transportation to the mer-town.

"I've got an idea about that," Herzer admitted as he loaded the mer-man back on his mount. True to his prediction the leather had stretched and was loose on the dragon.

"You mean other than siccing your girlfriend on them?" Pete asked.

The wyverns were warm, fed and balkish about flying. Furthermore there were no bluffs around and the omnipresent wind had died down to no more than a zephyr. So the dragons had to take off the hard way.

They turned into the wind and started hopping forward on their big hind legs, wings blasting downward with each hop. At each hop they got a little more speed and a little more height to flap with until they were finally, barely, airborne.

It was the first time Herzer had taken off that way and he didn't like it any more than Pete, who complained vociferously. Herzer had to bury his face into the dragon so that his head wouldn't be slamming into its back with each landing and he now understood, plainly, why dragon-riders hated to take off anywhere that there wasn't a bluff, a good wind or, preferably, both.

"So, you guys want us to fight for you or what?" Pete asked, as they flew back to the rendezvous.

"Yes, and or what," Herzer answered, honestly. "New Destiny is building a fleet to invade the UFS. We're going to fight it but there's a lot of the buggers. We're looking for the help of the mer for scouting and, probably, to attack the fleet."

"There's not much we can do to ships," Pete said.

"There's a guy on the ship that's on its way that could probably come up with some ideas," Herzer said. "But New Destiny has some seafolk on their side. Specifically the orcas."

"I'll have to admit I haven't met a single decent person who has turned themselves into an orca," Pete muttered.

"And we're willing to do more than just ask," Herzer continued. "The ship has some materials on it, things we thought you might need. Beryllium bronze knives and spearheads. Beryllium bronze is more resistant to corrosion than the usual type. There's even some things made of stainless steel that the dwarves dug up and we ground down. And wasn't that a job."

"Those would help," Pete admitted. "But couldn't we get the same things from New Destiny? Or by trading, for that matter?"

"It's a long way from the dwarves," Herzer pointed out. "What can't they get from others that are closer? And Raven's Mill has the best textile and rope manufacturing on the East Coast; we're where the cord for your nets is being made. We can sell *that* closer, too. I wouldn't say you need us more than we need you. But it's close to equality."

Pete didn't answer that, just gestured at the ground, which was already dark although the dragons were still flying in the last shreds of sunlight.

"Can the dragons land in this?" he asked.

"As long as it's not on a carrier," Herzer said with a laugh.

"A *carrier*?"

"How do you think we got here?" Herzer said. "You'll see. In a few days after it beats its way around to us."

They landed by the lighthouse, without incident, stripped

the harness off the dragons and unloaded Bast's catch. The wyverns immediately hopped over to the shelter of the bluff to be out of the wind and tucked their heads under their wings, nodding off into sleep.

"I'll go find Edmund," Joanna said, walking into the water.

"I'm for town," Pete said, gesturing at the fish and the lobster. "Can I take those?"

"And what do you think I caught them for, young mer-man?" Bast laughed. She picked up one of the fish and strode towards the water leaving her gear, and her clothes, in a trail behind her.

Pete picked up the string of lobster and looked at the other tuna.

"Herzer?"

"Got it," he said, hefting the fish with difficulty. He had long ago realized that Bast was stronger than he was but it was a bit shaming to have to struggle with the single fish when she had carried two of them easily.

Pete crawled to the water on his hands and submerged without a ripple and Herzer quickly followed him, fumbling with the combination of fish, mask and flippers.

The water trailed green phosphorescence around him as he strode into the water and he submerged quickly, following the faint luminous trail that Pete and Bast left. Bast was in the lead and seemed to know exactly where she was going.

"Bast?" Herzer called. "Two things. One, slow down. Two, how do you know where you are?"

"I was here years ago, Herzer," Bast said, slowing down to let him catch up. "I'm not sure how long ago, but I recognize it. And there's only one place for a mer colony around here."

"I've never heard of you," Pete said. It was clear that he thought he would have.

"The great grandfathers of the mer today were not yet born when I was here, young mer," Bast laughed.

"That was . . . a long time ago," Pete said.

"There was a mer colony in the Isles before the AI wars, mer-man," Bast said, softly. "Even then they were repairing the damage. I recall when the Port Crater was made. And why," she added in nearly a whisper.

The response from Pete was an untranslatable whistle.

The town when they reached it was lit in a fairy tale glitter. Luminescent fish swam around the square while the entrance of each canyon was lit by glowing globes.

"The fish are attracted here by feeding," Pete said. "Careful feeding. The lit globes are a type of sessile sponge; I think it was genegineered."

"It was," Bast said. "By the Bettel corporation as a type of underwater toy. Just as the wyvern were created by the Disney Brothers corporation."

"You were there?" Herzer asked.

"No, but in days when I was created genesis was still well known," Bast said. "These latter days . . . humans have forgotten most of their history. Fire lizards, wyverns, even great dragons, were all created by Disney genegineers. They've been tinkered with over years, but that is original genesis. Disney even did first work on mer, young mer-man. So owe your genesis to creators of dragons."

The arrival of the fish, and the lobster, was greeted with acclaim, and Jason pushed himself to the front of the mob that crowded around Pete.

"Good job, Pete," Jason said.

"Not me," Pete answered, waving at the naked elf next to him. "Thank Bast here."

"Bast," Daneh said, swimming up through the crowd. "I think we need to find you a bathing suit."

"Why?" Bast said. "I'm no more naked than the mer. Those slits on their fronts have a purpose, Daneh Ghorbani."

Daneh just chuckled and shook her head. "Whatever."

"This gift . . . it is a gift, right? This gift is much appreciated, Miss . . . ?" Bruce said.

"Bast," Bast replied, sticking out her hand. "Pleased to meetcha." She somehow retained her position in the water even while shaking hands with the mer-leader.

"How did you . . . ?" Bruce said, gesturing at the giant tuna she was holding by one gill-plate.

"Oh, no," Pete said, waiting for the dread pun.

"What's wrong?" Bast said with a grin. "Fish are curious. I just let their curiosity be their undoing. It's an old trick."

"Well, however you did it, we appreciate it," Bruce said. "Pete, can you divide it?"

"Here," Edmund said, swimming over most of the crowd. "Use this," he said, holding out a knife.

"Heavy," was all that Pete said as he used it to slide through the skin of the fish. "And sharp."

"Beryllium bronze," Edmund said as Bast passed out the lobster. Jason ensured that they were passed out to family groups but most of them simply opened up the shells and tore out the meat ravenously.

"Do you want some?" Bruce asked as Pete started handing out the thick steaks of tuna.

"We ate," Herzer said. "Grouper and hogfish that the dragons caught."

Pete had set aside a large fillet from the first fish and was starting on the second.

"Could you section that up, Herzer?" Pete asked. "It's for the delphinos."

"Sure," Herzer replied. His knife was of stainless steel, issued for the mission, and much smaller than the one Pete was using. But it sufficed to chunk up the tuna, if somewhat messily. When he had the meat cut up he looked at the chunks and realized that he had no way to move them.

"Here, let me help you," a mer-maid said. She had long, dark hair that was black in the pale phosphorescence and was slimmer than normal in what was generally a hefty group, with high, firm breasts, a nice smile and a tail that was apparently bright blue. What was strangest was that she had a moray eel twined around her neck like a collar. She held out a mesh bag so that he could load the chunks of meat into it. "I'm Elayna."

"Herzer Herrick," Herzer said, acutely conscious as her breast innocently brushed his arm, of the comment Bast had made about nakedness. Not to mention the fact that Bast, who was one of the most dangerous individuals he had ever met, was no more than an arm's length from him. But he had been celibate for an awfully long time.

"Come on," the girl said, picking up the basket. "The delphinos are usually down at the tip of the reef."

He followed her into the darkness and as they neared what he felt was deeper water he saw a group of shadows up near the surface.

"That's them," Elayna said. "The delphinos are really strange; as close to aliens as we'll ever find. We work together, but they keep a separate society from us."

"How do you 'work together'?" Herzer asked as they neared the group.

"They herd fish to us and we try to catch it in nets," the mer-girl said. "Try, I say, because our nets are really lousy."

"Fish smell," one of the delphinos blatted. He had been floating at the surface but now dove, followed by the rest of the pod.

Herzer felt more than heard a wave of sound cross him and he knew he was being sized up by the delphino. While he'd seen the occasional mer, this was the first delphino he'd seen in the flesh and was surprised by the size of the being.

"Herzer, this is Herman the pod leader," Elayna said. "Herman, Herzer Herrick. He and some friends brought tuna."

"Good is," Herman said. "Much is. Good hunting us, some take. Most take back, need not."

"Thank you, Herman," Elayna replied. "Jason didn't get much today so we need it."

"Know," Herman said. As she opened the bag he pulled pieces out and flipped them dexterously to pod members in some pattern unclear to Herzer. He stopped when only half the bag was gone and flipped his nose at Elayna. "Back take. Hunt tomorrow."

"Herman," Herzer said, diffidently. "I think that there might be a way to capture the big pelagics if you, the mer and the dragons worked together. It might not work at first, but I think we can figure it out."

Herman paused and Herzer felt another of those ripples of sonar run across him. He wondered what it would look like, what *he* would look like, to a delphino.

"Good is," Herman said. "Try will. Morrow?"

"I'll see," Herzer temporized. "Hopefully."

"Jason see," Herman said. "Breathe must. Morrow."

"Morrow," Herzer said as the delphino floated back to the surface to breathe.

"What's this idea you have?" Elayna asked as they headed back to town.

"I'm not sure of the particulars," Herzer said. "I need to talk to Pete and Jason." He paused as a shudder passed through his body.

"Cold?" Elayna asked.

"Very," Herzer admitted. "But I'll be okay."

"Maybe, maybe not," Elayna said in a concerned voice. "Hypothermia is no joke, and there's nowhere to warm up. I get that way sometimes, too. But we have a better heat regulation system than landies." She reached into the bag and extracted a chunk of tuna, biting into it as she swam. "Of course, it also requires more energy, so we have to eat stuff more than landies. And tuna's the best; lots of fat."

"I noticed that you're . . . heavier than most landsmen," Herzer said.

"You can say fat," Elayna said with a laugh as she fed some small pieces to the moray. "But the fat's really just a reservoir for us. And we've been losing a lot of weight lately; I know I have. With the way that we push water through our gills, fat doesn't help with the cold. Eating fat does, though," she added, taking another bite. "Want some?"

"No, I ate up on the surface," he said. He didn't add that cold, seawater-flavored tuna was not his idea of an appetizing meal.

They'd reached the town square and she spread the tuna around to the still hungry group, taking a few pieces for herself.

"Having fun?" Bast said, swimming up behind them.

"Uh," Herzer replied, brilliantly.

"Yes, we are," Elayna said. "And I haven't thanked you for the tuna."

"You're welcome," Bast said, smiling at her. "I wonder, were you going to ask Herzer if he'd seen the feeding stations?"

"Uh," Herzer said again.

"As a matter of fact, yes," Elayna said with a toothy smile. "Is that a problem?"

"No," Bast said, matter-of-factly. "Long celibate he has been; go take the edge off. He's good for more than once a night." She smiled at the girl and flipped off into the darkness.

"Uhm . . ." Herzer said.

Elayna just looked at him and batted her eyes. "Care to go look at the feeding stations, Lieutenant Herrick?" she asked.

Without a word he took her hand and followed her across the night-dark reef.

"Well, look what the sea tossed up," Rachel said as Herzer strode down the bluff from the lighthouse. She was squatting by the remains of the campfire adding driftwood to the coals. "Have a nice night?"

The wind had died overnight and backed around easterly. The sky was clear and the dawn sun was just starting to lift the remnants of early morning fog. The wyverns were awake and starting to mewl with hunger.

"Great, thanks," Herzer said, setting down a bucket of water from the spring across the island. "Is there any breakfast? I'm starved."

"Well, you have your choice of fish and sea plum or sea plum and fish," Rachel said. "And I'm not surprised you're hungry. I'm surprised you can stand."

"Herzer has the constitution of a bull," Bast said, following him down the bluff. "And other things like a bull, come to think of it."

"Oh, God," Herzer muttered. "It's going to be one of those mornings, isn't it?"

"You have only yourself to blame," Rachel replied with a sniff.

"Not if you'd make me an honest man," he retorted, then shrugged. "So I'm having fun. It's not interfering with the mission."

"Fooling around with Bruce's granddaughter isn't interfering with the mission?" Rachel asked.

"His *grand*daughter?" Herzer groaned. "Oh, hell."

"Yes, his granddaughter," Edmund said, coming up and squatting by the coals. "It's going to be a hot one today," he added, looking at the sky. "But don't worry about it, Herzer, we've got much worse problems. Bruce had word that New Destiny is sending a diplomatic mission as well."

"Crap," Herzer said, looking around at the sea as if to see a black sail on the horizon.

"We'll deal with it," Edmund said. "We'll deal with it . . . diplomatically."

"Who are they sending?" Rachel asked. "Do you know?"

"No. I only know what I picked up in town."

"Most of the people do *not* like New Destiny," Herzer said. "I know that for sure. But I'm not so sure they want to join with us, either."

"Well, we'll have to find a way to get them to see the error of their ways," Edmund replied. "Somehow. I wish the damned ship would get here, but with the winds the way they are it might be a week."

"What happens if they meet up with the New Destiny 'diplomatic mission'?" Herzer asked.

"Hopefully they'll deal with it . . . diplomatically," Edmund replied.

CHAPTER TWENTY-TWO

"Great day to be sailing," Commander Mbeki said as he reached the quarterdeck.

"Sure, if we were sailing the right way," the skipper said sourly. The ship was currently on the northerly tack, as it had been for a good half the morning. To sail to the east required turning first one way and then the other, tacking, so that the winds could be caught by the sails. They had been taking long tacks, far out to sea, to ensure that they avoided the shoals along the north side of the isles and the voyage was, unfortunately, taking longer than anticipated. "At this rate it'll be a week before we get to Whale Point. And what happens if they've hared off somewhere else by then?"

"We'll deal with it," Mbeki said.

"Sail off the starboard bow!"

They were well off from the islands so it was unlikely to be some stray fishing vessel. Chang and Mbeki both shrugged almost simultaneously.

"We'll stay on this tack," the skipper said. "We'll come up on it."

"If it's hostile, it will have the weather gauge," Mbeki pointed out.

"We'll figure that out soon enough. Get Donahue up on the mast with a pair of binoculars; I want to know what we're dealing with as soon as possible."

In no more than thirty minutes the midshipman called down.

"Square-rigged ship," he yelled. "Looks something like a

caravel. No flags that I can see. Looks like some dolphins swimming around it."

"If it's a caravel we can sail rings around it," Mbeki said.

"Sure, but we don't have so much as bowmen on board," the skipper replied. "Get me Evan."

When the engineer was shown onto the bridge he nodded at the news and frowned.

"I've been working on something, but I don't know that you'd want to use it on the ship," he admitted.

"What is it then?" Mbeki said impatiently.

"It was an idea that Lieutenant Herzer had," the engineer temporized.

"The materials he asked to bring on board?" the skipper asked.

"Yes, sir," the engineer said. "He wanted a way to make the dragons an offensive weapon. He was working on that but I thought I'd make something else."

"What is it, man?" Mbeki snapped.

"A flamethrower," the engineer said nervously.

"Shit," the skipper said, looking around at the tinder-dry wood of the ship. "You're right, I don't want that used on my ship."

"Sir!" the midshipman called down. "Sir! There's a flag hoisted now, I can't make it out exactly but it's red and blue! And they've changed course towards us!" The New Destiny flag was blue field with red ND on it.

"That caps it," the skipper said. "Clear for action, all hands stand by to repel boarders."

"I have an idea, sir," the engineer said after a moment. "But we'll have to have them to port."

"We'll figure that out later," the captain replied. "Get moving on it. And don't you *dare* fire that damned thing on my ship."

"Yes, sir. I mean, no sir!" the engineer said, hurrying to the companionway.

The two ships continued on nearly reciprocal courses, the caravel bearing down on the clipper. Normally it would be no contest; the clipper was far and away the faster ship. But the skipper kept her on her course, headed towards the other ship. After a few minutes he climbed up to the rigging for his own look and returned shaking his head.

"They've got a ballista," he said. "And those are orcas around their ship."

"Changed?" Mbeki asked.

"Probably." He stood there with his hands clasped behind his back, feet spread to counter the roll of the ship. "We *should* show them our heels. We could outrun even the orca over time."

"With all due respect, sir," the commander said. "That would look like hell on our report."

"It would look worse if we lost the carrier," the skipper said. "We should have brought armed sloops with us, I said it at the time."

"Yes, sir," the commander replied.

"But you're absolutely correct that it would look like hell," the skipper frowned. "I wonder if our wonder-boy has come up with anything."

"You want me to *what*?" the rabbit said. "No way in hell."

"You said one favor," Evan replied. "This is it."

"And I also said 'nothing unreasonable,' " the rabbit replied. "This is clearly unreasonable."

"No it's not," Evan said, doggedly. "It's more than likely that you'll survive. Especially if you have the flamethrower."

"I can do a lot of impossible things," the bunny said. "But I cannot swim with the flamethrower on my back! Well."

"You're not going to swim."

"This is your plan?" the skipper said, looking at the rabbit at Evan's feet.

"Yes, sir," the engineer replied, nervously. "This is all I could come up with on the spur of the moment."

The rabbit was wearing a black suit with a smoked-visor helmet. Attached to his harness, in place of the pistol crossbow, was a small circular tank with a, yes, rabbit-sized nozzle attached. But the harness still held all his knives.

"This is insane," Commander Mbeki commented.

"You're right," the rabbit said, hopping towards the companionway. "It's crazy. I shouldn't do it."

"Come back here," Evan said. "I don't know what happens to you if you go back on your promises, but I'm willing to find out."

"Damn," the rabbit said. "Does anyone think that this constitutes *unreasonable* as well as insane?" he asked hopefully.

"Nooo," the skipper said, thoughtfully. "Insane, yes. *Unreasonable*, no."

"But insanity is *defined* as unreason," the rabbit said.

"Not really," Commander Mbeki said. "Psychotics are, by definition, insane. But they can be quite reasonable people."

"You're really going to make me do this?" the rabbit asked. "That's unreasonable."

"But it doesn't matter, if the task is not. If it's stupid, but it works, it's not stupid," Evan replied with the logic of an engineer.

"We really don't have time to debate this," the skipper said. "Either you're going or you're not. On the other hand, you're an AI. I don't feel that I can, with conscience, force you to do something that is clearly insane."

"Damn," the rabbit said, trying to scratch through the suit. "I can't even get to my damned ear. Okay, put me on the catapult."

Evan had even rigged a small launching seat.

"How long have you been contemplating this?" the rabbit asked.

"When did you board the ship?" Evan said as the clipper fell off to starboard. A ballista bolt from the oncoming ship whistled through the air with an evil hiss and poked a hole in the mainsail.

"You made this suit, this helmet and this seat in that time?" the rabbit asked. "I'm impressed."

"No, I made the seat then," Evan said, stepping into the launching pit. "I made the suit and the helmet when I made the flamethrower. Have fun."

"If I end up in the drink I'm coming for you, Evan Mayerle," the rabbit hissed as Evan timed the roll and hit the launcher.

The black blob was fired into the air and as it flew across the gap two knives appeared in its hands. It hit the mainsail of the oncoming caravel face first but the knives went through the canvas like butter and it slid downward leaving two gaping wounds in the black sail. The last that could be seen of it was as it flipped off the base of the sail and into the crowd below it. As it landed, there was an inhuman scream.

"Poor bunny," Commander Mbeki said. "He didn't last long."

"I think that was whoever he landed on," Evan said, as a spurt of flame licked upward and caught the sail. It was quickly involved and turned to ash before their eyes. "You might want to have the captain sail out of range for the time being."

The wind was fair from the caravel and it carried the occasional sounds of screaming, pleas for help and from time to time someone leapt over the side, apparently preferring the briny deeps to whatever was going on on board. The ship had almost immediately lost way and now rocked from side to side in the waves, its helm clearly not manned.

The captain joined them and shook his head when blood started running from the scuppers.

"I'm glad he's on our side," the skipper commented.

"I don't think he is," Evan replied. "But he owed me a favor."

"Shall we send over a prize crew?" Commander Mbeki asked. The last, badly aimed, ballista bolt had sailed off into the distance some time before.

"No . . ." the commander said after a moment's thought. "I'm not sure that any sane human should see what is on board that ship." He eyed the orcas and an occasional raylike thing that were coming up and glancing at the ship they were supposed to be following. "But I'm not sure that he should have to swim back." There were flames licking from the aft of the craft by then and he shook his head again. "Let's lay her alongside, near the bow, and recover our . . . friend."

They jockeyed the ship over, carefully, and threw grapnels onto its bow to pull it alongside. Fire parties stood by because the aft had become fully involved, but shifted as they were that was downwind and for the time being the fire was held there.

As they pulled alongside the rabbit jumped from one ship to the other, a gap of more than three meters, which should have been impossible.

"Well," he said brightly, taking off his helmet, "that was fun. Let's go find me some more orcs to play with!"

"It was crewed by orcs?" Commander Mbeki asked as a division under Chief Brooks boomed the caravel away and the clipper got back under way. Some of the crew from the burning ship had climbed aboard and were lined up against the starboard rail under guard.

"No, they were their marines," the rabbit replied, pulling off the fire-scorched black suit. "I just kept telling myself it was a cruise of telemarketers and there just didn't seem to be enough of them. I haven't had that much fun since the last real telemarketer died of old age. I didn't track the bastard down until he'd keeled over from the heart attack. They said he'd seen a rabbit and that was it for him. The bastard."

Not a sound was heard from the ship as they sailed away, leaving behind a crowd of confused orcas.

Joel had watched the entire "battle," more of a massacre, from his battle station on the quarterdeck. He found it interesting, and instructive, that the enemy ship was there. Finding one ship at sea was not easy; as sailors said: "Lord, the sea is so large and my boat is so small."

It was an unlikely coincidence to find one of the New Destiny fleet placed right across their path. About as likely as rounding out a busted flush on a one card draw.

Which meant that it probably wasn't coincidence. Which meant that the vague possibility that there was an agent on board had gone from "vague possibility" to "high probability."

Furthermore, they had known more or less the ship's exact location and plans. That meant that the probable agent was among the officers, probably one of the primary navigational officers, either the captain, Commander Mbeki, Major Freund the navigator or one of the three lieutenants.

The rabbit was an outside possibility, as well. As an AI it could have an internal navigational system and even communications. He wished that he knew more about it, but everyone with prior experience had left with the dragons.

His hunch was still Commander Mbeki. But it was only a hunch and while he was willing to pay attention to his hunches, he wasn't willing to concentrate on them.

He needed more information.

"Orcas approaching to port," the masthead lookout called.

Martin had been pacing up and down the quarterdeck, waiting for word on the attack upon the UFS ship. He had spread the ships on a long line across the anticipated course of the dragon carrier and the caravels had only had occasional visual contact for the past three days. The lookout had reported possibly seeing some smoke early in the morning, but from what was impossible to determine.

Each of the ships, though, had a small pod of orcas attached. The orca sonar could transmit across significant distances and he was using that to keep in communication with the dispersed fleet. Why some were returning to *his* ship, however, remained to be seen.

He walked to the front of the ship and looked down at the pod that was riding in the bow wave. Suddenly he saw Shanol veer off and head in the direction of the oncoming orcas.

He waited impatiently for the leader whale to return and then walked back to the maindeck as Shanol and a smaller orca coasted to the side of the slow-moving vessel.

"What's up, Shanol?" he asked, leaning over the side of the gently heeling caravel.

"Your 'unarmed carrier' just took out the ship that was in its way like it wasn't even there," Shanol replied.

"What could have happened?" Martin asked. "They didn't even have the dragons with them!"

"Well, it's pretty hard to tell from down here," the orca leader said, sarcastically. "I had Maniillat report back in person."

"They didn't board or anything," Maniillat squealed. "The carrier never got near them until the ship was already st-stopped. Some of the sailors jumped over the side but they were just screaming about a fire-breathing imp."

"They couldn't have summoned anything," Martin snapped. "They don't have the power available. The only one that might have is Talbot, and he's already at the mer-town."

"Well, whatever it is took your ship out and the carrier is already past your line," Shanol replied. "What now, fearless leader?"

"Head to the mer-town," Martin said after a moment. "Time to start phase two."

"Yeah, well I hope phase two works out better than phase one," Shanol replied.

"Yeah," Maniillat squealed. "And no fire-breathing imps."

The skipper was walking down a lower deck corridor when he saw sailors bracing themselves against the bulkhead ahead of him. He wasn't close enough to have caused the reaction and he didn't understand the beads of sweat on their faces until he saw the rabbit coming around a corner.

"Mr. Rabbit," Chang said. "Just the bunny I was looking for."

"What do you want, Spiffy?" the rabbit asked.

"I wanted to show you something," the skipper replied, waving at him. He led the rabbit down the corridor to a locked storeroom and opened it from a ring of keys.

"The ships of the UFS Navy are dry . . ."

"Not something you have to tell me," the rabbit said, bitterly. "And no alfalfa either. And your women are mostly dogs."

"Well, I can't help you there," the skipper said, opening the door. Inside there was a large barrel, already tapped. He took down a half-liter pewter mug and held it under the tap until it was full. "But there are times, as the Navy recognizes, when it's medicinal to administer a small belt. For just such occasions it maintains the means."

He bent down and handed the mug to the rabbit, who peered into its depths suspiciously then took a sip.

"Rum, by God!" the rabbit said happily, drinking half the mug in one draught.

"High-proof rum," the skipper noted. "Royal Navy grog to be exact. I can't leave the room open, but if you'll step inside I'll come back in a couple of hours and have you carried to your bunk. You'll forgive me if I don't want you wandering the ship under the influence of alcohol, what with one thing and another."

"Nah, believe it or not I'm a happy drunk," the rabbit said. "Just let me fill up one more of these mugs and I'll let you lock back up." He beamed up at the skipper as he took another swig. "You know, for a stuffy son of a bitch you ain't all bad."

"I was thinking something similar, myself," the skipper said.

"Don't kid yourself," the rabbit said, taking another swig. "I'm all bad."

"Mistress Sheida," Joel said to the avatar. He had chosen the cable tier for the meeting on the assumption that there were multiple exits and hardly anyone ever came down there.

"How is your mission going, Mister Travante?" Sheida asked. Her avatar looked tired, which meant it was projecting "her" current state.

"Not fun, but that's not important," Joel said. "We were attacked today. The ship apparently knew our estimated course, location and speed."

"I see," Sheida sighed. "I guess sending you out wasn't just insurance, was it?"

"No, ma'am," the inspector replied. "I have a suspicion who the agent is, and even a feel for motivation. Could you give me some information on Commander Owen Mbeki's family?"

Sheida's avatar looked distant for a moment, then shrugged.

"The usual story. A wife, Sharon, daughter Sara. No last known location but his primary residence was in Ropasa. You think New Destiny has them?"

"Given one single comment, ma'am," Joel said, nodding. "I'd say that they have one or both and are using them as hostages."

"What do you intend to do?"

"I need to have more proof, even for myself, than one unguarded comment, ma'am," Joel admitted. "And I also need to know more about an AI rabbit that accompanied an elf to the ship. The attack took place after the rabbit's arrival. And while he was instrumental in destroying the New Destiny craft, I don't discount him being the agent."

"That rabbit, he is a scamp, isn't he?" Sheida said with a faint grin. "I'd love to hear more of the story at another time. He's another distinct possibility," she added with a frown. "I'll give you two items," she continued, holding out her hand and floating a pair of disks across the compartment to him. "I can ken those with very little power usage. Place them in strategic locations. If an avatar appears near them but not in the same room they'll indicate direction when you touch them. If an avatar *has* appeared in the room, they will record the conversation. Will that do?"

"Perfectly," Joel said, pocketing the disks.

"What do you intend to do?" Sheida asked. "Take the information to Duke Edmund?"

"The duke is currently at the mer-town," Joel told her. "We're sailing there at the moment. But, no, I don't intend to do that. With your concurrence, as soon as I'm sure who the leak is I'll take action. If it's the rabbit we will have to act quickly and decisively; he is a dangerous AI. If it is the commander I intend to turn him."

"What do you mean by that?" Sheida asked warily.

"It is often useful to let an enemy *think* they have perfect intelligence," Joel replied. "I would suggest that the commander be moved to a very important shore post where he can pick up various useful items of information. Most of them relatively low level, as, frankly, the movement of this ship is. But from time to time he'll forward important bits of information that are higher level. Some of them will be real information that we don't mind the other side having. I'm sure there are things that you wished you *knew* that New Destiny knew."

"Indeed," Sheida said, her eyes narrowing.

"Other things will be carefully crafted falsehoods. Carefully crafted because you don't want to burn an agent that good."

Sheida frowned. "And I certainly don't want to 'burn' his wife and daughter."

Joel paused and shrugged after a moment. "The time may come when that choice has to be made. The *preference* is to ensure the safety of the agent and their close kin. For example, if we catch someone that they don't want to lose, and if the commander has lost his utility, we could attempt to trade 'their' person for ours. But, sometimes, you have to cut your losses. If it meant harm to Commander Mbeki's family to prevent, oh, Paul winning the war, would you do it?"

Sheida frowned and shook her head. "I hate questions like that."

"You need to think about them, ma'am." Joel shrugged, his face hard. "I certainly do. Several times a day."

"Still no word on *your* wife and daughter," Sheida said, sadly. "I take it you haven't 'heard' anything."

"No, ma'am," Joel replied. "But if I do, you'll be the second person to know."

CHAPTER TWENTY-THREE

"Duke Edmund," Bruce said, coasting into the swim-through that had been set aside for the duke's party. "Would you mind joining me for a short swim?"

"Not at all, sir," Talbot replied, setting down the section of whale bone he had been carving.

He didn't ask, and Bruce didn't offer, where they were going. He just followed the mer-leader as he popped up above the reef and headed downward towards the open ocean.

The reef ended at about twenty meters or so and gave way to sand bottom. The light had trailed off, but it was still quite bright in the brilliantly clear waters. They turned to the right and swam along the edge of the reef and Edmund looked around himself with interest. He realized that while he had been enjoying the overall beauty of the reefs, he hadn't had the time, or, face it, the inclination to really *examine* them.

The reefs were covered with fish; schools of ones the size of his hand and nearly round of body with blue vertical stripes were everywhere. There were other schools of more "fishlike" appearance, fairly long to their height, with bright yellow tails. In among the crevices were more small fish, all of them in a rainbow of colors. It was only with great trouble that he managed to realize that there were drab fish there as well. And finally he picked out ones that were camouflaged so perfectly they were almost impossible to see. One that looked exactly like a section of reef popped up as they passed and swallowed a smaller fish whole. Edmund never would have noticed it if it hadn't moved and when it stopped to swallow its prey it nearly disappeared again.

Now that he was really looking around he realized there were many things about the reef that were puzzling. Some of it looked exactly like stone. He knew that it was limestone that had been built up by the coral polyps. But other portions seemed to be covered in fur. These portions were infrequent, but interesting. The covering didn't seem to be a slime or a mold; he wasn't sure what it was. And then, why were the swim-throughs there? They looked like gouged canyons, but there was nothing that he could see to gouge them. Did trickles of fresh water open them up? Or water or sand pouring down from the shallows to the deeps?

Furthermore, the reefs were not constant. The area with the swim-throughs, where the town was, was built up to several meters over the sandy bottom. But within a few hundred yards down the coast it had given way to scattered small rocks stuck up barely over the ground.

But even these were alive. There were delicate sea fans dangling from them, waving back and forth in the light currents. A turtle the size of a pony was lying with its belly on the sand, eating a sponge attached to the side of one of the outcroppings. There were brightly colored reef fish. There were even some larger fish that looked more of the open ocean type to him. But they had gathered around the rocks, one or at most two by each one. He thought, at first, that they were hunting something. But they were simply stopped, as much as possible, hanging motionless. When they drifted away from the rocks they would turn and come back into the current until they were over the rocks again and stop, as if they were using them as some sort of location beacon.

Intrigued he deviated from Bruce's wake and coasted over for a closer look.

The larger fish were shaped something like tuna, but had a more rounded head, a bluish sheen and a horizontal stripe along their midline. What was happening became clear as he got close enough to see details. Smaller fish, one colored bright blue, were darting out from the rock and swimming over the body of the larger fish. He waited patiently for the larger fish to eat one of them but it never did. Instead the small fish swam all over its body, picking at it from time to time as if eating the larger fish's skin. They even swam into its slowly opening and closing gills and as he watched in amazement

one swam right into the larger fish's mouth, poked around
and came back out.

"Cleaning station," Bruce said and Edmund realized that he
had stopped instead of following his host.

"Sorry, I was just watching this," he said.

"Good," Bruce replied, clearly willing to dally. "I'd hoped
you might actually look around you for once."

"Was it that obvious?" Edmund chuckled.

"You're a very focused person, Edmund Talbot," Bruce
replied. "And there are many things to focus on on the reefs.
What's happening there is that the small fish, that one's a
blue wrasse," he said, pointing at the bright blue one, "are
picking parasites off the larger fish. Which is an amberjack
by the way."

"Why doesn't it eat them?" Edmund asked. "It seems like
an easy meal."

"Sometimes they do," Bruce said. "But, by and large, they
don't. The small fish get the easy meal. The larger fish get
their parasites picked off. If they didn't have the small fish
around, if they ate them all, they'd end up covered in parasites. Both of them get what they need; it's what's called a
commensal relationship."

"I saw a turtle back there eating what looked like a sponge,"
Edmund said. "What does the sponge get?"

"Eaten," Bruce replied with a shrug. "Predation is predation. But . . . that type of sponge grows over live coral as well
as dead. If it was left unchecked it would spread over the
whole reef, killing it. Tide and currents along with storms
would eventually wipe the remnant coral out. So the whole
ecosystem would die. If you killed all the turtles, it might not
come to pass, there are other things that eat sponges and they
would increase as their food source increased, but you begin
to understand a small bit of the complexity of the web of life
that is a coral reef. Take away the damsel fish and algae grow
unchecked. Parrot fish eat the live coral, but their fecal matter
is almost pure sand because of the rock they have to ingest
to get to the polyps; their shit is what you see as crystal white
sand. But there's something in particular I'd like to show you;
it's not far."

"Let's go," Edmund said, turning away from the cleaning
station.

Down the section of patch reef a large coral head rose up
in the middle of an expanse of low rocks. It was about three
meters high and two across, tapering a bit like a teardrop. It

was colored a faint green, as if it had some algae all over it. Sections of it were covered with the mosslike growths he'd seen elsewhere.

"This is Big Greenie," Bruce said, coasting to a stop and letting the current carry him past the coral head. "It's a species called green coral and it is the oldest living organism on earth."

"I thought that was some tree in western Norau?" Edmund said, peering at the rock. "And is it alive?"

"Oh, yes," Bruce said. "See the fuzzy patches?"

"I'd noticed them before," Edmund admitted. "They look like it's covered in moss."

"Those are the live polyps," Bruce corrected. "They're actually related to jellyfish. Think of them as upside down jellyfish surrounded by a rock shell. They're filter feeders; they extend tendrils that catch plankton as it passes by. Once a year they reproduce, releasing clouds of sperm and eggs to drift on the wind. But Big Greenie, here, has been doing that for seven million years."

"Damn," Edmund said, impressed.

"It very nearly died," Bruce continued. "Water conditions in the mid-twenty-first century were terrible. There was, as it later turned out, a normal climactic shift to higher temperatures, then the cycle reversed and there was a sharp temperature decline, a mini–ice age. All of those created temperature stresses. Toxins released by industry into the water, divers touching the reef, industrial fishing that removed vital species, all of it nearly killed something that had lived for millions of years. There were sections of this reef where less than ten percent included live polyps; that was a recipe for disaster."

"Your point?" Edmund said, dryly.

"You are, as I mentioned, very focused, Edmund Talbot. But while it's important to focus on the trees, sometimes you have to let the forest speak for itself. I'm showing you the oldest tree in the forest because I thought it was something that you could focus upon. This is what the Work is all about; ensuring that the reef, Big Greenie included, is never brought to those conditions again."

Edmund thought about that for a moment, kicking against the current to carry him back to the coral head. He dropped down to the bottom and looked at it closely, then backed up when he saw the head of a very large moray stuck back in a crevice near the coral's base.

Finally he swam back to where Bruce was waiting patiently.

"I understand what you mean," Talbot said.

"There's a 'but' there," Bruce replied.

"There's a huge 'but' there," Edmund admitted. "The first 'but' is that the conditions that you're talking about don't apply. *Won't* apply. To get to the conditions you describe will require industry, major industry. Which cannot exist given the explosive protocols."

"Toxins can be created without internal combustion," Bruce said with a frown.

"Not on large scale, without internal combustion or electrical energy. The first is prevented by Mother under the explosive protocols. And any power production gets sucked up by the damned Net. So you cannot have large-scale industry. You have no idea what I'd give right now for a couple of tons of sulfuric acid, for example, but producing it in a low-tech environment is a stone bitch."

Bruce opened his mouth but Edmund raised a hand.

"Give me a second here." Edmund grinned. "You had your say. If we win this war, the entire system comes back online and all the conditions before the Fall hold. You'll be able to replicate all your needs again. There won't be any industry, any more than there was for a thousand years before the Fall. Nor will there be any more visitors, because there aren't that many people and even with the natural population increase that is going on, there won't be more than a billion and a half, two billion max, in the next hundred years. There's also a maximum even past that point; you can only support so many humans on preindustrial agriculture. You forgot nutrient run-off in your litany, by the way."

"It's in there," Bruce said, grimly. "Flora bay was nearly killed by it. And the bay is the nursery for half the ecosystem in this region."

"But that won't happen because you cannot transport the fertilizers from where they are to where they are needed," Edmund snapped. "God knows we're running into that already in Raven's Mill. My point is that while the war is going on, the reefs are still out of danger. But *you* are not."

"So you've said," Bruce shrugged. "But New Destiny doesn't have a reason to attack us."

"I'm not talking about New Destiny," Edmund replied. They had drifted away from the coral head on the current and were headed in the general direction of town. "Your people are excessively vulnerable. And they are valuable to more than just us and New Destiny. We passed a settlement on the way here in Bimi island. With your underwater abilities, you're a priceless asset to a group like that. How long until they come to the conclusion that since you're unwilling to assist them, they should force you to?"

"How are they going to do that?" Bruce said, angrily.

"I don't know," Edmund replied with a shrug. "But some of them, maybe not now, but soon, will figure out a way. "Why should they dive for lobster when you can do that for them?"

"We could ally ourselves with them, just as well," Bruce replied.

"They can't protect you from New Destiny," Edmund retorted. "And they have far less to lose than we do. You'd be the cleaner fish to their big fish. Sure, it's a commensal relationship, but if I had my druthers, I'd be the big fish. The cleaners can't snap me up."

"And you wouldn't be the big fish?"

"We need willing allies," Edmund said, reasonably. "We need you to scout for us, to fight for us if we can figure out a way. To communicate with the delphinos and the other cetoids. To find the New Destiny ships so that we can destroy them before they destroy us. Before they come to my land and I have to fight them at my damned *walls*. That's not big fish to little fish. We can't force you to do those things. How do we know that you intentionally missed some fleet? It's a big damned ocean, as I'm coming to understand. But I can damned well tell you that the fishermen will get out their whips if you don't come back with enough lobster."

"You create problems that don't exist," Bruce said, still angry.

"Maybe, but here's one that already exists: you're starving to death."

"We're getting by," Bruce said, defensively.

"Barely, as primitive hunter gatherers, dependent on what you can bring in each day," Edmund said, warming to his own anger. "Damnit, Bruce, you're responsible to your *people*, not just to this reef! I've got people under my protection that were members of the Wolf terraforming project. Are they working on it now? No, they're working on rebuilding civilization; not scavenging for food in the forests. And you're not even *good* hunter gatherers. You're losing body weight; Daneh can prove that. You've had people die from nutrient deficiencies. We can *help*. So you don't want gill nets, fine, they take too many of the fish you don't want and damage the reef. Fine. We can provide seine nets instead. You can target your prey that way. There are other things your people have asked for. Lobster pots, long lines—"

"No long lines," Bruce snapped. "They're nearly as bad as drift nets!"

"Whatever," Edmund replied. "Tell me what you want and we'll provide it. Within reason. You're not the only group we have to support with arms and materials."

"What's within reason?" Bruce replied.

Ah, hah. "That's to be worked out. We can provide the fighters with some weapons. The bronze is better for your purposes; it can be resharpened easily, unlike the stainless. But it's hard to make and there are no sources of made material whereas we can get blanks, have blanks, of the stainless in quantity. But that's hard to work as hell, it takes time which means money. We'll set up a credit system for support and ensure solid, and honest, trade, under UFS trading laws. We're not going to strip you of people and with our support there are products that you can trade for luxuries and that way you won't be entirely dependent upon us. As I said, the details have to be worked out, but they are *details*. As willing allies in a mutual protection pact we're not going to let you starve at the very minimum. Your mer-men and -women won't have to scrabble for every little reef-fish they can catch. And maybe even not have to eat sushi for the rest of their lives."

Bruce considered this for a pace and then shrugged.

"I come out here to convince you, and you half convince me," Bruce said.

"The reef will survive, with or without you," Edmund said. "But, here and now, the crisis is the war against New Destiny. Win the war and the reef will be waiting for you. As you yourself said, Big Greenie survived the worst that man could throw at her. She's survived natural and unnatural disasters for seven million years. She'll survive this. Assuming that New Destiny doesn't throw huge power bolts into her. Another thing that we can prevent."

Bruce shrugged again and then headed back towards the town. Edmund figured it was as good as he was going to get. For now.

Rachel pawed among the leaves and vines, her fins kicking at, and above, the water's surface to keep her in place. She was mostly finding hard, unripe fruits among sea plum growth.

"Sea plum's one of those 'good-bad' things," Elayna said, foraging in slightly deeper water. "It's more of a pest in the waters around Flora, but it has some really specific growing requirements."

The bed of vines was anchored near the spring on Whale Point Drop but the vines stretched for meters in every direction.

"It interferes with the sea grasses some," Antja said, sitting up so her head was out of the shallow water and looking around, then bobbing back down to continue to forage. "The roots have to have fresh water, but the fruits will only mature in salt. So it's *only* found where there's a strong freshwater flow that meets salt water. That means right around spring runoffs like this one for the most part. And it only grows so far. So it's not a terrible pest. And it supports most of the species that sea grass does, for that matter."

"There are all sorts of little fish and . . . stuff in here," Rachel said. "But not much in the way of mature plums. Elayna, can I ask you a question?"

"Sure," the girl said, her bright blue tail waving out of the water as she rummaged in the vines.

"Where's the eel?"

"Oh, I only bring Akasha out for special occasions," Elayna said, "And generally only at night. During the day she hides in her cave. I think this bed has mostly been picked over," she added with a sigh. "We need to go find something else. Conch? Lobster?"

"Conch is generally found around sea grass," Antja said, looking at Rachel. "But the nearest bed is klicks away. I think we need to go bugging."

"Bugging?" Rachel asked.

"Looking for crayfish," Elayna said, then added: "Lobster."

"Oh."

"Mostly the way that we do that is to swim upstream so we can coast back," Antja said, swimming towards the inlet's mouth. "But we've been here long enough that most of the upstream stuff has been picked over like the sea plum. The lobster move around; they come in to refill the niches they hide in, but that takes a little time. So, I'd suggest heading east, if you're up for a hard swim back?

"I think so," Rachel replied, picking up the string-mesh bag that had a few fruit in it. "What is this made of?" she asked as she followed the two mer-girls out to sea. They were swimming slowly since she was a virtual cripple in the water but it was still a little fast for her and she was glad when they caught the current and it pushed them to the east.

"Mostly seaweed stems," Antja said. "We make some from the sea plum, too, but if you cut the vine, you don't get the fruit. Hard choice."

"And both of them rot quickly," Elayna complained. "And aren't very strong to start with. They're not very good."

"This is something we can help with," Rachel said. "I don't know if cosilk or hemp would be best, but we have both. Not a lot, yet, but more every year as we break more ground."

"What I'd really like is a bathing suit top," Antja said, looking at Rachel's two-piece. "I'm really tired of having my breasts on display all the time. There are times that I don't like being looked at that way, if you know what I mean. I won't even comment on the occasional touch."

"Speak for yourself," Elayna said happily. "I like the looks. I don't even mind the touch, if it's the right hands."

"That's because you're a slut, Elayna," Antja said, without rancor.

"She's not a slut," Rachel challenged. "She's just . . . comfortable with showing off her body. But I know what you mean, Antja. Even this thing is too skimpy for me. I never really showed off, much, before the Fall. Except, you know, when I was younger . . ."

"Putting on as little as your mom would let you get away with and going out in public to flaunt?" Antja said with a grin.

"Oh, I'd shake it," Rachel laughed. "But then . . . some of the looks I'd get. They just made me shiver, you know? And I started putting my clothes back on. Since the Fall . . . with . . . some of the things that have happened, you never catch me anymore except in long skirts or slacks and a high-buttoned shirt. I don't want the looks. At all."

"Well, *I* don't mind them, thanks," Elayna said. "And I'm not a slut. A slut is some girl that sleeps with any guy that crooks a finger. I'm much pickier. Now, Bast, *Bast* is a slut."

"Not by your definition," Rachel said with a laugh. "By your definition, she's perfect. But she wouldn't mind being called a slut; she'd probably take it as a compliment. But Bast is *very* choosy and as far as I can see . . . sort of serially monogamous. I didn't realize it at first, but she really is. She's never even *looked* at another guy since she started dating Herzer, at least not around Raven's Mill. And, God knows, *Herzer* doesn't worry about hopping from bed to bed. If you'd like a slut, Herzer's the male definition. But Bast isn't. Hell, she chose my father when he was not much older than Herzer and they apparently were quite an item for damned near a decade."

"Really?" Elayna gasped. "Your *dad*?"

"*Oh*, yeah," Rachel said with a wicked grin. "Apparently back then, Dad must have really been something. Heck, he was living with Aunt Sheida before he met my mom and that was either post Bast or concurrent; I've never been sure and I'm not about to ask. And then he tossed them *both* over for Mom. Now *that* must have been a spectacular breakup."

"Aunt Sheida?" Antja said, picking up on the name. "Not the council member?"

"Yep, now *Queen* Sheida of the United Free States. Even back then she was number two or three on the list for a Key, and they don't hand those out at raffles. But here Dad is bouncing from Bast to Sheida and then finally settling on *Mom* of all women."

"So he's never slept with Bast again?" Elayna said. "That's hard to believe. She's so . . ."

"Sensual," Rachel finished the sentence. "After Mom left him, taking me along, he apparently had some time with Bast. But . . . I'm not sure what was going on there. I'd say he needed the company; he was really busted up when Mom left."

"When was this?" Antja asked.

"When I was about four," Rachel said, sadly, remembering the arguments vaguely as not happy times. "My dad was a really serious reenactor before the Fall. He lived in a stone house, cooked his own food, or had a nanny servant do it anyway, the whole thing. Like some feudal lord. I mean, it wasn't crazy living; he had hot and cold running water. But it was from a cistern on the hill and *that* was filled from a spring. When I say cold I mean *cold*. Anyway, the way I pieced it together, Mom wasn't willing to raise me like that and he wasn't willing to leave. So he clung to his life like a limpet and . . . Mom made a new one. He came and lived with us for a while but he just couldn't hack it. Technology really seems to drive him crazy if he's living with it every day. So by the time I was six or so, he was gone for good. I'd still visit him from time to time, especially for Faire. It was great when I was a kid. Dad was the local 'Lord' and I'd get all dressed up and people would fuss over me. But then as I got older, it just got so . . . old. So I stopped going to visit him."

"What happened?" Elayna said. "Why'd you go back?"

"Duh, the Fall, dummy," Antja chuckled, grimly.

"Duh, indeed," Rachel said with a frown. "Mom and I lived . . . hell, not that far from Raven's Mill. No more than a hundred klicks. Do you know how hard it is to walk a hundred klicks, carrying food, in the middle of the storms they had after the Fall?"

"Yuck," Elayna muttered.

"Yeah. But what more perfect place to go? Before the Fall it was 'This water is like ice and why do I have to use this old-fashioned flush commode? Why don't you just transport like any normal person, Daaadddy!' When I got there and saw a flush commode, and a hot bath being drawn, I cried like a baby. No more squatting in bushes! No more rough flannel and cold river water! Mom . . ." She stopped and breathed for a moment. "Mom got first crack at the tub. But, anyway, that's how Mom and Dad got back together. And . . . after a while they got back to being . . . friends. For a while there, it was really sickening, like two giggly teenagers. Now they're just . . . well, they're just about the most perfect couple I've ever seen. They discuss problems, rarely lose their temper with each other and compliment one another for what they do. And Bast, returning to the subject of the discussion, has been smart enough not to interfere. Why should she? She's got Herzer!"

"So what about you and Herzer?" Elayna asked. "I heard you were sharing a room on the ship? Care to pass on any tips?"

"He snores," Rachel said, sweetly. "As for the rest, Herzer's like my brother. I . . . we've never. We're not going to be doing that."

"Why?" Antja asked, reasonably. "I mean, I've got Jason and Herzer's got no tail to speak of, but that doesn't mean I can't see the attraction. Hell, you've only got to take one look at his bathing suit to see one attraction."

"I did!" Elayna snickered.

"Well . . ." Rachel said, coloring slightly. "If . . . if there's such a thing as an 'antislut' that's me. That doesn't mean I'm down on girls who enjoy bed hopping; Marguerite was one of my best friends before the Fall and she lost her virginity about the time she started blooming tits. And never looked back. But me . . . I've just never been interested."

"You mean in guys?" Elayna asked.

"I mean in sex," Rachel responded. "Guys or girls. I just don't care. I like guys, and girls, as friends. But I'm not interested in . . . all the squishy awfulness. It sort of makes me queasy to tell you the truth."

"That's weird," Elayna said. "I can't really imagine that."

"That's because you've got a sex drive," Rachel said with a sad frown. "I don't. It's like being tone-deaf. You can listen to the music, but all it is is noise. Unpleasant noise at that. The thought of . . . Herzer's dick in me is . . . ooooh!" she ended with a shudder of disgust.

"Okay," Antja said. "I have to agree, that's weird."

"Well if a normal sex drive is like a five," Rachel said with a shrug. "And Elayna here is, say, an eight, I'm like a negative one."

"And what's Bast?" Elayna said.

"Three thousand one hundred and fifteen," Rachel laughed. "More or less."

They had drifted to an area of scattered patch reef, most of them a meter or so high, and Antja suddenly darted downward, reaching into a crevice.

"Gotcha," she said, pulling the lobster out of its hole. It waved its antennae at her furiously and kicked with its tail but most of the motion stopped when she wrung the body off of the tail and dropped the latter into her bag.

"They generally hang out under ledges and in cracks," Antja said, dropping down to the sand bottom to swim along the side of the section of reef. She was peering into the ledges under the rock and then darted her hand in again. This time she drew it out with an expression of disgust.

"What we need is spears for this," she said. "It's not particularly sporting but we're not here for sport."

Rachel coasted a little farther down and picked out her own patch of rock. She got down on the sand and looked under the reef but it was nearly black to her eyes. The sun was high and shining down through the water as if the ten meters or so over her head wasn't even there. And the shadows under the rock were nearly impenetrable. But she could see stuff on the sides, little fish darting in and out. Then she saw a shadow move under the rock and backed up in a hurry as a small shark came sculling out lazily. At least, she thought it was a shark. It looked a little like one except that the mouth was pursed as if it had been eating a lemon.

"Nurse shark," Elayna said as she swam by. "They're harmless if you don't bother them. On the other hand, they'll tear you a new one if you do. A guy before the Fall, a mer and he should have known better, tried to ride one. Fortunately the nannites fixed him right up. But he Changed back to normal human and never got in the water again."

"How do you see under here?" Rachel said. She had changed patches and was now looking under the new rock, warily.

"You get used to it," Antja said, drifting past. She now had three lobster tails in her bag, one of which was huge. "Watch them, though, they've got spines. You have to grip them firmly but not hard. Firmly enough that they can't get away; they'll rip you up struggling out of your hand. But don't grab them so hard that you poke yourself."

"Great," Rachel said, catching a glimpse of some antennae waving just down the reef. She pushed herself off the bottom with her fingers and snuck up on the crayfish. It was apparently unworried about her approach, except for waving its antennae more aggressively. She moved her hand in closer and then lunged. She wasn't quite fast enough, but she got ahold of the antennae at the base, surprised by the struggle the lobster was putting up. She managed to get her other hand around it and then wrung the tail off quickly.

"Got one," she said, happily. Then noticed the small cuts in the fingers that had snagged the antennae. The salt water stung them but there wasn't much she could do about that.

"Gloves," Elayna said, popping up from a section of reef about ten meters away. "That's what we really need: Gloves."

"Not if you use a spear," Antja said. She was out of sight, only her golden-red tail sticking up out of the reef. The colors only really came out when they were close to the surface.

"Why do you guys all have colorful tails when the water makes them all look brown or green at depth?" Rachel asked, going back to her hunting.

"Our eyes process out the blue light," Antja replied, then paused as she apparently lunged for another lobster. "Until we get deep and that's all there is. But when we're at, say, twenty meters, we see things just as clearly, color-wise, as you do up here. But by the time you get down to say, thirty or forty meters, it kicks back over to 'normal' vision because just about everything but blue has gone away."

"Is it harder for you to see?" Rachel asked. "I mean, down by the town and stuff. Everything down there is blue."

"No," Elayna replied. "We've got superior night vision, too. Kind of like a cat. We can probably see better than you can. That might be why we can see under the rocks better, too."

"I see this one," Rachel said, darting in and getting ahold of the body this time. She'd figured out her grip and didn't get cut for her troubles, but her hand scraped on the rock as she drew the struggling crustacean out. She also realized that she was tired. And there was a long swim back against the current. "This isn't easy."

"No, it's not," Antja said. "I'm not sure we're getting more calories than we're going to burn off, especially with having to swim back against the current carrying the tails."

Rachel thought about that and then laughed.

"I'll carry them back," she said, spotting another lobster. "I can walk up on the shore. That way you guys don't have to wait for me to catch up."

"Works," Elayna said. "But we can keep in the shallows, that way you'll have company. That way you can tell me all of Herzer's terrible secrets."

"I think those are Herzer's to tell," Rachel said, pausing in her hunt.

"Oh, that's no fun," Elayna replied.

"Well, most of Herzer's life *before* the Fall doesn't contain many terrible secrets," Rachel replied as her hand darted in and just missed the more wary crayfish. It had been a large one, too. "He had a genetic condition that my mom cured, just before the Fall, fortunately. It got worse as he got older and especially worse around puberty. He . . . didn't have many friends and *no* girlfriends to speak of."

"That's pretty unbelievable," Antja said. Her bag was nearly full and she rested on the top of the reef for a moment. Rachel suddenly realized that the scales on their tails had more than decorative purposes; if she had tried that, with the mild swell that was pushing over the rocks, she would have come away with a scraped-raw butt.

"He . . . twitched," Rachel said, finding it hard to explain. "He worked out but he couldn't keep any muscle mass; he was like a shaking twig all the time. And he had a speech impediment. Sometimes he'd drool or one of his limbs would just start spasming. It was . . . awful to watch. He'd been a fun kid, played sports, and then this . . . disease just wasted him away. I admit I started avoiding him. I'm pretty ashamed by that but it was just too weird. Anyway, Mom figured out a cure just before the Fall. Basically she killed and brought him back to life." Rachel swallowed at another thought she didn't want to voice. "Which . . . makes them bound in a weird way. Anyway, that's why he didn't have girlfriends. Now *after* the Fall," she continued with an evil glint in her voice, "that's another story."

"So I'm just the latest?" Elayna asked. "I'd sort of figured; he was . . . pretty good. Actually, darned good."

"A lot of that is because of Bast," Rachel replied. She popped up over the reef to see Antja taking a bite out of one of the lobster tails. "Aren't we supposed to be sharing with the town?"

"I've got too much to carry back," Antja said, reasonably. "If I eat some, I carry it in my stomach."

"We can switch out bags," Rachel replied. "I'm never going to fill this one at this rate."

"Works," Antja said, finishing off the lobster tail and wiping her hands on her scales. "These things are a lot better cooked, though."

"So, why's it Bast?" Elayna said. Her tail was flipping back and forth savagely as she shoved an arm deep into a crevice. "Hah, gotcha ya bastard."

"Bast considers it a solemn duty to train her current boytoy," Rachel replied, dryly. "And she's been doing a lot of training with Herzer."

"It shows," Elayna laughed. "Although it took him a few minutes to figure out the differences in anatomy. After that it was great."

"Herzer has two great skills in life," Rachel said. "Fighting and . . . the other. I wish I could appreciate either one."

She snagged another lobster and carried it over to Antja, who was dragging what had been Rachel's bag behind her. It was more than half full.

"How do you do that so quickly?" Rachel asked.

"I've been doing it since I was a kid," Antja replied. "My parents were mer and they had me as a mer; I've been bugging my whole life that I can remember. For that matter, I've hunted this reef before; I know where they tend to hang out. Try over there," she said, pointing to a patch of reef that looked identical to the empty one that Rachel had just been working.

When Rachel approached the reef she could understand half of Antja's success; the ledge under the rock was packed with bugs from side to side, their antennae waving at her angrily. She reached into the mass and snatched one out while the others skittered from side to side, trapped by her body and the shallow ledge. As fast as she could reach she pulled lobsters out and wrung their tails. Some skittered by her, turning to use their powerful tails to skim over dangerous open ground, but she heard Elayna whoop behind her and dive on them.

In moments she had over a dozen tails lying on the ground among the scattered bodies of the lobster.

"So it's a trick," she said, smiling, as she gathered up the tails.

"Sure, isn't everything?" Antja replied. "I think that about does it. Three bags full as they say."

"So, you were born as a mer," Rachel said. "Did they, what?

Did they crack the can under water? Some sort of underwater uterine replicator? What?"

"No," Antja said, in a tone that showed she didn't want to discuss it.

"Sorry," Rachel replied, hurt. Given everything that they had been talking about it seemed a harmless enough subject.

"I'm sorry, too," Antja said. "I just don't want to talk about it, okay?"

"Okay," Rachel said. Then she paused and her brow furrowed. "Antja, after the Fall, all the controls on the landsmen, well, let me make this plain, the lands*women*, reproductive system turned off. We had an awful time with the first . . . menstruation. Did yours?" she asked, delicately.

"Yes," Antja said, tightly. "On the other hand, they designed mer better than 'normal' humans; we, thank God, don't menstruate."

"But, you *are* fertile?" Rachel asked, realizing that she'd just tiptoed into a minefield as Elayna came over a rock with a set expression on her face. "You and Jason could have a baby? Elayna, for that matter, might be carrying Herzer's?" She looked over at Elayna who had a stricken expression on her face as if that thought had just occurred to her.

"Yes, we are," Antja said. "I wish you would stop pursuing this line of questioning."

"Sorry," Rachel said, "call me incurably curious. Just one more: Antja, what happened to the babies?"

CHAPTER TWENTY-FOUR

Daneh had spent most of the day working with the mer healers. They had no trained doctors but a few of the mer had been familiar with basic first aid and had been pressed into service. Unfortunately, in the saltwater environment there was not much that could be done. The flip side was that many of the standard infections were unable to gain a hold.

Mostly what they had to deal with were poisons from the various denizens of the deep, rashes from running up against the wrong coral and the occasional shark bite. She was shown one such, a nasty gash on the mer-man's tail that had been clumsily stitched up. She gave a brief class on proper suturing, something that she had learned only after the Fall, and suggested some poultices for the rashes. They had about done the rounds when Germaine, one of the healers, drew her aside.

"Mistress Daneh," the mer-woman said, nervously. "There's something I need to show you, one case we'd like some help on. But Bruce said we weren't to tell you about it. You can't let on that I did this."

"I won't," she said. "Where is it?"

"It's a bit of a swim," the mer admitted. "I'll see if I can find a delphino that will give you a ride."

She came back some time later with one of the delphinos.

"This is Buttaro," Germaine said.

"Daneh, lady," the delphino spit. "Help baby?"

"Yes, I will," Daneh said. "If I can."

"Hold fin," the delphino said, rolling so that she could grasp the dorsal. "Go."

The delphino stayed low to the reef as they headed for the inlet overlooked by the lighthouse then turned towards where the spring was. On the far side of the spring it took a breath though its blowhole and then dove towards the bottom where there was a crack in the rocks.

The way led through a twisted series of tunnels and then Daneh saw blue light ahead. They surfaced in a cave.

She had noticed that some of the mer were pregnant, but had not seen any babies. As she entered the cave her ears were assaulted by the sound of at least a dozen, mostly crying. There were more than babies in the vaulted, but crowded, cave. Mer-women swam around the rocky shelves, leading some of the older infants in water games.

Germaine surfaced by her and looked at her pleadingly.

"Mer can't breathe water at first," she said, coughing out a lungful of water. "They don't have the mass to fight the cold and their lungs aren't strong enough. They have to be born on land. They have to *stay* on land for a year, generally, until they can live in the water."

"This is one hell of an Achilles' heel," Daneh said, quietly. "I can see why you didn't want us to know about it. You'd better hope like hell New Destiny doesn't."

She led the way to one of the ledges but was confronted by an angry mer-woman.

"Germaine, I can't believe you brought a landie here!" the woman snapped.

"Daneh is a doctor, Rema," Germaine replied, just as hotly. "Would you rather that Maturi die?"

"No, but . . ."

"I don't know if I can do anything," Daneh said, soothingly. "But I will try. And I promise that I will do nothing to endanger your babies."

The woman looked at her questioningly, then shrugged.

"Do what you can," she said. "For all it's worth."

Germaine led her to the ledge and then climbed out awkwardly, crawling to the rear where a very young mer-maid cradled a child in her arms.

Daneh took one look at the baby and made a reasonable diagnosis, but she wanted to be sure. She looked at the mermaid and held out her arms for the baby.

"Daneh is a doctor," Germaine said. "A real doctor. She might be able to help."

The girl looked up at her pleadingly, then handed the baby over.

Daneh walked carefully through the crowd of mer-folk, packed nearly hip to hip on the small ledge, to where the light was better and examined the baby closely. It, she wasn't sure if it was a he or a she because of the recessed genitals, was clearly a newborn, but the baby was far under what should to be normal weight and had a yellowish tint to the skin. It was sleeping but when she rolled back one eyelid it woke up and gave a pitiful mew of displeasure. The whites of its eyes were yellow as well.

"It's not serious," she said, returning to where the girl lay. "I think. If we can get it out of this cave. Is this a he or a she? I can't tell."

"He," Germaine said. "What is it?"

"Childhood jaundice," Daneh replied. "I'm relatively sure. It's definitely jaundice. In adults that comes from damage to the liver but in children it can manifest from birth."

"He's never been strong," the girl said, her mouth working. "And he's been that color."

"He needs sunlight," Daneh said, looking around the gloomy cavern. There were only a few slits that let in light. "Which clearly is in short supply. It helps if he can be given oil from fish livers, if I recall correctly. But sunlight alone might cure him."

"Just sunlight?" Germaine said, aghast. "Are you sure?"

"No," Daneh snapped. "I don't have medical nannites to make a diagnosis, nor do I have any to effect a cure. But I've seen it before and we had items at Raven's Mill that permitted me to research a similar case. And sunlight alone worked for her."

"He can hold his breath well," the girl said. "But if he swallows water he won't be able to cough it back out as weak as he is."

"Mer children, we have learned," Germaine said, "have a much stronger breath hold reaction than normal human children. But it's a long swim."

"Where would you take him on the surface?" Daneh asked.

"There's a sheltered cove that we use to wean the children to the outside," Germaine replied.

"Not far, I take it?"

"No."

Daneh stripped off her mask and placed it on the child's head where it conformed as well as to an adult. The mer-baby didn't like the sensation and gave off a tooth grating yowl of fear, thrashing his head from side to side.

"It's okay," Daneh said, putting out her hand. "He can use it to breathe on the way out. But, please, bring it back to me," she said, gesturing at the blue-lit water. "There's no way that I can make that swim on my own."

"Thank you," the girl said, crawling over and touching her on the leg. "Thank you."

"Thank me when he gets well," Daneh said, squatting down to hand the child to Germaine who was already back in the water. "It will probably be a week or so. And he may have sustained some permanent liver damage. And there's a possibility with infantile jaundice of brain damage. But if we caught it in time, he should be fine."

"Thank you," the girl said again, slithering over the edge of the rock into the water and heading for the entrance.

"You might not be so bad after all," Rema said from the water's edge.

Daneh walked over and dangled her feet in the water, looking around the sound-drenched cavern.

"Like I said when I surfaced," she sighed. "This is one hell of an Achilles' heel."

"Let me tell you a story from the bad old days," Rema said, hoisting herself out and sitting with her tail flapping in the water. "Fur seals give birth once a year. They congregate in colonies up in the Arctic. When the pups are born their fur is milk white, ice white to blend into the ice they are born upon. It's also very soft."

"I'm not going to like this story, am I?" Daneh asked.

"No, you're not," the mer-woman replied. "Well, at some point this was discovered by man. And men would go up into those seal rookeries and use clubs to bash in the heads of the seal pups. Up on land, there wasn't much that the mothers could do."

"I was right, I didn't like the story," Daneh said, looking around the cavern. The mer-babies were apparently born with almost gray tails, but over time they took on the whatever shade they were meant to have as adults. She could envision the genetic coding still. She shook her head and sighed again. "You need guards. Guards with legs."

"And give our hearts into the hands of the guards, you mean?" Rema asked. "You see our problem. Who watches the watchmen?"

"There's one group that, at least in this generation, I would trust with this treasure," Daneh said. "But only one group. And only in this generation."

"And what do we pay them with?" Rema asked. "Sex with mer-maids?"

Daneh laughed and waved her hand at the expression of fury on the mer-woman's face.

"No, it's not that," she said, still chuckling. "It's just that the only representative of that group has, unless I'm much mistaken, already been paid in that coin."

Elayna had invited herself along so it was a fairly large group: the three riders, Herzer and Bast, Elayna, Jason and Pete who took off, strapped to various dragons.

"Delphinos were signaling that there was a group of tuna feeding somewhere to the southwest," Jason called as the wyverns reached cruising altitude. They had fed skimpily and were hungry for more.

The group headed out in the indicated direction and soon saw the feeding school, spotting it first by a large flock of birds overhead.

"There's more than tuna down there," Herzer called as they swept low over the assembly. The school of fish—it was hard to call them bait fish since most of them were fair-sized eating for a human—was absolutely huge, stretching for nearly a klick in one direction and a half a klick in the other. The fish were mouthing at the surface creating a pattern of circular ripples while at the edges the larger predators churned the surface into froth.

"Mackerel," Pete called. "And there's everything on them. Sailfish, marlin, tuna. Hell there's probably wahoo and barracuda in the mix!"

"We can just fill this net with mackerel," Jason said. "Mackerel's good eating. Getting them *back* is going to be the problem."

"Dolphins," Koo called. "Or maybe delphino, bearing in from the northeast."

"How do you want to do this, Jason?" Joanna called.

"This was Herzer's idea," Jason pointed out. "The riders are going to have to stay up at the surface. And God only knows what's down there. Can they swim that long? How do we get back? Is something going to eat them?"

"Joanna, can you hold out on breakfast for a while?" Herzer yelled.

"Not happily," she replied. "But if you want me to play shark guard, I will."

"And you're positively buoyant," he said. "The riders can hold onto you if they get tired."

"I'm only buoyant up to a point," she replied. "But I see the logic. The wyverns can feed first."

"Then we get one or more of them back so the riders can hold onto them," Herzer said. "If the delphinos will let us, we'll ride back with them, the dragons following. Maybe the dragons can pull the net, maybe the delphinos. We'll scoop some of the mackerel for them, making their hunting easier."

"That's how we usually handle it," Jason said. "But with lots less fish."

"Well, let's get down, get the mer unstrapped, talk to the delphinos and get the net deployed."

The scene underwater in the bait school was a maelstrom. The sounds of the cavitation of literally millions of fish filled the water with a sound like thunder. Scales from dead and damaged fish rained down in a continuous silver-glittering cloud. And in every direction fish of various sizes were swimming chaotically. Besides the sound and the movement, the colors of the fish were confusing. A group of sailfish, swimming past faster than a dragon, were changing hue along their sides, rippling with blue and yellow stripes as they passed. Narrow, torpedolike fish that Pete identified as wahoo were marked the same way. The mackerels themselves changed hue constantly, presumably to make it harder for their predators to fix on any one fish. The chaotic patterns, the sound, the enormous sense of *movement* were oddly terrifying.

Herzer finally tore his eyes away from the spectacle and grabbed onto Joanna's spread wings. The delphinos had clustered in her shadow and he saw more forms clustering in the depths. As he watched a mackerel, squirted out of the school by the press of the predators, dart across towards the shadow and presumed safety. One of the forms rose in a way that at first seemed slow and lazy, then suddenly sped up, slashing in for a strike on the bewildered bait fish. The form turned out to be a massive marlin that quickly darted back into the deeps, the tail of the mackerel sticking out one side of its beak.

"I don't know where to start," Jason admitted.

"Don't really look at it," Herzer said. "Unfocus. Just let it all be a blur."

The dragons were clearly having some of the same problems but it hadn't slowed them much. They darted into the swarm, just a few more large predators to feast on the plenty, and started picking off fish at the edge, mostly the predators that had come for the mackerel.

Herzer had come for tuna, primarily, but they were running so fast it was hard to keep an eye on them. They would go by so fast that even by panning his head it was hard to see them as anything other than a blur. Their tails *were* a blur; they seemed to move faster than a hummingbird's wing.

He found himself getting overwhelmed again and took his own advice, grabbing a corner of the net as Jason spread it out.

"Right," Jason said, finally. "We'll just head into the school. When I give the word, Herzer and Elayna just try to hold steady and Pete and I will swing it around." He looked at the wall of fish of every conceivable size and gulped some water. "Follow me."

Pete and Jason headed straight into the baitball, through the wall of predators. Herzer saw one yellowfin tuna that was bigger than Bast slam into Pete as he neared the mackerel but Pete was merely buffeted for a moment and kept on heading in. Jason was at the top of the net and Herzer could see clearly when he entered the baitball because he simply disappeared.

The net in their way immediately affected the mackerel and a large slice of them, ten meters or so long and a few meters deep, turned aside and formed their own ball as predators slashed into them. Herzer tried to pull the net to a halt at the edge of the main ball but it was wriggling madly in his hands. A tuna slammed dead into his side and both of them rebounded from the impact, shaken. He stuck a hand out and jammed it into the momentarily drifting tuna's gills and was rewarded by a panicked frenzy for his troubles. The tuna, which was not much smaller than he and probably weighed more, thrashed against his side, dragging him off in an upward spiral. He got his hand free and grabbed the net with flesh and metal hands, striving with all his might to kick his way out into the open water. By this time he had been dragged fully into the mackerel and their flashing bodies were all he could see. They swarmed all around him, butting into his side, face, legs, like a thousand maddened cats. Suddenly his head crested the water and try as he might he could not get the net to budge; the weight of the fish in it, their frenzied fighting, Pete and Jason pulling on it, all combined to simply tow him through the water.

Suddenly a talon shot out of the water and grasped the net by his hand. He let go as Joanna took over, dragging the net, and a mass of fish, out of the main school. He gratefully swam out of the frenzy and into the comparative peace alongside.

The net was a gill net, long and relatively short, not the purse seine that would have been ideal for the purposes. But by tying it on the bottom and ends and letting it float to the surface they had gathered a huge quantity of mackerel, and several relatively small and confused tuna.

"You know," Joanna said. "Just when we need that damned ship."

Jason was pulling mackerel out with his hands, mostly those stuck in the net, and handing them to the delphinos. He pulled one out for himself and expertly stripped it of its skin, then tore into the flesh. Joanna dipped her muzzle into the net and caught a couple more along with one of the small tuna.

"Tuna," she said after she swallowed. "Tastes just like chicken."

"The question is," Herzer asked, floating at the surface, "did this work better than, say, diving in and grabbing them by hand or mouth?"

"Oh, yeah," Jason replied. He dipped under the water and blatted at the delphinos.

"Better," Herman said. "Less energy. Better."

"But we have to get the net back to town," Herzer replied.

"Eat fish, fill net, go town," Herman replied. "Fish fresh."

"Yeah," Jason mused. "They'll live in the net, so they'll be fresh when we get back. And they can stay in the net for a day or so, except for getting caught in the weave."

Herzer was watching Chauncey try to catch the big tunas. He had tried to snatch them on the run, but they were just too fast. Finally, he struck out with his half-folded wing and managed to temporarily stun one, which he quickly picked off. Others followed his example and the wyverns were quickly replete with fish.

"They learn," Herzer muttered.

"Oh, yeah," Jerry said. He and the others had swum over to the floating net, from which the delphinos were now stripping the gill-caught fish. "They'd never learn anything if it wasn't by example. When one sees something that works, it copies it. That's half of the way that they're trained."

"That's unusual in the natural world," Herzer pointed out.

"They're not natural," Jerry replied with a shrug. "All this swimming is fun, but this water is damned deep and we're way out here. How long are we going to stay?"

Herzer hadn't really noticed the depth, concentrating on the problem, but he realized they were out over the deeps for sure. The water was a deep, rich blue and the light from the sun formed a cone fading into the depths, his shadow in its midst.

"Dragons are fed, delphinos are fed, mer-dudes and dudettes are fed," Herzer said, tearing his eyes away from the attraction of simply going down and down. "I'd say we fill the net and head for home."

"Works for me," Jerry replied. "I'm getting tired of paddling."

"Try to get the dragons over to you," Herzer said. "They float. In the meantime, we have to try to fill this thing again."

The second time they left the bottom tied and swam the net, with both ends open, into the school. It quickly filled with mackerel, and in this case several very irate, very large, yellowfin tuna. They tied the top and end for good measure, then started dragging it back towards town.

The dragons were content to scull along on the surface and their riders, including Bast and Herzer, took that method of transportation. The mer switched off with the delphinos, who had stubby fingers on the ends of their pectoral fins, dragging the squirming net back to town. So it was a group of very tired, but triumphant, hunters that returned just as the sun was setting with enough protein, on the fin moreover, to last the town for a few days.

CHAPTER TWENTY-FIVE

Jason, Pete, Antja, Elayna and the weapons maker, Jackson, had dragged themselves up on land to join the landsmen for a good old fish fry. The fillets of mackerel had been wrapped in seaweed and left to cook on the coals while they feasted on lobster tails, sliced into cutlets and spitted over the fire. This was the group's share, and maybe a bit more, from the bags the girls had returned with.

"The question is," Jason said, around a mouthful of hot lobster, "can we do this *without* the dragons?"

"If the baitball is nearer the town," Herzer replied, juggling one of the cutlets from hand to hand to cool it. "If you can't swim out fast enough yourself, you can ride on the backs of the delphinos."

"The problem was always getting enough back to town," Jackson said. He was a short, burly mer-man with black hair and tail and the only one that Herzer had seen with a beard. "With nets that's fixed."

"Nets fix a lot of things," Pete said. "Nets, lobster pots, grouper traps, long lines. We can use them all."

"Only if we can get Bruce to go along," Jason pointed out. "He's death on commercial harvesting."

"He's going to find slow going fighting that battle," Antja said, popping a cutlet into her mouth. "This is the first time we've been well fed since the Fall. And while picking lobsters out one by one is fun when it's a game, I'd much rather go pick up filled traps. These tails took most of the day to round up."

"You can trade for all of those things," Edmund pointed out. "You might even be able to find a source for stainless steel. I doubt you'll find one for the bronze. But it's going to be slow going without some sort of support."

"We hear you," Jason said. "We've got the picture. The problem is that if we ally with you, we're New Destiny's enemies. And we have to consider that, carefully."

"You're already their enemies," Herzer replied. "They hate Change. They may have allied with the orcas, but that's a marriage of convenience. If they win, you can bet that their first action will be to round up their so-called allies and put them through a Change of *their* making."

"The ocean is big," Antja said.

"But places where you can birth your young are not so widely found," Daneh interjected.

"What?" Herzer asked.

"What?" the mer-folk all said at once.

"Who told you that?" Jason snapped.

"Someone who needed a diagnosis," Daneh replied mildly. "One that, if they hadn't gotten it, would have led inevitably to the death of the child in question."

"The yellow baby," Antja said.

"Correct," Daneh replied. "A simple case of jaundice that was easily corrected. But there are damned few trained doctors left in the world, and for sure you won't have access to them. That is something else that we can give you no one else can. And there's more."

"Oh?" Jason said. "What?"

"You know how bloody vulnerable you are," Edmund replied. He had obviously been talking to his wife. "We can provide the guards that can ensure your security."

"So we're just supposed to hand over the care of our children to you?" Jackson said. "That's a pretty huge leap of trust."

"It's not like you have a lot of choice," Edmund replied. "We're not going to be the last people to find out about it. You *have* to get guards somewhere."

"Why should we trust you?" Jason asked. "Why *you* as opposed to someone else?"

"Would you trust me?" Herzer asked.

Jason thought about it for a moment then nodded. "Yeah, you I'd trust."

"How about someone that I said could be trusted even more unreservedly than me?" Herzer asked. "Someone to train and command the guard force? We'd draw them from our best soldiers, each of them with experience."

"Gunny?" Edmund asked.

"He's getting a little long in the tooth even for the Academy," Herzer said. "But he'd be just the person to guard whatever you're talking about. And I can't imagine a better retirement spot than down here. We could cycle the Lords through on rotation. I think that most of them would scramble for the spot."

"Station a group of dragon-riders down here as well," Jerry said. "We've got the wyverns for it, but they'll have to be moved east and brought down on carriers. And we need more trained riders."

"If you ally with us, we'll establish a base," Edmund said. "A permanent station. There will be a permanent guard force that can watch over your birthing caverns. Hell, build something less makeshift; from what Daneh told me that place is a deathtrap. Probably not here, I'd prefer someplace more accessible. But we can do it."

"Why?" Jason said. "What is worth all that trouble and expense?"

"We need you, the delphinos even more, against the New Destiny forces," Edmund said. "And, hell, Herzer's right. Guards will give their eyeteeth for the posting. Especially in winter."

"Bimi's not the greatest place in winter," Pete pointed out. "Winds from the north turn it into an icebox from time to time."

"It's a hell of a lot better than Raven's Mill," Rachel replied with a grin.

"Would you have to trust us?" Edmund asked. "Yes. But we will be trusting you, in turn, to give us good information on the Destiny forces. And to be willing to attack them if it comes to it."

"Well, I have to admit, you've convinced me," Jason said. "But it's Bruce you have to convince."

"No," Edmund replied. "I just have to convince enough of the mer that I'm right and he's wrong."

"I don't know that I want to go there," Jackson interjected. "Bruce has a lot of supporters who are going to follow him even if it's the wrong idea and they know it. But we've survived by sticking together."

"That's what the mackerel said," Edmund replied, scooping out one of the fish and unwrapping it from its seaweed. "Right up until they got eaten."

✧   ✧   ✧

When Bruce, inevitably, found out, he was furious.

"I cannot believe that someone showed you the birthing cavern!"

"I'm a doctor," Daneh said, coldly. "There was a sick baby. He's probably going to get well now. He wouldn't have if they hadn't shown me."

"So to save one life they've threatened us all!"

"What threat?" Edmund said. "Seriously. You go on and on about all the history that you've studied, but I guarantee that I know it better than you. I know exactly what hostages those women and children make, but they're hostages *already*!"

"What?" several in the group said.

The discussion was taking place in the middle of the square. For once, thanks to the net full of mackerel and grouper dropped onto the town by returning dragons, there was enough to eat and leisure to gather and discuss the latest crisis.

"Your birthing problems are *always* going to be your greatest weakness," Edmund said. "A weakness you can't control without allies on the surface, allies you can trust unreservedly. There's no way, for example, to change out hostages. Humans, without breath masks, cannot survive underwater. Babies certainly cannot. So you can't force anyone who guards you to give you hostages in return. So, sooner or later, you're going to have to find allies to guard your babies, allies that you trust. Let me ask you this, would you ever, in your wildest dreams, trust New Destiny to guard them?"

From the mutterings from the crowd the answer was clear but Mosur had to pipe up.

"So you're saying we should trust you?"

"Yes," Edmund said. "With more than that. We'll establish a fleet base somewhere in the islands, probably near the Bimi chain. We'll rotate through our finest soldiers, the Blood Lords, Herzer is one, to guard your children. We'll establish a power shield so that if New Destiny strikes, the children will be shielded. Face it, we're the *good guys*. I know well what horrors are possible in war. But we guard *against* them. All of our beliefs, all of our philosophy, say that if we undertake this trust, we will guard it with our lives, our fortunes and our sacred honor. And there are only two choices, us or New Destiny."

As he said this shadows began to fall over the reef and a pod of orcas passed over the square. They started to circle and the largest detached himself and drifted over the gathering.

"So, landie, you say that our brethren should trust you tailless landsmen, do you?" the orca said, drifting to a stop. He paused and rolled one eye at Bruce the Black. "Etool Shanol," the orca said, bowing slightly. "Ambassador from New Destiny."

"Oh, bloody hell," Herzer muttered.

"We had a ship with us, carrying provisions to help you in your need," the orca continued. "But it was brutally waylaid by a ship from the so-called Freedom Coalition and burned, killing everyone on board."

"I'm sure that they approached the, effectively unarmed, carrier with parley flag flying and all good intentions," Edmund replied, dryly. "I'm sure they didn't simply open fire as soon as they were in range."

"We are on a mission of peace," Shanol replied. "Why ever would they attack your craft? So you see the lies that the Freedom Coalition spreads," he said, pulsing the sonar loudly. "They ask you to trust them; I suppose they ask for your support. While all that New Destiny asks is that you remain neutral. We have no need of your support; we orcas as well as other sentients of the ocean support New Destiny. As its name implies, it is the *destiny* of the world for it to grow and prosper. Peacefully, if possible. But the so called Freedom Coalition has thus far prevented it, attacking our leaders at the last peaceful meeting of the Council, so in fear of the historical inevitability of New Destiny that they stooped to violence. They always stoop to violence."

"If the triumph of New Destiny was so inevitable," Edmund replied, "Celine would not have introduced deadly poisons into the meeting. Nor would Paul be attacking us at every turn, building an invasion fleet, gathering forces on his coast. You could just sit back and let historical inevitability take its toll."

"The people of Norau suffer under their tyrannical rule of an *hereditary* aristocracy, *Duke* Edmund," the orca replied, nastily. "It is the duty of New Destiny to free them from their feudal bondage."

"The people of Norau voted upon the constitution," Edmund replied, tiredly. "Groups that have joined since have joined through plebiscites. We do not conscript soldiers, Change people horribly. *We* do not refer to the Changed as 'abominations.' "

"So you say, *Duke* Edmund, but I do not see these people here. I see a duke and his family."

"I am one of those 'people,'" Herzer responded, hotly. "I chose that life over yours, because I've seen the evil that comes wherever New Destiny touches! I will fight you with every ounce of my strength. With my last breath, I will curse you!"

"Ah, yes," the orca replied, smiling as only an orca can smile. "His family and his chosen lapdog. I trust that Mistress Daneh is recovering from her ordeal."

Herzer was halfway across the square before he felt arms holding him back. He struggled for a moment then shook them off and paused, panting.

"You finny bastard," the lieutenant replied. "If it's the last thing I do I'll see your bird-picked carcass floating on the surface."

"So you see the inherent peacefulness of the Freedom Coalition," Shanol replied to the group. "We send peaceful orcas, water dwellers, like you. And an unarmed freighter that is brutally waylaid and sunk. The Coalition sends an armed carrier, a general, and his hot-headed young lieutenant, a lieutenant that has been a party to crimes against *his own people*."

This time, Herzer was able to ignore the jibe.

"My demons are my own, fish-face," he said. "But at least I control them, not let them run at the head of the pack."

"Pod, young man, pod," the orca sighed. "So, you see the truth of the choice. The violent philosophies of the Freedom Coalition, whose stated aim is to take over the world and rule it as they see fit. Or simple neutrality and protection from them by aid of New Destiny."

"Yes, we can see it clearly enough," Jason replied. "Gentle lies in the mouth of the predators upon dolphins and whales or the simple truths spoken by people who have shown themselves to be our friends."

"You may believe who you wish, Jason Farseeker," the orca replied, calmly. "But we are simple eaters of fish, just as you are. Perhaps we do not survive on sea plum, but, then again, who would, given the choice?"

There was a chuckle from the crowd and Edmund looked around and shook his head.

"Bruce and I have been discussing history," Edmund said. "I remember other groups, as should he, who, in their time, claimed 'inevitability.' The strange thing about all such groups, the Nazis, the Communists, the Wahabbists, the Melcon AI, is that, in every single case, those who lived under their benign leadership suffered untold hardships. The Nazis disliked various groups within their control and they were marched to slave labor and gas chambers, killing nearly ten million all told. The Communists believed that things should go a certain way, that things should be done as they commanded, and in their blindness, and often quite open-eyed, they killed nearly a hundred million people before *true* historical inevitability dragged them off their thrones. And everyone knows the story of the AI wars; it is far too grim to repeat. Yet, in every case, the side that claimed inevitability was brought to the ground. By free peoples, going open-eyed to their deaths, aware that they were doing so so that their children, and grandchildren," he added, looking at Bruce, "would not suffer the fates of those *lucky* individuals caught in the clutches of 'historical inevitability.'"

"Yet, you speak of untold hardships," the orca replied. "How many died in Norau, *Duke*? Far more died in the Dying Time than in Ropasa. Because the leaders in Ropasa saw the need for a firm hand and ensured that their people were fit to survive. The people of Ropasa did not starve by roadsides, desperately searching for succor."

"Strangely enough," Edmund said, dryly, "I remember those days. And I seem to recall that New Destiny had a far higher energy budget than the Freedom Coalition. Something about illicit access to the terraforming project power budgets. An access, I might add, that Herzer and I had a hand in ending, preventing the project from total energy drain. But by the time they were done they had taken more than half the power out of the core, putting the project back by over two hundred years."

There was a mutter from the crowd at that. Even in the years after the Fall the Wolf 359 Terraforming Project was remembered, like a good dream at the end of the night. If there was anything to look forward to it was that at the end of the war they, or their children or their grandchildren, could continue the millennia-long project to create a new, livable, planet.

"Lies and damned lies," the orca said smoothly. "Show me proof of this. I would be very surprised if there was any."

"Well, I'd have to have access to Mother, wouldn't I?" Edmund replied. "And if I did, you would question the access. But I was there when Dionys McCanoc destroyed himself in a rush of power. It was I that put him in his prison of energy, a prison that was breached with the power equivalent of a nuclear weapon. Of course, he'd neglected to shield *himself,* so the prison became his tomb. Where, I wonder, did he get all that power? He, the New Destiny tool, who was the sole surviving member of the Project council. All the other members suffered mysterious, or not so mysterious, deaths just prior to and after the Fall."

"You call innuendo and supposition proof?" the orca asked with a blatted chuckle. "But we stray far afield. You want these good people to risk themselves in a doomed gamble. We but wish them to maintain themselves in neutrality. In proof of our goodwill we *had* brought goods to help them, nets, fishhooks, traps and harpoons. Unfortunately, all of them were destroyed by the Freedom Coalition. This is proof, not innuendo."

"And, as I said, I'm sure that it was just a friendly meeting on the sea," Edmund replied. "That your ship did not, for example, attack an unarmed clipper."

"And if it was unarmed," the orca snarled, "how did it sink our *ship*?"

"That, I'll admit, is a puzzler," Edmund said. "Honestly."

"All I know is that they fired some sort of device off of the clipper," the orca replied. "Black and small as a yellow snapper. But the ship stopped and the scuppers ran with blood."

Edmund turned as he heard a liquid chuckle and looked at Bast, who was staring at him with merriment in her eye.

"Are you not glad, Duke Edmund," she said, still chuckling, "that I brought that bedamned rabbit?"

Edmund started chuckling and ended up laughing heartily.

"You think?"

"Aye, methinks. A small object? Scuppers running with blood?"

"Poor doomed bastards," Herzer said, chuckling as well. He turned to Jason and grinned. "Let's just say that we have a secret weapon. It won't usually work, but when it does . . ."

"Scuppers running with blood?" Jason said, gulping. "I don't know."

"You haven't been through territory that New Destiny has ravaged," Herzer replied. "You haven't stood before their Changed orcs, come upon the ruins of buildings, and people, that they leave behind," Herzer said, trying to check himself but realizing that the fury that lurked always just below his calm exterior was coming to the fore. "You haven't seen the feeding pots, with the legs of children turning in the boiling water."

"Lies and damned lies!" the orca bellowed, looming over the unChanged human. "Recant those untruths!"

"When you recant your lies, you . . . you . . . I can smell the flesh of dolphin on your breath like the evil stench of the lies you have been spouting!"

The orca blatted him with sound and hooked his tail around, hitting the lieutenant with a blast of water that struck like a full body hammer. Herzer was thrown backwards through the water, half stunned. But he was used to fighting half stunned and before he had ceased to tumble his knife had appeared in his hand and he circled up and to the right, turning to try to get in on the flank of the orca.

Suddenly the orca found two strong fingers pinching his blowhole and a long, slim, dagger pointed at his eye.

"Take a bite out of my boyfriend," Bast purred, "and I'll drive this all the way to your brain."

"You wouldn't dare," the orca said.

"I've killed better orcas than you," she whispered, staring him in the eye. "And what *you* are is a psychopathic monstrosity. But, then again, so am I," she added and took a deep breath, letting it out in a long, unearthly sonar scream that echoed off the walls of the square.

Herzer shivered and froze as the reverberations of the unholy, multitonal shriek washed through his body. It was the most gut-wrenching sound he had ever heard, including the death shriek of horses, which was as close as he could come to identifying it with a known sound.

"Enough!" Bruce yelled. "Herzer, Bast, you're no longer to come into this town! Ambassador Shanol, I am forced to permit your continued presence, but one more such outburst and I will have you barred from the village as well, and your pod with you. Is that clear?"

"Yes," the ambassador said, blowing out bubbles as a sort of throat clearing. "I . . . regret my outburst. But the statement that I would eat the flesh of my good friends the dolphins . . . you understand."

"Fighting will not be tolerated," Bruce said. "That I understand. Duke Edmund?"

"Herzer is one of my staff," Edmund replied. "And, I might add, has made valuable contributions to this community. But I accept that he is not to come within, say, one hundred meters of the town square. That means if we need to meet, it is a reasonable swim for one or both of us. As for Bast," he sighed. "She goes where she wills."

"I'll not come back to this town until invited," the elf said. "But those *reshanool* had better stay far from me or I'll teach them what the myth of the food chain really means."

"Agreed," Bruce said. "And Ambassador Shanol, you and your pod are to stay away from the visitors from the mainland. The first sign of any further conflict and I am going to expel both groups."

Herzer had already sheathed his knife and now nodded at Edmund, then turned and swam towards shore followed by Bast. As he passed over one of the canyons, Antja and Elayna popped out of a swim-through and Pete and Jackson popped out of another.

"This sucks!" Pete said angrily. "That damned dolphin-eater turns up and you just get tossed out. It's not like you struck the first blow; he hit you solid."

"Yeah," Jackson added. "You okay?"

"I've had worse," Herzer said.

"I'd noticed the scars," Antja said. "But I hadn't wanted to ask. Or about the hand."

"Well, I think it's time to tell you all about it," Herzer said. "But not here. Up on shore where fish-face can't come."

CHAPTER TWENTY-SIX

Herzer was actually glad to get out of the water. He had been losing weight, too, on the high-protein diet and constant cold. The warm sun of the Isles felt good on his back.

"After the Fall, I fell in with a guy named Dionys McCanoc," Herzer said as the group dragged itself onto the shore.

"Met him," Bast said. "Bastard." She sat down behind Herzer and started massaging his neck. "Let me handle the orcas, lover. But if you *have* to fight one, remember they're really sensitive about their blowholes. Get them by that and it's like holding a man's balls. I mean, in a fight, not, you know . . ."

"I know," Herzer said, smiling. Bast could make everything a joke, which was just about the only way to live life he decided. "Anyway, McCanoc."

"Didn't Edmund mention him?" Pete asked, as Jason dragged himself out of the water.

"This sucks," Jason said, crawling over to the group. "I wanted to stick a spear in that arrogant New Destiny fisker."

"Didn't we all," Jackson replied. "Bast, that was unbelievable. I never saw you move, you were just there."

"Bast is an elf," Bast said, then raised a hand to forestall comment on the apparent non sequitur. "Everyone seems to think that elves are human. Not. Elves were constructed from ground up. No haphazard evolution for us. Look, somewhat, human, but are *not*. Better, stronger, faster, which is a *very* old joke. But also . . . happier. Less . . . serious than humans. Humans with their short lives always live in the *now*, which is good in a way. But elves are half the time in Dream, only way to spend a millennia or so. Me, I tend to spend most of my time in the *now*. Sometimes it hurts. I'll live on when Herzer gets gray and dick goes all flabby and then he dies. And I'll remember him, as I remember scores, hundreds, of others. And love them all. As long as Bast lives, they live on in one heart," she said, tapping her chest.

"But Bast is *not* a human, nor a Changed human. Bast is an elf. And what is impossible, even for most Changed, is normal to elves. Be glad elves so happy. If not, there be no more humans on earth."

"So you're not a Change race?" Antja asked. "Like the mer or the delphinos?"

"No," Bast said, shaking her head. "We're a *made* race, like the dragons. And, like the greater dragons, we have abilities that were, finally, recognized as just too dangerous to let breed unchecked. So most of us retreated to Elfheim and live in Dream."

"What abilities?" Jackson asked.

"That is for elves, and Mother and the Council, to know," Bast said with a grin. "But know this, I can take an orca, any single orca and probably more than one, in the water, mask or no mask. I'll give you one: I can hold my breath as long as delphino. Mask is really unnecessary so far."

"Damn," Jason said.

"I am as fast as a mer in the water," she added. "And can keep it up as long or longer." She nodded at a rock in the sand by Jackson. "Throw rock."

"This?" Jackson said, picking it up.

"Throw. Hard. To hit."

"I don't want to hit you," Jackson temporized.

"Won't," Bast said. She waited, leaning on one arm, the other hand languidly at Herzer's side, until Jason threw. She caught the hard-flung rock out of the air and, in turn, tossed it against the bluff so hard it cracked and left half of its mass buried in the limestone.

She stood up and pointed about a hundred yards down the beach.

"See big rock?" she asked and took off.

Her speed was phenomenal, especially since she was running on sand. The sand flew up behind her like a rooster-tail and by the end of the run she was striding nearly five meters at a time, bounding more like a gazelle than anything human. But she slammed to a stop at the end and then began cartwheeling and back flipping nearly as fast back to where the group was sitting with open mouths. She ended in a multiple flip and twirl that had her lowest point no less than two meters off the ground; she had jumped nearly twice her own height into the air.

"Not human," Bast said, dropping back to a lotus position and not even breathing hard. "Look, somewhat, human, but less human than chimpanzee." She smiled at Herzer. "Will not comment on what that means for mating, morality wise."

"The elves were created as super-soldiers, by the North American Union," Herzer amplified. "Bast . . ."

"Bast was created by Nissei Corporation during height of AI war," Bast said. "Is old joke, old even then, 'cheap Japanese knockoff.' " She grinned at the joke. "But not so bad knockoff, no?"

"Not bad at all," Jason said. "Jesus."

"Bast, I've got a question," Herzer said. "What was that . . . horrible sound you made when you were holding Shanol."

"That was the hunting scream of an orca," Jason said, shuddering. "I've heard it before."

"There are two types of orca," Antja amplified. "There are pods that generally stay in one area and hunt fish. And then there are nomad tribes, which hunt marine mammals. They're practically identical, but the nomads use that . . . sound when they are hunting. And for all they look the same, they're pretty much two distinct subraces of orca. And that sound . . . it's eerie as hell."

"It is indeed," Bast said. "Often thought that it was original of banshee's cry. But Herzer was explaining some of what Edmund and dolphin-eater were talking about."

"Yeah, Herzer," Antja said. "I want to know what he said that set you off the first time. Something about Doctor Daneh."

"As I said, I fell in with Dionys McCanoc," Herzer said, for a moment reliving those days and seeing the house-broad McCanoc as if he were alive. "This is . . . I have to give you the background, sorry. I . . . knew he wasn't the greatest guy in the world. No, I'll be more honest. I'd discovered shortly before the Fall that he was a bug-house nuts bastard. But . . . when I was growing up, I had a genetic problem that screwed up my nerves. I shook all the time, had a hard time speaking. And it was just getting worse and worse. So I didn't have many friends. And when it got worse I ended up with almost none. McCanoc . . . picked up on that and drew me into his circle. Generally as the butt of his jokes. But when I got better, when Dr. Daneh *cured* me, finally, I still hung around with him. Right up until just before the Fall, when I decided to give him a wide berth."

"What happened?" Elayna asked, cocking her head to one side.

"Dionys-fisker set up rape of homunculus," Bast answered. "Little girl homunculus, program to hate and fear sex."

"And . . . he invited me," Herzer said. "The problem being, as he had realized, I was . . . very tempted." He looked up at the group around him and saw responses ranging from disbelief to anger. "As I said, I have my demons."

"And very fine demons they are," Bast said, patting him on the leg. "Love it when you let them off leash."

"Bast!" Antja said.

"Hey, is fun play rough sometimes," Bast said. "Herzer very gentle lover when wants to, right Elayna?"

Elayna blushed bright red but nodded.

"Very nice," was all she said.

"Everyone demons have," Bast said, looking off to sea. "Question is, do we run demons or demons run us?"

"Don't get too angry with Herzer," Jason said, looking at Antja. "Unless you've never thought about some of the play that we do. 'Who's my pretty little baby?' with her hair tied up in pigtails?"

This time it was Antja's turn to blush but she just nodded at Herzer to continue.

"Anyway, that was when I started avoiding McCanoc. Up until the Fall," Herzer sighed. "I found him, or he found me maybe, shortly after. And . . . we were wandering with a group. No, not even wandering, waiting for something. McCanoc was always talking about his friends coming for him. And then we ran out of food and McCanoc decided that we needed to . . . take some from passersby."

"Bandits," Jason said.

"Oh, yes," Herzer replied. "He almost made it sound romantic. If it hadn't been for the constant rain and the hunger. I was thinking more in terms of begging food from them until whatever manna McCanoc expected dropped from heaven. Or, probably, just leaving the group, although McCanoc had said he considered that desertion. But before I could decide, one of the lookouts caught their first passerby. Who happened, by awful coincidence, to be Dr. Daneh."

"Oh, shit," Pete said. "What did you do?"

"Well, McCanoc, big-hearted guy that he is, offered me first rape," Herzer said, his face hard and cold. "There were eight of them, McCanoc was armed with a sword, others had knives. I was unarmed. So I did the only thing a true hero would do in the situation; I ran."

"Damn," Jason said, shaking his head. "Not much else you *could* do. Except die pointlessly."

"You didn't tell us about this," Antja said, looking at Rachel. "This was when you were on your way to the town, Raven's Mill?"

"Yeah," Rachel replied, tightly. "I didn't tell you. It's not something I tell everyone I meet. Even people I like. And . . . it took me a *long* time to admit it, but Jason's right, there was *nothing* that Herzer could have done except die and maybe get Mom dead in the process. In a way it took more courage, more *sensible* courage, to run and try to find a weapon than to stay and die."

"I guess we both had our secrets," Elayna said, looking at Herzer oddly.

"Yeah, but it doesn't make it a lot easier in the deeps of the night," Herzer said, his jaw working. "I *was* looking for a weapon, anything solid, but I got back after they were . . . done. I helped Dr. Daneh, and Rachel, on the way to Raven's Mill and then joined the Raven's Mill military at the first chance I got. I've always been into war games; I used to do enhanced reality before the Fall. But . . . I won't say that my demons weren't on my back about it, either. I'd gotten very good at being angry at that point. I wanted to kill something, to gut something, preferably McCanoc, but anyone like him would do.

"A few months later, lucky me, McCanoc turned back up at the head of a small army. We'd been training hard, but we were still outnumbered ten to one and most of the army was Changed, who are no joke to fight. They're strong, aggressive and very hard to kill. But we beat them, mostly by maneuvering them onto fixed positions and slaughtering them; McCanoc was no tactician. In the end, though, he attacked, himself, and he had powered armor and some sort of draining nannite field. I tried to stop him, and got this," he said, holding up the prosthetic, "for my pains."

"I tried to stop as well," Bast said. "Armor was too tough. Sword, any sword, just bounces off field. I hate powered armor. Unless I'm wearing it."

"Anyway, Edmund took him out," Herzer said.

"How?" Jason asked. "Powered armor, nannite field? What the hell did he do, drown him?"

"Ever hear of Charles the Great of Anarchia?" Herzer asked with a sly grin.

"Took over Anarchia, oh, a hundred years ago or so?" Jason asked, to a nod. "Ruled in peace for ten years, set up a representational government and left, disappeared?"

"He didn't disappear," Herzer said. "He took his dead brother's name. Edmund."

"Holy shit," Jackson said. "You're joking!"

"Nope, you've been dealing with him every day," Herzer chuckled. "Let's just say that the greatest master-smith in the world was not going to be fighting with unpowered armor and weapons. Bast, how would you take out Duke Edmund?"

"Strong crossbow," Bast replied seriously. "Two hundred meters, minimum. From behind. Only way be sure to live."

"Well, this is another fine mess you've gotten us into," Daneh said.

"That it is, love," Edmund muttered, "that it is."

They had parked themselves in one of the swim-throughs and now watched the suddenly much more nervous mer moving around in the square as the antenna of crayfish waved at them from just too deep under the ledges to reach.

"The ship's late," Rachel said.

"That's not what has me worried," Edmund replied.

"And dealing with orcas, in the water, is not going to be easy," Daneh said.

"And that's not what has me worried," Edmund replied.

"All right, Solomon," Daneh said, in an exasperated tone, "what *does* have you worried?"

"When I got here, I knew the name of Bruce the Black, but not what he looked like," Edmund replied. "I knew none of the other mer by name. And I didn't know that New Destiny was sending a mission."

"Damn, I didn't catch that," Daneh said. "He knew Bruce by sight. He knew *Jason's* name. He knew about Herzer and me."

"That indicates one damned effective intelligence agency," Edmund said. "And intel is half the battle. I'd let Sheida handle that end, assuming that she was doing as well as the enemy. No such luck. Damn!"

"What are you going to do about it?" Rachel asked.

"Not much I can do from here," the duke replied. "Except prove that it's only *half* the battle. But when we get back I'm going to be asking some hard questions, and not trusting the answers. They *knew* about the carrier. They were able to intercept it. On the other hand, they've made damned poor use of their intel so far. Letting slip that they knew that much was just *stupid*."

"Maybe there's even more that they know," Daneh said.

"I'm sure they do," Edmund said. "But that's not the point. How did they know that the ship was taking the northerly route? How did they know where it *was*? Intercepting a ship at sea is not easy, even if you know where it's going to be in general."

"You mean there's someone on the ship passing them information?"

"Has to be," Edmund said. "As well as sources on the land. And someone piecing them together and passing on the useful bits."

"Two guesses who the one on the ship is," Rachel said, bitterly. "And only one counts."

"If you mean the rabbit," Edmund replied, "you might be right. But don't jump to the conclusion. Admittedly, it fits its programming. But I'm not sure of the means. Does he have an internal sensor? If not, how did he know where they were? What was his means of communication? Why destroy the ship if he'd directed it in?"

"So, who?" Daneh asked.

"I'm not a mind reader," Edmund said. "But we'll do some discreet investigating when the ship gets here. We know that it's close, if the orcas were there and then here. That might, admittedly, be disinformation. But given the way they used the information they had, I doubt it. You can't always count on your enemies being stupid, but it's nice when they are."

Shanol coasted to a stop above the swim-through and then paused as if taking in the seascape.

"They brought dragons," a voice pulsed out of the darkness below.

"We were informed they would," the orca replied. "That's not a problem."

"That's what you think. They swim and can hunt underwater. The big one's developed a taste for bull shark; she bites them in half."

"Nothing that's bred for the air can match us in the water."

"Nothing is to happen to Elayna," the voice said.

"As promised, you can have your pick of the mer-women

when we are done. Although, I must admit she is a tooth-
some morsel."

"Elayna and Antja then," the voice said. "Although Elayna
doesn't have the best taste in the world; she's been swimming out with that jerk Herzer."

"An interesting datum, to be sure," Shanol mused.

"Where are the rays?"

"Nearby, waiting for my signal. If we can resolve this little
problem peacefully we shall. If not . . . other measures must
be taken. I've tarried too long. Be ready when the time comes."

"Just make sure the rays know who the good guys are,"
the voice said. "I don't want to get caught up in that."

"Oh, they know who the good guys are," the orca pulsed
in humor. "That's who they're aiming at."

Bruce had called both of the representatives to a meeting
in the town square. He looked at both of them and shook
his head.

"You're like two children scuffling in a schoolyard," Bruce
said. "All around you is beauty, and all you can see is your
conflict. Well, I will not let it come to us. I have sounded
the feeling of the community, and I hereby give you my
decision: The mer will have nothing to do with either of you.
We need nothing from either of you that is worth the trouble
it would bring. This is my decision. It is final and irrevocable.
I request that both groups leave and not trouble us again."

"For myself," Shanol said, "your neutrality is all that I
sought. My work here is done and I and my pod will leave
immediately."

"Well," Edmund said. "We're waiting on our ship. We request
to be allowed to stay until it arrives. I have some details to
work out with Jackson anyway; I still think that you need
more materials and I'm working on a list that I'll pass to
traders. But as soon as the ship arrives, we'll leave."

"Very well," Bruce said. "You can stay until the ship arrives,
it will be here soon?"

"Within a day or two, I hope. It is already overdue."

"It had to stop and burn a peaceful merchant," the orca
said, snidely.

"Enough," Bruce said. "This is what I want far from here.
Shanol, go now. Edmund, as soon as possible."

"Very well," Shanol replied. "I hope to see you again in better
times." With that he gave a flick of his tail, which blew water
across Edmund, and headed out to sea, whistling for his pod.

CHAPTER TWENTY-SEVEN

The next day dawned clear again and before the mists were off the ground, the dragons were aloft searching for a school of sizeable fish.

Koo and Vickie had stayed on land, so the only rider with Herzer was Jerry, who was the strongest swimmer. In the detritus from before the Fall, Jackson had dug up a set of fins and a conformable mask and snorkel, which fit the rider, and he intended to participate as much as possible in the hunt. Elayna had stayed back at camp, but the group included Jason, Pete, Jackson and an older mer-man named Bill, all of whom planned on working the net. Bast had also chosen to stay back at the town.

They spiraled upward, the dragons having to work for altitude with neither thermals nor wind, and looked for anything moving. But the surface of the ocean was glass smooth for klicks and there was no sign of migrating pelagics to be seen.

"I guess it's reef fish, today," Jerry said.

"Whatever," Joanna complained. "I'm damned hungry."

"If we can take just a little time," Bill said, "sometimes schools wait for the ebb tide by Roberts Inlet. It's not far down the coast."

"By where we went fishing the first time," Jason said.

"We can try it," Joanna grumbled. "And if they're not there we either eat reef-fish or mer-men that send us on wild goose chases."

Herzer looked back to the east, squinting into the rising sun, and saw a flash on the surface.

"Hang on," he said, spinning Chauncey practically on his own tail. "There's something back there."

"Dolphins," Jason said, as Nebka banked around to follow Joanna. "Or maybe delphinos."

"Delphinos," Joanna said. "I can see the rounded foreheads."

"From here?" Pete asked. He was riding behind Jerry and squinting to try to see what everyone was looking at.

"I can adjust my eyes for enhanced distance vision," the dragon said. "They're delphinos. But . . ."

"Why are they just standing on their tails?" Herzer asked. It was apparent the pod was not moving, just thrashing at the surface. As if they were *trying* to attract attention.

"I dunno," Joanna said. "But there's something closing on them from the direction of the town. Something underwater."

"Commander," Herzer said. "Will all due respect, I suggest we proceed immediately back to the town."

"It's an orca," Joanna growled. The whole group had been gliding in the direction of the delphinos and now the great dragon started flapping her wings, accelerating. "It's hunting them."

She entered a steep glide then pulled out as she swept over the delphinos. She stayed on level flight, wingtips just above the ocean, until she passed over the orca. She had timed the strike, by luck or planning it didn't matter, perfectly and just as she swept over the unsuspecting orca broached the surface. As it did, all four talons shot down and sunk into its skin.

She had banked upward as she struck and had nearly forty kilometers of forward momentum so the massive marine mammal was plucked from the waters as neatly as a fish being caught by an osprey.

But the massive orca weighed a good percentage of her own weight and Joanna quickly discovered that getting him out of the water was not the same as keeping him out. After a few desperate wing beats she released the whale and let him drop, bleeding, back into the water.

The orca, however, seemed to have had enough, and dove for the reef below, heading out towards deeper water and away from the delphinos.

"Just peaceful diplomats, huh," Joanna said as she gained altitude. She banked towards the village but took a look back at the trail of blood from the wounded orca. "Buh-bye, buh-bye now."

"We need to get down there!" Jason shouted.

"Let me and the dragons handle this," Joanna replied. "Herzer, the birthing cavern."

"Shit!" he said, banking Chauncey towards the land as the rest of the dragons thundered into the shallows. "I'll be back!"

Rachel was watching her father, who was talking to one of the older mer-folk in the shadows of a ledge. The merman was nodding his head as Edmund talked, clearly agreeing with what the general was saying. Edmund had been doing the rounds ever since Bruce had ordered them to leave, late into the last night and was at it again even before breakfast this morning. He seemed to reach some sort of agreement and was just starting to swim away when there was a shrill screeing in the distance.

Rachel had become inured to the constant low-level noises of the sea. There was a constant snapping, which she had been told were shrimp although she rarely saw them. And there was the semiconstant pinging of the delphinos that hovered near the periphery of the town. But this was different, it set her teeth on edge and made her want to get up and run.

When Edmund heard it he seemed to recognize it and headed up above the enclosing coral with Rachel following.

When she got above the coral she spun around, looking for what was making the noise but what she saw was a line of raylike forms heading in from the direction of the rising sun.

"Attack!" Edmund bellowed, just as the rays swept across the crowded square.

The creatures, Changed humans, were the size of manta rays, nearly three meters from wingtip to wingtip. But instead of the soft, plankton-gathering mouths of manta rays they had vertically slit mouths lined with sharklike teeth. Rachel saw a line with a bony harpoon head dart down from the belly of one of the leading ixchitl and strike the mer-man that Edmund had been talking to. The mer-man struggled for a moment then went flaccid as the line began to accordion back up to the ray. When the still-twitching mer-man reached the belly of the ixchitl the beast tore into his body, tearing off great strips of flesh as the shallow water turned red around it. More of the darts were dropping among the mer as those that could dashed for the relative safety of the ledges and swim-throughs.

Bruce the Black suddenly appeared from one of the swim-throughs, a bone-tipped spear in his hand, and shot up into the crowd of ixchitl. He caught one of the beasts in the maw and the hard-driven spear penetrated through its mouth and up out of the back in a welter of blood. But even as he took that one out, another speared him and the leader of the mer shuddered as its neurotoxin ran though his veins.

"Get under cover!" Edmund bellowed at her, drawing his knife.

Rachel ducked under the ledge but continued to watch her father, sure in her heart that he was as doomed as the former mer-leader. But Edmund seemed to dodge the ixchitl's darts as if he had been fighting them all his life. She saw him cut one that came at him and swarm up the retracting organ that dangled from the belly of the beast. When he reached the ixchitl he drove the knife into its anus and cut upward, gutting it from bottom to top. As the ixchitl thrashed in its death agonies the general shoved his arm into the slit and grasped something in the interior, dragging the ixchitl's body around to block another cloud of descending darts; he had created a giant shield out of the ixchitl's body.

The shield was unwieldy in the extreme but Edmund had not planned for simple defense. His free hand darted out and grasped the retracting cord attached to Bruce and let it raise him, and his shield, up to the ixchitl that was preparing to feast on the mer-leader. The ixchitl apparently divined his intent because it began to flap wildly, but because of the drag of the dead ray that Edmund grasped couldn't pull at any speed. It apparently had no conscious control of the retracting harpoon cord. Edmund was inexorably drawn up to the belly of the beast. He gutted it with another of those powerfully driven thrusts then cut the cord loose, leaving Bruce free to drift to the bottom.

More of the rays were gathering around him, though, and all the mer that were left had darted for safety. He managed to kill another of the beasts, who could seemingly only fire their darts straight down, but the crowd around him was eventually going to get a dart past his defenses. It seemed only a matter of time before the beleaguered general would be killed when a shadow passed over the square and Nebka dropped out of the sky into the midst of the rays, Bast hitting the water beside her like an avenging angel.

The dragon turned its head like a snake and caught one of the rays on the wing. The wyvern's broad, crocodilian head shook like a shark and ripped most of the wing off, leaving the mortally wounded ray to writhe in a death spiral to the reef below.

But the dragon was nothing compared to Bast. The elf moved with an unnatural grace and blinding speed, like some knife-wielding demon. She disdained the gutting technique of Edmund, instead whispering in from above and slicing along the back of the rays, cutting the muscles to their great wings, her knife slicing through their tough skin as if it were paper. She had taken out two of the rays before the rest of the dragons appeared, swimming over the reef edge like great birds of prey and descending upon the suddenly outgunned ixchitl.

The rays, at the appearance of the dragons, turned for deeper water and put on a burst of speed until the last one vanished over the reef edge, chased by the wyverns as Joanna coasted to a stop over the square.

"Commander Gramlich," the general said, tossing aside his ersatz shield, "get the dragons back; those damned rays can overwhelm them if they get their act together. And the orcas are going to be around somewhere. Daneh!" he bellowed as he drifted down to the twitching body of the mer-leader.

Rachel darted out of her shelter and to the side of the mer-leader who lay on the sand by the coral head at the center of the square. The mer-leader was still alive, twitching in the grip of the neurotoxin but Rachel could think of nothing to do for him. Suddenly, her mother was beside her.

"It's a paralyzing toxin," Daneh said. "Probably voluntary muscles only, which means he can't breathe. If we can get water over his gills he'll survive. But I have no clue how to do that."

"Get him to the surface," Edmund said. "Mouth to mouth."

"We can't get the water clear," Daneh said, desperately. "There's not enough air in our *lungs* to blow him out."

"He's trying to say something," Elayna said, dropping to the sand by her grandfather and grasping his hand. "Just clicks. But . . ." she leaned forward, holding up his head and cradling it to her. "Grandfather?"

"Cave," Bruce said. "Cave . . ." and then his eyes rolled back in his head.

"The birthing cavern," Edmund said, coldly, turning to look towards the land. "I'd wondered where the damned orcas were."

After Daneh had told about the birthing cavern, Herzer had taken the trouble to walk the crest of the island until he found the light-source of the cave. It was near the summit of the island, above the spring that had made the ancient lighthouse possible in its day. Now he winged Chauncey to a hard landing and sprang off the wyvern, slapping it on the flank.

"Go follow the other dragons, Chaunce," he yelled, pounding up the slope to the cracks in the rock.

When he got there he could hear the screams from below and his heart dropped, but he got down on his belly and peered into the fissure in the rock.

His eyes were blinded by the bright light on the surface but after a moment he could see the tableau below. A small orca was swimming back and forth in front of the main ledge, where most of the mer-women and their children were huddled, as far back as they could crawl. From time to time it turned and got up speed, finally lifting its body out on the ledge and writhing back and forth, trying to snap up one of the mer. Finally, it writhed back and forth and dropped down from the ledge, circling back through the water for another run.

The crack was narrow and the drop was at least fifteen meters. Not a problem if he was falling in water, assuming it was deep enough, but Herzer was well aware that he was not Bast; if he fell into the water the orca would be on him before he could react and Herzer would just be a part of the food chain. He turned and lowered himself into the fissure and then rammed his good fist into the rock, dangling over the drop below.

The orca came back for another run and got out of the water, just about reaching the tail of one of the mer-women. He snapped and writhed, but try as he might he couldn't, quite, reach the twitching tail. Finally, he started to hump himself backwards and was just about in the water when he was hit by a tremendous blow from above.

Herzer was half stunned by the impact and knew that he was going to feel it for days afterwards. He had hit the orca just forward of the dorsal fin with both feet, but they had both immediately slid out from under him on the slick skin of the beast and he had impacted on his hip and side, flipping sideways on the right side of the orca, entering the water with a tremendous splash.

The impact, however, had stunned the orca as well and Herzer was the first to gain some semblance of consciousness. He kicked himself back from the depths to which he had sunk and, taking a leaf from Bast's training, slid his prosthetic into the blowhole of the orca and grasped the flexible flesh on the side of it. Then he squeezed.

The sonar blast that the orca released was like nothing that Herzer had ever heard, the shriek of a dying child the size of a whale was the closest he could imagine. It thrashed its way to the surface and blasted out air, flailing its tail and spinning around the cavern until it impacted nose first on one of the unyielding rock walls.

"Quit this!" Herzer shouted. He put his knife by the eye of the beast and it quieted.

"Leb go ob my ho!" the orca said as distinctly as it could. Its surface method of communication was its blowhole, which Herzer still gripped, although less firmly.

"The hell I will," Herzer said. "I've got a cutting edge on this thing. I can cut right through the muscle. You won't be able to submerge for weeks until it heals. You'll starve to death first."

"Baberd," the orca said. "Pleab?"

"No," Herzer replied. He suddenly realized that the orca, by its dorsal fin, size and, hell, demeanor, was no more than a teen, probably a young one. "Where are the rest of the orcas?"

"Nob gonna te'," the orca said. "Leb go."

"Fisk you," Herzer said, engaging his pinky muscles and bearing down with the internal gear.

There was another shriek from the orca and it sobbed in pain.

"Where are the rest of them?"

"A' da fron," the orca sobbed. "Wai'ing."

"For you to bring them little mer-snacks?" Herzer said, nastily. "I don't think so. Turn around and put your tail up on the ledge. And no tricks; I can press harder than I have. Not to mention putting this knife right into your brain-case."

He maneuvered the orca's tail onto the ledge and had one of the mer-women secure it with his leather belt to a projecting rock. Then he let go of the creature's blowhole and swam around to where it could see him with eye and sonar. Herzer ducked below the water for the conversation.

"I know what it is to fall in with the wrong companions," Herzer said. "Which is the only reason you're still alive. I'm going to ask the mer-ladies not to kill you. On the other hand, did you catch any of the children?"

"No," the orca said. "I didn't want to do this, but Shanol . . ."

"I know," Herzer said. "And I also know that having power over the defenseless can be a rush. I know that you enjoyed yourself, even while you hated feeling that way. Am I right?"

"Yes," the orca whispered.

"I don't have time for this, but you need to think about something while you're tied up here. Which side do you really *want* to be on? Who are you, inside? A good guy or a bad guy? Think of this as a chance to correct a mistake. And use it."

He popped up to the surface of the water and looked at the mer-women, still huddled on the ledge.

"Ladies, this young man is very sorry for causing you all this distress," he said. "For that reason, and because he's a source of information, I'd appreciate the hell out of it if you could see your way clear to not beating him to death with rocks."

There were a few half hysterical giggles at this speech but one of the mer-women crawled forward in a furious slither.

"He nearly ate my Gram!" she shouted. "I want him dead!"

"Yes, well, as I said he's sorry," Herzer replied, heartily. "And we all have our character flaws. I, for example, get angry when a reasonable request isn't granted. Am I making myself clear, ma'am?"

"Yes," she said, gulping.

"Glad we've got that sorted out," Herzer replied. "Now, I think I need to go see what's waiting at the entrance."

"You're crazy," the mer-woman said. "The rest of the orcas are going to be out there!"

"Well, better out there than in here," Herzer pointed out. "And if this youngster doesn't bring them out little mer-snacks they might try to wriggle their way in. I think I need to go make sure that doesn't happen."

"Why?" the mer-woman asked. "Why are you doing this?"

"As I said," Herzer replied, sadly. "We all have our character flaws." Then he ducked under the water and headed for the blackness of the tunnel.

The tunnel was pitchy black, a solid darkness that seemed to creep into his soul. It also was so tight in places, he had no idea how the orca had wormed its way in. Possibly there were better ways through, ways that would be visible to a creature with sonar. But Herzer could only grope his way along, hoping against hope that there were no side turns that would take him off into some tunnel from which he might never find his way. Again and again he hit projections of rock, once solidly on his forehead, and he brushed against things that he really was sure he didn't want to see. Once his hands settled into a mass of corruption that burned his skin so that he flailed back wildly, shaking his good hand as it tingled and burned.

Finally, when he was sure that he had lost his way and would be wandering around in this watery tomb forever, or until his air ran out, there was a faint gleam of blue light. His eyes, adjusted to the darkness, started to let him distinguish the walls around him and he sped up, headed for the light, headed for hope. Until the light was extinguished as an orca head popped into the opening and blasted him with sonar.

"Well, what do we have here?" Shanol said. "If it isn't the little lieutenant. What happened to Tomas?"

"He saw the error of his straying ways," Herzer said, suddenly tired. He could see the other orcas cruising back and forth; it looked as if most of the pod was out there. He could hold the entrance against them, he was sure, but his every bit of training resisted simply standing on the defensive.

"You'd better hope he's still alive," Shanol said.

"What do you care?" Herzer said. "You were the one that sent him into a tunnel that could have killed him."

"I knew he could get through," Shanol said. "There's a lot I know. Like what happened with you and Daneh. Do you dream of her at night, Herzer?"

"Oh, man, you have been reading too much pop psychology," Herzer laughed. "There's a degree of anger there. But anger is such a useful emotion when you learn to properly channel it." With that he darted forward and slammed his knife into the orca's eye.

Shanol had opened his mouth to dart forward and catch the human but the narrow entrance of the tunnel prevented him from moving and Herzer's sudden attack caught him off guard. He screamed in sonar, bubbles pouring out of his blowhole and backed up, his tail flailing wildly.

Herzer lost his grip on the dagger as he was slammed into the roof of the tunnel and he backed up into the entrance as the orca swam backwards, blood streaming from his eye, the hilt of the knife standing out like some bizarre ornament.

"Kill you!" the orca screamed, heading to the surface and getting a breath of air. But the sound he made was as much sob as scream.

"Come on and do it, then," Herzer shouted back. "Come into the tunnel! I can stay under as long as I like. You have to *breathe*. Come into my parlor, little fly!"

"I'll kill you," the orca sobbed. "Kill you and eat you! Eat you alive, from the legs up! Nittaatsuq!" he continued, leaning the knife towards one of the other orcas.

Like the delphinoids the Changed orcas had stubby fingers and the indicated orca drew the knife out of the eye socket with a quick jerk and a scream from his leader. Then Nittaatsuq got what he thought was a brilliant idea and swam forward, thrusting his pectoral fin with the knife gripped clumsily in its fingers into the narrow crevice.

Herzer simply laughed and grasped the blade with his prosthetic, wrenching it out of the grip of the orca with an expert twist.

"Thanks for my knife back," Herzer laughed. "I was sure I'd lost it for good."

"*BASTARD!*" Shanol bellowed, charging at the entrance, then turned aside, trailing blood.

"Hey," Herzer said, in a thoughtful tone. "Don't *sharks* home in on the smell of blood?"

"I'm going to kill you," the orca ground out.

"You keep *saying* that," Herzer responded. "I don't think you're orca enough. I've had much better people than you try to kill me and so far they've all failed. By the way, the orca that was after the delphino found out that he *really* doesn't like dragons. And as soon as they get done with the ixchitl, they'll be back for me. I'd suggest you beat feet before they get here."

"We will," Shanol said after a moment's pause. "But we'll be back. You wait."

"Breathlessly," Herzer replied. "I'm *so* looking forward to it."

When the orcas were gone he took a deep breath, noticing for the first time a slight constriction on his breathing caused by the mask. He started to panic, his breath coming faster and faster, feeling that he couldn't get enough air into his lungs. Finally, he got a grip on himself, thrusting the dagger into a convenient crack and holding onto the walls as he strove to conquer his breathing. Finally, when he stopped hyperventilating, he started to calm down, as the mask finally had enough time to pump the built-up carbon dioxide from the fight out of the area. Eventually he hung, limp, from his deathlike grip on the rock until Chauncey and a group of worried, spear-wielding mer-men appeared in the entrance and he could finally leave his lonely vigil and swim to the surface to gulp in lungfuls of good, clean, salt-tainted air.

✧   ✧   ✧

"I *warned* you about the dragons!" Mosur said.

"I am in no mood for you," Shanol replied, tightly. The salt water in his wound stung like fire.

"We need to get out of the area," Shedol said. The orca second in command had returned covered in punctures and slices from Joanna's attack. "We can't stay down long enough to keep out of the vision range of those damned dragons."

"We can just go back," one of the pod pinged nervously. "There's too many of them."

"No," Shanol replied.

"The ixchitl are calling for us to ambush them," Shedol noted. "They have a plan."

"*BE DAMNED TO IXCHITL PLANS!*" the big orca boomed. "No. *I* have a plan." He turned to Mosur and ran a wave of sonar over him. "You're of no use to us now."

"Good," Mosur said. "I'm quit of this."

"And we have a long way to go," the orca continued, running his sonar over the mer again. "And I'm hungry."

With the small bone that they used to communicate underwater, it was almost impossible for the mer to scream.

CHAPTER TWENTY-EIGHT

The wind was fair from the northeast and the carrier rolled over a slight sea with a string of islands to its north.

"If this holds we'll be up to the mer-town by dusk," Commander Mbeki said.

"Three days late," the skipper growled. Beating around the edge of the islands had been a slow process, especially since they'd had to negotiate some tricky shallows.

"You can't control the winds, sir," the commander replied.

"No, and I can't control New Destiny, either," Chang replied. "We lost half a day with that little encounter."

"Well, so far, so good," Mbeki said.

"Something in the water to port," the lookout called.

"I think I should have knocked on some wood," Mbeki said. "Could you be clearer than 'something'?" he yelled.

"No, it's . . . coming up from the depths. Looks like a . . ."

Before he could complete the sentence a gigantic tentacle snaked over the side of the ship, smashing the rail and twisting into the ratlines of the mainmast. The ship heeled hard over to port and shuddered as the weight of a giant squid caught it.

"KRAKEN!" the skipper yelled. "Chief Brooks! Axemen! Sound general quarters!"

More and more tentacles slithered over the side of the ship as the beak of the immense squid was revealed. One intelligent eye was just visible below water level and it rolled from side to side, searching for prey. It found it as one of the sailors

285

dashing at the tentacles was caught around the waist and hoisted, screaming, over the side of the ship. The screams were abruptly cut off as the sailor's head was thrust into the half-meter-wide, parrotlike beak of the squid. It crunched with bitter finality.

Mbeki found himself down on the deck, snatching up the fallen axe of the sailor and hacking at a tentacle that had wrapped itself around the mainmast. The beast was trying to turn the clipper over on its side and its immense weight might just manage it. The body of the beast was half out of the water, its tentacles given free play around the maindeck. It caught another of the crew, one of the marines who were stabbing at the tentacles with boarding pikes, and the marine was dragged over the side, still stabbing at the immense tentacle wrapped around his waist.

Mbeki and Brooks were hacking at the tentacle around the mainmast, in a rhythm with one striking as other raised his axe, when one of the blindly thrashing tentacles wrapped itself around the commander's ankle and started dragging him towards the edge. He grabbed a stanchion and his arms were nearly ripped from their sockets as he struggled to keep from being taken to the beast's maw.

Brooks leapt over the half-severed tentacle attached to the mast and hacked downward at the one wrapped around the commander's ankle. The tentacle had only caught him with a tip and a single blow from the chief severed it to lie flopping on the deck. But even as he turned back to the one around the mast, the ship heaved over on its side and the water came up over the bulwarks as the squid half humped itself onto the ship. Now that it could see what it was doing, its tentacles attacked the axe-wielders and Brooks found himself wrapped in its slimy clutches.

He hacked futilely at the thigh-thick tentacle around his waist but it was to no avail and he found himself in the air, being lowered to the beast's maw. He saw it open to receive his head just as a jet of fire went past his ear, and impacted squarely on the beast's mouth.

The tentacle around his waist tightened convulsively and he felt his eyes practically pop out of their sockets as the air was driven from his lungs. The next thing he knew he was flying through the air.

Evan heard the screams from the deck and felt the ship heave over as the big kettle drum on the deck began to pound the signal for battle stations. Without a thought he caught up the flamethrower and started to make his way onto the deck. The ship heeled again and he was thrown against a bulkhead, the flamethrower half thrown over his shoulder catching his arm painfully. He saw the damned rabbit in the corridor, and shouted at him.

"What the hell are you doing just loafing along?" Evan yelled, getting the other strap over his shoulder. "We've got a problem!"

"And that means what to me?" the rabbit said, stopping and nibbling at his shoulder. "Me, I'm heading for the lifeboats. You can deal with whatever it is."

"Damn you," Evan said, stepping over the rabbit and heading for the companionway.

The rabbit looked after him then pointed a finger at himself.

"I damn thee," the rabbit muttered. "Shoot, didn't work."

Evan stumbled onto the deck to a scene of pandemonium. Tentacles were slithering across the deck in every direction or were already wrapped around pieces of the ship. As he stepped out of the companionway the ship tilted to an alarming degree and water shipped over the side as the kraken hoisted itself up. He saw Chief Brooks chopping at a tentacle that had caught the XO and then the chief was caught by another tentacle and lifted into the air.

Evan found himself screaming as he ran through the jungle of writhing arms, desperately clicking at the self-starter for the flamethrower. Finally the pilot light caught and he slid into knee-deep water and pointed the device over the side, triggering it for its first test.

The stream, he noted in a strange abstraction that made the whole experience dreamlike, was darned near perfect, some droplets coming down from the stream but most of them impacting in the target area. As the jellied gasoline hit the squid just above the mouth—he'd been aiming directly for the maw but close was good enough with a flamethrower—the squid convulsed, its jets closing to pull it back. The tentacles thrashed wildly and then with another massive pulse it slithered off the edge of the ship and disappeared back into the depths so fast it was gone before the ship had heaved back up onto an even keel.

Evan found himself on the deck, the end of the flamethrower dripping jellied gasoline onto the, fortunately water-covered, deck. He stumbled to his feet and shut down the valves as sailors grouped around him, pounding him on his shoulders in lieu of his tank-covered back.

"Mister Mayerle!" the skipper bellowed from the quarter-deck.

"Sir," Evan said, spinning in place and giving the skipper a salute that, as a civilian, was not strictly necessary.

The skipper returned it anyway and then grinned.

"Damned fine job," the skipper said. "Thank you. But before you use that thing on my ship again, kindly find something that allows us to extinguish those little fires you just left behind."

"Yes, sir!" Evan said. Buckets of sand had already been dropped on the dribbles that had hit the deck and looking over the side it was clear that the ship had drifted clear of the puddle of burning fuel the scorched squid had left behind.

"Commander Mbeki?" the skipper called.

"Sir?" the commander said, getting to his feet.

"We've got some damaged rigging," the skipper said, turning to look at the sails, some of which were flapping in the breeze. Fortunately the wind was not strong or they would have shivered themselves to pieces. "Get a damage party to work. How's the chief?"

"I'll live, Skipper," Brooks said, getting shakily to his feet.

"Bridge!" the lookout called. "Dragon, fine on the port bow! Signaling. Number Twenty-three, forty-seven, fourteen!"

" 'Enemy in area,' " Midshipman Donahue said. " 'Under attack. Make all sail.' "

"Bit late," the skipper said. "Get to work, Commander!"

"Wait," Joel said as one of the deck apes started to flip a severed tentacle end over the side.

"What?" the seaman asked, tired and unhappy from the battle and the cleanup. What he didn't need was one of the damned wardroom stewards slowing him down.

"We need to keep a souvenir," Joel said, stooping to pick up the tentacle. "We'll put it in alcohol and set it up in the mess or something."

"Whatever," the seaman replied. "I've got work to do."

"As do I," the steward said, picking up the tentacle and taking it below.

Now if he could only get a gene scan out of Sheida, one of his cases might at least get closed.

He rounded up a jar and wood alcohol in the galley and

then carefully stored the chunk in his seabag. After that he went and checked his telltales.

The rabbit roamed all over the ship, mostly being a minor nuisance and bugging people. But the external telltale, when he touched it, pointed to the aft of the ship and he went to pick up the data from the one in the wardroom.

The latter was occupied, however, by Commander Mbeki who had a pile of documents spread out on the table. He was sitting at the far end, fountain pen in hand, staring at the papers with an abstracted expression.

"Sorry, sir," Joel said. "Anything I can get you?"

"Not right now, Joel," Mbeki said, looking up with dark eyes.

"You look worn out, sir," Joel said. "A mug of herbal tea? Some food?"

"No thanks, Joel," the commander said, shaking his head.

"Sir, I can see you're busy," Joel said, nervously. "But, could I talk to you for a moment?"

"I don't know," the commander said, looking stern for a moment. "What about?"

Joel shut the door and then shrugged. "I sort of need to . . . go out of the chain of command, sir. It's about something you mentioned. And I've been thinking about it a lot."

"What's that?" the commander said. "And you know I don't like sailors breaking chain of command."

"Yes, sir, but it's about my family, sir," the seaman said, gulping. "What you said about New Destiny, sir. Just before we shoved off one of the civilian laborer guys asked me if I knew where my family was."

"And what did you tell him?" Commander Mbeki asked.

"I was sort of surprised, it wasn't like we were talking or anything," Joel replied. "He just up and asked. Then he said that if they were in Ropasa, he knew some people who were smuggling people out, those they could find . . ."

"Indeed," the commander said, frowning. "You realize that there are several possibilities here."

"I hadn't thought about it at the time, sir," Joel shrugged. "But I have since. It might be legit. Then again . . ."

"It might have been a New Destiny agent trolling for sources," Mbeki replied, his face hard.

"Yes, sir," Joel gulped. "The thing is, I *told* him who my wife and daughter were. What do I do now? I feel like such an idiot."

Commander Mbeki rubbed the bridge of his nose with thumb and forefinger and grimaced.

"Well, don't think you're the lone idiot," he muttered. "Joel, for now, you've brought it to my attention. I'll think about what to do with it. I *should* pass it on to the Criminal Investigation Division. But those idiots can't find their ass with both hands. For now, I'm going to sit on it. If you get any more contacts, *any* more, tell me. Clear?"

"Yes, sir," Joel replied. "What should I do if, you know, if they're from New Destiny and they found them? What if they tell me to . . ."

"In that case *definitely* contact me, not CID," the commander said.

"Yes, sir."

"Take care, Joel," the commander said, picking up his pen and uncapping it. "And we did *not* have this little conversation."

Edmund scrambled up a ladder dangling over the port side as the ship heeled to starboard; the carrier was getting its dragons back.

"Belay that," he said, waving at the receiving party. "No time." He looked up in the dim light at where teams of sailors were rapidly rerigging the damaged cordage. "What happened?"

"We were attacked by a kraken, General," the skipper said. "That was the *second* attack that we sustained. And I doubt that the kraken was some generic denizen of the deep; it was definitely aiming for us."

"Damn, damn and double damn," Edmund snarled. "We have a hell of a situation here, Skipper. Let's go below."

Edmund sketched out the attack on the mer-town and listened as the captain detailed the two attacks on the ship.

"Well, we're in a fine pickle," Edmund admitted. "The mer need to move. They say that there's a much more defensible position over by the Bimi islands and they want to go there. Soon. Normally that's not a problem. But they can't protect, or even carry for that matter, their babies, not if they're under attack. And I'd guess that as soon as the ixchitl and the orcas lick their wounds they *will* be back."

"You want us to transport the children?" the skipper said, frowning. "We can do that, but I can't guarantee that we won't be attacked again. That kraken . . . was frightening. And I can think of ways that it could attack that we wouldn't be able to counter with Evan's flamethrower. Grab us from underneath and gnaw through the hull comes to mind."

"It's the best chance that we've got," Edmund said, well aware that with a spy on board it was more dangerous than he was making out. "Bruce is dead. Jason hasn't been elected as their leader but he's already taking charge, and he's on our side. Hell, all the mer are on our side except a couple that are dead set on supporting New Destiny and they have made themselves scarce since the attack. We've got the mer, and the delphinos for that matter, on our side. But we need to get them to this Key Harbor or whatever and get their babies protected. And the only way to get the babies there, is by sending them with you. I'm putting the lives of the mer in your hands, Skipper. Can I trust you?" Edmund realized very well that he might be putting them in the hands of an agent of New Destiny, but looking in the eye of the skipper he saw not a flicker of misdoubt.

"Before anything happens to them I will die in their defense, sir," the skipper replied. "And so will every one of my crew."

"I need some of the dragons," Edmund said with a nod. "I'll take Joanna, Chauncey and Donal. You take the rest and the regular riders. They've shown they can take on just about anything that New Destiny has thrown at them; I'd be surprised if the three of them, working together, couldn't even take on a kraken."

The skipper nodded seriously at this, then started to crack a smile. Finally he put his hands over his face, trying very hard not to laugh. Edmund could tell it was half hysterical.

"Are you finding something humorous, Colonel?" he said coldly.

"It's just . . ." the skipper said, taking a breath and wiping his eyes. "General, just for a moment, step back and think. I'm commanding a *dragon-carrier*. And I'm fighting *kraken* and black-sailed caravels. Every now and again . . . it just catches me off guard and I have to giggle. I got this job because I was a tall ships' sailor. I took out barkentines so that groups of people could experience what it was like to sail in the tall ships. Now I'm figuring out how to use *dragons* to protect my warship. It just . . . gets me sometimes. I wouldn't do this in front of the crew, but . . ."

Edmund stared at him coldly for a moment, then grunted. Before he knew it he was laughing as well.

"Okay, you got me, but I just *gutted* a Changed human being and stuffed my arm into its *chest*, to use it as a *shield*," he said, chuckling blackly. "You think *you've* had a strange day?"

✧   ✧   ✧

"Daneh," Edmund said, coming up behind the doctor as she was tying off the last suture in one of the injured mer.

The square had been a shambles after the battle, but most of the debris, dead ixchitl and pieces of dead mer, had been cleared out. The ixchitl had been disposed of by the simple expedient of feeding them to the dragons.

Some of the mer had taken less of a dose of neurotoxin than Bruce, who had been hit by at least two harpoons. They had been able to maintain a ragged breathing and Daneh had concocted, on the spot, a form of tail-to-chest resuscitation that had let them live long enough for the fast-decaying toxin to work itself out of the body. Others had been badly bitten by ixchitl or had simply injured themselves in the flight to safety. It was one of the latter she was finishing work on, a young mer-man who had gashed his arm, badly, on the coral, jamming himself into a crevice.

"Hold on, Edmund," Daneh replied. "You're going to need to favor that for a few days or the stitches will tear out. I'd put a bandage on it if we were on the surface, but nothing really stays here in the water. Just be careful of it."

"I will, ma'am," the boy said, wincing at the pain of the wound.

"Daneh, I want you and Rachel to go on the ship," Edmund said as the boy swam away.

"I'm going to be needed with the mer," Daneh said. "There's going to be more fighting. I'm not just going to run for safety."

"Daneh," the duke said, drifting closer and lowering his voice. "You and Rachel are the only ones I can send that I *know* aren't the leak. You're going to have to find some way to figure out who it is."

"You know it's that damned rabbit," she replied, quietly. There were mer around and it would do their morale no good to know that the women and children were being sent on a ship that had a potential agent onboard.

"No, I don't know it's the rabbit," Edmund said. "And neither do you. Don't assume that. The one person I refuse to suspect, though, is Evan."

"Why?" Daneh said, then frowned. "Not that I would, either."

"Because he's such a perfect little engineer," Edmund replied. "You can tell what he's thinking just by looking at him. I don't think he could carry it off. I may be wrong, but I also think that he might have an idea how to ferret out the mole. Whoever it is has to be communicating somehow. Even if he's being visited by an avatar, there are traces of their presence.

Evan should be able to figure something out. If he can't, I'm out of ideas."

"Okay," Daneh said. "I can see that. But Rachel could go."

"I want both of you to go for the same reason you both came down here, I trust you more than Rachel and, really, it's going to need two. Just go, okay?"

"Okay," she sighed, reaching out to stroke his face. "Take care of yourself."

"I will," Edmund said. "It's you I'm worried about."

Getting the mer-women out of the cavern was easier than retrieving their babies. But the latter, well swathed in sail-cloth, were lifted out through the light fissures and then both groups were ferried out to the ship and hoisted over the side on slings.

While that was going on the ship was discharging its cargo. Since there weren't enough of the bronze-headed spears that had been brought as friendship gifts, they were supplemented with boarding pikes. The pikes were made of low-carbon steel and would rust quickly in the salt environment but they were all that were available. As this was going on, Edmund went over the side and rounded up Herzer and Jason.

"Here," he said, when he finally found them going over plans for the retreat. He thrust out two scabbarded short-swords, wrapped around by heavy belts of a synthetic fabric.

Herzer drew his and tried to whistle. The blade was bright silver and surprisingly light. The design was identical to the Blood Lord blades that he had trained with but while they were light and maneuverable, this blade felt like a feather.

"What is this?" he asked. "Titanium?"

"No, it's a high-tech alloy from the twenty-third century," Edmund replied. "Angus showed it to me just before the Fall. It takes power to work initially, but I had some prepped when the Fall came. I made those just before we came down here as a bribe to Bruce. It's much better than titanium; among other things you can shape it to a damned near monomolecular edge. Don't run a finger down the blade to see how sharp it is."

"I won't," Herzer said, strapping on the sword. The belt was just long enough.

"Thank you," Jason said, sounding weary.

"We're taking Donal, Chauncey and Commander Gramlich," Edmund said. "Put that in your calculations."

"Thank you again," Jason said. "I thought you were going on the ship."

"No, I'm sending Rachel and Daneh that way," he admitted. "But I'll hold on to Joanna to keep up."

"The straps aren't going to take the strain," Herzer pointed out. "It's going to be a long ride. And they're only half as effective if they're stuck in the water all the time."

"I know," Edmund said with a grin. "I think it's time to find out if you can ride a dragon bareback."

CHAPTER TWENTY-NINE

"Evan, we have a problem," Daneh said, coming into the engineer's crowded office with Rachel trailing her.

"There are female members of the ship's company," he said, uneasily. "The dispensary has everything that . . ."

"Not *that* kind of problem." Daneh sighed. The engineer, while brilliant at what he did, had the social skills of a rhinoceros. Which made what they needed to do a bit of a problem. "Edmund is convinced that there's a spy for New Destiny on the ship."

Evan opened his mouth to protest and then closed it, nodding.

"They do seem to find us with remarkable regularity," he replied.

"And they knew too much about our party when we got to the Isles. Now, it could be anyone . . ."

"It could be me," he said, looking at her suspiciously. "Or you. No, not you. You weren't on board when they intercepted us before."

"And, sorry, Evan," Rachel said with a smile. "I don't think you could bring it off."

"No, probably not," the engineer said with a grin.

"But you might be able to find out who it is," Daneh said. "Edmund told me to tell you 'avatar traces.' I have no idea what he's talking about."

"Hmmm." The engineer frowned and nodded. "When avatars, or any manifestation of Net energy, are formed, they give off a minute electromagnetic field. It's caused by the not quite perfect intratransmission of data among the nannites or fields that are formed. And in the case of straight projections, because it's a quantum field projection, the energy is actually quite high. In cases where they pass through grouped pieces of metal or other conducting materials they tend to create a static charge area that is similar in some respects to Saint Elmo's fire . . ."

"Okay, okay," Daneh said. "You don't regale me with the physics and I won't tell you about DNA interactions."

"You're a genegineer?" Evan said, delighted.

"No," Daneh replied. "Before the Fall, I fixed their screwups. But the point is, if he, the spy that is, is using a transmitter or being visited by an avatar, there should be traces."

"Well . . . yes," Evan said. "But very faint ones. I don't know how . . ." He paused and murmured to himself. "Perhaps if I . . ."

"I'll leave it to you," Daneh said, patting him on the knee. "But this is between us. If you find anything, report it to Rachel or me. *No* one else. Clear?"

"Not even the skipper?" Evan said.

"Not even the skipper." Daneh paused and then shrugged. "Whoever it is, they always appear to know our exact position. If they're not using a position locator, and I don't see why they would have access to one, then it has to be someone who has access to the updated navigational charts. How many members of the crew does that make?"

"Oh."

It was nearly midnight before the work was done and all the gear of the mer was loaded on the ship or on their backs. The group at the surface waved to the women and children on the ship in farewell. The younger mer, even those that could free-swim, had been loaded on board as well, most of them protesting furiously. Finally all preparations were complete and the ship raised anchor, filling its sails with the dying landwind, and moved off to sea.

"The faces of the women aren't something to take with you on the ship," Herzer muttered.

"What?" Jason said at the apparent non sequitur. "They're the ones on the ship."

" 'Bird of Prey March,' " Herzer said. "I really need to teach you some Kipling." He paused and frowned as they swam back to where the dragons were gathered. "Actually, there's one that's more fitting."

"Oh Danny boy, the pipes, the pipes are calling,
From glen to glen, and down the mountainside.
The summer's gone, and all the flowers are dying.
'Tis you, 'tis you must go, and I must bide.
But come ye back when summer's in the meadow,
Or when the valley's hushed and white with snow.
'Tis I'll be here in sunshine or in shadow,
Oh Danny boy, oh Danny boy, I love you so."

As he sang the clustered delphinos echoed the song back in weird harmony, the siren song drifting across the dark waters until finally it died away.

"That's a damned sad tune to start this journey on," Jason said.

"It's a damned sad journey," Herzer replied, taking his place in the protective hemisphere. The plan was to have Joanna take the point with dragons near the surface on all four sides and the armed mer-men in a hemisphere with the unarmed women and a few of the older males in the middle. The latter weren't there just to be guarded. The landsmen and the dragons needed fresh water and they were dragging along barrels of it. The fresh water was denser than the salt so the barrels tended to float but it was still going to be hard going. The delphinos were ranging out as scouts, but at the first sign of trouble they were to enter the protective bubble; there was no way for them to fight either the orcas or the ixchitl. Much less the reported kraken.

"You know a lot of songs like that?" Jason said as the group moved off.

"I love war," Herzer admitted. "It's a damned sad thing, but it's the one thing that I'm really good at. And if you love war, you have to know its face, the good, the bad and the ugly, and there really are all three faces. War has a beauty that is almost addictive, winning or losing. An ancient general said: 'It is good that war is so terrible, lest we grow too fond of it.' Music is to war what food is to sex, a very nice accompaniment. So, yeah, I know a lot of songs and poems about war. For that matter, I'm a pretty good cook," he added with a chuckle.

"You're weird, Herzer."

"So I've been told," the lieutenant admitted. "On the other hand, there are some that aren't quite so dreary. Old Ireland was called the land of sad war songs and happy wars. But

Norau was the land of sad, or at least unwilling, wars and happy war songs. Let me teach you one of those."

And so, with the delphinos echoing back the tune through the night-dark seas, he taught the group of mer-warriors the words to the song "March of Cambreadth."

The ixchitl struck at dawn.

The day dawned clear with scudding winds from the north. On them the clipper rolled south under nearly full sail at almost forty klicks per hour.

"Great day to be sailing, sir," Jerry said as he scrambled up the ladder to the bridge. "Do you want to launch?"

"Hell, yes," the skipper said, bellowing for all hands to turn the ship into the wind. When the crew was engaged he turned back to the rider. "I want constant top cover. Keep an eye out for that damned kraken. And, of course, any New Destiny ships. We're not going to bother parleying; I am not willing to be Mister Reasonable with this cargo."

"Aye, aye, sir," the warrant said, saluting. Shep had already been brought from below so Jerry settled his gloves, glad for the first time in nearly a week to be in proper gear, and loaded her on the catapult. As soon as the wind was off the port quarter he launched for the dawn patrol.

Jerry had been recovered and Koo was aloft when the lookout called down to the bridge.

"Dragon signaling, sir," the sailor called. "Number twenty-four, and four dips!"

"Enemy in sight," the signal midshipman read off. "Five ships."

"Bloody hell," the skipper growled. He had the weather gauge of the ships and more speed than they, either with or against the wind. But the position they had chosen was a narrows that he had the choice of passing through or beating around for another two or three days, maybe a week. And there was another thing.

"Damnit, XO, they're waiting for us," the skipper snarled.

"Maybe, sir," Mbeki said, with a shrug. "But this is the logical path if we're taking the southern route. They might have another force on the northern turn as well."

"I don't buy it, XO," the skipper said, shaking his head. "Once is happenstance, twice is coincidence, three times is enemy action."

"Yes, sir, nuke Mars now," Mbeki said, completing a joke so old its genesis had been lost. "But this is only twice."

"No, that damned kraken as well," the skipper said. "Well, it doesn't matter, one way or the other. We have to pass through. But we're still below the horizon to them. Bring the ship into the wind, I need to talk to Warrant Officer Riadou."

Evan knocked on the door of the wardroom and entered without permission to the frown of the skipper.

"What?" Chang snapped.

"I heard that there are more ships ahead," the engineer replied, seeming not to notice the rebuke. "I was looking for Jerry. Herzer asked me to make something for him, but in all the bustle we never got to test it."

"What?" Jerry asked.

"Well, the skipper was saying that he wanted the ship to be more offensive."

A leather-and-wood device had already been strapped to the breast of a protesting Shep when they reached the deck. It was mostly wooden box, with three partitions, and some leather reins and wooden levers, apparently to open the partitions.

"I'm afraid it's . . . somewhat dangerous to the ship, sir," Evan said. "Loading is the worst part. You see, each of the compartments has a pottery jug of jellied gasoline in it."

"Ouch!" Jerry said. "But . . ."

"Oh, it also has a fuse," Evan said. "It was that that took me so long to make. The first few designs tended to detonate prematurely."

Jerry had a sudden clear image of what it would be like to be riding a flaming wyvern and closed his eyes against it.

"They'd better not prematurely detonate on my ship, Mr. Mayerle," the skipper said angrily.

"Well, I'm fairly confident in this design," the engineer said with an abstracted expression. "There's a vial of sodium and a vial of water in the base of the jar. When the two hit something solid, the sodium ignites and that, in turn, ignites the gasoline. As long as they're not dropped . . . That was why I was commenting on the loading."

"We're going to need to come up with some *very careful procedures*," the skipper said in a definite voice.

"Yes, sir," Evan replied. "But, there they are."

"I just pull the straps?" Jerry said, looking the device over. There were three straps and three boxes. He noticed that the boxes had pins through their covers; until those were released, they couldn't be opened. The pins had white pieces of canvas on them that fluttered in the wind. If they hadn't been pulled, it would be evident.

"Well, I suspect that hitting the ships will be harder than you anticipate," Evan replied. "Wind drift, differences in speed. But . . . yes."

"Skipper," the dragon-rider said with a feral grin, tightening up his gloves. "I think we've got us a *strike* carrier."

"As long as we have something to sail to," the skipper noted, looking to the north where the ship was now pointed. "Okay, I'm going to stay below the horizon; it's up to you riders. Go show them why they don't mess with the UFS."

The ixchitl had been lying doggo in the sand but one of the delphinos just ahead of Joanna spotted them and raised the alarm. However, before it could turn to run back to the ring of defenses one of the ixchitl erupted from the sand and passed over it, firing down with its nematocysts.

Joanna reacted immediately but even as she clamped her jaws shut on the ray it was too late; the harpoon had done its work and the delphino rolled over on its back as the neurotoxin coursed through its body.

The group was suddenly surrounded by a white cloud as the school of ambushing rays erupted out of the sand, filling the water with their wings. They rushed the bristling hemisphere but could neither penetrate the shield of spears, nor get above the group to fire down.

The dragons, meanwhile, were ravaging through their school, chopping at the rays. Ridden by Bast, Edmund and Herzer, they kept near the surface where the ixchitl's rays could not reach them, but they could bite downward. The ixchitl found themselves trapped between the dragons above and the hemisphere of spears.

Finally they backed off and one of the larger ixchitl turned on its side, its normally white underbelly flashing through a range of colors. At apparent command two of the rays on the far side broke off and then came back at speed, leaping high into the air and into the midst of the crowd of mer-maids and huddling delphinos.

They arrived with a tremendous splash and the impact momentarily broke the spear line. They also fired their harpoons immediately, and apparently at random, hitting one of the mer-girls and a delphino.

Even this did not avail them much. The spear line reformed before the ixchitl to the outside could do anything to help their comrades and at a squealed command from Herman two of the delphinos grabbed the nematocyst cords, practically before they could begin pumping poison, and rolled with them, like great crocodiles, until the cords were ripped from the bellies of the beasts.

Furthermore, the mer-women were not unarmed and they fell on the ixchitl with the fury of anger and desperation. Two of them were badly bitten but the steel and bone knives jabbed and fell and before long the ixchitls' carcasses drifted downward on the light current.

At this the ixchitl leader flashed his belly again and the whole group broke off the attack, heading for deeper water.

Herzer directed Chauncey up to the surface with his knees and pulled back his mask for a breath of real air. They had attached sailcloth collars to the dragons, even Joanna, and the riders held onto them while riding. But the dragons spent most of their time under water, like a dolphin, and it meant spending all his time breathing through the mask. Since the battle with the orcas he'd developed a distaste for the mask, all mental he well knew, but real for all that. So he took every opportunity to get a breath of real air.

Jason surfaced beside him, lifting himself on Chauncey's wing to blast out his lungs as Joanna, Bast and Edmund popped to the surface.

"Well, breakfast for the dragons was catered," Joanna said, swallowing the last of an ixchitl.

"You'd better hope that neurotoxin is digestible," Herzer said, looking around at the placid sea. The wind was from the north and with the islands blocking the breeze there was barely a chop where they had been attacked.

"We need to rest," Jason said. "And we've got wounded."

"Well, we can't rest in the middle of the water," Edmund said. "Those damned orcas will be back sooner or later and they can break the spear line if they're willing to take some casualties. Break up the hemisphere and we're done."

"The mer can pull themselves out on the beach," Herzer said. "But the delphinos can't."

"A bay," Bast said. "One with a narrow entrance but enough water in it for the delphinos to float."

"There's one up the coast," Jason said after a moment's thought. "But . . . it's a ways."

"No help for it," Edmund said, pulling his mask down over

his face. "The orcas and ixchitl will be dealing with fatigue, too."

"Fatigue!" Jason said. "We've been fighting or swimming since yesterday afternoon! And we're out of food."

"We just keep going," Edmund said, pointing Nebka into the water. "That's all we can do."

"Fight until you die and drop," Herzer said, looking at Jason steadily as he pulled his own mask down. "Now you know what it really means."

"What are you? Iron?" Jason snarled. Even though Herzer had been on the dragon most of the way, he knew that the landsman had been doing more than his share of fighting.

"No," Herzer said, "I'm a Blood Lord. Works out to the same thing, though. Blood to our blood, steel to our steel."

Jerry waved Koo back to the ship and took up station overlooking the black-sailed caravels. Koo, though, flew alongside and made a questioning sign at the device slung under Shep. Jerry thought about it, realized that they were going to have to come up with a sign for "bomb rack" and made the sign for "weapon." Then he added "Weapon Yazov. Send Yazov," and waved Koo away.

He watched the ships as he waited for the other dragon to first be readied and then reach his position. They were tacking back and forth across the narrow passage in a ragged line, clearly intending to block the passage. Since the only boats they had seen were local fishing boats, and none of them near here, they were clearly waiting for the clipper. And the war between New Destiny and the UFS was already declared. But he still felt uncomfortable about what he was about to do.

By the time Vickie and Yazov had reached him, he had come up with a tentative plan. He had been watching the boats and noticed that besides going forward, they had a nasty tendency to crab sideways away from the wind. The term "to leeward" came to mind from conversations among the ship's officers. So he had to account for that when he was dropping his . . . bombs. Fire bombs, technically. When Vickie reached his position he waved her closer so they could talk.

"I'm going to make my runs," he said. "Watch what I do and we'll try to figure out the best way to work this."

"Okay," she yelled. "Is it just me, or does something feel wrong about this?"

"It's not just you," Jerry yelled back. "But that's why they call it war."

He lined up to come at the front of the boat, high enough that arrows wouldn't reach the wyvern. He had to mentally judge the drift of the boat, and the dragon, and released his first bomb when it was where he thought it would hit the ship. He had lined up long-ways on the ship, since that made for a bigger target area, and the bomb dropped clean but over the windward side; he'd made too much correction. The ship was also closing too fast, so he lined up from astern this time and tried again. This time the bomb fell off to the leeward side. Finally, he came to the conclusion that he needed to get closer to the ship. He banked around and got back up to altitude again, but this time he waited until he was almost over the boat and then put Shep into a steep dive, pointed right at the mainmast.

He could clearly see figures in black armor on the deck, pointing crossbows up at the dragon. But most of them loosed far too soon and the arrows hissed back down into the sea. He dove to well below his previous point and then released, pointed just forward of the mainmast, and pulled Shep up and to windward.

The dragon could not pull out of the dive immediately and he ended up banking out and to the side, nearly at the level of the mast. A flock of bolts from the crossbows followed him as he banked up and away, but most of them struck the nearly invulnerable wings. Jerry could distinctly hear the guttural cries of the orc marines and the shouts of the crew, as well as several awful screams but he waited to see the effect until he got the dragon up to altitude again. Shep was whimpering and Jerry craned around but couldn't see any damage.

"You've got a bolt in his leg," Vickie said, drifting over him. "It's barely in, but you're going to have a fun time landing."

"Don't go as low as I did," Jerry said.

"I won't. Look at that sucker burn, though."

Jerry banked around and looked down at the caravel. The bomb had apparently hit just forward of the mainmast and the maindeck was fully involved. He could see fire parties trying to stop the flames but the jellied gasoline simply spread out when hit by water. As he watched, the mainsail caught fire and was whipped into ash in a moment. The mast had caught as well and even as he watched men and orcs were jumping over the side to escape the flames. The orcs, in their armor, sank like stones, but the crew was lowering the boats and some of the unChanged humans were going to survive. Some.

"A shallow dive doesn't seem to do it," Jerry called. "Come

from the rear and drop towards the mainmast. Watch the way they fall off to leeward, but the wind is pushing the bombs, too. And don't get as low as I did."

"Will do," Vickie yelled.

"I'm heading back to base," Jerry called, turning the dragon towards the carrier.

The ships had come into the wind and were beating to the north. They had apparently figured out that the carrier was up there somewhere. Jerry made a mental note to pass that on to the skipper.

Martin watched the object drop away from the dragon in puzzlement until it burst into flame.

"So much for there not being any way for the dragons to harm us," the captain said. He was a squat man named Gebshe with a cynical outlook on life. He raised an eyebrow at Martin and shrugged. "That's one fine barbecue. What now? We apparently cannot shoot them down."

"They came from the north," Martin said. "Turn that way and sail this tub as fast as you can. Try to find that carrier. If we can close with it, we'll destroy it. If not . . ." Martin shrugged.

"I think we'll do that," the captain said. "But I also think we'll have the boats standing by, just in case."

Martin had placed the ship that he was on one wing of the formation of caravels. The dragon-rider, naturally supposing the center ship was the leader, had concentrated his fire on that one, which was now well on the way to burning to the waterline. In his haste, he hadn't thought of what raising signaling flags would mean and as soon as they went up the mast the replacement dragon-rider, which had lined up to drop on the far ship, banked around and headed for his.

"Gebshe," Martin said, "you have my authority to maneuver independently."

"Why, thank you, kind sir," the captain said, judging the line-up of the rider. "I can't imagine that I would do so entirely on my own."

Martin grinned. At least the captain was retaining his sense of humor in this disaster. Because disaster it was. He knew there was no way that the ships could catch the carrier if it kicked up its heels. Which it would as soon as it heard they were headed its way. And the dragons were impossible targets; they just stayed too high for the crossbows to reach. But that might mean they could avoid their bombing, for now. If they could just hold on until dusk. In the night they could slip away and be well away by dawn. He didn't care what his orders were; there was no way he was going to sit here and be used for bombing practice.

The dragon had lined up on its bombing dive and he looked at the captain.

"Just waiting for it to get too deep in to correct," Gebshe said, then "Port your helm! Jib sheets!"

The caravel came around slowly, too slowly, and the dragon expertly corrected, making minute changes in its wingtips to keep the round-hulled ship in its sights. It loosed, high, but accurately, and the bomb dropped just behind the mainmast.

The effect was much more hideous up close. A group of sailors were trimming the mainsail and the bucket of liquid fire dropped over half of them, clinging to their skin as they ran, screaming, over the edge of the ship and jumped in the water. As they ran they spread droplets—Martin could track the progress of one by the blazing footprints he left—spreading the fire even wider.

A crew had been standing by with buckets and a pump, but even pouring water on it simply spread the fire around. As he watched, the ropes of the mainsail caught fire, the fire traveling quickly up the tarred cordage and catching the sail on fire. It disappeared before his very eyes. By the time he looked back to the deck, the whole center of the ship was a blazing inferno.

"So much for the boats," Gebshe said, philosophically. He looked to the west where land was just in view on the horizon. "Long swim," he said, taking off his coat and cutlass. "Last one there gets eaten." With that he dove over the side.

Martin was looking at the inferno and wondering what to do. It was, indeed, a long way to the coast. Too long for him; he was no great swimmer. But there were always options.

He pulled the communications cube out of his pocket and said: "Conner."

In a moment a projection appeared. Brother Conner apparently heard the crackling behind him and turned around.

"Fascinating," Conner said.

"Your report that the dragons had no offensive capability was, I hate to tell you, quite inaccurate," Martin said, pointing to where the dragon was lining up on another of the maneuvering ships. As he did the screams of the orcs below showed that the fire was getting to their quarters.

"Quite distressing, I admit," Conner said, cheerfully. "But important data that Chansa will, if not be pleased, appreciate knowing."

"Well, it also got the ship's boats," Martin said. "So I'd appreciate a lift out."

"Ah, well, sorry old friend," Conner said with a shrug. "But my power budget isn't quite up to a teleport. Other projects to support. Seems you're on your own."

"What? You little weasel?" Martin paused, furious with anger. "You bully me out onto the ass end of nowhere and then you're just going to dump me?"

"Seems like it," Conner said with another shrug. "Take care." And then he was gone.

"Conner?" Martin said, shaking the cube. "Conner. Damnit!" He looked at the rapidly approaching inferno and chucked the useless cube over the side. Then he took off his boots and shirt, sorrowfully. Both had been custom-made for him and he had grown attached to them, especially the boots. But needs must. He then cut the legs of his finely woven silk pants just below his crotch, in a circle, leaving him in short shorts and holding two tubes of fabric. He tightened his belt around his waist, tied one end of each tube, put his knife away and followed the captain over the side.

CHAPTER THIRTY

Back on the carrier, with Shep having the bolt removed from his thigh, Jerry watched nervously for any sign of Vickie. At his warning the carrier had continued into the wind, running far to the north, and he was afraid that it was too far. Koo was out there, as well, but both of them had faded over the horizon and Vickie should have been on her way back by now.

Finally there were two dots to be seen and the carrier prepared to recover dragons.

"Worked like a charm," Vickie said, hopping off of Yazov as the dragon was led below. "I got three for three. One of them was right up in the bow of the boat, though, and if they were fast they might have gotten it out. But it burned up their front sails before I turned back. There's only one ship that's unscathed, and the other three are sunk or were burning to the waterline when I turned back."

"Good job," the skipper said. "How are the dragons?"

Jerry looked at the sky and shrugged.

"Shep is out for today anyway," he said. "We can send one more sortie out if you want."

"Do it," the skipper said. "We're fair for launching now. As soon as they're in the air I'm going to turn around and head back downwind. Make sure there's nothing in my way when I get there."

Shep's bomb-rig was loaded onto Nebka and the two dragons took off, one after the other, climbing fast to the south.

"All hands wear ship," the skipper called. "Let's go chase some dragon."

It was late afternoon when the lookouts spotted the dragons, flapping wearily north against the wind. The captain actually sailed down past them before turning the ship about and came up to the LSO position for their landing. This time Nebka had a bolt in his leg and when he landed it crumpled under him. But a sling was put in place and the piteously wailing wyvern was lifted up and lowered into the stable area.

Koo had been thrown clear on the landing but stumbled to his feet and blearily saluted the skipper.

"They're all burned, sir," the rider said. "I went too low on my second pass. The one that Vickie winged had put out the fire and they were apparently a little upset about it. They were learning to maneuver, too. But we got both of them. I had one bomb left but I dumped it on the way back."

"Damn fine job," the skipper said, shaking his hand. "Now, get below and get some rest, we still have Vickie to recover."

Vickie made a perfect landing, but she was clearly tired.

"You know, I think landing is worse than fighting?" she said as she slid off her wyvern. "We got 'em all, though. How's Koo and Debka?"

"Debka's leg looked bad," Jerry said. "Worse than Shep. Right now, you've got the only hale dragon."

"Well, we won't need them for those guys," Vickie said. "Some of them were in boats headed for the islands. I suppose they'll be a problem for the islanders but we can always send some marines or Blood Lords down to fix that." She shook her head tiredly. "It really takes it out of you."

"So does the waiting," the skipper said. "And the wondering. This is a strange sea battle. You expect boarding actions, but this is all . . . at arm's length. It just feels . . . wrong."

"Not particularly heroic," Jerry said. "But I wonder . . ."

"What?"

"I wonder when they'll start having carriers of their own," he said, looking to the south.

"Now *that* will be something," Vickie admitted.

"And *I* wonder how the mer are doing," the skipper said.

It was near dusk when the weary group of mer and dragons reached Charzan Inlet. The broad, flat banks were visible through the entrance and warm, almost hot, water boiled out to the ocean on a descending tide.

Herzer reveled in it. As the day had progressed he had gotten colder and colder until by the late afternoon he was shivering uncontrollably and continuously. The warm water of the inlet was like a balm to the soul.

The mer quickly writhed their way over the sandbar at the entrance of the inlet, which on the falling tide had less than a meter of water covering it. They then clustered in the shallow waters, lying back and breathing in the warm salt.

"Up," Herzer said, wearily. He had dismounted from Chauncey and now waded through the thigh deep water, thumping the mer with his foot. "The delphinos need the space; you're for the land."

"Oh, God, Herzer," Elayna said, sitting up and blowing water from her lungs. "We can come on land, but it's not comfortable."

"I don't really give a rat's ass," Herzer said, tiredly. "Get your pretty little tail up on land and make room for Herman and his people."

Between Herzer, Edmund and what Herzer had come to think of as the mer-leaders—Jason, Pete, Antja and Bill—they got the mer up and out of the inlet as the delphinos started to fight their way over the bar.

They had far more trouble with it than the mer. The delphino bodies were ill suited for crossing the spit—they were purely marine creatures—and in the interval the tide had fallen still farther, making the water over the bar barely the depth of their bodies. But with some assistance from Herzer and Bast they all made it into the inlet. The water in the inlet was deep enough that they weren't going to have to support their weight, which was the important part. And if they and the mer had hard going getting into the inlet, so would the ixchitl and the orcas, if the latter ever showed up.

But even after getting everyone in the inlet the work wasn't done.

"Jason," Edmund said. "We're going to have to post sentries, about one person in four. They'll take two hour shifts. One of the command group is going to have to be awake at all times as well."

"Okay," Jason said, wearily. "I'll go start finding people."

"General," Herzer said, "I want to go check the back of the inlet."

"That's the banks back there, Herzer," Pete said. "None of the ixchitl can make it through the banks, even at high tide. And it won't start flooding for a couple of hours."

"Fine, Pete," Herzer said. "But you don't make assumptions. We need to watch that as well as the *land*. There's nothing saying that they won't have help from landsmen and if we get attacked by orcs we're all up shit's creek."

"Do it," Edmund said. "Joanna."

"General?" the dragon said. For the first time in Herzer's experience she actually looked ragged, her wings hanging slightly limp.

"Go hunt with the wyverns. Keep an eye out for enemies. Try to bring something back if you can find enough, but get yourselves fed."

Herzer walked to the back of the inlet as the dragons waded into the water to hunt. From the spit of land at the back of the inlet he could see far out over the banks in the dying light. The water on the north side was deeper than at the entrance but he could see that it shoaled out quickly and large areas of the banks were already exposed to the dropping tide. Ixchitl probably couldn't make their way through that, but better safe than sorry. He waded into the warm waters of the inlet, noting that the breeze was turning colder as the sun set, and hunted up Herman.

The leader of the delphinos was floating at the edge of his pod, dropping below the surface from time to time until his pectorals hit the bottom then floating back up to breathe.

"Herman," Herzer said as the leader resurfaced.

"Herzer man," the delphino squeaked. "Safe are?"

"I'd like a couple of delphinos awake in shifts, posted near the inlet on the north. Probably nothing can come across the banks, but we shouldn't take 'probably' for an answer right now."

"Will," the delphino said, dropping below the surface and clicking his sonar. A couple of the delphino males, clicking irritably, moved to the north and stationed themselves by the entrance.

"I'll get someone to tell them when to find relief," Herzer said. "I'd suggest you get some sleep."

"Hungry," Herman replied. "Pod hungry."

"Hopefully the dragons will bring something back," was all Herzer said.

He waded wearily ashore and found that Bast had, somehow, gotten a fire started.

"Get some water," Edmund said, pointing at one of the barrels that had had its end opened. "No more than a liter; we need most of it for the dragons."

Herzer dipped out a cup of water and drank it carefully, avoiding slopping any despite his thirst. He had been in sun and salt water all day and his body felt like a drooping plant.

The water seemed like the finest wine and he felt refreshed with just one cup but he carefully drained another; he knew he needed it.

"There's some mackerel left," Edmund said. "But until the dragons get back I don't want to share it out."

"I found some conch," Pete said. He had already extracted the snail from the shells and was now cutting the foot of the mollusc into slices. "Wish I had some lemon. It's pretty good marinated in lemon juice."

"I'll just toast mine if you don't mind," Herzer said, accepting one of the slices and going up into the brush to find a stick. He returned with four of them and managed to whittle a point that would penetrate the rock-hard flesh. He held it over the fire, turning it carefully, until the flesh became limp, then pulled it out, nibbling at it before it even cooled.

"Bleck," he said, struggling with the rubbery flesh. "I never thought I'd eat anything *worse* than monkey on a stick."

"I'm not sure I want to know," Antja said.

"Field rations," Edmund said, struggling with his own conch. "Dried and pressed meat, basically."

"But I'd kill for a handful of parched corn about now," Herzer added.

"Wine-baked venison," Bast said.

"Stalled ox," Edmund added with a chuckle. "With the meat red at the bone."

"Trigger fish in wine and cream sauce," Pete added. He hadn't bothered to cook his conch and it was already gone.

"How about grilled grouper?" Joanna said from the edge of the fire. The voice was muffled because she held one the size of Bast's torso in her mouth.

"Nothing that big should be able to move that quietly," Jason said as Chauncey dropped a smaller grouper by Herzer.

"We're going to have to share this with the delphinos," Herzer said as Edmund started to gut the fish.

"Donal is taking them the largest," Joanna said. "And I'm ready to collapse."

"Lie in the entrance, if you don't mind," Edmund said. "You're not going to get too cold?"

"No, I'm fine," the dragon said, then yawned hugely. "But ready to sleep. And when the time comes, you owe me one of those stalled oxen, barbecued. With sauce."

"Will do," Edmund chuckled.

"See ya," the dragon said, moving out of the firelight.

The wyverns had already backed up against the cliff and

were nodding off to sleep. Herzer realized he could barely keep his eyes open but he waited for the fish to cook, nodding from time to time. Many of the mer hadn't had that much discipline, or hunger, Elayna included, and were sprawled on the sands asleep.

When the fish was cooked he took portions and went among the mer, waking them up and forcing them to eat. Many of them protested that they weren't hungry but he made sure that they all were eating before going back to his, small, portion.

"A liter of water and, what? Two hundred grams of grouper? This is like the Dying Time."

"No," Edmund said. "More water then." He popped his own morsel of grouper into his mouth and swallowed it nearly whole. "I'm for bed."

"I'll take first watch," Herzer said.

"No, I will," Bast said. "But you're going to lie down here beside me."

Herzer soon found himself in a pile of bodies as the mer and landsmen huddled together for warmth against the cold wind. Herzer, Edmund, Bast, Elayna, Antja, Jason and Pete were all there. He realized that it wasn't just warm, it was comfortably warm, and that was the last thing he remembered. Except a memory of gnawing hunger through the night.

He awoke to a bellow and was on his feet, sword drawn, before he realized that it was dawn, with the sun peeping over the horizon to the southeast.

He looked around for danger but then saw Joanna, stretching and yawning hugely in the dawn light.

"Sorry about that," Joanna said, yawning again, which came as a bellow from the belly of the immense beast. "Can't help it."

"Well, the good news is we're all awake," Edmund said. He, too, was on his feet but his sword was still sheathed.

"And how are you this morning, Commander Gramlich?" Herzer asked.

"Fine," the dragon replied, yawning again. "Except I had to keep waking up all night to let the water in and out."

It was apparent that the sand of the entrance had been gouged by water and dragon claws. It was also deeper than it had been on their entrance, with the water going out again. They had slept through the flood and high tide and now were in the ebb again.

"Dragons have to forage first," Edmund said, looking around at the mer, who were wiping at their eyes. "Landsmen and dragons get some water first. If the delphinos want to run some scouts out, I wouldn't mind. When the dragons get back, if they bring anything, we eat. Then we take off."

"We're going farther out this time," Joanna said. "We pretty much hunted out this area last night."

"Go," Edmund said. "Take as much time as you need, but no more."

"Will do, General," the dragon said with a grin. She rounded up the wyverns and between the three dragons they finished off the water barrel. Then they headed for the crest of the island to get some room for takeoff.

"I was supposed to take a watch last night," Herzer told Bast, who looked wide awake.

"I don't need that much sleep," Bast said. "And there were no threats. On that you may trust me, lover."

"I do," Herzer admitted. "And thanks."

"You can thank me properly later," she said with a grin. "There's been so little time!"

"Where the hell are the orcas?" Edmund growled. He was looking out to sea, frowning. "The ixchitl can be down in the sand. But the orcas *have* to surface some time or another. I expected them to be waiting right outside the entrance when we woke up."

But neither the orcas nor the ixchitl made their appearance even after the dragons returned with a fine haul of large fish.

"We saw some rays in the distance," Joanna said and burped hugely. "But I don't know if they were ixchitl; we didn't get that close. There's a really productive reef just down the coast; we could see all the fish on it as we flew over."

"This is great, Commander," Edmund said. The three dragons had returned with huge grouper and there was more than enough for everyone to, if not eat their fill, at least get a good portion.

"But we need to get on the move," Edmund said. The sun was already well up. "Dragons out, with riders, then the armed mer, then the delphinos, then the unarmed mer. We'll set up a perimeter until we can get the hemisphere reformed."

Herzer chuckled as he buckled the sailcloth halter on Chauncey, and Bast smiled at him as she climbed on Joanna's back.

"You see it, too," Bast said.

"Yep," Herzer replied, leading the dragon down to the water; it was nearly impossible to ride the dragons without their full harness until they were laid out in the water.

"What?" Edmund asked.

"You," Joanna said as she walked out into the water until she was deep enough to partially submerge. "Did you think about how to get out of this bay last night? Or did it emerge, full blown, from your forehead like Athena from Zeus?"

"I thought about it before we left Raven's Mill," Edmund replied. "It's a simple modification of the way that Roman Legions, or the Blood Lords for that matter, exited their camps."

"Except we don't have to take it down behind us," Herzer said with a nod. "I just hadn't thought that far ahead."

"You'll learn, Herzer," Edmund said, climbing on Donal when he lay down in the water. "You'll learn."

They weren't hit as they debouched from the inlet, or even after they reformed the hemisphere and started off down the coast.

"Where are they?" Herzer asked.

"Waiting in ambush," Edmund replied. "That's their way."

Herzer had taken the comment about thinking ahead to heart and used the time now. Something about the narrows that entered the channel through the banks had been bothering him for a while and how he had it.

"I think they're going to hit us at the entrance to the banks, sir," he said. They were traveling beneath the water, the dragons swimming for a while and then broaching like whales for a breath.

"That's my guess as well," Edmund replied.

"And there's only a few ways for them to do it," Herzer replied. "And . . . I think I have a way that we might be able to round up the whole set. But I'm afraid it might take too much coordination, that it's too complicated."

"If a plan is too complicated, the way to use it is to decomplicate it," Edmund replied. "So what's the plan?"

Herzer told him and he nodded.

"You're right," Edmund said after some thought. "That's too complicated. And you haven't allowed for it to go to hell in a handbasket. Let's see if we can decomplicate it and come up with a go-to-hell option."

They talked about it for a while, as, reinforcing their suspicions, the ixchitl failed to attack, until Edmund finally nodded.

"It doesn't take into account the orcas," Edmund said. "Or the kraken. But it will do. If one appears it still might work. If both appear we're on the go-to-hell-plan."

"Which is?" Herzer asked.

"The mer get on land, as far up as they can and the

delphinos are on their own," Edmund said, brutally. "If there's an orc force, we just pull into the shallows and fight until we're all dead. That's why it's called a 'go-to-hell' plan. You're all going to hell, anyway, so you might as well take as large an honor guard as possible. Go brief the mer, I'll handle the delphinos."

CHAPTER THIRTY-ONE

Rather than follow the coastline all the way around, since it would be two longer edges of a triangle, they cut the chord across deeper water. This was one of the potential attack points, in Herzer's opinion, and he kept a careful eye on the blue depths. But as no attack materialized, he relaxed, only to realize that they were approaching the entrance to the banks.

A long, narrow passage cut through the banks from the deeps side to the Stream side which was their destination. Most of the passage was up to thirty meters deep and almost a klick across. But at the edge of the deeps it narrowed and shallowed to only a few meters and no more than fifty meters across. Yet, within less than a click from the entrance into the deeps the water had deepened to over two thousand meters.

The group had reached no more than a hundred meters from the entrance when the sandbar to the northeast erupted in ixchitl.

There were more of them than had survived the first ambush, at least forty, and they swept around the formation, disdaining their nematocysts to close with the spear-wielding mermen.

Most of them disdained their nematocysts, that is, but others swept in, targeting the dragons in particular and Chauncey let out a bellow as a harpoon entered his back. He bellowed past the body of a dead ixchitl, however, and the poison did not seem to affect him as greatly as it did the humans. He turned on his side, wrapping his wings around his body and using the technique of the delphinos to wrap the cord of the harpoon about his body and bring the beast down to where his teeth could sink into it, turning the water around him bright scarlet with its blood.

But others were swarming on the wyverns and the lesser dragons had to break off to the south, pursued by at least twenty of the great rays. The rays were, in turn, pursued by Joanna.

The rest of the ixchitl gathered around the mer, trying to strike into the formation past the spears.

Herzer, Bast and Edmund had released the dragons at the first sign of attack and now formed a reinforcement team at the center of the hemisphere. But the group could not press past the ixchitl, without going under them and risking their nematocysts. By the same token, the ixchitl were finding it impossible to break the line of spears held by the mer-men. It seemed as if it was a stalemate until one of the delphinos squealed a distress cry, pounding his sonar to the southeast, into the deep. Rising out of the deep was a leviathan of tentacles and beak. The kraken had returned.

"Jason!" Edmund bellowed. "We're going to have to break low and proceed to the second phase. NOW."

The bottom of the mer burst open like a flower, sweeping up and under the ixchitl to the west, braving their toxic harpoons in the face of the greater threat. The delphinos burst through their formation, doing their best to catch the harpoons, with most of them hanging back by command.

The mer-women and older males dropped their burdens and broke under the mer-men, swimming as fast as they could for the entrance with the delphinos screening ahead of them, pounding the sand to check for a second ambush of the rays.

Herzer grabbed Herman as he went past, holding onto the big dolphin's dorsal fin with his prosthetic since there was no way that a landsman could keep up in this fast-paced underwater battle. He heard a scream from his side and looked over to see a harpoon pulsing poison into Elayna's arm.

His sword swept out without thought and slashed through the cord, then he grabbed one flailing arm and held on. The big dolphin had sensed his movement and slowed to allow him one moment to recover the girl but now accelerated hugely, heading as fast as he could for the shallows. Herzer felt as if both his arms were going to be torn from the sockets but he somehow retained his grip on sword, girl and delphino.

As the delphino came opposite the shallows on the near

side of the entrance he turned to the side sharply and threw Herzer and his burden off into the shallows. Without a word he then sped to the west, following his pod.

The mer-men, in apparent panic, were now streaming through the entrance to escape the combination of the ixchitl and the kraken. In the same apparent panic they made the same wrong turn in the tricky shallows as the mer-women, and ended up in a small, landlocked bay on the southwest side of the entrance.

There was no escape. The sides were relatively steep and while they could climb out onto the land they could never struggle over the steep cliffs around them. And the ixchitl controlled the only entrance to the sea. Unless someone came to their succor, the kraken could easily enter the relatively shallow bay and pluck them from the sides.

All of the ixchitl had followed them into the bay, even the group that had been pursuing the dragons, and the kraken waited at the entrance to the narrows, apparently preferring the deeps to the shallows that might be dangerous to his depth-adjusted design.

Herzer dragged Elayna farther up the shore, far enough that the kraken could not pull her to her death, and looked across the narrow entrance to the bay. It was almost exactly as he'd remembered it from his reading of the maps and he waved at Edmund, on the far side of the entrance, as he pulled the heavy package off his back.

"We still lost too many," he called.

"No plan survives contact with the enemy," Edmund replied. "This one came damned close. At least, it will, if you'll hurry up."

Herzer unfurled the monomolecular net from his back and took a section of it, whirling it around his head until it had good speed, and hurled it across the entrance.

At the splash, some of the ixchitl turned towards the sole opening to the bay, but Edmund had already splashed out into thigh-deep water and was scrambling back to the far shore.

The heavily weighted net quickly sunk to the bottom as Herzer and Edmund pounded the ends into the ground with the stakes they carried.

The ixchitl began to swim back and forth in the bay, flashing their bellies at each other. One jumped into the air to cross the net but the water on the far side was shallow as well and Herzer waded thigh deep before he spitted it to the sand below with his sword. The adamantite cut through flesh and cartilage, ripping a huge gash in the ixchitl, which was reduced to thrashing in the shallow water.

Another got a run up and jumped the net into slightly deeper water just as a shadow passed over the pool and Chauncey landed on it with both talons. One bite tore through the head of the ray and it, too, was left quivering as Donal landed next to the feasting wyvern. The latest arrival turned to the bay of penned rays and spread his wings, hissing in hunger and clashing his jaws as if to catch one in the air.

The kraken, seeing the dragons in water that was just deep enough for it to maneuver, jetted forward but stopped as Joanna landed in the inlet in water that was over her back.

"Hi," Joanna said. "Wanna play? I *like* calamari."

The kraken seemed to consider this for a moment and then jetted backwards in a cloud of black ink.

"Oh, no you don't," Joanna shouted leaping to the land and then running forward to get up in the air. "I'm *hungry*, damn it!" she bellowed.

She pounded her wings, ascending like an elevator and then turned over, pointed at the kraken, which was still, apparently, visible. She folded her wings back and, still accelerating, arrowed into the water like a dart.

"Commander!" Edmund yelled, but the dragon had already submerged.

"Well," Herzer said, bending to Elayna, "I guess we get to answer the eternal question."

"What?" Elayna asked, wincing.

"In a fight between a sea serpent and a kraken," Herzer said, seriously, "which one wins?"

Joanna had timed the dive perfectly and even as she started to slow in the water her mouth closed over the body of the squid.

It was the foulest taste she had ever experienced, a combination of ammonia with a hint of long-dead fish. But she bore down and felt something pop in its vitals.

It wasn't a killing blow, though, and the great kraken writhed in her grip, wrapping a tentacle around her neck and others around her wings, body, its beak tearing at her, searching for something that wasn't invulnerable wing.

Joanna's eyes bugged at the pressure from the tentacle and she shifted her grip to its base, ripping it off after a long struggle with the rubbery tissue. She spat the still-writhing tentacle out and bit down again, looking for something vulnerable, ripping at it with her talons, as the jets of the beast churned and they shot into the depths. She could feel the water growing colder and the light change from light blue to dark and then the deepest twilight. The pressure on her lungs was building enormously as she struggled to rip with talon and teeth.

Commander Gramlich, she thought, her brain growing foggy with the pressure and cold, *this was not the smartest thing you have ever done in your life.*

"I can't feel my arm," Elayna said, lifting it up from where it lay bonelessly on the sand.

"Daneh says it's only a paralysis agent," Herzer said. The bonelike harpoon was deeply embedded in her arm, though. "I think we should wait to try to get that out." He took his sword and cut the dangling cord off.

"Okay," she replied. "Thank you."

"Don't thank me," Herzer said. "We'd both be dead if it weren't for Herman."

"Where'd they go?" Elayna asked, sitting up.

"Down the passage," Herzer said. "They're *faster* than the ixchitl. It's the orcas that they're worried about, but the orcas weren't going to go into the shallows; they would have been out in the deeps somewhere."

"So now what?" Elayna asked.

"Now, we wait for the tide to go out," Herzer said, looking out to sea. "And we count the breakage."

The breakage had been heavy. Jackson the toolmaker was missing as well as a half a dozen of the mer-men who had given their lives to screen the retreating forces. Two of the mer-women were missing as well. Leaving Donal to hold the entrance, Herzer took Chauncey back into deep water to try to find them and Joanna, who hadn't returned.

He found one mangled body of a mer-woman, her identity a mystery, and another was found by one of the greatly daring delphino scouts that darted out of the entrance. But no further sign of the mer-folk, or of Joanna, was seen.

"I can't believe she's dead," Elayna said, when Herzer returned.

"She might be invulnerable to most harm," Herzer pointed out. "But she can't hold her breath forever."

"She said she can hold it a long time," Edmund pointed out.

"It's been nearly an hour," Herzer replied.

"We've got time," the general replied, looking up at the sun. "It's several more hours to low tide."

The ixchitl had apparently divined the plan and had been making more rushes at the entrance. But some of the armed mer-men had worked their way over the rocks to the entrance and the delphinos clustered there as well. One ixchitl that worked its way under the net was torn apart by the enraged delphinos even before the dragons could swarm on it. After that Herzer cut stakes and the net was staked all the way across the entrance.

Still they looked out to sea, hoping to see any sign of a sea serpent's head. The sun was descending in the west and they had virtually given up hope when Chauncey gave a startled cry and flapped his wings.

Herzer ran up to the shoulder of the ridge that formed the embayment and looked out to the darkening sea. Sure enough, there was a snakelike head slowly making its way back to shore.

Thirty minutes later Joanna dragged herself up onto shore. Her belly was ripped in numerous places and her back was covered with broad, red welts. But she was alive.

"Cristo," she muttered, collapsing in a heap. "Remind me not to do that again."

"So did you *escape*?" Edmund asked. "Or eat?"

"Neither," she answered, wearily. "I swear I died. But I *know* it did. And I didn't eat; have you started serving ixchitl yet?"

"No," Edmund said, looking at the rapidly shallowing water. "Soon."

"Good," she said, "wake me up when some's done. I'd like mine medium."

"The kraken is *definitely* dead," Edmund pursued.

"Cracked its brain case with my own teeth," Joanna said, her eyes closed. "Poke me if I lie."

"And you didn't eat it?" Herzer asked, aghast.

"Worst stuff I've ever tasted," she answered. "Now, if you please, I vunt to be alun." In moments she was snoring hugely.

It was after dark before the tide had gone out fully, but Herzer and Bast had gathered quantities of firewood and the water in the bay was lit with red when they and Edmund walked across the sandy bottom.

The ixchitl were crowded into the narrow stretch of remaining water, their wings flapping as they fought for the remaining breathable liquid, the firelight reflecting from madly churning wings, backs, eyes.

Herzer stopped as he raised the boarding pike and looked over at the general.

"Question, sir," he said, lowering the pike as one of the ixchitl rolled an eye upward at him, gill openings on its back flapping in distress. "Is this a violation of the laws of land warfare?"

"Good question," Edmund said, leaning on his own pike. "They're sentient beings, so they can't be treated like animals. On the other hand, they're not signatory to any agreements with us and they have all participated in their own illegalities. On the gripping hand, we're planning on feeding them to our dragons. And, honestly, I'm thinking of having a couple of wing-steaks myself. What's your feeling, Lieutenant?"

Herzer looked down at the flapping rays and raised his pike. He thought about the tail of a mer-child lying on the sand of Whale Point Drop. Of Bruce, Jackson and all the others, paralyzed and dying for a breath of water or air. Eaten alive.

"Kill them all, sir," the lieutenant growled, spearing downward and flipping the wounded ray out of the mass onto the hard, dry sand where it would die like a fish out of water. "God will surely know his own."

"It tastes like . . . scallop," Herzer muttered around a steak the size of a large Porterhouse.

The band of ixchitl had yielded enough food for the entire party to eat their fill. Cutting along the backbone and peeling back the skin of the wings revealed huge chunks of white, linear sections of meat separated by cartilaginous tissue. The dragons had simply torn into the ixchitl given to them, but Pete had shown how to separate out the steaks and these had been grilled over the fires, using the monomolecular net to keep them away from the flames. The produced meat was succulent and juicy, heavy in fat, and Herzer realized he'd eaten his steak without a pause.

"Back before replicators," Edmund said, "they would catch rays and chunk them up, selling the meat as scallop meat. When replicators were introduced they used that meat as the template rather than real scallops. Real scallops got called 'bay' scallops. They're sweeter and less chewy."

"It's still good," Herzer said.

"You realize that this is cannibalism, right?" Pete said, chewing slowly.

"For you," Bast said. She had produced a fork from her apparently infinite pouch and was delicately cutting slices from her steak. "I'm an elf. It doesn't count."

"They're still sentient beings," Jason pointed out.

"I'm not telling you you have to eat it," Bast said. "In fact, if you're done . . ."

"No," Jason said, popping a piece into his mouth. "Just wanted to point it out."

"For me, it helps," Elayna said, chewing on a mouthful of the juicy meat. Her arm was tender and swollen around the harpoon still in it and had been bound up in a sling. But the other more than sufficed for current needs.

"Why?" Pete asked.

"The next time we have to fight them, I'll just be thinking about the barbecue afterwards," she said with a feral grin.

The barrels of water had been recovered but the island hosted a small spring and Herzer had had a chance to drink his fill and wash some of the salt off. All in all, he was feeling better than he had since the first attack on the town.

"Sentries are detailed, General," he said formally. "I've got the second watch, so I'm for bed."

The flood tide was making and there was enough room for most of the delphinos to fit in the bay again. The rest, mostly young males, hovered nervously at the dragon-covered entrance. But the two wyverns were posted by the water and if there was any attack they would be ready.

"I'd join you," Elayna said, "but out of the water I'm not much fun."

"If Herzer will carry you, feel free," Bast smiled. "I wouldn't mind a threesome."

"Oh, Lord, what have I done to deserve this?" Herzer asked, holding up his arms.

"Is that thanks or a plea?" Elayna laughed. "No, you two go. I'm going to stay here by the fire and finish off the rays."

"Do you want some help with that?" Pete asked.

"Yes, as a matter of fact," she replied, smiling at him. "I'd love some help."

"Come along, love," Bast said, pulling Herzer to his feet. "You got plenty of sleep last night."

Jason watched them as they walked up the hill and winked at Antja. "Care to try it on land?"

"Not on your life," she said. "General, what happens tomorrow?"

"I think the ixchitl, if there are any left, aren't going to be a problem anymore," Edmund said. "But the orcas are still unaccounted for."

"They're not going to go in the shallows," Jason pointed out. "They get beached too easily."

"So I don't think we have to worry about them until we reach the far side," Edmund replied. "But we shouldn't let our guard down. We're not safe until we're linked back up with the carrier and everyone is safely in your bay. Maybe not even then. I won't be happy until there's a serious guard force down here and a solid defense set up. Then we can start striking back."

"I look forward to the day," Jason said. "But I've got third watch, so I'm for bed."

"I'll snuggle with you, but that's all," Antja said, crawling into the darkness. "Understand?"

"Snuggle," Jason said with a grin. "Right."

CHAPTER THIRTY-TWO

"Mr. Mayerle," Commander Mbeki said, "what are you doing?"

The engineer was in the process of attaching a small box to the mainmast. It had a brass dial on the front and a winding key on the side, which he proceeded to wind up.

"Gravitic anomaly detector, sir," the engineer replied. He had finished winding the key and headed for the rear of the ship. "It detects small changes in the gravity as the ship passes over. By taking the punch tapes in them, and comparing them to the course, I think I can figure out a back-up navigational system for when we're under cloudy skies. I thought of it when we were having all that trouble finding the shoals when we were clouded over."

"It wasn't *finding* the shoals we were interested in," the commander said with a chuckle. "It was *avoiding* them."

"As you say, sir," the engineer said, seriously. "I need to attach one by the captain's cabin. It will just be on the wall in the corridor. Is that okay?"

"That's fine, Mr. Mayerle," the commander replied. "Carry on."

Joel was back on night duty, the day watch steward having been put back on limited duty. So he was surprised to see the odd box on the wall when he walked down the corridor to the wardroom.

"What's that?" he asked the sentry on the general's door.

"Somebody said it was a gravity detector." The marine shrugged. "Something about navigation. Ask one of the officers."

Joel walked over and examined the box curiously. He could hear it faintly purring and at first feared that it might be some sort of trap or bomb. But without an explosive, it could only hold a small charge of fire-making material. Or, perhaps, poison.

"Who put it here?" Joel asked.

"How the fisk would I know?" the marine said, grumpily.

"Just asking," Joel replied, heading to the galley again.

If that was a gravity detector he was Paul Bowman. The question was, who had put it there and why.

By the end of the shift he had determined that it was the civilian engineer who had put them there and that there were three, one in the officer's corridor, one on the mainmast and one in the forecastle.

The question remained what their real purpose was. Or, maybe he was just being paranoid. But he knew enough of basic Newtonian physics to question that you couldn't get a reasonable reading of gravity using that small of a device. Especially without advanced technology. Now, that it was measuring *something*, was possible . . .

Like avatar emissions. Bloody hell, that meant that someone else was stumbling around looking for the leak. He recalled, bitterly, what Sheida had said about "not stepping on each other's toes." At this point it had to be clear that there was someone passing information to New Destiny; three attacks, each right on their course, was just *too* much coincidence.

His only contact point was Duke Edmund. Admittedly, the duke's wife was Queen Sheida's *sister*, but that didn't mean she was a viable contact. He didn't go blabbing his missions to Dedra and Miriam.

He decided he'd wait until they rendezvoused with the duke and hope like hell that nobody did anything stupid until then. Let it be soon

The delphinos had had to quit the bay before dawn, as the tide sucked the water back out, but there was no attack from any quarter and the party, after finishing off the leftover rays, started down the passage to the west.

They overnighted in a small bay near the exit to the banks. There weren't islands around them, but the shoals on either side were shallow enough that no ixchitl or orca could pass over them. In the morning the dragons woke up hungry; there hadn't been anything for them to scavenge on the trip across the banks.

"Take them out feeding," Edmund told Joanna. "The deep water is just to the west. Keep an eye out for the carrier; the rendezvous is just to the north of the entrance."

"Will do," Joanna said, climbing up onto the shallows. The tide had come in and the shallows were ankle deep to the dragon but she and the wyverns were still able to get aloft.

"Where does all this sand come from?" Herzer asked, picking up a handful and letting it slide through his fingers. "On shore it's from runoff from eroded quartz. But this isn't quartz."

"It's mostly eroded coral," Jerry replied. "Which is calcium carbonate. I say 'eroded' but much of it, believe it or not, comes from parrot fish . . . droppings. But it's also some pure carbonate. The banks are one of the few places in the world where the temperature is just right for carbon dioxide to form carbonate. It reacts with the calcium in the seawater to make it. Not so much on this section, but over on the far side of the deeps there's a huge bank that is constantly making."

"Which makes it a carbon sink," Edmund noted. "Back when there was hysteria about 'greenhouse effect' and global warming, all that people would talk about is how it was impossible to correct. Admittedly, cutting down ninety percent of the rainforests was silly, but the people who were hysterical about its effect were lousy atmospheric scientists. Tropical rainforests aren't any sort of carbon sink; they recycle too quickly. And they're actually a net oxygen consumer. Oxygen production, and carbon sinkage, occurred mostly in the temperate regions. And carbon sinks were everywhere that the hysteriacs weren't looking. In the banks, in industrial farmlands, in a huge current off the coast of Anarchia. In fact, Norau, which was considered the most wasteful country on earth at the time, was a net carbon *consumer* because of its plant coverage, despite being a heavy source of carbon dioxide and methane. But nobody particularly cared for truth. They just wanted Norau to quit producing carbon, not realizing that if they did half the sinkage would go away with it. Nor that the warming that was occurring was part of a natural cycle that had been repeatedly proven from historical research. Not that humans have changed that much or we wouldn't be in this war."

"But there *was* a man-made heat wave," Herzer said.

"In the twenty-*third* century," Edmund pointed out. "When you're producing sixteen to thirty terawatts of power, the heat efficiency gets very bad. But the carbon dioxide hysteria was just that, hysteria. As real as the Dutch Tulip Frenzy or the Beanie Baby Recession of the late twentieth century when the sudden drop in Tyco sales set off a market panic. Plenty of scientists, most of the atmospheric scientists, were saying it at the time, as well as pointing out ways to increase the rate of carbon deposition. But nobody wants to listen to the voice of reason when there's a good hysteria to be had. Humans are like that."

"Humans were evolution created," Bast said, sitting down in the shallow water. "Must have been evolutionary positive to hysteria in small groups. Whole tribe to pile upon the leopard, perhaps."

"Perhaps," Edmund said with a grin. "The history of the period is so *funny* at a distance. As deadly in its own way as the present war. The world was in a golden age, and no one would *pay attention* to it! It's maddening, like looking at the Inquisition histories and going 'Well, duh, why didn't you just try to get along?' Science, engineering, were both expanding, lifestyles, across the world, were improving. The environment was improving. More people were living longer and better lives, in the areas that had decent governments at least. But everyone was screaming that the world was coming to an end."

"Why?" Herzer asked.

"Why did Paul start this war?" Edmund replied with a sigh. "He saw the present trend, falling birthrates, and felt that the human race was on the edge of extinction. The people of the time took present trends, present methods of production, present resources, present population growth rates, carbon dioxide output, temperature increases, and created a straight line model, ignoring the fact that the *historical* models were anything but straight line. And every time that their doomsday pronouncements were disproved, they just shouted louder about some new looming catastrophe. Over a *thirty* year span, the same group of so-called 'scientists' first predicted a coming ice age, then that the polar ice caps would melt, then the ice age again! Instead, population growth fell off. Industries became more efficient. Every year a new, previously undiscovered, carbon sink was found. New energy sources were discovered, each of which created a new cry that a resource would be exhausted. People just seem to prefer that the world be a bad place, even when it's clearly not. For chicken little, the sky is *always* falling."

"Well, I wish I could grab a few of them and drag them into this world," Herzer growled. "Show them what *bad* really means."

"Nah," Edmund said with a grin. "Bad was the Dying Time. The war is just *challenging*. Herzer, you're sitting waist-deep in warm water. There's a beautiful elf maid by your side. The sun is shining. The wind is light. Take a look around for a second and tell me you're not in heaven."

"I'm hungry and I need to go to the bathroom," Herzer said, but he grinned as he said it. "Okay, point taken."

"The war will wait for us," Edmund said, sighing. "It's waiting for us right now, unless I'm much mistaken, just off the coast. But in the meantime, let's just enjoy the sun and water, okay? And not look for a reason for hysteria."

"Unfortunately, Miss Rachel, your father was right." Evan sighed. "There is a steady power source in the rear of the ship and another that comes and goes. I think, though, that I've traced *one* of them to your father's room."

"That I know about," Rachel said. "There's a datacube in there. It's also designed to protect the ship against a direct energy strike, assuming that Paul can free some up long enough to attack us."

"That makes one headache go away," he sighed. "Unfortunately, the other one is coming from the wardroom. And it's intermittent. There have been two surges in the last day. But I've been unable to determine who was in the room when they occurred."

"Damn," Daneh said. That narrowed it down to the officers and the stewards; nobody else used the room. And another thing. "I've never seen the rabbit in officers' country."

"Nor have I," Evan said. "It is *possible* that he's coming up with the reports and then giving them to a steward. But the stewards don't go in the wardroom unless there's an officer that needs something. Or, occasionally, to clean up when they're not there."

"I think I need to ask some more questions," she said, frowning. "I'll be back. Keep monitoring."

"I shall," the engineer said. "Be careful."

"I'll try."

Rachel had prowled most of the ship but for various reasons she hadn't been down to the marine quarters. For that matter she hadn't paid much attention to the marines; they were just ornaments as far as she could determine. But at the moment, they were going to have the information she needed.

She opened up the door to their bunkroom and then stepped back, closing her eyes.

"Sorry, miss," the marine said. "I've got my pants on, now."

"Not your fault," Rachel said, opening her eyes. There were a round dozen of the marines in the narrow room, most of them in their bunks since they were off duty. The half-dressed marine finished toweling, looking at her questioningly.

"I need to speak to your CO or the senior NCO," Rachel said.

"Gunny's off-shift," the marine said. "He was up most of the night. The CO's awake." The marine gestured with his chin to a door at the end of the corridor.

Rachel walked down the corridor and knocked this time, waiting for permission to enter.

"Yes, miss?" the marine captain asked. He was sitting at a small desk, working on paperwork.

"Captain, I need to ask some of your marines some questions," she said, pulling out a sheet of paper and proffering it. "This is my authority."

The captain frowned and glanced at the paper, stopping to read it more thoroughly.

"This is a pretty blanket authority, Mistress Ghorbani," the captain said, his lips pursed.

"Yes, it is," Rachel said. "And it gets worse. I need to ask them some questions and I need to do so privately. You cannot ask them what was said and you cannot report the questions to *anyone* on the ship. Is that clear?"

"Very clear," the marine said, his face hard. "Which means you have a problem with something on the ship that you can't even bring to the skipper."

"Not the skipper, not the naval officers, none of them," Rachel said. "Clear?"

"Clear, ma'am," the marine said, shaking his head. "Who do you need to see?"

"The marines that were on duty in the officers' corridor during last shift," she said. "One at a time. Now, where?"

"Here," the captain said, getting up and buckling on his tunic. "You can have my chair. Let me ask you a question; should I turn out the duty guard?"

"Not yet," Rachel said. "Hopefully it won't come to that. Hopefully this is nothing."

✧   ✧   ✧

"Nothing," Joanna said as she landed. "Fish, yes. Orcas, ixchitl, the carrier, no."

"The orcas could have just given up," Jason said.

"Not Shanol," Herzer replied. "Not with one eye gone. He's got it in for me, bad."

"They might not know where we're going," Elayna interjected. "I mean, there are lots of places we could go."

"Their intelligence has been too good," Edmund replied. "They've known our movements all along. I doubt that whoever is feeding them intelligence is unaware of our destination, route or rendezvous."

"You mean there's a spy?" Jason said. "Who?"

"I don't know," Edmund said. "I suspect more than one. But I notice that Mosur has been missing since the first attack. And I didn't see him in the square when the ixchitl attacked."

"But he was around for a while after," Antja said, looking unhappy. "He talked to me. He wanted me to leave with him."

"Why didn't you tell me that?" Jason asked, angrily.

"Why do you think?" Antja said. "He's been hanging around a lot lately. I didn't tell you because I could handle it."

"He said something like that to me, too," Elayna said. "But it was before the attack. He said that he thought that you guys," she pointed at Herzer and Edmund, "would bring trouble and he had a place to hide. I just laughed at him and told him to get lost. After the attack I was around people too much, I guess. He probably didn't feel safe coming near me."

"But he would know where we were going," Jason said. "Everyone had been told."

"So we can assume, I think, that the orcas know," Edmund said. "Don't let your guard down."

"Have a seat on the sea locker," Rachel said to the young marine. She vaguely recognized him as one of the marines who had guarded her father's quarters. "I need to ask you some questions. You're not to tell anyone what I asked. Anyone, is that clear?"

"Yes, miss," the marine said, swallowing nervously. "The captain said the same."

"Not even the other marines I'm questioning," she said. "Don't go comparing notes. Understood?"

"Yes, miss."

✧   ✧   ✧

Rachel was on the sea locker now, with her mother pacing nervously in the captain's office and the marine CO sitting back behind his desk.

"All three of the guards, independently, stated that the only person to be in the wardroom alone during their shift was Commander Mbeki," Rachel said, glancing at her notes. "The CO was in his quarters most of the time. He left, but only to go to the quarterdeck. The navigator and the three lieutenants were never in the corridor. One steward was in there, but only while Commander Mbeki was present."

"Okay," Daneh said. "Damn. *Mbeki?*"

"Can I ask, now, what is going on?" the marine asked.

"Not yet, Captain," Daneh said. "But on my husband's authority, get your guard ready and armored up. Rachel and I need to go see the CO."

The skipper tossed the letter onto his desk and looked up angrily.

"It is not normal, nor wise, to turn over full military authority to a civilian, Mistress Daneh," the skipper said, his mouth pursed. "Can I ask the reason for this extraordinary document?"

"Let me ask you a question first," Daneh said. "Have you noticed anything about the New Destiny attacks?"

"Other than they have been inept?" the captain asked sarcastically.

"Have they?" Daneh asked, pacing up and down. "The first attack they were beaten off by using the rabbit, an attack that no one could have anticipated who wasn't aware of his full capabilities, not to mention the deal he had set up with Evan, correct?"

"I suppose," Chang said.

"The caravel would have carried fifty or sixty Changed warriors. Despite the valor of your crew, between them and the ballista, it is likely that they would have captured or destroyed your ship, unless you ran. And you couldn't really run, could you?"

"Not without losing days in the voyage, no," the skipper admitted. "Effectively we had to fight our way through. On that Commander Mbeki and I agreed."

"The second attack was by *five* ships. Even if the rabbit could have been induced to help you, again, there wasn't much you could have done, was there?"

"No," the skipper said. "Thanks for pointing that out."

"But, again, Evan had a device that he had concocted, more or less without anyone knowing."

"I knew," the colonel said. "Nobody gets on my ship with sodium, gasoline and all the rest without my knowledge."

"The kraken is another example," Rachel said.

"The point is that at each attack, they knew your location and *thought* they knew your capabilities," Daneh said, stopping her pacing to face the skipper.

"You suspect a spy," the skipper sighed.

"Edmund *suspected* that New Destiny had an agent on board," Daneh said. "But he didn't know who it was. There were, however, some clues."

"It had to be someone who knew our course and plans," the skipper said with another sigh. "Which means it *could* have been me. It's not; I'd know," he added with a grimace.

"But that does explain the orders," Daneh said, gesturing at the paper. "The agent had to be communicating. We have managed to track the communications to the wardroom."

"How?" Chang snapped.

"I'm . . . going to decline to answer that," Daneh said. "I'm not sure I want the knowledge getting around. Sorry."

"Don't be," the skipper said. "And who used the wardroom during the period? I guess it wasn't me or we wouldn't be having this extraordinary conversation."

"Sadly, only Commander Mbeki," Daneh said.

"Owen?" Chang said. "I've known Owen Mbeki for *years*. He's the most trustworthy man I know. There's no *way* that he's a spy for New Destiny!"

"Unfortunately, skipper, that's who it points to," Daneh replied. "And the evidence, while slim, is going to be more than enough for Edmund."

"It won't be for a court-martial," the skipper replied, his face hard. "And that is what this is going to come to. You'll have to reveal your methods for that at least."

"Not if we catch him in the act," Rachel said, frowning.

"How do we do that?" the skipper asked.

"We can't if we don't all act normal," Rachel replied. "It's gonna have to be a surprise . . ."

CHAPTER THIRTY-THREE

The squeal of a delphino scout was all the warning that they had and then the orcas were on them, coming up from behind where there wasn't a dragon guard.

The group had nearly reached Hope Harbor. It was late afternoon and the formation had started to get ragged. Herzer had had to, more than once, shove one of the mer-warriors back into the hemisphere as their excitement and nervousness got the best of them. Everyone was worried because they had expected the carrier to beat them to the harbor, but so far there was no sign of it or the mer-women and children that it carried. The mer tended to stick their heads up out of the water, hoping for a glimpse of the elusive ship.

So it was in a gaggle more than a disciplined formation that they were hit by the orcas exploding off the bottom.

Their black bodies had blended into the shadows of the reef and they had apparently created a sonar image that hid them from the oncoming delphinos. Furthermore, they seemed to care nothing for the ring of spears, slashing through them to get to the interior.

Herzer was ripped from his seat as Chauncey turned hard right to attack into the formation. As the two wyverns slashed into the group it exploded outward with a swirl of orcas, mer-women and confused spear-wielders.

Herzer dove deep and came up from below the formation, slashing his sword through the belly of an orca that had just caught one of the mer. The cut was too late, though; the orca's jaws crushed the mer-girl before he even realized his guts were trailing in the water.

"Form a globe around them," Edmund yelled, "women to the *outside.*"

But as fast as the mer tried to regroup, the orcas were faster. Their powerful flukes smashed any attempt at formation and after their first attack on the women and older men they turned on the broken formation of spear-wielders and attacked them.

Herzer saw Pete caught that way, one of the orca catching him by his tail and tossing him up and out of the water like a play toy. Jason was fighting a desperate action against another, jabbing with his sword to keep the orca at bay.

It was the dragons, and Bast, that saved the day.

Herzer thought that the orcas were fast until he saw Bast. Her fins blurred like the tail of a tuna as she cut through the water like a shark. Her saber wasn't well suited for killing the big whales, but where she went orcas were left bleeding with huge gashes in their side, back, stomach, guts hanging out and fins cut away so they had to swim lopsidededly.

Donal had a nasty bite in his side but he still drove through the pod of orcas like a killing machine, tearing huge chunks out of their sides, catching fins and flukes and ripping them off to stain the water with crimson.

Chauncey was more methodical. He had caught one of the orcas with both claws and tore at it as it struggled. He didn't let go until the orca went limp and floated up to the surface, dead or so injured that it could struggle no more.

Joanna was more like Donal, her snakelike head darting through the formation and slashing at any orca that was stupid enough to get in range. One managed to get its teeth in her tail only to find out how well sprung it was; the two-ton orca was spun through the water, raising a wave on the surface for a moment, until he was brought in range of those killer teeth and when they closed the orca fought no more.

As fast as the attack started it was over and the water was filled with dead and dying orcas and mer.

"Oh, God," Jason said, looking around.

Bill and three of the other mer-warriors were clearly dead, horrible jaw marks on their chests and abdomens, their entrails drifting in the current. Pete was floating at the surface, his tail bitten half-way through. Herzer wasn't sure that he'd live, even if Daneh had been there. Several of the mer-women were dead as well and others were badly injured.

"Get to land," Edmund said. "Get them up in the shallows. The ones that are whole all the way out of the water. We'll . . . see what we can do for the rest."

"Grace is all we can give most," Bast said, wiping her sword on the flank of one of the still-twitching orcas.

"We'll see," Edmund replied.

Herzer floated up to one of the injured mer-warriors and grabbed him by the wrist, towing him towards shore. Everyone was dragged shoreward, the injured and the dead. None would be left for the sharks, as the bodies of the orcas were being left.

The sharks and the dragons. Chauncey grabbed the tail of the one he had killed and dragged it along as Donal grabbed another. Joanna got two.

"You're not going to eat them, too, are you?" Jason asked.

"Why not?" Joanna replied. "They'd eat me if they got a chance."

"They didn't eat any of us," Herzer replied. "We're all here."

"Are we?" Edmund said. "That's a damned good question. Jason?"

"Anyone notice anyone not here?" Jason said. "I never bothered to really get a list." He looked around and blanched white. "Antja?"

"Elayna," Bast hissed. "Where's Elayna?"

By the time they reached the shore it was clear that the two mer-girls were missing.

"Where could they have gone?" Herzer asked. "They would have come out if they hid in the reef."

"That was why they went for the women, first," Edmund said. "I thought it was a brilliant tactic. But I bet that they made off with them while we were still fighting, come and gone before anyone noticed."

"Herman," Herzer said, ducking under the water. "Did you see Antja or Elayna taken?"

"No," the delphino responded. "Too fast. None of ours injured."

"They ignored the delphinos," Edmund said, shaking his head. "They went for the girls and ignored the delphinos."

"Why?" Jason shouted. "Why them?"

"Tender mer-girl snacks?" Joanna asked, craning her head up to look around. "I can find them."

"Me too," Herzer said, climbing on Chauncey who had just started to rip into his lunch. The wyvern snarled at being kept from his meal but turned to look at Joanna.

"I'm coming," Bast said, climbing on Joanna. "At least seven whales. Two dragons; Donal's too hurt to fly. We'll do."

"Herzer?" Jason said, looking up at him.

"You take care of your people," Herzer ground out. "Time for this to end."

"Oh, we'll end it," Joanna replied. "They're not getting away from me this time."

The marine sentry at the skipper's door shook his head as the telltale on the box next to him sprung up.

He didn't bother to turn, simply knocked quietly on the door behind him.

"Yes," the skipper said, sticking his head out.

The sentry pointed at the telltale and motioned to the door of the general's quarters. The marine there was looking at them with a raised eyebrow.

The skipper nodded and walked swiftly and silently down the corridor as a group of marines in armor exited Talbot's quarters. Moving the marines around without, it was hoped, anyone noticing had been difficult. But with any chance it was about to pay off.

Daneh and Rachel trailed the group. They knew their place and in the front of battle, if it came to battle, was not it.

The skipper started to open the door to the wardroom and then stepped back, letting the marine corporal in charge of the group enter first.

The corporal drew his sword silently and then threw open the door, entering the wardroom and moving to the side to let the rest of the marines in.

Commander Mbeki was at the far end of the room, looking up at a projection of a tall, fair man with black hair. The projection turned to look at the group and snarled, tossing up his hand and throwing a red bolt of power at the skipper in the doorway.

The bolt, however, stopped in midair and faded as the datacube protecting the ship was activated.

"Well," the projection said, turning to look at Mbeki. "It would seem that your utility is at an end." He reached out and his hand entered the commander's chest.

The skipper bellowed in anger, rushing forward and throwing the commander to the ground as the marine threw himself on the projection. But it was nothing but a hologram that faded with a mocking laugh.

Commander Mbeki was already turning blue at whatever

the projection had done to him. He grabbed the skipper's arm and shook his head.

"Why?" Chang ground out. "You were my *friend*."

"Wife," Mbeki said. "Sharon. Ropasa. Bastards . . ." His eyes widened in pain and then his head rolled back.

"I'd guess that the projection crushed his aorta," Daneh said, clinically. "Blue tongue and fingertips. Maybe introduced cyanide but why do that when you can just give him a heart attack."

"He'd always wondered what happened to Sharon, after the Fall," Chang said, lowering the body of the XO to the deck. "She was in Italia visiting the museums when the Fall hit. He'd hoped . . . Damn them."

"Yes," Daneh said, thinking her own thoughts, of her own memories. And nightmares. "Damn them all to hell."

"What now?" Rachel asked.

"Find the mer," Chang said. "Keep fighting. Until New Destiny is destroyed or we are."

Antja had discovered that punching was useless against the orca and that the grip of his pectoral fins was impossible to break. So she had spent the entire wild ride alternately fuming and terrified.

Shanol and one of the other orca males had left the fight almost immediately. Antja couldn't believe that they had attacked the group just to steal two mer-girls, but it was starting to look as if that was exactly what had happened.

"Okay, I give up," Elayna said. "Why are we here?"

"I don't answer existential questions," Shanol said with a ping of mocking laughter.

"Okay, to be more precise, why have you kidnapped us?" Antja snarled.

"I didn't think we could win," Shanol answered, truthfully. "So I had to ask myself, what was the worst thing I could do to Herzer and Jason, who are the two people I've come to hate the most in this world."

"And kidnapping us is the answer?" Antja asked.

"Oh, it's more complex than that," the orca said. "You're Jason's girlfriend and Elayna is Herzer's."

"I'm not Herzer's girlfriend you freak," Elayna shot back. "I'm his girl in the local port. *Bast* is his girlfriend. And when she's done with you, there won't be big enough pieces to interest the sharks!"

"I thought at first of just eating you," the orca continued, "and sending back your heads. Or maybe the tail; there's good eating in brains."

"You are sick," Elayna said with a quaver in her voice.

"But then I thought, 'is there anything *better*?'" Shanol continued, ignoring her. "And I'd heard that there were some interesting crosses happening with Changed on land."

"You've *got* to be joking," Antja said, deadly serious.

"Why? I have to wonder, what do you get when you cross an orca with a mer?" the orca said, slowing. "And I think we've come far enough to find out."

"An intelligent orca?" Antja said, slapping at him with her tail. "A mer with no morals? I don't *think* so. Let me go!"

"You know this is how orcas and dolphins mate," Shanol said, pinging her with laughter again. "And the difference between consensual mating and rape is hard to tell with us. Me for you and Shedol for Elayna."

Antja flailed against him with her tail and writhed in his grip, but she could feel his member sliding out of its protective slit even as she did so. Most cetacean males were designed for nonconsensual sex, and she was discovering just how well designed.

Elayna was flailing in the grip of her own captor and Antja had just about given up from exhaustion when the water above the orca exploded.

"Never ride a dragon bareback," Herzer groaned as Chauncey finally made it into the air. Staying on one with saddle and grip straps was hard when it took off on level ground. As for staying on bareback, the only reason he'd retained his grip on the strip around Chauncey's neck was his prosthetic. He was bruised across half his body. And he didn't even want to *think* about how his balls were feeling.

"Quit to complain," Bast said. "Look around."

"There's a pod of five headed out to sea," Joanna said. "Ones from fight; lots of blood trail. Sharks on their tail, too."

"I don't think that whoever took them stayed around to fight," Herzer said, sitting up slightly and regretting it immediately; without the straps his seat on the dragon was *not* stable and it was a long way to fall. Not to mention the . . . discomfort. "Bast, I may not be too good for you for a couple of days."

"Bast has remarkable curative powers," she laughed. "There, to the south. Two spouts!"

"Orcas," Joanna said, zooming her eyes. "Which group do we follow?"

"South," Herzer and Bast said together.

"Shanol?" Herzer asked.

"Elayna and Antja," Bast replied. "It is *good* that we did not bring Rachel."

"Yeah," Herzer growled, kicking Chauncey in the back. "Go!"

The dragons drove their wings as hard as they could and quickly overtook the orcas, who had slowed. They seemed to be struggling with the two mer-women.

"Is that what it looks like?" Joanna said, circling the pair. "Because if it's not, it's something very strange."

"Yes," Herzer shouted, pulling at the throat-piece of the wyvern and pushing him over into a stoop.

Chauncey had watched Joanna and he threw his wings back in a v, aiming at the right orca with minor corrections of his wingtips.

The stoop had started from over a hundred meters up and Herzer realized that he had just done a very stupid thing. Water, as he had learned as a lad jumping off a cliff on a dare, gets very hard when you hit it at high speed.

"Oh, shit!" he yelled, jumping off the dragon and pointing his feet at the onrushing ocean. As the water came up he pulled his arms into his head, pointed his feet, pinched his nose and mentally kissed his ass goodbye.

Antja was slammed downward by the orca and wondered what he had done to manage that. But at the same time, he let go his grip and his member retracted so she was thankful for small favors. She wriggled out from between the pectorals and headed in towards shore. There was always a reef somewhere around here, and once she got into one of the crevices he could be buggered for all she was coming out.

But she stopped and turned back, remembering Elayna. The younger mer-girl, however, was right behind her. And behind Elayna was a battle royale.

Chauncey had gripped Shedol on the back and was now tearing at the orca for all he was worth, with Bast sliding in and out, her sword flickering like lightning.

Shanol, bleeding from a dozen wounds, had somehow managed to escape from Joanna and was heading for the depths, with the dragon in hot pursuit. Herzer was holding onto Joanna's tail and working his way up her back, hand over hand.

"Herzer, where do you think you're going?" Antja said, as loudly as the bone in her forehead would let her.

"Down," the boy replied, getting a grip on one of Joanna's spineridges. In a moment they were both lost in the gloom.

Shanol could hear the dragon behind him. He should have been faster in the water than the damned lizard but despite everything it was gaining on him.

"Shanol . . ." he heard Herzer calling behind him. "She followed the kraken into the depths and killed it. You can't run. And she can fly above you, so you can't hide either. Just give up." The voice was eerie, distorted by the depth. Suddenly a cry rang out behind him and he shuddered. It wasn't the hunting cry of an orca but something weirder, bass and deadly. He realized it was the dragon. He didn't know it could do that.

What else didn't he know about them?

Desperately he dove deeper.

"Joanna," Herzer croaked. "I can't breathe."

There was a rumble under him and he realized that despite the underwater roar she had let out, the dragon couldn't exactly talk.

"I think it's the mask," Herzer said. His vision was going funny. On the other hand, it was getting darker as they went deeper, so maybe it was just that. But the purple spots weren't part of the light change from the depth, he was pretty sure.

"You may be able to do this, but I don't think I can," he muttered. But for some reason he kept his grip on the dragon's spine. The ridges flattened out along the back and he could only make it as far as the rear legs. That was going to have to be good enough. But he was getting very tired. And it was getting really cold.

The mask wasn't giving him air. He didn't know why and he wasn't sure that even if he let go he could make it to the surface anymore. He realized that he'd just killed himself, but that seemed a small price to pay if he could watch Shanol's end. He'd always realized there was a bone-deep vengeful streak in him, but he'd never realized it was going to kill him.

Oxygen, that was it. Too much oxygen was deadly. The mask was trying to keep from killing him by giving him too much oxygen. But there weren't enough other gases in the area for it to mix something else in. At that point, his limited knowledge failed. And he really didn't care anymore. He could see the orca ahead of him and just as he was sure he was going to pass out, it turned towards the surface. Probably as desperate for air as he was; it hadn't breached since before the last fight. Then Herzer saw the bottom of the ocean flash by. He had no idea what the depth was around here, but he was pretty sure this mask was *not* rated for it.

Joanna, on the other hand, seemed to have a limitless lung capacity. She held onto the trail of the orca, her sinuous glide getting her nearer and nearer with each passing second.

Shanol didn't seem to care anymore. He was just trying to make it to the surface.

As they got into shallower water, the light going from deep, dark blue to a lighter translucence, the mask started to feed Herzer air again and he sucked it in as fast as he could get it. Joanna's side-to-side motion was particularly bad by her rear legs, so he started working his way up her back, getting minor purchase in her immense scales. His prosthetic was particularly useful and he was afraid he was pinching her, but he wasn't going to be riding at the back the whole time.

"Give it up, Shanol," he called, as soon as he had a lungful of air to speak. "She's not going to."

"Fisk you, landsman," the orca pulsed. But it had a tinny quality, as if he was panting or on the ragged edge of exhaustion. "I'm the greatest predator in the ocean. I'm not going to die to any damned flying lizard."

"This flying lizard eats sharks," Herzer said. He'd almost made it up to the collar around Joanna's neck. He finally got a hand on it, then his prosthetic, and gripped like there was no tomorrow. "And she's going to eat you."

"Not if I can make it to the surface," the orca panted.

"Gob ya," Joanna said as she bit down on his flailing fluke.

The orca screamed, no more than ten meters from the air he so desperately needed, but Joanna wasn't letting go. She pulled the thrashing body back and got a talon around his tail, then swam to the surface, hauling him up behind her. She stuck her head out of the water and breathed deeply and rapidly, holding the thrashing orca down.

"Let me go!" the orca pulsed, blowing air frantically. "Let me get a breath!"

"Don't think so," Joanna said, turning towards the shore, dragging him backwards. "Sometimes you eat. Sometimes you get et."

The orca continued to thrash and pulse wildly until, finally, he was still.

CHAPTER THIRTY-FOUR

"Now that's just *wrong*," Antja said.

Herzer had dragged himself out of the water and ripped the mask off, swearing that he was never, *ever* going to wear one of the damned things again. Bast, Elayna and Antja were waiting for him on the shore, sitting on a projection of reef that was just above the tideline.

To one side, Chauncey was ripping huge chunks out of Shedol, holding the body of the orca down with one talon and then lifting the meat skyward to bolt the flesh down his gullet.

"The ixchitl were Changed humans as well," Bast said.

"I know, but that's just *wrong*," Antja exclaimed again.

"Well, maybe it is, and maybe it isn't," Herzer replied. He was lying with his head in Bast's lap but he lifted up to look at Chauncey, then over to where Joanna was starting to feed on Shanol.

"But if you really think so, *you* try to get them to stop."

And he passed out to Bast's delighted chuckle.

"Hi, Daneh," Edmund said, tiredly, as he climbed over the side of the carrier. "You've got some work ahead of you."

The wounded mer were being hoisted over the side and carried down to the sickbay but Daneh walked to her lover first.

"You look . . . worn," she said.

"I am that," Edmund replied. "Any luck?"

"Mbeki," she said, shaking her head. "Long, sad story. Later."

"Do we have enough evidence to convict?" he asked.

"He's dead," she replied, shaking her head. "Talk to the skipper, I have to get to work."

Joel seriously considered breaking cover to "discuss" some ramifications of his family's "handling" of Commander Mbeki. Not just that a potential double agent was dead. Not just that his family was now in unnecessary danger. But that in the future, doubling agents was going to be that much harder.

Bottom line, Duke Talbot was a fine soldier but he didn't know *shit* about intelligence matters. It irked him to realize that this was the case of almost everyone around Sheida. A bigger bunch of Boy Scouts was hard to find.

He was going to have to have a *serious* talk with Sheida when he got back.

In the meantime, one of the officers who had interrogated survivors from the ships let slip that some of the commanders had tried to make it to the nearest island. Rounding them up was a high priority; he might as well get *some* information out of this debacle.

Time for another cover to go away. And probably for one Joel Annibale to go, officially, AWOL.

"You took your time getting back, Lieutenant," Edmund said as Herzer climbed over the side of the ship. The general had had time to wash up and change into uniform and it was well after dark. "I thought you'd gone AWOL."

"I came back on the surface," Herzer admitted. "If I never put one of those masks on again, or see emerald water again, it will be too soon. Dragons belong in the air."

"Speak for yourself," Joanna replied, hoisting herself over the side to the now familiar heeling of the ship. "I kind of like it down here. Any chance of a permanent posting?"

"Maybe semipermanent," Edmund replied. "What with the Fleet base, there's no reason that there shouldn't be a dragon weyr as well. But don't get settled in; the main brawl is going to be up north, not down here."

"Understood, General," the dragon replied with a grin.

"Antja and Elayna?" he asked.

"Back with the mer," Herzer replied. "And happy to be there. Shanol and his second in command are well and truly dead."

"Vickie saw," Edmund replied. "And apparently threw up all over her dragon."

"And the last five surviving orcas were last seen headed out to sea, trailing blood, and hotly pursued by a group of sharks," Herzer added. "I'd say we won this one, boss."

"Yes," Edmund said, somberly. "But at a hell of a price. On the other hand, groups of mer from all over the islands are flocking this way, from reports. We always knew that there were more than just the mer at Bruce's village. Apparently having seen, and heard through the delphinos, about the attacks, they've decided that they have to choose sides. And most of them are choosing ours."

"Mission accomplished," Herzer said, looking out at the blue waters of the Stream. "As to the breakage, that's why they call it war, sir."

"Herzer, sometimes you are too bloody-minded even for me," Edmund replied. "I understand that there is some medicinal rum aboard. I'm going to go raid the stores. Why don't you wash up and join me in my cabin for some medicating."

"Sounds good," Herzer replied. "But I'm also going to go find where they hide those captain's crackers. Anything with some damned *carbohydrates*. A pure fish and fruit diet gets *old*."

"Don't tell me," Edmund laughed. "What you'd really kill for is a cheeseburger."

"Sounds good," Herzer said with a lifted eyebrow. "Why?"

"Another song I'll have to teach you," Edmund replied. "Probably on our fifth or sixth glass. I've got some bad news, though."

"What?" Herzer said. "The ixchitl and orcas are dealt with, the mer are safe and part of the Coalition. Rachel is okay?"

"Rachel's fine," the general replied. "But a dispatch sloop arrived. The bad news is from back home. Harzburg has flipped to New Destiny. The little army you trained is now on the other side."

"Son of a bitch," Herzer muttered. "Son of a fisking bitch. Those *bastards*."

"Yep," Edmund said, shrugging. "I think they're going to get a sharp lesson in why you don't piss off the Blood Lords. Especially with fire-dropping dragons backing them up. Especially since they're pressuring Balmoran, militarily, to switch sides as well. Balmoran has, officially, requested Federal support. So . . . pack your bags."

"Well," Herzer said, tossing the mask to the deck and looking around at the ship and thinking about the last few days. "At least I got my Caribbean vacation. Sun, surf, hot women. And, okay, some emerald seas. It'll have to do. Now, you said something about rum?"

EPILOGUE

Martin waved the remnants of his pants back and forth on the stick, trying to attract the attention of the passing boat. It was a small craft, no more than three or four meters in length, with a dirty, patched triangular sail. The man at the tiller had been looking shoreward and turned the boat inshore in a controlled jibe, bringing the boom in and then turning to bring the north wind across the rear of the boat.

Martin had been subsisting for the last two weeks on brackish water found in pools and whatever looked mildly edible along the shoreline. He'd managed to make it to land with his knife, his sorely depleted money pouch, a tinderbox and his clothes. Over the time he had gotten first burnt and then blackened by the sun.

The islander was, if anything, darker, almost a true negro black for all his features were the motley polyglot that was common these days. He was tall and had a fair growth of beard, although it looked like a new addition.

"Hello," Martin called as the skiff ran up on the shore. He seized the bow and pulled it farther in as the islander sat in the stern and looked at him.

"Didn' need to do that, mon," the man called. "Push ee back off. I'd guess you want to be get someplace else and I've fishing to do."

"Okay," Martin said, pushing the boat back into deeper water and scrambling aboard. The fisherman expertly brought the stern around and set the sail and the boat skipped back towards the distant reef.

"Man, am I glad you came along," Martin explained. "Got any water?"

"Jug at your feet, mon," the islander said. "The rounder gourd dere. The tall one's me rum. Thomas don't be sharing his rum wit' any old castaway."

The bottom of the boat was half full of empty baskets made of woven palm fronds. But by the mast were two stoppered gourds, one of them much rounder than the other.

"Well, thank you for the water, Thomas," Martin said, taking a solid slug but leaving plenty in the jug. "The packet I was traveling on sank off-shore four weeks ago. I've been trying to signal someone to stop ever since."

"Don't many be coming this far south," Thomas replied easily. "Plenty of fishing up thee coast. But Thomas he likes it down here. Plenty of good big fish, plenty of hogfish on the reef. Thomas, he like hogfish."

"Never had it," Martin replied, leaning back against the side of the boat. The sun was beating down and it was positively hot. Of course, a couple of times in the last week the wind had been downright vicious at night. He'd made a miserable job of weaving some palm fronds for cover, but they weren't much against the wind. He'd take the heat.

"Be grabbin' the boat hook, mon," Thomas said after about a half an hour. "Be pickin' up the gourd in the water."

Martin found what was probably the boat hook, a solid pole of wood with a withy on the end bound into a crook by what looked like tree bark. The boat was rapidly approaching a floating gourd and Martin, after an initial hook that missed, pulled it over the side. The gourd had a rope tied around its narrow end and Thomas came forward, dropping the sail onto the deck with an expert twist of the halyard and grabbing the rope.

"Thomas will pull," Thomas said, pulling in the rope hand over hand. "You be yankin' out the fish."

As the rope ascended it was clear it was attached to a net. As soon as the net cleared the bulwark Martin saw his first fish. The fish, about twice as long as his hand, had a whitish body with a blue stripe and a bright yellow tail. Its head was caught in the openings of the net by the gills. Martin grabbed it and tried to pull it out backwards but the gills were firmly caught. The whole time he was wrestling with it, Thomas continued to pull in the net.

"Pull it through, mon," Thomas said, somewhat angrily. "It small enough."

Over the next hour, or so it seemed, Martin pulled one fish after another out of the gill net. Thomas slowly told him what they were; the yellow-tailed ones were snapper as was a red-colored one. Hogfish had three tall spines on their back. There were at least three kinds of grouper. Scamp, bar jack, after a while he stopped trying to memorize them.

Finally they were done with the net, the fish in one of the baskets and the net piled untidily in the bottom.

"Thomas could have done it nearly as fast without help," the sailor grumped, raising the sail and setting the boat into motion.

"Hey," Martin said, slumping in the bottom of the boat and looking at the direction they were going. "Isn't that north?" He pointed to the rear.

"Thomas don't have just one net, mon," the captain chuckled.

Thomas, in fact, had five nets out, and it was very near dark before they turned to the north. Martin was exhausted, and all he had done was pull the fish out. His hands were covered in fish slime, and no matter how many times he washed them over the side they didn't seem to come clean. For that matter, most of his body was covered in one sort of filth or another. And he had been badly stung by some sort of jellyfish.

This was for the birds. He loved work, he could watch it all day, but this was just ridiculous.

The sun set fast and the tropical night was as black as pitch. The stars overhead shone down clearly, but at the surface of the sea it was like being in a cave. But the wake of the boat was filled with green phosphorescence. It was so bright, Martin swore he could see by it.

The captain was a barely glimpsed figure at the rear of the skiff and Martin couldn't for the life of him figure out how he could see.

"You know where you're going?" Martin asked.

"Oh, yeah, mon," Thomas replied. "You just be lying back. Thomas get us home safe and sound."

He had enough in his pouch to pay his way to the mainland. Once he was there, well, something would come up. It always did. With that thought, Martin lay back and looked at the stars until he fell asleep.

The change in motion of the boat woke him and he rolled

over, stiff from lying on the bottom of the skiff. They were entering a harbor that could be dimly glimpsed by the light of occasional torches and lanterns. There was a rough stone dock but the boat headed for a low shoreline. As it grounded, Martin got out stiffly and grabbed a painter, pulling the boat up onto the shore as far as he could go.

"How did it go?" a voice said from out of the darkness.

"Rather well," "Thomas" replied in a much more cultured tone. "Duke Edmund Talbot, meet John James the Third, aka Martin Johns, aka Martin St. John, aka . . . well I won't do the whole list."

Martin darted away from the voice on the shore and into the darkness. He had covered three steps when he ran into a metal-covered mass that picked him up by his hair until his feet dangled off the ground. His eyes immediately filled with tears of pain and he found himself still trying to run in place. It had been a really bad day.

"What you want I should do with him, boss?" the metal-clad figure asked grimly. The muscle-bound moron was apparently supporting Martin's full weight with one extended arm. Effortlessly. At that, Martin quit trying to run. Fighting had been out of the question all along.

"Oh, don't harm him, Herzer," Talbot chuckled out of the darkness. "There are so *many* things we want to ask him."

Author's Afterword

I've gotten into the habit of these; I really need to start breaking it. But I thought that a few items in this book needed attention.

I had too much fun writing this novel, in case it's not clear. My normal "output" is something on the order of a thousand words a day, when I'm "cooking." At times I was writing ten or, once, eighteen thousand a day on this novel. The underwater sequences, in particular, practically wrote themselves. Eight hundred hours of "down time" (last time I bothered to update my log, which was in the early '90s) will do that for you; blood really is emerald green at about sixty feet and turns black as you go deeper. And the Blackbeard trip to the Bahamas last January certainly didn't hurt. Indeed, it was on the deck of the sloop that the basic outline of the book came together. Then there are the dragons.

I've never really been interested in dragons; I'm certainly not one of those people who go around with an online persona of one. In fact, to the extent that I have an online persona it is "DaGiN" which stands for "Da Guy in Nomex." I have to wear Nomex because I like to bait the online dragons. (And, yes, that's what the rabbit was wearing. Asbestos, actually.)

But I'd evolved the idea of what was first called "The Caves of the Mer-folk" and as it developed in the back of my mind, dragons became more and more integral to the story. I've had many problems with fantasy dragons over the years and it gave me a chance to point out some of the unlikelihoods. At the same time, I'm of the opinion that almost nothing is unbuildable that mankind can envision. And, someday, someone *is* going to genegineer a dragon. Count on it. And it'll probably be Disney. Take a close look at the pictures around their "Safari" attraction if you don't believe me. Disney thinks *big*.

But they are still going to be constrained by the problems of aerodynamics and biology. Birds of prey are the closest current analogue to dragons (indeed, they will probably be the template for them when they are created, as they were for the wyverns in this book) and birds of prey have to eat an enormous amount of food, relative to their body weight. Given the much greater size of flying dragons, they are going to be a logistic nightmare if used militarily and I strongly doubt that they would be able to survive in the wild. Not to mention that muscle and bone will not permit the stresses involved in normal flight for such enormous wings. Build up the bone too much and the wing is too heavy. Etc. So they'll have to have some very artificial materials involved, such as the "biologically extruded carbon nanotube." And if you can figure out how that works, call Dupont and they'll make you a billionaire.

Still, I had this image, glorious and terrible, of dragons fighting orcas (go watch *Blue Planet: The Open Oceans* to see where that came from) and I had to get them to where the book was based. The world did not permit a base in south Florida (yes, this all takes place on Earth in the far future) so they had to be transported there by ship. But . . . why not have it be a ship that they could take off and land upon?

You begin to see the ugly truth of how stories are created, at least by me. Kind of like legislation and sausage.

Thus was created the dragon-carrier. And that's when I really got carried away.

I grew up on tales of naval aviation; my late uncle was a Navy fighter pilot in WWII. And while I'd never care to be a crewmember on one, much less a pilot (a bigger bunch of suicidal adrenaline junkies cannot be found), carriers are fascinating.

Carriers are the most complex system ever created by man and it is only with enormous difficulty that they function at all. (As the French, Chinese and Russians all have learned to their dismay.) Packing all the planes; people, fuel and parts to support the planes into a ship—much less having it all arrive where and when it is needed in a carefully choreographed dance—has taken the U.S. Navy generations to perfect. Just so that airplanes the size of WWII bombers can leap into the air and return to decks not much larger than WWII carriers with regularity. It's an amazing feat and makes me proud of my country and my countrymen. Yes, even the Airedales. (Slang term for Navy pilots.)

So it is with the dragon-carrier that I have taken the greatest liberties. Many of the items in this book were not invented until late in the development of carriers. Yet all of them were imagined and then engineered by the bright characters in my book in the space of a few short weeks. I'd considered having the different groups of carrier operations personnel wear different colored uniforms, but I felt that was pushing it.

I also played fast and loose with many of the seascapes. There are no specific inlets as described, but there are places very like them in the Berry Islands. Big Greenie is real, but it's by Bimini, not in the Berrys. Nor is the entrance to the Bahamas Banks on the east side exactly as described, but it is very close. And, who knows, in a few thousand years it might be *exactly* as described; hurricanes, erosion and the continuous build-up of the Bahamas Banks change things drastically in decades much less millennia. Whale Point Drop, however, is real, and much as I described, minus the spring and the cave. If you don't believe me, go check. The lighthouse, however, is private property. I wish it was *my* private property, but I haven't sold *that* many books yet.

So, permit me the liberties that I take, and I hope you enjoyed the book. That's, really, all that matters.

As usual, I'd like to thank the people who aided me in this book, either through information or by providing the characters that make it so rich.

Evan Mayerle, who is indeed a very inventive aviation engineer.

Bast, who, while not quite the character in the book, can see it on a clear day.

Hank Reinhardt for chopping pork shoulders so artistically.

Chief Robin Brooks, the best damned chief in the Navy.

Elayna for heroic baby-sitting beyond the call of duty.

Pete Abrams for the rabbit. If you want to know where the rabbit came from, google "Bun-bun" and prepare to lose two weeks of productivity. Start at the beginning, read the first month, and then prepare to laugh yourself sick, probably at work with your boss watching.

And, most especially, I'd like to thank the crew of the Blackbeard Cruise Ship, Pirate's Lady: Antja the Deck Wench,

Jason the Divemaster, Jackson the engineer, Pete the cook, Bill the mate, and, yes, Bruce the captain, owner of Blackbeard Cruises. All of whom put up with such truly insane questions as "If you were a mer-man, where would you live?"

If you're a diver and stout of spirit, I recommend the Blackbeard Cruises for the fun, price and the rum punch. Especially if my brother is directing the ratio of rum to punch. Although, sorry Bruce, not in January. Yes, the hypothermia was from experience. As was the seasickness. Including the thyme. On the other hand, if you're a Canuck, go for it. Scopolamine patches are over-the-counter in Canada and sixty-four-degree water is, apparently, positively balmy to our northern neighbors.

Thanks for reading my books and I hope to bring you more adventures with Herzer, Edmund, Bast and Daneh in the near future.

Who knows, maybe even the homicidal rabbit.

John Ringo
Commerce, Georgia
July 2003
Abn1508@mindspring.com

WARNING:
ABANDON ALL HOPE
YE WHO ENTER HERE!

The following story, while not pornographic, does contain erotica. If it were a movie it would probably be rated NC-17, possibly X. Since as an author I'm best known for my combat science fiction and "closing the bedroom door," I thought this warning in order. The erotica, for reasons that should be obvious in the story, is necessary and central to the development of both characters and plot. I've previously posted "Megan's Tale (The Harem Girl's Story)" so that a large group of fans could comment. (On Baen's Bar which can be accessed via the Baen website, www.baen.com. I'm there pretty much every day in Ringo's Tavern. Trolls will be ejected at waist height.) Their comments ranged from "this was a bit much for me" to "flesh it out." (Pun intended.)

Megan is an important character whose experiences in this story will shape her, and the world of the Council, for some time to come. I think that the majority of my readers are mature enough to not have a problem with the following story. I don't exactly read these things as bedtime tales to my own kids. To those of you who do, my apologies and be glad for the warning.

In a Time of Darkness
(Megan's Tale)

PROLOGUE

The girl washing clothes by the side of the rushing stream might once have been pretty. Now, with the exception of her forearms, she was filthy and skinny, her long, brown hair hanging in tendrils around her face. She wore the remains of a fine, blue cosilk tunic, which had been tied up in the heat, and matching pants that had been cut off at midthigh. She was barefoot and her feet were heavily calloused.

Less than a year before Megan Samantha Travante, like all the humans of her time, had lived the life of a god. Before the Fall, with the omnipresent Net to care for every need, humans wallowed in almost inexhaustible luxury. A person could live anywhere, even under the sea or in the photosphere of the sun, Change themselves into almost any form. Food was available with a word, replicated in any form. Safety was guaranteed by personal protection fields capable of surviving in any possible conditions.

Megan's life had been slightly different from the norm. Her father was one of the few remaining "police" of the era, a man who tracked the limited criminal element that sprung up even with enormous luxury. And he was very good at his job. Good enough that he had pressed his only daughter into studying more than was normal for the period and developing a high degree of personal paranoia, not to mention defensive capabilities, which made her strange to many of her friends. Joel Travante knew that even in Paradise the serpent always lurked in the human breast, and he was sure that his daughter knew it as well.

With pressure from her father, and her mother who was an expert on preindustrial art, Megan had used the resources of the Net to develop herself in ways strange to many of her peers. She attended few of the innumerable parties; she, in fact, had very little social life. Her life had been dedicated from an early age to intensive mental and physical training. Teaching methods had advanced along with every other art and science. Besides audio-visual systems that practically hammered knowledge into the young mind there were direct input methods available. Between the two, no realm of knowledge was closed to even the youngest. At first under her parent's pressure, and then on her own for the acorn does not fall far from the oak, Megan had used them to amass an education that would have astounded most professors of previous eras.

The Fall, though, had caught almost everyone by surprise. The Net was managed by the Council of Key-holders, thirteen people who between them held the keys to the program that managed the Net. They had fallen out, the reasons given ranged from their own statements to wild rumors, and started a civil war that had drained the power from the Net and thrown the world into a state of instant barbarism.

Megan had been seventeen at the time of the Fall, not yet officially "released" by her parents, but free to wander at will. She had been visiting a friend in Ropasa when the Fall came while her mother was, presumably, home in the Briton Isles and her father on assignment "somewhere" in the world. Thus she had been left to her own devices. She had managed, through the smarts and paranoia that her father had inculcated, to avoid the worst aftereffects of the Fall. She hadn't been raped, unlike some of her friends, and she hadn't been one of the women chosen as "consorts" to the Changed legions of New Destiny. But it hadn't been easy to avoid either. Finally, she had found work as a washing girl and general servant for one of the elders of the local town. It wasn't a great job, but she had plans. She had skills that were rare in the post-Fall world. Most of those skills required an industrial base that was sorely lacking in the small town she had stumbled into. So she bided her time, watched for opportunities and kept her head down. In time, she'd work her way out of squalor.

In the meantime, she had clothes to wash.

"Excuse me, young lady," a quavering male voice said behind

her and she sprung up, holding the stick she had been beating the laundry with as if it were a club.

But the voice had come from an old man who was leaning, wearily, on a stick. Even with the stick, he was no threat.

"Excuse me for startling you," the old man said. He was dressed in rags and his feet were as worn as her own. "I was hoping that you might help me across the ford."

The girl cocked her head at him and, keeping her hand on the stick, walked to support his off-side.

"This is very kind of you," the old man said. "There is not much kindness to be had in this Fallen world."

"It's okay," the girl replied as they entered the stream. "I'm surprised you're able to survive."

"Well, I make my way, you know," the old man replied. He was skinny and his long hair hung in greasy locks over his face and he stumbled on the round stones of the knee-deep ford. "Food is where you find it and I can work, sometimes. Not much to steal from old Paul so no trouble from bandits. I could wish that that damned Sheida hadn't caused all this trouble, though."

"I wish all the Council were damned to hell," the girl snarled. "I wish . . . oh, I wish too much."

"Sometimes we feel we are," the old man muttered. "And tell me your wishes, young lady."

"Just the usual," she laughed, bitterly. "To be home. To be fed. To not have to worry about the cold or having to dodge gangs of men."

"Where do you live?" the old man asked as they reached the far side of the ford. He stumbled over the slight bank and then sat down, resting his feet in the water.

"With a couple in town," the girl replied, sitting down next to him. "They took me in after the Fall. I . . . well I do their cleaning and laundry and stuff. The man is one of the town elders and it's a good enough life. They protect me, at least."

"Do you . . . perform other services for him?" the old man asked, delicately.

"No, he's never even asked," the girl replied. "I don't exactly dress up around them, though. I . . . don't know what I would do if he made it a condition of staying. But I think Master Jean's wife would have something to say about it if he did. He lives in fear of her."

"Yes, yes," the old man said, looking at her out of the corner of his eye. "Not the most idyllic life, though." He peered at her and then nodded. "Good genes, good phenotype.

I think you'd clean up well. Yes, you'll do. You'll most definitely do."

"What?" the girl said, suspiciously, getting to her feet. She held the laundry club protectively in front of her and looked around, afraid that the old man was a scout for some group of thugs. "I'll do for *what*?"

"As it happens, I can make your dreams come true," the man said, suddenly standing without the club and holding out his hand. "I can make it all better."

The girl felt the world swirl around her and she lost consciousness.

In a moment, the two were gone.

CHAPTER ONE

When the girl awoke it was in a stone chamber. She lay
on a soft bed covered in a fine cosilk coverlet. Her filthy clothes
were gone and she wore a robe of light yellow silk, or something so like it she couldn't tell the difference. The room had
a desk, on which sat a fine silver vase and a washing basin.
There was only one door and a barred window high on the
wall.

She got up and walked to the door, expecting it to be locked,
but it opened easily. On the other side was a corridor lined
with other doors. One end ended in a blank wall, but there
was light and an open area at the other end. And female voices.

She walked down the corridor uneasily but was surprised
at the sight that greeted her. There was a high-ceilinged
chamber at the end, with slits near the roof to let in light
and several corridors leading off of it. There were several
women in the chamber, lounging on pillows strewn around
on the floor. Some of them were sewing but most were simply sitting, talking in low tones, or playing board games. Some
of them were just . . . sitting. They seemed vacant. They smiled
happily all the time, but didn't talk or play the games. They
just sat and stared at space, as if fascinated by the walls.

All of the women were dressed . . . scantily. Most wore robes
like the one she was wearing, their legs slipping out reveal-
ingly at the open bottoms, while a few were wearing cami-
soles and panties or even lighter lingerie. All of them were
more well-fed and healthy looking than any but the most

successful of the post-Fall women that she had known. They were all also, even by the standards of the time, very good looking.

"Ah, our sleeper awakes," one of the women said, getting to her feet. She was a tall, thin brunette wearing a camisole outfit and high-heeled strap-sandals.

"Where am I?" the girl demanded. "What . . . what is this place?" She had a sinking feeling that the answer was evident.

"Well, food and a bath first," the woman replied. "I'm Christel Meazell, by the way. And you are?"

"Megan," the girl said. "And I want some answers."

"As I said," Christel answered, smiling brightly but clearly in no mood for back talk. "First some food and a bath. I suspect you're starved and you *definitely* need a bath."

Christel led her down one of the corridors and into a long room with a table occupying most of it. Christel clapped her hands imperiously and in no more than ten seconds a woman came in bearing a platter heaped with food. The woman, who was much older than those in the chamber and not nearly as good looking, slid the platter dexterously onto the table and laid out the plates and cups she had carried.

There was roast pork, hot from the oven. Mashed potatoes. Hot loaves of bread. Butter. A huge bowl of steaming broccoli. Gravy. Spring carrots. Megan's mouth watered at the sight.

"Sit," Christel said. "Eat."

Megan started to sit down and then looked at her still dirty hands.

"I hate to eat this as filthy as I am," she admitted.

"Eat first, then a bath," Christel said. "I'll be back in a few minutes. *Don't* gorge yourself and then throw it all up."

"I won't," Megan said as both of the other women retired from the room.

She carefully served herself small portions of everything. The bread was succulent. The carrots were heaven. The broccoli was ambrosia.

None of this kept her from scoping out her surroundings. The door at the end of the room clearly led to the kitchen. One of the other corridors, at least, was going to lead out of what was clearly a prison. On the other hand, she was being fed and there was the promise of a bath. She also suspected that there was more than one layer she would have to penetrate. And she had no idea where she was. The "old man" had clearly used power to knock her out and then ported her here. Wherever "here" was; it could be anywhere on earth. Whoever the "old man" was, he *had* power. Which meant he was either a member of the Council or in their employ. Which meant escape, if even possible, would be problematic at best.

Better to reconnoiter the territory rather than make a break and fail. Gather information. Interrogate, carefully. Get the lay of the land.

Lay of the land. That had a bad ring to it because if this wasn't a harem, she was a kraken. Thus far, even given the Fall, she'd managed to avoid spreading her legs for anyone, much less someone not of her own choosing. It looked like her luck had run out.

Even though she'd eaten hardly any of the food she was full and knew that if she ate more she probably *was* going to spew everywhere. Especially given that last thought. So she took a sip of the wine that had been brought with the food and went back to the main chamber to find Christel.

"Bath next," Megan said. "Then you'll answer my questions."

"You're fitting right in," Christel said, getting to her feet. She led Megan down the same corridor and opened a door on the opposite side from the dining room.

The "bath" was sumptuous and occupied most of the wing. There was a long, deep pool, with water running into it in a waterfall and then spilling out the far end. There were showers along one wall. Heaped towels. Soft soaps. A vanity with various ointments and cosmetics. And more of the light, silk robes in various colors.

"Dive in," Christel said. "Shower first, then the bath. Wash *thoroughly*."

"What about . . . feminine needs," Megan asked, insulted. Did she think she wasn't going to wash her butt or something? Then she realized that the older woman recognized the dirt as a mask and was warning her not to try to use it here.

"It's not your time of the month," Christel replied. "I checked."

"You *checked*!" Megan said, angrily.

"It's my job," Christel said, coldly. "Now take a bath and we'll discuss the rest when you're done."

As soon as the woman was gone Megan stripped out of the robe, dropping it in a hamper, and turned on one of the showers. The water ran hot quickly and she gratefully started working off the grime of months. She washed her hair three times before it finally felt *clean*. When she was done she glanced at the baths and then shrugged. There was no need for them after the shower and she wanted answers. But she knew that she had better pretty up so she sat down at the vanity. Her hair had gotten long since the Fall—it was easier to just let it grow—and dropped nearly to her butt. This was the first time she'd seen a mirror in a long time and she was surprised, and shocked, at how much weight she had lost. Even her breasts had shrunk.

She had never gone for the standard "look" pre-Fall, which had been for a skinny, buttless, breastless, waiflike body that was more boyish than anything. She had a natural hourglass shape, with rounded buttocks and high, firm breasts. Which, it appeared, had just led her into serious trouble.

"Good news," she muttered at the stranger in the mirror. "You're fed, you're bathed, and you have clean clothes to wear. Bad news. It's because you're about to be raped." She flexed her jaw and for just a moment saw an echo of a parent in her blue eyes.

"So, what would Daddy do in this situation?" she asked, then paused. First of all, he wouldn't say something like that aloud; there was every likelihood that there was at least intermittent monitoring of the harem. And what he would do was gather information and then when he had a good plan, escape. He'd *stay alive*, whatever that took. Her eyes teared for just a moment and then she shook her head. What he wouldn't do was start crying because he was afraid he'd never see her again. He'd just go on. And hope for the best, planning for the worst.

She shook her head again and then stood up, donning one of the robes and wondering if there was some way to at least get *panties* for God's sake.

"Time for the briefing," she said. "Let's get out there and slay 'em."

"You clean up quite well," Christel said.

She had taken Megan to a small chamber off the main room. The chamber had a low desk, designed for a person sitting on the floor or, as Christel was, on a cushion. And it had more of the ubiquitous cushions found in the main room. Megan had taken one of these and was sitting cross-legged with her back against the stone wall.

"Thank you," Megan replied, coldly. "Okay, where am I? I can guess *what* this is. Given the way the world is run these days I won't ask 'by what right' but I will ask 'what council member keeps this harem?' "

"Smart and pretty," Christel said, smiling thinly. "Don't be too smart for your own good. Did you notice the young lady out there that didn't seem to care if it was night or day?"

"Yes."

"She was . . . too smart for her own good," Christel said, giving that thin, humorless smile again. "This is the . . . seraglio of Paul Bowman."

" 'We feel the same way,' " Megan said, nodding. "And he even called himself Paul."

"It is not just for his idle amusement," Christel added. "I was one of Paul's . . . biological consorts prior to the Fall. We made a child together, using replicators of course. After the Fall he ensured that I and Jean, who is a grown man now, were provided for. As he did with his other four consorts." She paused and looked up as if bringing some rehearsed speech to mind and then nodded.

"Paul's purpose in trying to bring a new age to this fallen world is just," Christel said, primly. "He was terrified that, given current trends and the way that the world was slipping into lotus eating, that the human race would simply wither away. Since the Fall he has worked incredibly hard to ease the suffering of his people. But he feels it important that there not only be breeding, but *good* breeding. And therefore he has established this retreat for the purposes of breeding a finer quality of human. You are here to be one of his consorts. Your purpose, from his point of view, is to breed good children. When you become pregnant you will be moved to another area where you will be pampered and cared for carefully until the birth of the baby. You will then move to the creche for two years so that your baby will develop a good early infancy bonding. At the end of the two years you will return here."

"And never see them again?" Megan said, perhaps more aghast at that than the rest of the litany.

"No, you will visit them from time to time; they will be well cared for, I guarantee it. And when they reach an age where they are amenable they may visit the seraglio from time to time. When Paul is not here. He . . . believes in the importance of children but . . . does not care for them as *children*."

"Oh, that's just great," Megan snapped. "He wants babies bred but doesn't want to be bothered with them himself. Some leader. Some visionary. What a hypocrite."

"Watch your tone," Christel said, dangerously. "We are here for Paul's pleasure and needs, not the other way around. He is a very important man, to the world and to us. Keep that in mind. I will add that Paul works *very* hard. And the *other* purpose of this group is to make him *happy* when he has the time to visit us. If you find it impossible to make him happy, steps will be taken."

"Such as a mind-wipe?" Megan said, coldly.

"There are preliminaries," Christel replied. She held out her hand languidly and mouthed a series of syllables.

Megan's whole body was suddenly seized by pain and she couldn't even gasp, much less scream at the agony. In a moment the pain stopped and she was left panting and sweating in reaction. There was no side effect except a lingering memory, but she felt as if she was going to throw up her good supper.

"Paul has given me access to a small amount of power and a few programs," Christel said, smiling thinly. "I use the power sparingly. Don't make me use it on you."

"I won't," Megan said, trying to act meek.

"Why do I suspect you're lying?" Christel said. "Megan who watches everything as if she were the predator rather than the prey. But you'll learn your place. Everyone does eventually. One way or another."

Megan stumbled out into the main room still feeling the tingling aftereffects of the pain lash. Most of the girls ignored her quite pointedly but one, who was sitting beside one of the mind-wiped, smiled at Megan and patted a pillow next to her.

"Isn't she just dreadful?" the girl whispered when Megan collapsed on the pillow.

"It wasn't fun," Megan admitted.

"I'm Shanea," the girl said. She was a short, heavy-breasted blonde with a happy but vacuous expression. "Shanea Burgey."

"Megan Sung," Megan replied, holding out her hand. "Your name is actually Shanea?" Megan continued.

"Yes," Shanea said, looking at her sideways. "Why?"

"Your parents gave you that name?" Megan asked with a faint smile. "Did you kill them in their sleep?"

"No, silly," Shanea said, smiling. "I like it. This is Amber," Shanea continued, turning to the girl next to her. "Say *hello*, Amber."

"Hello," the girl said, softly. Amber was a tall, absolutely exquisite brunette with slender hips and waist but very firm, large breasts. Megan had already noticed that Paul seemed to be eclectic in his taste for women except on the order of breasts. Amber continued looking off into the distance while her hands worked at the knitting in her lap. It didn't seem to be intended to be anything; she was just making a long piece about as wide as the knitting needle was long. The wool was lovely, a light gray shade that looked as soft as silk. From time to time the girl would stop knitting and stroke the fabric, a look of pleasure crossing her perfect features.

"Her real name is Meredith," Shanea said. "But she likes to be called Amber. She doesn't talk much. She . . . had some problems adjusting."

"I can imagine," Megan said. She wondered what the girl had been like before. In a way she'd rather be dead than mind-wiped. And most mind-wipes didn't leave the person a relative vegetable as Amber seemed to be.

"Really, it's not that bad," Shanea said, earnestly. "Paul's actually rather sweet in his own way and we don't have to worry about . . . other men. It's much worse on the outside."

"I'd love some more clothes," Megan replied. "Even panties for God's sake."

"You can make them," Shanea said, perkily. "Come on."

She led Megan down one of the corridors to a side door and opened it up to reveal a small storeroom just about crammed with fabrics. There were bolts of lace and silk, some of them woven so sheer as to be transparent.

"And, look," Shanea said, opening up a basket, "there's all sorts of needles and things."

"I've never . . . done any sewing," Megan said, looking at the room and thinking in terms of rope ladders. Silk could be awfully strong, especially if you braided a section of cloth. She also didn't know much about braiding, but somebody in the harem probably did. Not that a rope was going to do her much good if she couldn't even find a window she could fit through.

"I'm not that great but I'm learning," Shanea said happily. "Come on, we'll work on some shorts for you."

"Not pants?" Megan said. "A shirt? Maybe a dress?"

"No, not pants," Shanea said, for the first time with a serious tone. "Megan, please don't say things that don't make sense, okay? Did you see *anyone* wearing *pants*?"

"No," Megan said, slowly. "I guess that was pretty stupid, huh? I guess, maybe, a halter top? Short shorts? What was that thing they used to wear, I've seen it sometimes. Oh, yeah, a *mini*skirt?"

"What's that?"

"Think 'school-girl look.'"

"Oh, is *that* what they used to wear in schools?" Shanea said, her eyes widening. "Were they harems, too?"

"Sometimes you have to wonder," Megan frowned. "Sewing. Bleck."

CHAPTER TWO

There had been a pair of cutting scissors in the room, chained to the shelves. Other than that they had small cutting blades about the size of her thumbnail to section the cloth. Megan noticed that she hadn't seen anything resembling a knife or any serious bladed weapon in the whole harem. They had cut sections of cloth and headed back to their seat by Amber.

"What are you going to make?" Shanea asked.

Megan looked around at the other girls. Most of them simply wore the light robes that were provided, but a few had other items. One girl had a lovely blue pair of panties and bra with lace on the edges. But Megan knew that was far beyond her ability, even if she felt "right" wearing nothing but panties and a bra in public.

But she really wanted some support for her breasts. And something down lower would be good as well.

"I think . . . something to go around my top and bottom," Megan said, then shook her head at Shanea's incipient worried frown. "Nothing too . . . covering, damnit. Something that just covers the breasts, maybe buttoned. Just a few buttons. And pretty much the same thing on the bottom. If I can use those to figure out *how* to sew, I'll look at making things like bras and panties."

"Oh, those are *hard*," Shanea said, sadly. "Mine always look terrible. Only Mirta is that good. She's so good nobody picks on her even if she isn't one of *Ashly's* friends."

"Ashly?" Megan asked, picking up a length of heavy blue

silk that rippled like water in her hands. "What about this?" she said, wrapping it around her breasts over the robe.

"Shorter," Shanea said, darkly. "Narrower, whatever."

"Great," Megan snorted, folding the cloth almost in half. "They're going to hang out the bottom if I go this narrow."

"Trust me, go with narrow," Shanea said. "If Christel thinks you're trying to 'cover up' too much you're not going to like it."

"Got it." Megan frowned. "Shorter. Now, Ashly," she said, setting the cloth down and trying to figure out what to cut off. And how; the narrow cutters were hard to figure out.

"She's the one playing backgammon," Shanea whispered, gesturing carefully to the far side of the room where a tall, heavily built blonde was lying on her stomach looking at the board, one foot raised in the air and lazily waving back and forth.

"What about her?" Megan asked. She was trying to cut a straight line in the cloth and failing miserably despite going with the weave. The cutters were wooden crescents with two small blades embedded in them. When pressed into the edge of the fabric they would start a triangular cut and they maintained it well, as long as the fabric was kept taut. But when she'd stop to tighten the fabric the cut would waver. And it wasn't particularly straight to begin with. She suspected her first effort was not going to be useable in public.

"She's next after Christel," Shanea said. "Christel doesn't say that, but Ashly does, and she's *really* mean. She's the one that turned in Amber for talking about escaping. And she's got some friends that help her. She'll hurt you; she likes to hurt people."

"Some people are like that," Megan replied. *I'm one of them. At least when I'm this angry.* "So does she hurt you?"

"Not so much anymore," Shanea said, sadly. "I just try to keep my head down and not bother anybody. Most of the time they don't bother me. Mostly."

Imprisonment experiments. Dad had talked about that one time, too. Take any random group of people. Make one side the "guards" and the other side the "prisoners." Within weeks the guards are sadistic to the prisoners and the prisoners have separated into packs for mutual protection.

Something else about prison society. "It's human society with all the stops off, honey. You have to establish that you're not the bottom of the pecking order. And you have to establish that fast."

Prisons were as much a part of the past as . . . well, war, come to think of it. But her father, it seemed sometimes, knew everything. And a lot of it he had passed on.

"Sometimes they want me to have sex with them," Shanea continued. She had cut out a triangle of cloth and was contemplating it idly, as if thinking about something in the past. "It's . . . sometimes it's not so bad."

"Shanea?" Megan said, gently.

"Yes?"

"Let me handle Ashly and her friends," Megan said, then smiled, nicely.

"Don't try to fight them," Shanea said. "Christel doesn't like fighting."

"I'm sure it won't get that far," Megan replied. "Leave it to me." She looked at the strip of cloth, then folded in an edge and wrapped it around her top again. "What do you think?"

"Narrower."

"It will be when I'm done." Megan sighed. She measured where it met in the front and then cut it off with some extra cloth in case she messed it up. Then she folded over one edge, which immediately unfolded.

"Pins," Shanea said, handing her a handful. "Fold the edges and then pin them."

"This is a pain," Megan snapped.

"It passes the time." Shanea shrugged. "There's sewing, talking, bathing and playing board games. Except when Paul is here."

"And then there's getting raped," Megan said, darkly.

"It's really not that bad," Shanea said. "Really. There's nothing you can do to stop it, so just have as much fun as you can. Think of your boyfriend or something. Or girlfriend if you go that way."

"Which is it for you?" Megan asked.

"Oh, I dunno," Shanea smiled. "I think for fun, guys. For comfort, mostly girls."

"And the only 'guy' is Paul," Megan said.

"Yep."

"What's he like?" Megan asked, almost against her will. She told herself she was just gathering information about the enemy, but she knew she was lying. If she was going to spend the rest of her life "servicing" some guy, it made sense to recon the territory as well as possible.

"Not too big, thank goodness," Shanea said with a shrug.

"I kind of have to clamp down on him. Too quick. He really seems to think it's just a duty."

"Wham, bam, thank you, ma'am." Megan said, thinking that if it was "just a duty" a test tube and artificial insemination would work as well. Although, somewhere, she'd heard the term "live cover" which supposedly worked better. She shuddered at the thought. *I'm a brood mare.*

"Yep. 'Oops, I gotta go now.' And he switches around, too. I haven't been with him in . . . a while. I mean, I don't know how long. No way to tell time in here."

"Does he just . . . arrive, do one of the girls and then leave?"

"Usually. Sometimes he stays for a while talking and then chooses another."

"Just one of his myriad 'duties,' " Megan snorted.

"I guess. And he's looking worse and worse, too."

"What do you mean?" Megan had gotten the edges pinned and took up one of the fine needles. Shanea had insisted on little needles for the silk and Megan found herself squinting at the hole, trying to get the incredibly fine thread to fit the even finer hole in the needle.

"Well you saw him," Shanea said. She was apparently working on one breast piece of a bra and her movements were far defter than Megan's.

"He looked old and worn out," Megan said. "From the little I saw. But I thought that was a disguise?"

"The old might be," Shanea said, picking up one of the needles and trying to thread it as well. After only a few tries she got the thread through. "Try licking it."

"What?" Megan said, aghast at the apparent non sequitur.

"The thread, silly," Shanea said with a grin. "Try licking it. It makes the end a little smaller, it slides in better and it stays . . . firmer." She grinned again.

"Harem humor," Megan snorted. "Great." She tried licking the thread though and it *was* easier. It still seemed to take her forever to get it though the needle.

"See? Lick it and it goes in easier," Shanea grinned.

"Shanea?"

"Yeah?"

"Once is funny; twice is annoying."

"Okay."

"You were saying Paul is looking worse?" Megan said after an overlong silence.

"Yeah," Shanea replied after a moment. "He just keeps getting thinner and weaker-looking. Like he's sick or something."

"Or wondering if destroying the world is a really good idea?" Megan muttered.

"No. He's really worried about people, though," Shanea said. "It's really all he talks about, how hard it is for the people."

"Maybe he should have thought about that *before* he tried to overthrow the Council," Megan replied quietly.

"Well if Sheida hadn't fought back . . ." Shanea said, hotly.

"Shanea, let's not argue about that, okay?" Megan smiled. "You're the closest thing that I've got to a friend in here. I won't say anything else bad about Paul, okay?"

"Okay," Shanea replied, shrugging. "I mean, I wish it hadn't happened, too. But if Sheida had just seen what he was trying to do . . ."

"I'm sure she did," Megan said, as placatingly as she could. "But, really, let's not argue about it, okay? We can't *do* anything about it. And, you're right, Paul is probably a nice guy. I'm sure we'll get along fine."

"Well, he is a nice person," Shanea said. "He's been very nice to us."

"Of course," Megan replied. *He gets sex whenever he wants it and all he has to do is give us some board games and cloth. Great guy.*

"Dinner time," Christel announced, as she opened up her door.

"I'm not really hungry, yet," Megan whispered.

"Eat it while you can get it," Shanea replied. "Three meals a day, none in between."

"What about the sewing?"

"We'll just leave it here," Shanea said, standing up and touching Amber on the arm. "Ami, time for dinner."

"Dinner," Amber replied, standing up and walking towards the dining room. She had a graceful stride and, again, Megan had to wonder what she had been like before.

"Settling in?" Christel asked.

"Yes, ma'am," Megan said, trying to imitate Shanea's bright vacuousness.

"Have you ever sewn before?" Christel asked, stooping and picking up the pieces of fabric.

"No, ma'am, but Shanea is showing me how," Megan said, gritting out a smile.

"What is this?" Christel picked among the fabric, looking at the way it had been pinned. "This isn't a shirt or something, is it?"

"No, ma'am," Megan said.

"It's more of a breast-band," Shanea interjected. "It's going to be quite fetching, really. I hadn't thought of it, but I think Paul will like it."

"And a short skirt," Megan continued. "*Very* short."

"We'll see," Christel looked at the other girls who had paused to see if the new girl was going to get a tongue-lashing. "Get into the dining room!" She tossed the fabric on the pillow and put her hands on her hips. "We're here to make Paul happy. We make Paul happy by being pretty. Anything that is not pretty doesn't get worn in here. Do I make myself clear?"

"Yes, ma'am," Megan said as Shanea nodded her head. "I'll do the best I can."

"Now, go eat," Christel said, pointing. "And don't overeat; half the girls are starting to look like balloons."

When they reached the table the only spaces were at the far end. The food was brought through the door to the kitchens and then served to Christel first who passed bowls down the table. By the time they got to Megan, Shanea and Amber, who had somehow been driven to their end, there was very little left. The meal was the same that she had been served before, roast pork, broccoli and potatoes. The only pieces of pork left were ends and gristly bits, the broccoli was all gone and there was only a smidgen of potato.

Megan didn't mind, she wasn't particularly hungry, and she gave her servings to Shanea and Amber. But she noticed that several of the other girls had taken huge servings and then eaten barely half of them; as if they were *trying* to starve the girls at the bottom of the pecking order.

"Who's the skinny brunette by Ashly?" Megan asked, pointing with her chin at a thin-faced brunette who had started to become one of the "balloons" Christel had mentioned. She was sitting next to Ashly and wolfing down a huge plate of food, even though Megan hadn't noticed her doing anything in the afternoon but sit watching Ashly play backgammon.

"That's Karie, Karie Szymonic," Shanea whispered. "She likes to start stuff and then Ashly and the others join in."

Christel was at the head of the table working on a much smaller portion and taking delicate bites. On her right was Ashly and then Karie, across from them was a delicate, birdlike, redhead, who had also taken a small serving. Megan had noticed her earlier doing sewing in the corner.

"The redhead?"

Shanea leaned out to look down the table.

"Oh, that's Mirta. She's okay and Ashly doesn't pick on her because she does the most beautiful needlework. If you want anything nice, you ask Mirta. But she'll want something in return."

"And, unfortunately, I don't have anything to trade," Megan snorted.

"You'll find something," Shanea said.

"When can I stand up and leave?" Megan asked.

"Not until Christel," Shanea replied.

Megan continued to observe the other girls covertly. She caught one absolutely poisonous look from Karie, for no reason she could determine. Ashly seemed to be ignoring her so far. She knew from what her father told her that she should try to establish dominance, but the time didn't seem right. And if she made too many waves there was Christel with the threat of the neural whip. And mind-wipe on the other side of that. Neither thought pleased.

For some reason, her mind kept coming back to the scissors in the store room. Chaining them there was probably to keep the girls from using them on each other. The tiny cloth cutters would be almost useless as weapons, even in a catfight. She doubted that the scissors were secured to defend Paul; he had to have a personal protection field on at almost all times.

Almost. There's one time when a PPF had to come down, and that was during sex; any personal intimacy, really.

Interesting.

But he'd be able to summon it almost instantly. And practically any damage a person could inflict by hand could be repaired by medical nannites.

Almost, again. Her father had not talked a lot about his investigations but sometimes she was able to pry information out of him. Sometimes she had wished she hadn't, one time . . .

She was about . . . fourteen. He had been . . . mean to her for nearly a week. He'd been pressing her, hard, about her boyfriends and what she had been doing with them. Usually he was more than willing to let her do her own thing. As he put it: "I gave you the skills to live your own life and I can't be there all the time. I have to trust you."

But he'd been . . . pressing her. He'd gone into what she called "Full Inspector Mode." Who was she hanging out with, were they having sex, what were they like, how old were they, how did they act, how did they treat her? Finally she'd lost her temper with him and told him to mind his own business. And it came out.

There was a predator who had been stalking little girls. Most of them just postpubescent, as she was at the time. He'd sweet-talk them into a little cuddling, not sex, oh no. Then when their shields were down he would hurt them, confuse them, teleport them out to somewhere and keep hurting them, continuously, never letting them get a moment to even think about summoning shields. He'd rape them while he hurt them and then usually kill them. He'd made a mistake with one, finally, and she'd had just enough presence of mind to call her shields and teleport out so they finally understood what had been happening.

He'd gone into some pretty graphic detail, probably to convince her of the seriousness of the threat. She hadn't liked it at the time and didn't really like thinking about it now. But that was the answer. But if she managed to kill Paul, really kill him, brain dead fully, against the fight of his nannites, what would she do then? And how to do it, how to hurt him that badly?

She realized that while she had been dreaming Christel had gotten up without a word and left. Most of the other girls were getting to their feet and filing out as well.

"What about the plates and stuff?" she asked Shanea, who was getting up and taking Amber's arm.

"The servants clear them," Shanea said. "Come on, Ami."

"That's silly," Megan replied, taking Amber's other arm and pulling the girl, who was still eating in very small, fine bites, to her feet. "Why don't we clear?"

"Because we can't go in the kitchen," Shanea replied. "You can't pass through the door and it zaps you if you try."

"Oh." So much for that way out.

CHAPTER THREE

When they reached the main room, they found their sewing scattered all over the place. Her breast band and the other large piece she had intended for the skirt had been cut into ribbons as had the triangular piece Shanea was working on. Karie was standing over the damage with a smirk on her face.

"Oops," the girl said, looking at Megan. "It looks like somebody had an accident."

"Oh, that's okay," Shanea said, getting down on her hands and knees and picking through the pillows. "But watch your feet, those pins could jab into your foot and really hurt you."

Megan looked at the girl, standing there with a vicious smile, and then sensed someone moving up behind her. She suddenly looked to the side where Mirta was watching her from over the piece of complicated brocade she was sewing. The girl raised an eyebrow as if to say: "Okay, what are you going to do now?"

Megan gave her one, brief, hard look, which she was pretty sure Karie wouldn't notice, and then . . . dissembled.

"Yeah, that's okay," she said, at her absolute meekest. "I think there's a pin there on the floor by your feet." She got down on her hands and knees, keeping her eye on the ground, and picked up the pin. "You need to watch yourself, really; you don't want to get hurt." All of this was said in the saddest little humble tone she could manage.

"Pathetic bitch," Karie said, kicking her in the side.

Megan rolled with it expertly and came up on one knee in the most helpless pose possible. Amber's knitting needle was right by one hand but she knew if she used that sort of weapon she wasn't going to like the consequences. Two of the other girls had closed on her as well and she was just as positive that showing that much ability would make her a threat, to Christel if not to Paul. She was pretty sure she could turn all three into mincemeat, especially if she used nerve and joint techniques. But it would not be a good thing in any sort of long term.

"Oh, come on," she whimpered, holding her hands up to Karie. "Can't we be friends?"

"Like I'd be friends with a pathetic little bitch like you," Karie replied. She darted forward and grabbed Megan's hair, hard enough to bring tears to the girl's eyes. "You think you're better than me?"

"No, Karie," Megan whined. The other two were standing back, letting the leader have the fun. "I just want to be your friend."

"You're gonna be my bitch is what you're going to be," Karie smirked. She pulled aside her robe and thrust her crotch in Megan's face. "Lick it, bitch."

"Karie," Ashly drawled. "Get a room."

"Okay, I will," the girl said, dragging Megan to her feet by her hair and dragging her down one of the corridors. She pulled open the first door and threw Megan into the room.

"Down on your knees, bitch," Karie said, striding over to Megan who had rolled, again, to one knee.

"Please don't hurt me," Megan whimpered.

"I'll hurt you if I feel like it," Karie said, catching her up by her hair again. "I won't hurt you, much, if you lick me till I come."

Megan whimpered again and then leaned forward, placing her left hand, lovingly, humbly, on Karie's thigh and then driving a knuckle-punch upward into the girl's crotch.

Women are very nearly as sensitive in the crotch area as men and, like men, it tends to take their breath away when struck there, hard. It certainly does so when followed up by a rock-hard fist to the solar plexus.

Then Megan really got to work on her.

"Mustn't make marks," Megan whispered as she pinched the base of the bully's nose then drove another fist into the woman's gut.

"Don't want anyone getting upset," she added, slamming

one open palm into the girl's right kidney followed by another to the left.

After the second kidney strike, Megan realized that she was letting her bad out just a little too much and wrapped the sadistic bitch up in an unbreakable hold that included some very nice joint work.

"Having fun?" she asked Karie, who was whimpering softly and half unconscious from the pain. The last kidney punch had probably been over the edge; the girl was likely to piss blood for a week.

"Moan," Megan said.

"Wha . . .?"

"Moan!" Megan whispered, fiercely. "Like you're having fun with your new girlfriend." She increased pressure on the elbow joint until she felt sweat bead out on the other woman's body. "You're having fun with me right now, aren't you?"

"I don't . . ."

"Moan!" She gave the elbow an extra twitch and what came out was a gasp followed by a moan.

"I can take the whole lot of you, but I have no reason to want to," Megan said, softly. "But you need to know that Megan's the top bitch. Say it: Megan's the top bitch."

"Ooooooah!" Karie moaned. "I can't . . ."

"Say it," Megan snapped, bearing down on the wrist this time. "Megan's the top bitch."

"Megan's the top bitch!" Karie gasped.

"Now moan like you're having the orgasm of your life."

"Oooooaaaahooooo . . ."

"Lousy acting," Megan said, standing up by pressing a nerve point in the girl's shoulder so hard she gasped. "When we go out there, your acting had better be better. You'd better have a big happy, I-just-came, post-orgasm smile on your face. Moan."

"Ooooohhh . . ."

"Better. I'll be crawling. Don't think you can get your mad out because I'm on my hands and knees; you really don't want me to show you how mean I can get. Who's the top bitch?"

"Megan."

"Moan."

"Oooooohhhh . . ."

"Very good. Much better. I think you like this too much. Who's Megan's bitch?"

"Karie?"

"Bingo, moaner. Let's hear a low, growly one this time."

"I . . ."

"Loud!"

"Ooooooaaaagggaaaa!"

"Good. Now, fast pants, moans, and then orgasm gasp . . ."

"Ah, ah, ah, ooooo . . . ooo . . . ooooh, AAAAAH! Oh, my God!"

"Good. You're good at faking it."

Karie suddenly lashed out a leg and tried to sweep Megan's out from under her. Megan jumped lightly over the leg and landed with both knees in the girl's back, driving the wind out of her lungs. Then she hit nerve points a couple more times, lightly, to get the point across. With each strike the woman let out a moan of pain. Close enough to pleasure for anyone listening in the hall.

"You can't beat me, you can't sneak up on me, and all of you together if I was asleep and stone drunk couldn't take me," Megan said in a feral whisper. "Now get on your feet, be a good little bitch and I'll quit hurting you."

As Karie stumbled up Megan drove her heel into the girl's stomach.

"That was for calling me pathetic." Megan smiled broadly. "Now you can really get up. And, remember, big smile. Oh, I almost forgot." She stood still for a moment and then slapped herself as hard as she could, once on each cheek.

"You hit in the face?" she asked Karie.

"No," the girl said, looking at her wide-eyed. "No bruises."

"Nothing Paul might not like, right?" Megan snarled, working her jaw from the slaps. "Who's the best bitch?"

"You are, Megan," Karie said.

"And who's Megan's bitch?"

"I am," Karie said in a defeated voice. She wouldn't meet Megan's eye. "I'm gonna piss blood."

"Too bad," Megan said coldly. "I'm sure I wouldn't have enjoyed the recovery from what you were going to do. And this is just between us, right?"

"Yeah."

"And leave Shanea alone," Megan added. "She's my friend."

Megan got down on her hands and knees and headed for the door.

"Big smile. Big shit-eating smile."

"I am," Karie said. "Ashly's gonna eat you alive, though."

"Ashly's got no idea who she is fucking with," Megan replied, then opened the door.

✧   ✧   ✧

"Are you okay?" Shanea said when she crawled over and sat down.

"Fine," Megan replied quietly. She looked over at Mirta who was staring at her somberly. The girl continued to stare and then raised one eyebrow. On an impulse, Megan winked. Mirta looked over to where Karie was clearly regaling the other girls with her tale of the rape of the new girl and then frowned and looked back at Megan. Megan just smiled, her eyes cold, and turned away.

"I managed to salvage some of it," Shanea said.

"Well, I think Karie got her mad out," Megan replied, smiling sadly. "So maybe she'll leave us alone for a while."

"Maybe," Shanea said. "But sometimes she decides we need extra training." Shanea looked sadly at the scraps in her lap. "I don't like that."

"Maybe she'll concentrate on me," Megan replied. "I can survive it."

She'd gotten another piece of cloth and pinned it when Shanea nudged her.

"Time for baths," the girl said. "Almost lights out."

The sun had set long before and the lamps had come on. They were clearly powered but instead of the normal diffuse lighting of pre-Fall these were globes, some of them colored, hanging from sconces set in the walls. They illuminated the area, but not brightly, and Megan had discovered why Mirta sat in the same place all the time; it was where the light of three lamps fell and just about the most brightly lit place in the room. The brightest spot was Ashly's seat and the girl, who had continued to play one game of backgammon after another, glowed in the light.

"I had a bath," Megan said.

"You take one every night," Shanea replied.

"I think I'll put this stuff in my room," Megan said with a shrug, picking up the sewing.

"No locks, it won't help," Shanea pointed out. "But I don't think they'll cut it up again. Christel doesn't like us wasting cloth. I don't know why; there's enough of it and more."

Megan took the pile of sewing to her room and set it on the bed, then headed for the bathroom. Most of the girls were in there and the vast majority had already climbed into the long, low bath. Warm water flowed in at one end and out at the other and the pecking order remained; Ashly was having her hair washed by one of the other girls while the far end, which was already filled with oils and soap scum from the upper end, was reserved for Shanea and Amber.

"I think I'll take a shower," Megan said with a grimace.

"I sometimes do after the bath," Shanea whispered. "But you don't want to stand out."

"I think, this time, I'll stand out," Megan replied, glancing over at Ashly. Mirta had just finished washing her hair and gave her a long, considering, look as Megan strode to the showers.

Except for relaxation, she'd never been much of a bather. She much preferred showers; she just ended up feeling cleaner. And since she'd already had one she did a sketchy wash of her pits, toweled off, grabbed a new robe and was out of the room before most of the girls had gotten done with their careful soaping.

When she reached her room she considered it carefully, then dragged the desk across until it was in front of the door. It wouldn't stop a concerted assault, but it would wake her up if and when.

She lay down and considered the day. It had been a long one. And there were probably going to be more long ones in the future. Right now, though, she was very tired. Before the lights dimmed she had closed her eyes and breathed into sleep.

Shortly afterwards, however, her eyes sprung open as the desk scraped on the floor.

She rolled to her feet in a defensive crouch but the movement had stopped.

"Megan?" Shanea whispered.

The lights were down and she was pretty sure the girl wasn't supposed to be walking around.

"What?" Megan said. She stepped over to the door and it was open enough to see that it, apparently, was just Shanea.

"I wondered . . . sometimes when bad things happen I have nightmares," Shanea said, uncertainly. "Would you like somebody to sleep with?"

"Is that okay?" Megan whispered.

"Christel doesn't care," Shanea said, "as long as it doesn't . . ."

" . . . bother Paul." Megan sighed. She really wanted nothing more than a good night's sleep and there weren't enough pillows for that. They'd have to be constantly in contact. On the other hand, she rather doubted that Shanea was there for Megan's comfort. After a moment's thought, Megan pulled the low desk out of the way and led the girl inside.

"The active term here is 'sleep,'" Megan muttered as she pushed the desk back into place.

"I know," Shanea said settling down with her back to the wall and Megan on the outside. The girl laid her head on Megan's shoulder and put one leg across her thighs. "I . . . just like someone to hold at night."

"Remind me, if I ever learn how to sew, to make you a teddy bear," Megan said, shaking her head.

In remarkably short order, Shanea was snoring very faintly. It was unpleasantly regular but Megan put it out of her mind and mentally composed herself for sleep.

I have got to get out of this place.

After the events of the first day, things mostly settled down. Their sewing project was not disturbed and the clique around Ashly seemed to have decided to ignore them for the time being. Megan slowly learned to sew and as the days passed discovered the true horror of the harem: boredom.

There was nothing to do and, of course, nowhere to go. Their day was a regular, monotonous routine. Get up in the morning, clean themselves and their rooms, have breakfast, which was usually very tasty, flaky rolls with fruit, fruit juice and milk, play games, talk or work on sewing projects all morning, lunch, generally light, more killing time in the afternoon, dinner, more killing time, bathing, lights out.

She found herself unable to sleep at night after the stresses of the first few days wore off. More often than not Shanea came by, scratching at her door. She'd at first expected the clique around Ashly to attack her in the middle of the night. Then she'd dreaded it. Then she'd anticipated it as *something* to break up the monotonous routine.

Christel left the harem to more or less run on its own. She spent all her time in the inner sanctum. Which left Ashly to run things. Badly.

Megan had taken to leaving the main room for most of the day, although Shanea was aghast at that as well. It Just Wasn't Done. But Megan *had* to get some exercise. She retreated to her room and would spend hours in there, first limbering up, then doing katas, which segued into dance. Snatches of tunes would come to her mind and she danced to all of them, running one into the other as they could be recalled. She didn't sing, she didn't hum, she just danced, sometimes furiously, for hours.

She was getting to be in the best shape of her life. And she *still* was bored out of her gourd.

✧   ✧   ✧

From time to time there had been verbal jabs from the girls around Ashly but since the incident with Karie nothing more. Then, at the end of the second week, when she had finished her sewing project, she returned to her room one afternoon, planning on getting in some solid exercise, to find that someone had placed the skirt and top on her pillows and then peed all over it and them.

She was pretty sure it wasn't Karie. The girl was a bully of the first order and unlikely to want to brave her wrath again. But it meant it was probably one of the girls in Ashly's little clique. And the way to deal with that was to kill the rot at the source.

She picked up all the material and walked through the main room to the baths with a sad expression of woeful misery on her face. Once in the bathroom she attacked the material, cleaning it as well as she could. The silks were too stained to be worth using, though, and all her work was ruined. She also couldn't get the smell of pee entirely out of the pillows. It infuriated her that she'd have to live with that smell for who knew how long.

Somebody was gonna pay.

CHAPTER FOUR

Megan waited a few days until the others had decided she'd decided to take the injury lying down. She had started work on another outfit and planned on making *sure* that this one was wearable. Then, one day, she noticed that Ashly was getting a bit squirmy and casually got to her feet, headed for the toilet.

The toilet was just off the bathroom and just as well appointed. There were more vanities inside as well as four stalls with doors so the girls could have some privacy. Megan waited in her stall until she heard someone come in and then walked out. When Ashly emerged from her stall, still adjusting her panties, Megan looked at her with eyes wide with sadness.

"Ashly, I know I'm not your friend, but it wasn't nice for somebody to pee all over my bedding," Megan said in her meekest little-girl voice.

"Well, I guess some of us just don't like you," the girl said dismissively. She was a head taller than Megan and carried herself with assurance.

"I was just hoping that maybe we could be friends," Megan said. "I'd like for us to be friends."

"Why would I want to be friends with a little turd like you?" Ashly said, brushing past her.

Megan waited until she was almost past and then drove a knuckled fist into the other girl's solar plexus. When Ashly doubled up, choking, Megan lifted her by one shoulder and drove her fist into the girl's stomach twice more.

391

"Well," Megan said, neutrally, as she grabbed the girl by her long, blond hair and drove a knuckle into her kidney. "For one reason, I wouldn't beat the shit out of you."

Ashly fell to her knees and whimpered.

"Christel's gonna . . ." the girl started to say, just as Megan grasped the base of the girl's nose and pinched, hard. There was a very sensitive nerve juncture there and clamping down on it effectively ended rational thought for Ashly.

"Christel is going to what?" Megan said, sweetly. "I don't think Christel is going to hear about this at all. Because if she does, you're going to find out that this is love taps. Now, you're going to talk to *all* of your friends. And you're going to explain that the little games are stopping, aren't you? Because if you don't, we'll have to . . . talk again. You might think that you can gang up on me, but if you do that it will be obvious. Besides, you might want to have a quiet *chat* with Karie about what happens when I get *really* angry. And then Christel *is* going to know. And then she'd better mind-wipe me. Because otherwise, you're not going to be good for anything but a kitchen slut. Do I make myself clear?"

She didn't wait for an answer. She just pinched the nerve point so hard the girl must have thought she'd been hit by a neural lash and then walked out, twitching her robe into place.

She didn't know if the girl would take it lying down or not. But when she got back to the main room she gave Karie a significant nod and then strode over to Mirta.

"Hi," she said, squatting down in front of the seamstress.

"Hi," Mirta replied neutrally. "Could you move over, you're in my light."

"Sure," Megan replied, moving over. "What do I have to do to get you to make me something?"

"Oh, I think you've already done it," Mirta replied, lightly. She was hand-embroidering the edge of a bra that was made of silk so transparent it was like glass. "I've been waiting for months for someone to take down that arrogant bitch."

"I have *no* idea what you are talking about," Megan said with a broad smile.

"Yes, you do," Mirta replied. "I wasn't sure at first, but Karie steps aside when you walk past. And she never gives just one lesson to the new girls. She didn't give *me* just one lesson," the woman said in a low but fierce tone. "And I notice that Ashly seems to be taking a long time in her toilet. But she only went in there to pee. She'd have been out at least two minutes ago."

"You notice a lot," Megan said, sitting down.

"I notice that you spend a lot of time in your room," Mirta replied. "That when you come out you usually go to the shower because you need it. I notice that you don't walk quite like a dancer, either. You walk more like some martial artists I've known. You walk like a panther, except when you play that meek little girl role. I notice that you watch all the time, too." She looked up and pinned the girl with her eye, tying off a section of the embroidery and picking up the next color without looking down. "And your hands have calluses. But not from sewing."

"How old *are* you?" Megan asked.

"Me?" Mirta squeaked. "I'm just like you, just a little girl, not even twenty! And some man picked me up by the side of a stream and then . . . oh, it was So! Terrible!" The entire performance was delivered in a frightened little voice while cold eyes stared back at Megan.

"Yes, it is so terrible," Megan replied neutrally. "Will you help me?"

"With sewing?" Mirta replied, finally looking down. "Happily." She had been stitching the embroidery, tiny stitch after tiny stitch, without looking at what she was doing. And doing it perfectly.

"You do it so well," Megan pressed.

"Most of my life," Mirta replied. "My parents were reenactors. You know what that means?"

"Yes, people who had a hobby of doing stuff the old ways," Megan said. "The town elders where I . . . was . . . were sort of like that. At least, they lived in an old house and had some stuff that they used from time to time."

"My mother taught me to sew when I was very young," Mirta said. "We'd make stuff and then take it to Faires." Her face cleared of the cold lines it normally had and she smiled. "I used to love to go to Faire."

"I hope we all can some day again," Megan said.

"Don't talk that way," Mirta said carefully. "We are Paul's servants. That is all that we are or ever will be."

"Doesn't mean *he* can't take us." Megan grinned.

"Hmmph," Mirta grunted, but she smiled as she did. "So what do you want?"

"I really don't know," Megan replied. "Some *simple* panties, for God's sake. I'm just too clumsy with a needle to get the fine sewing for them."

"Easily done," Mirta said, then looked at her. "I saw what you were trying to do with the other outfit. I have some ideas. I don't know if you'll like them."

"As long as it . . ."

"Pleases Paul." Mirta grinned evilly. "Yes, I think it will. Do you want me to do it?"

"Please," Megan said. "How do I repay you?"

"Oh, you already have," Mirta replied calmly. "Although breaking the bitch's neck and boiling her in oil would have been preferable."

"Once you break the neck, they don't feel the oil," Megan pointed out. "Details. You have to decide."

Mirta shrugged. "Okay, just lowering her into a vat of acid."

"What?" Megan said, frozen.

"I said . . ."

"Yeah, okay," Megan replied, her mind racing. "I guess I'll get them in a few days?"

"That . . . works . . ." Mirta replied.

"Thank you," Megan said, suddenly looking her in the eye. "You have been very helpful."

"I'm glad to hear that," Mirta said, staring at her. "Very glad."

Megan gave her a nod and walked back to her room. She refused to whistle as she walked.

Shanea was there when she arrived. The girl had gotten over her fear of being out of the main room and now hid in Megan's room much of the time despite the still-noticeable smell of urine. It was a pain in the ass in some ways and in others quite comforting. Megan had never really had many girlfriends and certainly none that looked to her for protection. It was pleasant and cloying simultaneously.

She was working on another outfit and looked up happily when Megan entered.

"Where were you?" Shanea asked.

"I had a . . . conversation with Ashly," Megan said. "And Mirta is going to make me an outfit."

"How did you talk her into that?" Shanea asked, eyes round.

"I was very charming," Megan said, throwing herself on the smelly pillows. "Shanea, I need to think for a bit, okay?"

"Okay," Shanea said, going back to her sewing.

After a while Megan threw herself to her feet and paced back and forth.

"Shanea, what does Christel do in her office all day?" she asked. It bothered her that the woman almost never came out except for meals. For that matter, she was never at the evening bath.

"She's working on the accounts," Shanea said. "You didn't know?"

"No, I didn't know," Megan said, stopping her pacing and looking at the girl. "All day?"

"There's a lot of them," Shanea replied. "That's why she's always so angry. She hates doing them. I saw them one time and they're really really complicated. I couldn't make head or tails of them."

Megan stared at her, unseeing, for quite some time, then smiled broadly.

"Shanea, you are the most wonderful person in the world."

"Thank you," Shanea smiled. "Why?"

"Just because," Megan said. "I'm either going to be stumbling back in just a minute or I'll be quite some time."

She walked to the door to the office and knocked, knowing that all the other girls were watching her. What was that feely she had watched? *Oliver Twist.* "Please, sir, can I have some more?" That was just how it felt.

"What?" Christel said angrily from beyond the door.

"I'd like to speak to you," Megan replied, as meekly as she could manage.

"Come in," the woman said.

Megan stepped in, half expecting to end up on the floor, doubled in agony. The older woman was behind the desk, which was littered with paper.

"Shanea just told me that you're in here doing the books all day," Megan said, standing more or less at attention. "I . . . think I could help."

"You?" Christel snapped, throwing a pencil on the desk. "What do you know about it?"

"I . . . was studying numbers before the Fall," Megan replied. "I know something about accounting. And . . . you seem like you really hate it. That makes it hard on the rest of us. If I can help, that makes it easier. And, frankly, I'm bored to tears."

Christel looked at her, cocking her head slightly to the side, then shrugged.

"You really think you can make head or tails of it?" Christel asked.

"Yes, ma'am," Megan said, walking over to the table and looking down. The papers were covered in columns with notations and numbers by them. They also were covered in equations, most of them scratched, rubbed or in some cases ripped, out. It was pretty clear that math was not Christel's strong suit.

She pulled one of the papers around to her and read it, then blanched.

"Oh, my God," she exclaimed. "You use single-entry book-keeping?"

"What?" Christel said.

"Single entry," Megan replied, shaking her head. "You've got both your expenses and your income on the same line. Not to mention mixing up your purchases and your use. No wonder you've been having problems."

"How else do you do it?" Christel asked, bewildered.

"Okay, okay," Megan said, dropping into a cross-legged position next to the desk. "You've got food purchases here and a new shipment of cloth. Not to mention housekeeping items and cleaning supplies. By the way, can I get some new pillows?"

"What happened to the ones you have?" Christel asked, angrily.

"They got . . . damaged. Look, what you do is separate this out by category . . ."

For the next two days Christel led her over the accounts, although it was quite often the other way around. It turned out that the woman was responsible for managing all of the needs of the harem. She had to track, and account for, all of the food that was consumed, the supply of bedding, the raw materials the girls used in their sewing, their "feminine" supplies and everything else that went into a functioning harem.

By the second day, Christel was in a more jovial mood. Megan hadn't been lying when she said she knew something about accounting. It was clear that the younger girl was far better at organizing the accounts than Christel had ever been.

"The worst part is that Paul is always checking on them," Christel admitted early the next day. "He wants me to account for every single item and explain why they were used. The food budget is the worst. He's always harping about how much food the girls eat. So one time I cut them back and then they didn't have enough and were complaining."

"Well, from the looks of some of them they could use a diet," Megan noted. "But not all. What we need to do is manage the diets individually. But that will mean working more closely with the kitchen staff. Also . . ."

"What?" Christel asked, looking at her sharply.

"Well, there's no reason they have to sit around all day," Megan pointed out. "I'm sure some of them know how to dance, for example. And they could use some toning up. Dial in on the food consumption, maybe have weigh-ins and track their body fat, and start having classes in, oh, dance, singing; can any of them play a musical instrument?"

"We're a harem, not a choir," Christel noted.

"Yes, but you said that one of our purposes is to keep Paul happy," Megan said. "Is he going to be happier with a bunch of roly-poly slugs? Or a group of girls that are healthy, happy, in good condition and maybe can entertain him other than on their backs?"

Christel made a moue and shook her head.

"Think of it this way," Megan said, carefully. "It's not going to cost anything more, except maybe for some instruments, and it's going to *look* good. Look, *I* can dance for Paul, at least. And I can teach the other girls, if there's no one else."

"You?" Christel asked.

Megan stood up and took off her robe, uncomfortably aware that it left her entirely naked, and went through a series of simple dance steps, lifting on a toe, turning, bending. She wasn't about to show her advanced moves, much less katas, which looked very much like a dance when she did them.

"Me," Megan said when she was finished. She picked up the robe and put it back on, belting it tightly. "Not to mention stretching exercises and gymnastics. I'm sure that Paul gets tired of the missionary position all the time."

"Well, you'll just have to find out, won't you?" Christel said cattily and then sighed. "You do have a point, though. And you're not the only one who can dance, girl. In fact, you don't dance all that well at all."

"No, I don't," Megan said, meekly.

"I'll see about it," Christel said.

Megan had been working all day, skipping lunch in fact, getting the books in order. She had broken out most of the items by category and had started to get a handle on in-flow and out-flow. Some of it still didn't add up, but she wasn't sure if that was Christel's execrable bookkeeping or something else. But she realized that she was so tired of staring at columns, and so hungry, that she wasn't making any more sense, so she stood up and walked out into the main room.

Christel, once Megan had demonstrated she knew what she was doing, had been spending most of her time in the main room. Ashly had been displaced from the position of prominence and Christel spent her time chatting and playing Yahtzee while Ashly sulked off to the side.

As Megan walked out and headed for her room, she heard her name called.

"Megan," Mirta said. "I've got your outfit finished."

"Let's . . . see it in my room if you don't mind," Megan said, gesturing at the corridor.

Mirta merely nodded and headed down to the room where Shanea, inevitably, was ensconced. Megan noted that her friend was one of the ones who needed to go on a diet. Since Megan had befriended her, mysteriously larger portions had made it down the table. Amber was in there as well, knitting something golden this time.

"Here it is," Mirta said, holding up two pieces of cloth that together might have made one decent skirt.

The top was at first glance a simple halter, with *very* brief coverage of the breasts; the triangular fabric might just cover the nipples. But the fabric was of some odd material that changed color as the light hit it. Small as it was, it was quite spectacular. The "skirt" that accompanied it, in the same fabric, was brief to the point of scandal in any other environment. Short, *very* short, and slit up either side.

"I made you some panties as well," Mirta said. "But with that, well, even a thong might show."

"It looks . . . tight," Megan said.

"It is tight," Mirta replied. "I got the outfit you were working on from Shanea for sizing and figuring that you went a little loose, I tightened it up, because . . ."

"Paul will like it," Megan said, making a moue of distaste. She slipped off the robe, despite the company, and slipped on the skirt, which had two buttons in the back. She found it easier to slide it around to the front to button because it *was* tight. The buttons gave no sign of straining loose, but she had a struggle to get them in the holes. She also had to pull it down onto her hips to maintain any shred of decency. The halter top was tight as well and as she had feared the tiny triangles barely covered her nipples.

"Oh, that's . . . lovely!" Shanea said.

"Pretty," Amber said, looking up at her with a fixed expression. "So pretty."

"Just right," Mirta said, pushing Megan's breasts up into the halter; the bottom of her breasts showed a goodly bit of rounded flesh. "Perfect."

"I think I'd rather wear a robe!" Megan said.

"I think that *Paul* would rather you wear this," Mirta replied. "And Christel will certainly have no problems with it. The other girls will be clamoring for one just like it."

"I want one," Shanea blurted. "But I don't have anything to trade!"

"I'll see if I can fit you into my busy schedule," Mirta replied. "Now that I've got the pattern in mind, turning more out won't be all that difficult. Some . . . small, strong stitches involved, but not hard ones."

"I can't wear this out of here," Megan complained. "Every time I sit down I'll show all I've got!"

"Not so," Mirta said, stepping to the side. "The method for sitting is thus. You point your toes and roll down onto your legs." The woman demonstrated, gracefully sitting without spreading her legs or showing anything she didn't care to show to the audience.

"Where did you learn that?" Megan asked.

"That's for me to know, dearie." Mirta laughed, getting up with almost the reverse motion. "When you sit, you stay in the same position, with your feet tucked under your butt. Nobody gets to see anything you don't want to show. Drives guys nuts. Try it."

After a few tries Megan had managed to sit without collapsing or spreading her legs and she realized that it was how Mirta *always* sat down. It was both elegant and, she suspected, alluring. A graceful and sexy motion. Grand.

"Now, go show it off," Mirta said.

"I'm not going to parade around in this . . . this . . ."

"Go show it to Christel," Mirta said, definitely. "You will *too* 'parade' around in it. You're my walking advertisement. Get out there and advertise."

"You evil old . . ."

"Ah, ah," Mirta smiled. "Me?" she added in a little girl voice. "I'm just . . . just a little girl . . ."

"Right," Megan said, facing the door. "And I'm Sheida Ghorbani."

She strode down the corridor and into the main room, walking over to where Christel was playing Yahtzee. The other girls watched her and she had to admit that based on their reaction she had to be the most hated girl in the harem. Many of them had some minor form of lingerie or panties and bras. But the outfit Megan sported was, to those, what a nuclear weapon is to a firecracker. It was the sexual equivalent of a weapon of mass destruction.

She stopped in front of Christel and pirouetted in place.

"Will this *do*?" she asked, sharply.

"It will do very well," Christel replied with a nod. "I'm sure Paul will love it."

"As am I," Megan said tightly.

"Dinnertime," Christel said. "Why don't you go get your . . . friends. And put a robe on; that thing is scandalous."

Megan went back to the room and stripped off the outfit, replacing it with a robe. She felt more dressed with a robe on. She felt more dressed *naked*.

"It was a hit," she told Mirta sourly. "Christel's going to want one."

"I might make her one," Mirta replied, with a malicious smile. "And she'll never understand why she doesn't look as good as you do in it. But the next outfit I'm going to make is for Amber."

"Amber?" Shanea said. "Why?"

"Because I want to." Mirta grinned. "You'll see. And one for you, dear, of course."

"One that will suit her?" Megan asked. "Dinnertime, by the way."

"Oh, yes," Mirta replied, as they walked out the door. "Definitely one that will suit her. And I think that Amber's will cover her almost completely. And make Paul want to tear down walls. The human body is a lovely thing, but never so lovely as when properly covered. It's using clothes to create a mystery that is the truest art."

"Not much mystery in what you made for me," Megan said, sourly.

"Enough." Mirta smiled. "Just enough and no more."

When they reached the dining room the food still hadn't been served and Megan sat down with a puzzled frown.

"Girls, listen up," Christel said, clapping her hands for attention as Mirta sat down. "Starting tonight, you will be served individually. And for tonight all the portions will be equal. As soon as I can obtain a scale, all of you will be weighed. Those of you who are overweight, and you know who you are, will be placed on reduced servings."

"What?" Karie said.

"Yes, Karie, you're one of them, and Shanea and Demetra. But we're also going to start having classes in dance and exercise. They will be mandatory for most." There was a general unhappy muttering at that and she looked around at the group with a hard smile.

"Paul maintains a harem, not a palace for lazy slugs. It is about looking good for Paul and, frankly, most of you are starting to look a bit soft in the middle. That is going to change." She waved to the kitchen and the servants began carrying out plates that had been pre-served. Megan carefully kept her eyes on her plate and tried very hard not to smile. One change effected.

CHAPTER FIVE

After another week, Megan had the books in order and Paul still hadn't put in an appearance. And after struggling for that week, maintaining things became easy enough that she got bored again. But she still didn't go out of the room, much, preferring to use the excuse of "keeping up the books" to maintain some relative privacy. She was also exempt from the regular exercise and dance classes, but she kept in shape by working out in the office. Everything was on track except one: The kitchen books still wouldn't add up; the harem was paying for at least twenty percent more food than was being consumed.

After going over the numbers repeatedly she reached the point that she was positive it wasn't just sloppiness. Which meant she knew darned well where it was going. The problem was what to do with the information. She could inform Christel in which case the head cook could look to being on the wrong end of a Change. Or she could manage it more . . . obliquely.

She was also fascinated by some of the items available for order through the kitchens. There weren't only foods and spices but cookware, distilling materials, cleaning solvents . . .

An idea was starting to tick over in her head one afternoon when the door opened and Christel waved at her imperiously.

"Megan, go to your room and put on that *lovely* outfit Mirta made for you," Christel said, smiling viciously. "There's someone you need to meet. Again."

401

✧   ✧   ✧

"Ah, the washing girl," Paul said, smiling. He was no longer the old man he had appeared, but the face was the same. As was the long hair that hung in lanky strands. But his clothes were clean and finely made. He had the look of being about two hundred, slightly below normal height. Megan suddenly realized that she had met him before, years ago. She truly hoped that he would never remember the meeting.

"Her name is Megan," Christel said. "Megan Sung."

It was the name she'd used after the Fall. She didn't know why she had changed it; it wasn't like her father was well known. But, then again, the sort of people who would react to the name "Travante" were precisely the sort she *didn't* want interested in her.

"How have you been, Megan?" Paul said, holding out his hand. "You look much better than the last time I saw you."

"Oh, I am much better, sir," Megan said, not taking the hand but instead dropping in a curtsey that kept her legs modestly crossed. She stayed in the curtsey for a moment then straightened back up, not meeting his eye.

"What a delightful young lady," Paul said, running an eye over her like a horseman with a likely looking filly. "Beautiful bone structure. Love the outfit."

"Thank you, milord," Megan simpered as well as she could. *Let him choose one of the others, let him choose one of the others . . .*

"I think we should get to know one another better," Paul said, taking her hand and leading her to the room reserved for him.

"Yes, milord," Megan said, trying to sound happy and failing miserably. She bit her lip and the last thing she saw before the door closed was Ashly looking at her with an expression of malicious delight.

"The first time is always hard," Paul said, raising himself off of her and rolling to the side. "It will get better."

Megan rolled onto her side, away from him, and curled into a fetal position, clenching her hands so hard that her nails dug into the palms of her hands.

I will not attempt to kill him, she thought. *It's not possible. He's protected. I'm in a prison in a fortress. It will only get me killed.*

"It was . . . wonderful, milord," she heard herself say.

"That is, in fact, a lie," Paul said, neutrally. "But I appreciate the effort." He patted her on her rump. "Get up. Clean yourself. It will help you feel better. And it will get easier with time. What you do here is of great importance. You are a fine group of potential mothers. Good genes should be perpetuated and here you are protected from harm to you and your children. Understand your importance and it makes the life much more pleasurable."

"Of course, milord," Megan bit out. *I'm supposed to be thankful for being a well-kept broodmare. Gee.*

Paul rolled to his feet and pulled on his clothes than tapped her on the rump again.

"Get up," he said, not unkindly. "I will give you a few moments to yourself but then you *will* come out of this room."

When he had left Megan grabbed one of the pillows and hugged it to her stomach, fighting against tears. She wanted to cry, she wanted to scream. She wanted, oh, how she wanted to escape. But neither tears nor screams would do anything. As she lay there, feeling fluids trickling down the inside of her thigh, she had a clear vision of her hands pushing Paul's head into a bucket. And she realized that the bucket was *not* filled with water, for all that the liquid was clear.

With that thought, she rolled to her feet, her face hard and her eyes like agate. She walked to the silver basin and carefully washed herself, then, recomposing her features, she donned her "outfit" and walked out the door.

"Marlene, thank you for meeting with me," Megan said, sweetly.

She was sitting in the dining room by the door to the kitchen when the head cook came in. The cook was a slightly overweight, older woman with piggy eyes buried in her flesh.

"What do you want?" the cook asked, brusquely. "I've got work to do."

"I know, I know; it must be terrible slaving over a hot stove all day," Megan said. *There were enough cooks on the payroll, if they all existed, to do the work three times over. She doubted that the fat old bitch had been near a stove in a year.*

"I work for my keep," the cook snarled. "I don't make it on my back."

"Well, we all do what we can." Megan sighed. "Speaking of doing what we can, I just had a couple of teensy questions. Nothing really."

"Oh?" Marlene said, suddenly wary.

"I was just looking at this item for meat last week," Megan

said, her brow furrowing in clear perplexity. "You see, based upon what we've worked out in the individual diets, there should have been seven kilos of beef used in last Friday's meal. And it appears that we paid for *ten* kilos . . ."

"Well, there's wastage," the cook said, huffily. "I mean, we order it on the bone. Bones, gristle cut out, you ladies have to have everything perfect . . ."

"And I know you make your own noodles, aren't they delicious? But there's another ten kilos of flour listed as used. And, by golly, the servings should have only worked out to *five* kilos. I'm just *so* perplexed!"

"You had better get unperplexed, missy," the cook said, nastily. "You have no idea what can end up in your plate."

"Oh, I rather think I do," Megan said. "I rather think I do. And anything . . . untoward would be easy enough for Paul to detect if one of his concubines turned up dead. And he *would* wonder, wouldn't he? Let's just drop the bullshit, okay? I've been over the books for the last several months. You're not just skimming, you're stealing a council member blind. What do you think his response would be?"

The cook just looked at her, her jaw working in anger.

"Now, let's be friends, shall we?" Megan said, after a moment to let the cook consider her position. "I see no reason to cut in on your little . . . peccadilloes."

"What?" Marlene replied, suspiciously.

"I don't, frankly, care if you steal that bastard's shorts," Megan said, making the point clear. "On the other hand, there are a few things I need. And I see no reason that you can't get them for me."

"Oh."

"If you're stealing and I catch you out, I'm a hero," Megan said, smiling sweetly. "On the other hand, if you're stealing and at the same time slipping me things I need, while I'm covering you up in the books, that makes us . . . partners."

"What do you need?" Marlene said, after a moment. "And is this . . ."

"It's not going to cut in on your take at all," Megan assured her. "But you really need to be a bit more discreet. I can point out some areas that are easier, and more profitable, to cover up than others."

"Okay," Marlene replied. "What do you need? And how are you going to get it past the Gorgon?"

"I'll handle Christel," Megan replied, handing the cook a

sheet of paper. "Here's a list. I'll also handle the books on those items. We'll just list most of them as . . . spice."

"Christel," Megan said as she was carefully walking the older woman though the last week's receipts, "you know what this harem needs that it doesn't have?"

"Dildos?" Christel said snippily. She had been spending less and less time on the books and liked that state of affairs. But she wasn't going to entirely trust "the new girl" either.

"No, easier to just get cucumbers from the kitchens," Megan replied with a chuckle. "No, it needs *perfume*."

"Perfume?" Christel said, then smiled. "Yes, as a matter of fact it does. I think Paul would like that."

"Perfume and cosmetics. I know all the girls are gorgeous, but there's nothing that a little cosmetics can't improve upon. The problem is, I talked to Marlene and there aren't any suppliers available."

"Paul could probably find one," Christel said, thoughtfully. "Or just ken it."

"He probably could," Megan admitted. "But wouldn't it be better as a surprise?"

"Yes," the older woman replied. "But you said there aren't any suppliers."

"There aren't. But the raw materials are available." Megan pointed out. "In fact, there's some indication that most early perfumes were invented in harems. Still-rooms used to be common in them."

"Stills?" Christel said, cautiously. "One of the reasons we only serve a little wine is that I could easily see us all getting to be drunks . . ."

"A still can be used for much more than making alcohol," Megan said, shaking her head. "What you do is you get raw materials for the perfume and you distill them down, concentrate them. That's how you get the concentrated scent. By the time of the Fall they were mostly based on nannites, but this is the old way of doing it."

"How do you know that?"

"I said I was studying numbers," Megan replied. "That wasn't . . . entirely accurate. What I was studying was *chemistry*. Early perfume production was part of the history I audited. I can make some simple cologne just from stuff available in the kitchen. But with a few other items, nothing expensive or complicated, I can make some really nice perfume. I think. I know the theory, anyway."

She looked up and saw the older woman eyeing her warily.

"Look, I'm talking about some rose hips to start, okay?" Megan said, shrugging. "I promise I won't be making brandy in my spare time. If I do anything out of line you can always zap me, right? There are two spare rooms. All I need is a table, some glassware, a catchment for runoff and some spices. Perfume, scented candles. I can't sew, but *this* I can do."

"Okay," Christel said, suspiciously. "But if you're trying something . . ."

"For the last time," Megan said, letting a note of anger enter her voice. "We're in an impregnable fortress in the middle of Paul's territory. I'm not even sure where we are except up in the mountains. And I'm well fed and well housed. Running away would be stupid, impossible and pointless. I like my brain the way it is. And, let me note, so do you. Otherwise *you're* going to have to manage all this damned accounting. At this point the last thing *either* of us wants is me brain-drained."

"True," Christel chuckled. "Are you going to have enough time for this and all your other duties?"

"Yes, I will," Megan sighed. "All of them. Including . . ."

"Keeping Paul happy."

Cosmetics turned out to be easier than perfume. There were people who were making the former and if it was available anywhere in Ropasa it was available to "Paul's Girls." The expense of the material made her blanch when she got the bill, but in time she'd find a better, meaning less expensive, source. But within a week she had a supply of rouges, mascara, lip gloss and powders that the girls cheerfully dug into with abandon. So much abandon that she knew immediately that she had to find another source.

Perfume was another matter; no one seemed to be making it anywhere in Ropasa. Certainly not commercially. She felt a twinge of anger at being trapped in this damned harem; if she was back on the outside she could make a killing in the perfume business. But needs must and she instead ordered the materials she needed to make it, including a good workbench.

The material for the table was brought into the harem by Changed. They were not the half-wild orcs that made up the bulk of Paul's legions but heavy-bodied, dull-witted beings wearing gray smocks that took no note of the women who shrieked and hugged the walls as they came through carrying balks of timber and tools.

They were followed by another Change. He was short with preternaturally long arms and legs. He did notice the women but only to wink at them and leer as he followed the bearers into the room set aside for the perfumery.

"I want it over there," Megan said, pointing to a wall that got a decent amount of light.

"Build it, build it," the shorter Change said. "Sammy build it he will!"

The Change started pulling out tools with what appeared to be complete randomness but he worked incredibly quickly, all the time singing and humming to himself. In less than thirty minutes he had taken the raw wood and constructed a heavy-duty table without using a single nail or glue.

Megan watched the proceedings with interest. The Change had never bothered to measure anything but the table appeared to be perfectly level and was extremely sturdy. As he was sanding the top she shook it, but it barely budged.

"Build!" Sammy yelled. "Solid. Live longer than Sammy it will!" He smoothed the top as the bearers left the room to another cacophony of screams, then began applying lacquer to the whole thing.

"Well, Sammy, you did a very nice job here," Megan said. "I'm going to go see about some glassware."

"Build!"

She thought about the construction as she walked back to the dining room. Paul wasn't only building legions of fighters, but other specialties. She suddenly had a vision, as if she had been there, of rank upon rank of "Sammies" specialized for metalwork turning out weapons and armor for the legions. Of more Sammies building ships and engines of war.

She wondered, if Paul's faction won this war, if this was the fate of mankind. If, with the unlimited power and knowledge of Mother available, the New Destiny faction would turn everyone into narrow, specialized, insects. What, then, would be the fate of Megan "Sung"? Would she be specialized for providing sex to a wretched old pervert, so far beyond the bounds of sanity that he thought the women of his harem were happy to be here?

In all honesty she knew that most of the women in the harem *were* happy to be here. The life was far easier than anything since the Fall. And, as Marlene was only too happy to point out, all you had to do was lie on your back and spread your legs from time to time.

All.

And who was Sammy? Who had he been *before* he was Changed? What had caused them to Change him into this . . . builder-goblin? Had he angered some council member, one of their staff? Or had he simply been chosen at random. "Five orcs, next one's a builder . . ."

She shuddered at the thought and, deep inside, admitted that maybe there were worse things than having to fake enjoying being raped every few weeks. Even if the person they happened to no longer knew it.

CHAPTER SIX

Megan was in the still-room trying to convince rose water not to boil when Shanea came in.

"Paul's here," Shanea whispered.

"I guess I should go get dressed," Megan said, looking down at her spotted robe.

"And fix your hair," Shanea replied, pulling at her arm.

Megan turned down the oil lamp and went up the corridor. Other girls were rushing past her but she ignored them. Once in her room she stripped off the robe and started to pick up another.

"You probably should wear . . . you know," Shanea said, picking up the few decimeters of material.

"I probably should," Megan groaned. "God help me."

"Have you seen the one that Mirta made for Amber?" Shanea asked, helping her into the skirt.

"No, is it as bad as this?"

"Covers practically everything," Shanea answered. "In gauze. I don't think she's wearing it, though. And Mirta's not done with mine."

"I need to talk to Mirta about the fabric closet," Megan said, making a mental note. "I think she probably has some suggestions."

"Probably," Shanea said, taking Megan's hair down from the bun she'd had it in and brushing it out. "It's snarled."

"I can't keep it down around the flames; I'd end up burning it." Megan sighed and winced as the tangles were pulled out. "That will have to do."

"Everyone else is made up," Shanea pointed out.

"This will have to do," Megan stated.

The two girls walked down the corridor to the main room. Paul was still there, talking with Christel, who did not look happy. Paul looked, if anything, worse than the last time they had seen him and Megan noticed that his hands were worn and almost white. It looked, impossible as that seemed, as if he'd been washing clothes by hand, probably with lye soap.

"Ah, Megan," Paul said when she walked in the room. "I was wondering where you were."

"Megan has many projects at the moment," Christel said, subtly shifting to be between them.

"Surely none that require her attention right now," Paul replied, walking around Christel to take Megan's hand. "You look lovely."

Most of the girls in the room had made heavy use of the cosmetics Megan had procured and had donned their best outfits. She got vile looks as Paul led her into the room.

This time she tried very hard to if not enjoy the act, at least appear to. After the first "session" she had had nightmares three nights running. The worst was when she awoke with the face of her father over her. That had brought her as close as she had ever gotten to suicide. But she had tried to mentally prepare herself for the next time, knowing that with no way to avoid it, the better she could make it for herself, the better off she would be.

However, there was no foreplay or even time for her to prepare herself. Paul took her practically as soon as the door was closed, pushing her to the floor and thrusting into her, hard. She tried to loosen up, to moisten up, moaning, badly, as if she enjoyed it. But he came quickly and then rolled off of her, pulling on his pants quickly and not looking at her.

"I guess you like the outfit," Megan said. He'd pulled the halter away from her breasts and she'd managed to get the skirt out of the way of any outflow. But the outfit had never really come off.

"Maybe too much," Paul said, getting up and starting to retrieve his shirt.

As she wiped herself she looked at him out of the corner of her eye.

"Paul," she said. "what's wrong?"

"Nothing," he replied, dismissively.

"Was it me?" she asked with a plaintive note in her voice.

"No, sweetling," he said, sitting down by her. "It's just work."

"You look tense," she said. "Lie down."

"Why?"

"On your stomach," she replied, pushing him over. She rolled over and straddled his back, the skirt hiking up out of her way. She thought for a moment of simply hammer-driving his upper vertebrae, but she wasn't sure if his healing nannites would cure it. And whoever took over from him was sure to kill her, even if she succeeded. Instead, she took her thumbs and started digging them into his back, rolling upward with strong, firm, strokes.

"God that feels good," Paul exclaimed. He pillowed his head on his hands and rolled his back up. "Thank you."

"Now, what's so troubling at work?" she asked. "Don't you dare tense up on me," she added, pushing at the muscle that had bunched at her words until it had eased back down.

"It's nothing I think you'd be interested in," Paul said.

"Probably not," Megan said. "But verbalizing a problem is quite often a way for the unconscious to find a solution. You talk, I'll massage. Call it division of labor."

Paul laughed at that but was quiet for a while as she continued massaging his back.

"Minjie Jiaqi's aide killed him and took his Key," Paul said, finally. "He's willing to join with New Destiny, but he's putting too many conditions on it for me to feel that I can trust him. Minjie had been a friend for years. I don't feel happy just letting the son of a bitch get away with it."

"Good God," Megan said. "I hope the Coalition doesn't know."

"They don't," Paul replied. "We have a very good source close to their Council. But the problem is . . ."

"You're tensing up again," Megan warned. "Talk, don't tense."

"The problem is that if he feels he can go his way, the others will too," Paul snarled.

"Calm," Megan said. "Shuuuh. Talk it out."

"I'm holding a tiger by the tail, honey," Paul said, rolling out from under her and sitting up. "The council members that side with me don't *understand* the importance. Really, only Minjie ever did. Celine wanted to be able to make her damned abominations. Chansa . . . Chansa just wants power, direct power. The kind that the Council couldn't really wield before the Fall. Reyes has his . . . girls." Paul stopped and looked to the side, shaking his head. "Every time I come in here I think of the . . . the horror that they are suffering and it just makes me want to throttle that perverted bastard."

"You need some more massage, Mister Paul, sir," Megan said, grabbing him by the shoulder and pushing him facedown again. "So how do you keep them in line?"

"Subtly," Paul muttered. "For one thing, all their guards are bound to me. They didn't notice at first and since they have I've been quite pleasant but very definite about it. The thing is, if one of them decides to defy me, I can take them out at any time. Furthermore, it's *my* guards who hold the power plants and *my* word that locks the shields. And I'm very careful to remain shielded myself. When I'm in here, no one can enter or leave and there's a shield up to ensure that. But this Patala bastard had all my guards killed and refuses to have them replaced. He doesn't have access to much power; I could destroy him in an instant. But I'm afraid if I do, it will cause the others to react."

"How was Minjie killed?" Megan asked. She lay down on his back, pressing her breasts into his muscles and rolling them around. "Now, doesn't that feel better?"

"Oh, very much so," Paul said, rolling over.

She mounted him, smiling sweetly, trying hard to enjoy it enough to get moist and started moving up and down. To her surprise she actually *did* start to enjoy herself, at least partially because she was looking at his unguarded neck. She clamped down on him and leaned in, stroking up and down, imagining cracking his hyoid bone and watching him choke to death on his own blood. When she realized she was finding sexual pleasure in the thought, she tried to think of something, anything, else.

"How was Minjie killed?" she asked, panting.

"You want to know *now*?" Paul gasped.

"Um, hmmm."

"Binary toxin," Paul said. "Part in his food, part in his wine. By the time the nannites could react, he was already effectively dead." He rolled her over and began thrusting until he came and collapsed onto her, burying his face against her neck.

"Kill him," she said, grabbing his hair and pulling his head back to where she could look in his eyes. "Have him assassinated. Quietly. Then make a deal with *his* aide. Don't fuck with me, I won't kill you."

"How?" Paul asked as he drew out of her.

She knew the answer but wasn't about to tell him.

"That should be easy to figure out," Megan said. "Have Celine do it."

"Hmmm . . ."

"There," she said, using a corner of a towel to wipe herself, "don't you feel better?"

"Yes," he replied, kissing her on the lips and running his tongue into her mouth. He needed to use a toothbrush and he smelled. "Thank you."

"I live to serve," she said, running her hands over the back of his neck. She knew damned well how *she* would kill this unnamed usurper. The only problem was escaping after she did it.

Paul returned over the next three days in quick succession, each time looking more worn and wan. Each time he chose at least one of the girls, sometimes two. Twice in the three days it was Megan, to her well-hidden disgust.

After the quick succession of visits Paul didn't come back for two weeks and then another long pause of almost a month. The last visit he bedded Ashly and Velva, one of Ashly's little clique, giving them something to talk about for *days*.

This pattern continued for months. From time to time one of the girls would begin showing signs of being pregnant and after a brief check by Christel she would be whisked out of the harem and into the confinement quarters.

Each month, Megan secretly prayed that she wouldn't be one of them. If she was taken out of the harem, away from her "experiments," away from the books that at least gave her a few hours of work during the week, if she was simply cooped up and fed like some damned brood mare, she was sure she would go completely insane.

She wondered, as the time passed, about the pregnancy rate. She had spent enough time on the outside to know that farmers' wives spent most of their time "knocked up." But over a six-month period, only two of the girls tested pregnant. A similar group on the outside would be at least an order of magnitude more efficient as "breeders."

But given Paul's infrequent visits, the rate was not so surprising. A couple of visits a month, one maybe two of the girls "taken" at apparent random and there was no way that the rate was going to be much higher. And he was getting to be in terrible shape. She had to wonder if his nannites were bothering to maintain his sperm count. It was just another of Paul's studied blindnesses. He had a "duty" to perform, even if he was performing it badly. The fact that this "duty" happened to be sex with voluptuous young females, none of whom had a say in the matter, was quite beside the point, of course. It was just another proof that Paul was absolutely crackers.

But, as the time went on, despite the many things she now had to occupy her, Megan looked forward to his infrequent visits. The disgust was starting to fade and that terrified her. By the sixth month of captivity, she was beginning to look forward to the act, to the sex. It no longer felt like rape and she was horrified that she was actually starting to enjoy Paul's company. He was smart, very smart, and when he did bother to talk he was interesting. The chance to know something of what was happening outside the harem was delightful. To listen to the intrigues that were going on among the New Destiny faction and, from time to time, to hear about the actions of the Freedom Coalition that fought against them.

What was even more horrible was, she began to enjoy him as a bed partner and he definitely seemed to prefer her to the other girls. The dreams continued but more and more they tended to be erotic rather than nightmares. Or, they *were* nightmares, because the dreams never really changed; she'd see his face above her, taking her. But the fear and anger and disgust drained out of them as time went by. The helplessness was still there, but something in *her* was changing. When she had him at her relative mercy, she no longer looked at him as a target. The plans were still there, remaining in the background, waiting the proper time, but she no longer thought of killing him when he was inside her. She wanted him. And she hated herself for it.

"Here it is," Megan said, holding up a small bottle filled with yellow liquid.

The still-room was now filled with odd scents, a complex of strong musk, rose water and an undertinge of sulfur. Ceramic bowls bubbled over charcoal braziers and a small complex of distilling equipment dripped liquid into a small glass jar. The end of the table was covered in a pile of spices and several sealed bottles were scattered around them.

Christel took the bottle and removed the stopper, sniffing at the liquid.

"Oh," she said, tipping some of the liquid out and rubbing it on her inner wrists. "Wonderful!" she exclaimed, sniffing at her wrist.

"It's not very potent," Megan noted. "The scent will wear off quickly. I need a secondary distilling apparatus to get it to be real *perfume* as opposed to a very light cologne."

"Can you do that?" Christel asked. She sniffed at her wrist and noticed that the scent had already begun to fade.

"Oh, yes," Megan said. "But it will have to be ordered from a glassmaker. The cost is well within our . . . well I've got it listed as 'fripperies' budget. The cloth to make clothes, board games, that sort of thing. We haven't really touched the budget on that. And the glassware isn't all that expensive."

"All right," Christel said, sniffing at her wrist again and touching some of the cologne behind her ears.

"Um. I'd sort of hoped that I could . . . use this to trade," Megan said. "I can't *sew* and I was hoping I could trade this with the other girls. Obviously, you have first dibs."

"Obviously," Christel smirked. "But that's fine. Just don't start *too* many fights, okay?"

"Okay."

Christel looked around the room and then under the workbench.

"What is that big bucket?" she asked.

"That's sort of the junk left over," Megan said. "I'm going to have to have it hauled out sooner or later, but there are two hogsheads for it. They're plastic lined, so they won't leak."

"Okay," Christel replied, looking around and shaking her head. "You really do surprise me, Megan."

"Thank you, ma'am," the girl said as the older woman left the room. "I certainly hope so."

CHAPTER SEVEN

Megan was frowning at the latest bill for cosmetics when Paul suddenly appeared in the office. She let out a slight shriek and the paper she was holding flew across the room.

"Jesus, Paul!" she snapped. "Ding a bell when you're porting or something!"

"I'm sorry," Paul said, then frowned at her, looking at the papers scattered across the desk. "What are you doing in here?" he added severely, the frown creating a furrow between his eyebrows. He had lost weight even in the last few weeks and was so thin his ribs showed. His clothes weren't as elegant, either. Actually, he looked like a walking corpse.

"I'm doing the accounts these days," Megan said, waving at the papers and worrying about the change in his appearance. Paul dying from malnutrition was not part of her plans. "And other things."

"What 'other things'?" Paul asked, dangerously. There was an almost feral light in his eyes as he stared at her. "And why are you doing the accounts?" he asked, harshly.

"The 'other things' is making perfume," she said, coming gracefully to her feet and walking over so he could smell the underside of her wrist.

"Nice," Paul said, mollified. "You make it?"

"I have to." She frowned in turn, returning to the desk, and sitting in the graceful motion Mirta had taught her. "Do you know that there's not a single perfumer in all of Ropasa? Saving me, of course. You want to *make* some money instead of spending it for a change?"

"Making perfume?" Paul snorted.

"Perfume was a major trade item in preindustrial days, Paul," Megan replied, hotly. "Given what I'm paying for cosmetics for the girls, I could make a *killing* if I was still on the outside. Setting up a perfumery would be expensive, but I'd recoup the investment in a year!"

"You're not getting out of here, Megan," Paul said, kindly, squatting by the desk. "You have more important work to do. Don't . . . don't make the mistake that some have made."

"Paul, I'm not trying to escape, okay?" Megan replied, wondering and fearing at the truth in the statement. "I don't even know where we are. Okay, I got up to a window, that I couldn't fit through, and looked out. We're in a castle. Big surprise. We're in a castle on a mountain. We're in a castle on a mountain that has a valley down below and other mountains in the distance. Paul, I could be *anywhere* in Ropasa, okay? And I got enough of a look to see that there are about a billion Changed guarding the castle. There's a town in the valley. Why do I think it's probably crawling with your forces? Paul, I'm not trying to run away. I'm just saying that you're leaving money on the table, here!"

Paul looked at her for a moment and then laughed, finally sitting down on a pillow, some of the tension going out of his face.

"You've changed," he said, still chuckling.

"What do you mean?" she asked, cautiously.

"Where's the meek little Megan that I found by the side of the stream?" Paul said. "Meek, scared little Megan. She's disappeared and been replaced by a coldhearted business woman who wants to make a killing in the perfume business."

"Little Megan is still here," she said, smiling. She shook her head at his appearance, though. "Paul, what have you been doing to yourself? You look like a damned ghost. How long has it been since you've laughed?"

"Too long," he admitted, frowning. "The world is such a terrible place right now, Megan. That bitch Sheida and her lackeys . . ."

"Paul," Megan said gently. "You need to get some rest."

"There's too much to do," he said, almost wailed. "I'm holding on with both hands, as tight as I can, and I can feel it all slipping away!"

"Paul," Megan said, severely. "Go take a shower, maybe a bath. No, wait . . ." She thought for a moment and then nodded. "Stay here. Don't go anywhere. Promise?"

"Promise," Paul said. "But why?"

"Why do you come here, Paul?" Megan asked.

"Because I have a duty . . ." Paul started to say.

"And we have a duty, too," Megan replied, cutting him off. "More than just to make babies. You're the most important man in the world, right now. Our duty is to make sure you can do yours, and we've clearly been falling down on the job."

"That's what Christel says, but . . ."

"Christel, Schmistel," Megan snorted. "I'm sorry; she's good for keeping the girls in line but there's a reason I'm doing the accounts. Face it, Paul, she's not the brightest leaf in the tree. I know what you need, and you're going to get it. So you wait right here."

She got up and walked into the main room, pointing at Shanea, who was talking to Mirta, and then at Mirta. She walked over to Christel and squatted down.

"Paul is here and he looks awful," she said to the woman.

"In the office?" Christel said, flustered and getting to her feet. "He'll want to check the books . . ."

"I'll handle it," Megan said, laying her hand on the woman's arm. "Let me handle this, okay? He needs rest. You've tried your arguments, let me try mine, okay?"

Christel looked at her, and at the door, frowning.

"Christel, I don't want your job," Megan said, softly. "I don't want to try to keep the girls in line. I don't want to hold the whip. I *don't*, okay? But what happens if Paul kills himself from neglect?"

The woman gulped and shook her head. "I don't know, I suppose . . ."

"You suppose what?" Megan said, softly but fiercely. "That Chansa would take us under his wing? Not hardly. We'd probably go to Reyes, who goes through women like a shark though a school of fish. Or to service the Changed. Or *be* Changed. Maybe even turned over to *Celine*." The latter council member was the source of most of the monsters that had been created for New Destiny's war. Most of them had started off as human beings. Under the rules pre-Fall they still *were* human beings. But nobody who had seen them or heard of them could think of them that way.

"They wouldn't . . ." Christel said, desperately.

"Yes they would and you know it," Megan replied. "So we have to make sure that Paul survives. You were right all along; we're here for Paul's needs. But he has more needs than the 'duty' to turn up from time to time and inseminate us. And I'm going to prove it to him."

"Go," Christel said, finally. "Try it."

"I will," Megan replied. "Shanea, Paul is in the office. Go get him. Take . . . Velva. Take him to the baths. Bathe him, don't let him do a thing for himself. Don't have sex with him. If he says he wants to, tell him 'not now, later, just bathe now.' Got it?"

"Give Paul a bath," Shanea nodded, gulping. "Don't have sex with him, even if he wants it. What if he *really* wants it?"

"Really tell him, 'later.' When you two are done, bring him to his room in a robe," she turned to Mirta. "Mirta, get Amber into her costume, then go to the kitchen door. Get a platter. Light foods. Bread, fruit, cheese, a small carafe of wine. Then bring it and Amber to Paul's room."

"Paul has . . . problems with Amber," Christel said. "Are you sure . . . ?"

"I'm sure," Megan said, looking around. "Girls, go get into your new costumes. When Paul comes through from the bath, I want you to stand up and move in around him saying nice things. Nothing important, just that we're glad he's here. *Don't* be suggestive. And don't try to follow him in. If this works out I'm going to keep him here for at least a couple of days."

She looked at Shanea and Mirta, then gestured. "Go."

Megan stood for a moment, pulling at her hair, then turned to Christel.

"I have things I need in the workroom," she said. "If I could . . ."

"Go," Christel said, "you're doing fine. I think you're right, okay? Girls, what are you doing just sitting around? Up on your feet, go get dressed . . ."

Megan rushed to her room and grabbed up various pots, then to the abandoned still-room. Shanea had taken to watching the bubbling substances for her but with the girl otherwise occupied Megan turned down the heat on all the crucibles, grabbed some bottles and headed for the toilet.

There were other girls in there jockeying for position in front of the mirrors but Megan shoved one of them out of the way with her hip and carefully deposited her bundles on the countertop.

"Ashly," she said, looking over at where the blonde was brushing her hair in front of a mirror. "My next-stage perfumes;

they're a little more concentrated. And I need somebody to mix something for me while I do my makeup."

Ashly looked at her as if she had grown another head, then nodded.

"Okay, Karie, you do the mixing," Ashly said, walking over to look at the bottles and pots. "What is all that?"

"Perfumes, oils, massage creams," Megan said. "Karie," she continued, opening up a jar and dropping a few milliliters of oil onto the cream inside. "Mix that up for me, please?"

"What is it?" Karie asked, sniffing at the contents.

"Almond massage paste, the oil is sesame," Megan said, looking in the mirror. "I don't have *time*," she muttered, picking up a flat of eye shadow.

"Vita, do her hair," Ashly said. "Megan, calm down. What the hell is wrong?"

"Did you *see* him?" Megan asked, turning to the girl. "He looks like a zombie."

"I saw. Megan, don't tell me you're falling in *love*," Ashly said, smirking.

Megan closed her eyes and decided not to "explain" to Ashly the facts of life, again. But it was tempting.

"No, I'm not falling in love," Megan replied, wondering if it was a true reply or not. "But if Paul dies, all this will go away and very bad things will probably happen to us, okay? I don't want that to happen. Do you?"

"No," Ashly said. "I hadn't thought . . ."

"Neither had Christel," Megan replied as Vita combed her hair and Ashly took the eye makeup out of her shaking hands.

"What are you going to do?" Vita asked. She was brushing Megan's hair up and out to make it appear larger.

"I'm going to make him the one happiest son of a bitch in the world," Megan replied. "I'm going to make him never want to leave. And then I'm going to convince him that, for the good of the world, he shouldn't for a while. A few days at least. And we're going to feed him up and primp him and pamper him until he's able to take care of himself again."

"And if you can't?" Ashly asked, brushing on the makeup expertly.

"Lightly, please," Megan said. "Then we might as well all cut our own throats. Do you want to be turned over to Reyes? Or the Changed?"

"Oh, God!" Vita said.

"Right, so we'd better make him *really* happy," Megan said, looking in the mirror. "Got it?"

"Got it," Ashly replied.

Megan picked up the pile of cloth at her feet and put on the new "outfit" that Mirta had made for her; a bikini bottom with a long "loincloth" front and back and a tight matching top like a sleeveless shirt that completely covered her breasts except for a swelling that dropped out from the bottom. It practically begged to be pushed up.

"You look like . . . well you look good," Ashly said.

"You all need to get dressed, too," Megan replied. "Hurry."

She picked up the pots, nodding at Karie and Ashly and practically ran out the door.

She dropped the pots in Paul's room and then ran back to the office, getting the synopsis of all the accounts that she had prepared. She knew that Christel usually covered them with Paul but that had to stop soon, too. There were too many inconsistencies that Christel, bless her black stupid heart, wouldn't know how to explain.

She piled the reports by the pillows and then assumed a modest position and waited. Before Paul got there Mirta came in with the platter of food and Amber. As Mirta left, she settled Amber in place, positioned the tray of food and wine, with the addition of a carafe of water, which was smart thinking on Mirta's part, and settled down to wait again. She had barely had time to rearrange the pillows when she heard a murmur from the main room and the door opened up. She could see that the girls were all in their finest and as Paul came in the room she imperceptibly waved at Velva not to follow him in. The girl looked nonplussed but closed the door behind her.

"Megan," Paul said, weakly, "this is all quite unnecessary . . ."

"Hush," Megan said, standing up and unbelting his robe. "Lie down."

"Megan," he said, looking at the other two girls.

"Have you bedded each of us?" Megan said, pushing him down.

"Well . . . yes . . . but . . ."

"Hush," she replied. "No talk. No work talk, no talk at all."

She rolled him over on his stomach and positioned Shanea and Amber on either side.

"Like this," she said, taking up a fingerful of the massage cream and dabbing it on his upper arm. She took Amber's hands and pushed the thumbs into the muscle, working down the arm. "Slowly and firmly, all the way down the arm. You understand? Don't pinch."

"Down the arm," Amber said with a nod, pressing into the flesh of his triceps. "Don't pinch."

"Shanea, you do the other arm," Megan said, rubbing the cream into his back, then beginning to massage.

"Oh that feels good," Paul murmured.

"You need to take better care of yourself, Paul Bowman," Megan replied, pressing into his muscles. They were firm from work but he was so skinny. "What happens to us if you die?"

"I won't die," Paul said, starting to push up.

"Don't you dare get up," Megan said, sternly. "We've barely gotten started."

She worked his back as the other girls worked on his arms and shoulders, then the three of them worked down his legs. As they massaged he began to relax and at one point gave a faint snore. He started at that and began to rise.

"And you haven't been getting enough sleep apparently," Megan said, pushing him back down. By then they'd worked most of the way down his legs and she pushed on him to roll over. She began massaging his pectorals and nodded downward at Shanea.

Shanea looked at her with a happy grin and slid downward, taking him in her mouth.

"Megan!" he said, his eyes flying open and his arms coming up.

"No, Shanea," Megan grinned. "Now lie there and enjoy."

"This isn't right," Paul said, lying back anyway. "People are starving and . . ."

"And if you die, who will care about them?" Megan asked. "Chansa? *Celine?*"

"You have a point," Paul admitted.

She slid over and propped his head in her lap, then gestured at the platter. Amber had to think about it for a moment but then her eyes lit up and she slid the platter over, taking a plum from it and offering it to Paul.

Megan picked up a loaf of bread, still warm from the ovens, and broke off a piece. As soon as Paul was finished with the plum she handed him the bread and he tore into that as if he were starving.

"Softly," she said. "Slowly. You need to build your strength back up. And I'll tell you something, Paul Bowman, you are not leaving this . . . building until you are looking better than when you came in. And you had better be back soon for more pampering."

"This isn't right," Paul muttered, but he also didn't try to rise.

"My neck's getting tired," Shanea admitted. "You never give me enough practice at this, Paul."

"See?" Megan said, trying not to either laugh or cry. "You've been neglecting Shanea shamelessly, forcing her to lose the best of her arts."

"Oral sex does not get babies made," Paul pointed out.

"Babies won't get made, or have a protector, if you don't take care of yourself," Megan said, ruthlessly. "Amber, can you remember . . . ?" She pointed to where Shanea was idly stroking at his member.

"Yes," Amber said, moving down to replace the other girl. As she started, Paul groaned and reached out a hand to her.

"Amber," he said, sadly. "Of all the things I've done, I feel the worst about you."

Worse than throwing the world into barbarism? Megan thought, surprised at the sudden intensity of her anger.

"I think she's probably happier this way," was all she said. She picked up another piece of bread as Shanea snuggled into his side.

"Sometimes the caged nightingale won't sing," Paul murmured stroking the hair of the woman who was fellating him. "Did you know she was a . . . friend before the Fall?"

"Like Christel?" Megan asked, neutrally.

"Yes, I care for our daughter as well. But Amber could not adjust to the confinement I had to impose on her." He looked up and back at Megan. "You seem to have adjusted well."

That's because I'm working on the key to the lock at this very moment.

"Some people can't handle change," she replied, picking up another piece of bread and feeding it to him. Shanea had slipped out of her top and was now lightly licking his chest, and he groaned again.

"Amber," he said, breathlessly.

The suit Mirta had made for the brain-drained girl covered her almost entirely, somewhat like a jumpsuit. But it was made of nearly transparent material that shifted in color and opaqueness as the light hit it, hiding and revealing in apparent randomness. It also had well-placed buttons and ties, and Amber obediently opened up the bottoms and mounted Paul.

He groaned again as she began to stroke and then came quickly.

"This is all too much," Paul said as Amber lifted herself

off. Shanea picked up a cloth and wiped him clean, then ensured the job by lowering herself onto him again, working the area with her tongue, her head moving like a cat.

"This is all too much," Paul murmured again, then his head lay heavy in her lap.

Shanea looked up with an unhappy expression when she heard the snore.

"Stay here with him," Megan said, slipping his head off her lap and deftly sliding a pillow under it. "When he wakes up, send Amber to me and give him whatever he needs. No, let me make that clearer, when he wakes up, make sure he comes again, one way or another. But send Amber to me first."

She picked up the platter and stood up, walking to the door. It was only when she was through it that she realized she was the only one in the room who hadn't gotten involved in one form of sex or another and she was horrified to find herself regretting it.

CHAPTER EIGHT

"How is he?" Christel asked.

"Sleeping," Megan replied. Mirta took the tray from her and she thanked the seamstress with a nod.

"He never sleeps here!" Christel said.

"He will for the next few days if I've got my ducks in a row," Megan said. "He needs the rest."

"He's supposed to be guarded when he's sleeping," Christel pointed out. "Did he ask about the accounts?"

"The accounts never came up," Megan said. "Although other things did," she added with a grin.

"He'll never stay," Christel said. "He has things to do."

"Look, when he wakes up, first he gets screwed then we feed him," Megan said, lifting her fingers in order. "We feed him heavily, lots of meat and carbohydrates; he's bound to be hungry after two bouts of sex. When he's fed, we get him to come again. Between the food and the sex he'll fall asleep *again*. When he wakes up *again*, we might have an argument out of him. But if we have to, all the girls strip naked and pile on him in a giant scrum of bodies. There's not a man on earth who will try to run away if he's got fifteen naked girls holding him down and begging him to take them."

"You have a point," Christel said with a grin of her own.

"This is really important," Megan pointed out, again.

"I know," Christel replied. "Should somebody else go in there?"

"You know anyone else who has the patience of Amber and Shanea?" Megan asked, raising her eyebrows. "Why do you

427

think I'm not in there. It's going to be lots of fun watching him snore."

"What about guards?" Christel asked.

"What about them?" Megan shrugged. "He's got a PPF; what more does he need?"

"They don't activate automatically anymore," Christel pointed out. "He has to summon it. What if someone broke in and tried to assassinate him?"

"Who?" Megan said, exasperated. "They'd have to get through the Changed guards around the castle and then through us, which, admittedly, wouldn't be hard. But by then he'd be up and prepared. He's *safe*, Christel. The only person who is going to kill Paul is Paul himself. And that's what we've got to convince him not to do."

Megan was in the distillery when Amber came to get her and she hurried at once to Paul's room, pulling off the robe she'd used to cover her outfit as she went.

When she entered Shanea was already fellating him, stroking up and down hard. Paul looked up in annoyance as the door opened and then in something like shame when he saw who it was.

"I don't like being watched," he said, his face wrinkling up in worry.

"Then why don't I join in?" Megan said, stripping off the panties of her outfit and pushing Shanea aside as she slid onto him.

"Hey, mine," Shanea said, jokingly.

"Later maybe," Megan said, sliding up and down on him. Fortunately he'd been premoistened and she found herself rapidly lubricating the area. After a short time she rolled over and pulled him onto her, grabbing his buttocks and digging her fingernails in. He pumped at her hard and rapidly and, as always, came a bit too soon.

"I need to go," Paul said, getting to his feet.

"Not until you've had something to eat," Megan said, gesturing at his robe. Shanea obediently picked it up and put it on him.

"Come on out in the common room," Megan said. "The rest of the girls want to see you, too."

She cleaned up, put on her bottoms and led him out into the common room, settling him on some pillows with girls on either side. The she went to the dining room, dragging Shanea with her.

"Marlene," she called from beyond the doorway. She had already determined that a field extended out for at least a meter into the dining room. If one of the harem girls moved into the field she got a very unpleasant pain jolt. She wondered if it extended to the other side of the doorway as well. If not, it might be possible to throw yourself through the field. On the other hand, she had no intention of trying to find out.

"You rang?" Marlene said, coming through the door with a tray covered by a silver lid.

"Thank God," Megan said, taking the tray.

"And I've made up another with cakes and other goodies so the girls can eat, too," Marlene said as a servant came through the doorway. "He might not if they don't have anything."

"Thank you," Megan said, nodding at Shanea to take the second tray.

"I heard why you are doing this," Marlene said, looking her in the eye.

"Just my duty to help my lord and master," Megan replied, smiling.

"Mirta says more with a glance than you do with a sentence," Marlene grinned. "Paul might like a couple of those cakes as well; make sure the girls don't stuff themselves silly."

"I will," Megan said. "Later."

Megan walked back to where Paul was listening to Ashly tell about her latest triumph in backgammon. It was apparent that he was trying to be interested and failing miserably.

"More food?" he asked, as Megan sat down and opened up the cover.

Marlene had outdone herself. There was some sort of meat covered in a red wine sauce and beautifully sculpted portions of potatoes, lightly grilled tomatoes and a green mash that had been shaped into the form of a flower. Shanea had opened up the other tray and was distributing small, glazed cakes to the girls, one apiece, and whispering that they were supposed to make them last.

"More food," Megan replied, picking up a fork as he reached for it. "Ah, ah, you don't do *anything* for yourself."

"I can *feed* myself," Paul said, but he let her section small bites of the food and shovel them in his mouth. When a few crumbs fell off the fork, Ashly helpfully leaned forward and licked them off of him. By then Christel had turned up with another carafe of chilled wine and fed him sips between bites.

"What are you doing to me?" Paul asked, looking at Megan.

"Pampering you," Megan said. "We'll stop when you learn to take care of yourself."

"Okay, I promise not to learn to take care of myself," Paul said, laughing as the last of the food was served.

"Good," Megan said, honestly. Having him here a lot worked perfectly. She unbelted his robe and kissed his chest, licking at it lightly.

"Megan, not here," he groaned.

"Here," she said, reaching over and pushing Ashly's head towards his crotch. She would have grabbed Shanea, not knowing how Ashly would feel about it, but Shanea was just out of reach.

Suddenly she found a breast in her face as Karie sidled up on one side and she backed away as the rest of the girls closed in on him.

She stood up and looked at Christel who winked back at her. So there was more than one plan afoot; good.

Megan backed away from the pile and gestured with her head at Christel.

"How do we get him back to sleep?" Megan whispered.

"Oh, I think when they're done with him he'll sleep," Christel chuckled quietly.

"I think they'll all sleep," Megan said, turning her head to the side. Paul wasn't the only one who was having fun in the pile. Ashly, who was still stroking for all her neck would bear, was sitting on Shanea's face. And there was no way that Shanea had been forced to the position; she'd been on the other side of the pile to start. But Shanea wasn't lacking as somebody's hand was down in her crotch and that led to . . . maybe Velva . . .

"It looks like an erotic M.C. Escher painting," Megan muttered, shaking her head.

"Good work." Christel chuckled again.

"Sure, laugh," Megan replied. "I've got distillation to attend to."

"Go for it," Christel said, stripping off her clothes. "I've got better things to do. All this needs is a half a ton of whipped cream and five more males."

Megan shook her head as Christel writhed into the group. She fully intended to just go back to her, lonely, workroom and keep distilling the various substances she had concocted. But the more she thought about it, the more she watched, just standing there as the pile writhed in a tangle of limbs like some giant fleshy amoeba.

But far more attractive.

"Oh the hell with perfume." She sighed, aware that she had reached a point where she wasn't *about* to go to her workroom. Although the bath had some interest. Finally, she took a deep, shuddering breath, stripped off her clothes and dove into the pile.

Christel was right; it needed whipped cream.

CHAPTER NINE

Paul looked slightly shamefaced when he woke up in a pile of female limbs. But the first thing he saw was Megan, leaning on one arm, watching him.

"Was it just my imagination, or did I see your face in the middle of . . . this," he asked, gesturing at the girls, most of whom were still sleeping.

"It wasn't your imagination," Megan replied, shrugging.

He watched the way that moved her breasts and shook his head.

"I . . . didn't figure you for this sort of thing," he said, carefully.

"Neither did I," Megan admitted. "But it was pretty fun once I got over the idea."

"I have to get up," Paul said, trying to figure out how to crawl out and disturb the least number of people.

"You are staying here at least one more day," Megan said, sternly. "You looked like death-on-a-cracker when you came in and you still don't look good."

"I've got things I *have* to do," Paul said. "Besides go to the bathroom."

"It's over there." Megan gestured with her chin. "But you'd better come back out, too."

"I will," Paul said.

When he came back out he was wearing one of the standard robes and he sat down on a pillow, turning his head to the side as he contemplated Megan.

433

"What are you doing awake at . . ." he paused and obviously consulted the Net, "three A.M.?"

"I get enough sleep in the harem." Megan shrugged. "I wasn't tired. I was watching you."

"Watching me sleep?" Paul asked. "Or watching over me?"

"A little of both. Watching and thinking."

"How easy it would be to kill me?" Paul asked.

"Damage you, yes," Megan said. "Kill would be for all practical purposes impossible. And if I even tried, well, the best that might happen is that I'd wind up like Amber. And, hell, I don't want to kill you. I did at first, but I don't want to anymore."

"Do you know why?" he asked quietly.

"No," Megan replied, sitting up. "Tell me, O Wise One."

Paul smiled and said something softly.

"Have you ever heard of the Sabine women?" Paul asked.

Megan thought about it for a long time and then shook her head.

"I think my mother mentioned the term," she said. "But I don't recall anything about it."

"Very old legend," Paul said, taking a sip of wine. "The Romans were short on women so they invited a neighboring tribe, the Sabines, to a festival in honor of the gods. Under a binding truce of course. At the height of the party, the Roman young men took off with the Sabine's wives and daughters while the older men held off the Sabines. Then they raped them and took them as their wives. Quite a few years later the Sabines had built up enough force to fight the Romans and, hopefully, destroy them. But the Sabine women convinced them not to kill their new husbands. After a while the Sabine tribe was absorbed by the Romans."

Megan frowned. "It's a legend."

"A legend that has had a ring of truth to this day." Paul sighed. "Because the psychological basis of it started to be understood in the twentieth century, starting with something called the Stockholm Effect. People tend to bond to their captors in personalized imprisonments. Most of the real-life examples have faded over the last few millennia but there are tens of thousands of them that have been studied. And the psycho-physiological effects, even the evolutionary bases, are easily traceable. Women who have been kidnapped and imprisoned tend to bond to their captors even more readily and to fall in love with them. Tend. Not always, humans are individuals. But it's the majority."

"I've fallen in love with my kidnapper," she said, hanging her head.

"You've fallen in love with your kidnapper," Paul confirmed. "It's not nice, it's not the way that things are 'supposed' to be. But it's very real and it's very human and it's something that I counted upon when I set up this . . . group. It probably goes back to prehuman conditions. Young female chimpanzees that are thrown out of their packs are often found by males from other packs. When they are, they are forced back to the area that the females stay in and are brutalized until they stay there of their own free will. To the point of preventing new females from attempting to escape. I have not brutalized you girls, but do you think Christel, for example, would support any plans to escape?"

"No," Megan said.

"I could postulate a race which is different," he paused and chuckled grimly. "Actually, I don't have to. The elves *are* different. Attempt to rape or imprison an elf and you'd better have lots of chains. And a gag."

"You haven't . . ." Megan said, her eyes wide.

"Never," Paul replied, definitely. "But some have tried from time to time, especially in the years when they lived among humans; elves were always beautiful. But the elves have no submit in them. They do not change their . . . emotions under stress. Put them in an imprisonment situation and they will *always* try to escape. They will tend, very hard, to try to kill their guards, even if it means their own deaths. Humans, though, tend to make the best of a bad situation. Even to the point of falling in love." He looked at her tenderly and smiled. "I take it you're human?"

"Very," she admitted.

"Amber, though, seemed to be part elf," Paul sighed. "She never would submit to this necessity and when she plotted to kill Christel and escape I was forced to make her . . . more compliant."

Megan shuddered and shook her head. "Paul, do me a favor. If I ever go insane and do something that makes you have to do that, just kill me, okay?"

"I truly hope it never comes to that. You can't kill me, you know," he added, looking at her. "And if you even managed it through some miracle, it would be worse than it is now. That is part of this effect; faced with unpalatable choices humans choose the lesser of the evils and live through them as best they can. But you don't want to anymore, do you?"

She thought of all the nights that she had cried for her loss and the pain. And of all the times they had talked. She probably knew more about the inner workings of the New Destiny faction than anyone not a part of it. And she knew that she no longer wanted to kill him. It didn't mean she wouldn't, but she didn't want to.

"No," she answered honestly, dipping her head again and fighting not to cry.

"If it helps you at all, I love you, too," Paul said. "You're . . . very precious to me. Sometimes when I come here it is only to see you. I can't talk to other people as I can with you. I certainly can't to anyone outside this group and of all the ones in it, the only other one that had your clarity of mind and ability to listen and make useful comments was Amber. And in the end, I had to make her safe."

"I won't force you to do the same to me," Megan said. "At least, I hope I never do."

"Do you know why the caged nightingale won't sing?" Paul asked.

"You said that before," she said, looking up with unshed tears in her eyes.

"It is because it knows that it is supposed to fly free," Paul said. "When you can't sing anymore, I'll know that it is time to release you . . . or know that you will never sing again." He looked at her sadly for a moment then stood up. "I have to go."

"Paul, you are not going anywhere," Megan said. "You're still not strong enough."

"I have things I *have* to do, Megan," Paul said. But when he stood he swayed on his feet.

"There," Megan said, triumphantly.

"Blood flow, that's all," Paul said. "I stood up too fast."

"I'll wake everybody up again and we'll start all over," Megan warned. "Where do you have to be? What can't you do from right here?"

"I need . . . I don't *have* to be anywhere. But I need to recall my avatars and find out what they have been doing while I've been . . . busy."

"You've got projections running and not monitoring them?" Megan asked.

"They're sentient avatars," Paul corrected. "For all practical purposes they *are* me. It was proscribed pre-Fall, but it's the only way to keep track of what is going on. I need to recall them, soon. They're not . . . fully stable. I need to recall them and then send out new ones."

"Well, you can do that here," Megan said. "Right?"

"I need to be undisturbed," Paul pointed out.

"There's an empty room right there," Megan said, pointing at his chamber. "And I'll make sure you're not disturbed. And when you're done, I'll make sure that you're fed and comforted and cosseted and . . ."

"Okay, okay." Paul laughed, hushing himself as one of the other girls stirred and snaked a hand across the body next to her. "I'll go in there."

"And I'll watch. Is there anything I should be aware of?"

"No, it's a harmless procedure," Paul said, walking to the room. "Mostly."

Paul reclined on one of the pillows and closed his eyes, appearing to go back to sleep or into a trance. But almost immediately he began to twitch as if hit by some invisible force. And he muttered.

"Bloody hell . . ." Pause. "No, no, no how stupid can one vacuous bitch be? Released?" Pause. "Ekmantan." Pause. "Ships? Dragon-carriers?" Pause. "Damn them." "Talbot." A hiss of anger.

It went on for what seemed like hours and he became drenched with sweat, the increasing anger boiling off of him like a vapor.

She rose after a while and left quietly. All of the other girls were still in sodden slumber so she picked through the detritus of the orgy until she found the remains of the carafe of wine and a jug of water. She carried both in and resumed her vigil.

Paul finally settled down, stopped twitching, mostly, and appeared to dream. He muttered from time to time unintelligibly. She listened as closely as she could but there was nothing that was understandable. Finally, he opened his eyes, looking wan and pale.

"Harmless, huh?" she asked, sitting him up and propping pillows behind him. She held a glass of wine to his lips and then followed it with water.

"This one was harder than normal," he admitted. "I'd been away too long."

"And you do this regularly?" she asked.

"Usually every day," Paul admitted. "It's how I keep track."

"What are dragon-carriers?" she asked.

He looked at her sharply, then shrugged.

"The UFS has rigged out one of the warships to land and launch wyverns and greater dragons," Paul said. "I'd heard about it, but didn't really expect it to work. Well, it did. They destroyed the force that we sent down to the Isles to disrupt their negotiations with the mer. Now Chansa wants to build some of his own, so he can protect the invasion fleet."

"What do you think?" Megan asked.

"I think we're playing to their game and that's what I told Chansa," Paul replied. "We're just about evenly matched for power at this point, so we can't use that against them. But just making our own carriers isn't going to win us control of the sea. We need something to deal with the dragons. I told him to consult with Celine about modifying our dragons and get a group together to consider how to counter theirs."

"Do you think it will work?" Megan asked, handing him the water.

"We have to take Norau," Paul shrugged. "There are five power plants in Norau. We've tried everything from sedition to infiltrating attack teams, but most of them are well away from the coast and we can't use teleport. If we take the plants, or capture that bitch Sheida Ghorbani, the war will be over. But taking it will be . . . difficult. They've armed every peasant in the field and they make them train with the arms. There are areas that haven't done that, though, because Sheida's too stupid to make them. We're going to concentrate our attack on those areas. But we have to get there first, which means controlling the ocean. And we can't do that if one carrier can destroy six of our ships, five of them without ever coming in *sight* of the ships. And the carrier had less than a full complement of dragons."

"What are dragons afraid of?" Megan said. She'd wished for a month now that she had some way to get word to the other side. This was operational intelligence, stuff that could be acted on. Especially if she found out the counter plans. She *had* to figure some way to smuggle out information. There had to be a way.

"Nothing that I'm aware of," he said, getting a far away look as he accessed the Net. "Their wings are monomolecule fibers, so no hurting them there. Their underbellies aren't, though. I'd say that a well-placed ballista bolt would take one down."

"Lots of dragons?" Megan prompted.

"Lots of bolts," Paul smiled in response. "Chansa's problem, I'll let him come up with the solution."

"Who is Talbot?" Megan asked. "You've mentioned him before."

"Duke the Honorable Charles or Edmund, take your pick, fucking Talbot," Paul said with a frown. "He was one of

Sheida's little fuck boys before she became a council member. He apparently threw her over for her sister. He's now the commander of the eastern defenses in Norau and he was on the mission to the mer-folk. Apparently he put some spine in those Changed abominations, because they killed everything that Chansa sent at them. Chansa is simply furious. He not only lost the orcas and a kraken but a reasonably competent field agent and a very good source. All thanks to Duke Fucking Talbot."

Megan decided that she much wanted to meet "Duke Fucking Talbot" someday and give him a very friendly kiss.

"And the rest?"

"We've settled the negotiations with the replacement for Minjie's replacement," Paul said with a grin. "You had a perfect plan there, my dear. I let Celine handle all the arrangements. I understand they almost have the blood off the walls. She sent a very small and somewhat intelligent spider into his quarters. When he was in flagrante delicto, it bit him and paralyzed him. Then its momma came in and finished off the job."

"What happened to the girl?" Megan said, horrified.

"Boy as it turns out," Paul replied. "Nothing, the spiders had very specific instructions. I made that clear to Celine. Much more horrible that way."

"Paul," Megan said, glancing around. "I can't guarantee I'd notice a spider."

"I would, my dear," Paul smiled. "I don't keep up a PPF when I'm with you ladies, but nothing can come in or out."

"I got food and drink from the kitchen," Megan pointed out.

"Only because I relaxed the protocols to let you," Paul replied. "And the kitchen itself is sealed. I also sweep for anything that might be one of Celine's little monsters, not to mention poisons. You have a few lovely items in your lab, by the way. What do you use sulfuric acid *for*?"

"Reagent," Megan said. "It's used to transform some of the products that I get to add a sulfur molecule. That makes them more volatile."

"Ah," Paul said, getting a far-away look. "Actually, most of the stuff that you use for perfumes is poisonous in sufficient concentration." He looked at her and smiled. "But not to me, of course. It takes something much more subtle than concentrate of rose hips."

"People used to die from cosmetic poisoning," Megan shrugged. "Heavy metals. And painting. Painters didn't always *start* mad, but lick enough paint brushes that have been covered in vermilion, which was basically mercury, and you get a little brain addled. Not to mention that lovely yellow from lead."

Paul got a far away look again and then smiled. "You are a font of knowledge my dear."

"I like chemistry," Megan said with a shrug. Of course, mostly from a forensic side, but let's not go there. "Half of chemistry is knowing what you don't want to swallow."

Paul yawned and smiled at her.

"Could I convince you to snuggle down here with me?" he asked, patting at the cushions. "Just like two people who enjoy each other? Not one of my girls who feel they have to . . . service me. Just . . . friends?"

"Yes, Paul," she said, lying down in his arms. "I think we could do that."

"Always sing for me," he murmured as he coasted on the edge of sleep.

"Always, my dear," she whispered. *Till death do us part.*

Appendix

New Destiny Key-holders

1. Paul Bowman, Leader of New Destiny, Minister for Ropasa
2. Chansa Mulengela, Minister for Frika, Marshall of the Great Army
3. Celine Reinshafen, Minister for Ephresia, Chief of Research and Development
4. Lupe Ugatu (Vice Minjie Jiaqi), Governor of Hindi (in dispute)
5. Reyes Cho, Minister for Soam
6. Jassinte Arizzi, Minister for Chin (in dispute)
7. Demon, lone actor

Freedom Coalition Key-holders

1. Sheida Ghorbani, Her Majesty of the United Free States, Chairman of the Freedom Coalition
2. Ungphakorn, Lord of Soam
3. Ishtar, Counselor of Taurania and the Stanis States
4. Aikawa Gouvois, Emperor of Chin
5. Lenora Sill

Neutral:

The Finn